Lisa Kleypas is the author of a number of historical romance novels that have been published in fourteen languages. In 1985, she was named Miss Massachusetts and competed in the Miss America pageant in Atlantic City. After graduating from Wellesley College with a political science degree, she published her first novel at age twenty-one. Her books have appeared on the *New York Times* bestseller lists. Lisa is married and has two children.

Sugar Daddy is Lisa's first contemporary novel. Her second and third, *Blue-Eyed Devil* and *Smooth Talking Stranger*, are also published by Piatkus.

Visit her website at www.lisakleypas.com

D0230574

Also by Lisa Kleypas

Contemporary:

Blue-Eyed Devil
Smooth Talking Stranger

Historical:

Mine Till Midnight
Seduce Me At Sunrise
Tempt Me At Twilight

Sugar
Daddy

LISA KLEYPAS

piatkus

PIATKUS

First published in the United States in 2007 by
St. Martin's Press, New York, USA
First published in Great Britain in 2007 by Piatkus Books
This paperback edition published in 2009 by Piatkus

A CIP catalogue record for this book
is available from the British Library

ISBN 978-0-7499-4219-9

Printed in Great Britian by Clays Ltd, St Ives plc

Papers used by Piatkus are natural, renewable and recyclable
products sourced from well-managed forests and certified
in accordance with the rules of the Forest Stewardship Council.

Mixed Sources
Product group from well-managed
forests and other controlled sources
www.fsc.org Cert no. SGS-COC-004081
© 1996 Forest Stewardship Council
FSC

Piatkus
An imprint of
Little, Brown Book Group
100 Victoria Embankment
London EC4Y 0DY

An Hachette UK Company
www.hachette.co.uk

www.piatkus.co.uk

To my husband, Greg, who is my true love, my best friend, my adventure, my comfort, and the compass in the map of my heart. For giving the best hugs, making me feel beautiful, being funny and smart, choosing the perfect wine, taking care of the family, and always being the most interesting person in the room.

ACKNOWLEDGMENTS

While writing this book, I was blessed with help from as well as the knowledge of many people. It would require the equivalent of a novella to describe all they've done for me. I hope they know how grateful I am.

Mel Berger, an extraordinary agent who has accompanied me through each phase of my career with wisdom, patience, and humor, and has never stopped believing in me.

Jennifer Enderlin, who said she wanted me to have wings, and helped me to find them. Not only is she a brilliant editor, she is a beautiful person, inside and out.

Sally Richardson, Matthew Shear, George Witte, Matt Baldacci, John Murphy, Dori Weintraub, Kim Cardascia, and the rest of the team at St. Martin's Press, for all their talent and amazing work.

Linda Kleypas, Lloyd Kleypas, and Ki Kleypas, for their emotional support and insights, for helping me to know and understand the people we came from, providing answers to a million questions, and being great company and a loving family. Most of all, for being a small and perfect constellation of guiding stars. Because of you, no matter where I go I can always find my way home.

Special thanks to my smart and exuberant mother, who is, as Marie Brenner would say, a great dame.

Ireta and Harrell Ellis, for giving me the right advice at the right time, helping me to believe in myself, and for showing me the strength and steadfast love that always provide a safe place to anchor. Also for the wonderful evening spent sharing memories of Mac Palmer. Cristi and James Swayze, for their love and encouragement, and for changing my life all those years ago by arranging a Very Good Blind Date.

Christina Dodd, the dearest friend in the world, who told me I could write a "contemporary," and turned out to be right. And Liz Bevarly, Connie Brockway, Eloisa James, and Teresa Medeiros, who always pick me up when I fall, defend me right or wrong, and surround me with a circle of love. I couldn't do it without you.

Geralyn Dawson, Susan Sizemore, and Susan Kay Law, who listened patiently, offered invaluable insights, showed me how to make caramel cashew bars, plot vampire stories, and eat cereal out of teacups, and became friends I want to keep forever.

Stephanie Bascon and Melissa Rowcliffe, two dynamic and beautiful women, for sharing their legal expertise, and even more for the gift of friendship.

Billie Jones, the most generous woman I know, and her husband, James Walton Jones, for their love, wit, and wisdom, and for the dinner party one summer evening, spent with friends who shared precious memories and helped me to understand the real issues of my story. Thanks to these friends who have inspired me in a multitude of ways: Mayor and Mrs. Norman Erskine, Mena Nichols, Betsy Allen, J. C.

Chatmas, Weezie Burton, Charlsie Brown, Necy Matelski, Nancy Erwin, Gene Erwin, Sara Norton, Hammond Norton, Lois Cooper, Bill Reynolds, and Mary Abbot Hess.

Patsy and Wilson Kluck, for their priceless reminiscences and their love, and especially to Patsy for showing me all that is best about Texas women.

Virginia Lake, who influenced me to write the story of a woman who triumphs over hardship with grace, determination, and humor—all qualities she has in abundance.

Sandy Coleman, for her friendship, support, and love of the romance genre.

Michelle Buonfiglio, a woman of great intelligence and charisma who makes me proud of my profession.

Amanda Santana and Cindy Torres, not only for answering technical questions about the hairstyling profession but also for sharing personal observations and memories.

Most of all, I am thankful for my children—my two miracles—who fill my heart and every corner of my soul with joy.

Sugar Daddy

CHAPTER 1

When I was four, my father died in an oil-rig accident. Daddy didn't even work for the drilling outfit. He was a company man who wore a suit and tie when he went to inspect the production and drilling platforms. But one day he stumbled on an opening in the rig floor before setup was completed. He fell sixty feet to the platform below and died instantly, his neck broken.

It took me a long time to understand Daddy was never coming back. I waited for him for months, sitting at the front window of our house in Katy, just west of Houston.

Some days I stood at the end of the driveway to watch every car that passed. No matter how often Mama told me to quit looking for him, I couldn't give up. I guess I thought the strength of my wanting would be enough to make him appear.

I have only a handful of memories of my father, more like impressions. He must have carried me on his shoulders a time or two—I remember the hard plane of his chest beneath my calves, the sensation of swaying high in the air, anchored by the strong pressure of his fingers around my ankles. And the coarse drifts of his hair in my hands, shiny black hair cut in layers. I can almost hear his voice singing "Arriba del Cielo," a Mexican lullaby that always gave me sweet dreams.

There is a framed photograph of Daddy on my dresser, the only one I have. He's wearing a Western dress shirt and jeans with creases pressed down the front, and a tooled leather belt with a silver and turquoise buckle the size of a breakfast plate. A little smile lingers in one corner of his mouth, and a dimple punctuates the smoothness of his swarthy cheek. By all accounts he was a smart man, a romantic, a hard worker with high-carat ambitions. I believe he would have accomplished great things in his life if he'd been given the gift of more years. I know so little about my father, but I'm certain he loved me. I can feel it even in those little wisps of memory.

Mama never found another man to replace Daddy. Or maybe it's more accurate to say she found a lot of men to replace him. But hardly any of them stayed around for long. She was a beautiful woman, if not a happy one, and attracting a man was never a problem. Keeping one, however, was a different matter. By the time I was thirteen, Mama had gone through more boyfriends than I could keep track of. It was sort of a relief when she found one she decided she could stick with for a while.

They agreed they would move in together, in the east Texas town of Welcome, not far from where he'd grown up. As it turned out, Welcome was where I lost everything, and gained everything. Welcome was the place where my life was guided from one track to another, sending me to places I'd never thought of going.

On my first day at the trailer park, I wandered along a dead-end road that cut between rows of trailers lined up like piano keys. The park was a dusty grid of dead-end streets, with a newly built loop that circled around the left side. Each home sat on its own concrete pad, dressed in a skirt made of aluminum or wooden latticework. A few trailers were fronted by patches of yard, some featuring crape myrtle with blossoms crisped a pale brown and the bark shredded from the heat.

The late afternoon sun was as round and white as a paper plate tacked to the sky. Heat seemed to come equally from below as above, uncurling in visible waves from the cracked ground. Time moved at a crawl in Welcome, where people considered anything needing to be done in a hurry wasn't worth doing. Dogs and cats spent most of the day sleeping in the hot shade, rousing only to lap a few tepid drops from the water hookups. Even the flies were slow.

An envelope containing a check crackled in the pocket of my denim cutoffs. Mama had told me to take it to the manager of Blue-bonnet Ranch, Mr. Louis Sadlek, who lived at the redbrick house near the entrance of the trailer park.

My feet felt like they'd been steamed inside my shoes as I shuffled along the broken edges of asphalt. I saw a pair of older boys standing with a teenage girl, their postures relaxed and loose-limbed. The girl had a long blond ponytail with a ball of hair-sprayed bangs in the front. Her deep tan was exposed by short shorts and a tiny purple bikini top, which explained why the boys were so absorbed in conversation with her.

One of the boys was dressed in shorts and a tank top, while the other, dark-haired one wore a weathered pair of Wranglers and dirt-caked Roper boots. He stood with his weight shifted to one leg, one thumb hooked in a denim pocket, his free hand gesturing as he talked.

There was something striking about his slim, rawboned form, the hard edge of his profile. His vitality was almost jarring in those heat-drowsed surroundings.

Although Texans of all ages are naturally sociable and call out to strangers without hesitation, it was obvious I was going to walk by this trio unnoticed. That was just fine with me.

But as I walked quietly along the other side of the lane, I was startled by an explosion of noise and movement. Rearing back, I was set upon by what appeared to be a pair of rabid pit bulls. They barked and snarled and peeled their lips back to reveal jagged yellow teeth. I had never been scared of dogs, but these two were obviously out for the kill.

My instincts took over, and I spun to escape. The bald soles of my old sneakers slipped on a scattering of pebbles, my feet went out from under me, and I hit the ground on my hands and knees. I let out a scream and covered my head with my arms, fully expecting to be torn to pieces. But there was the sound of an angry voice over the blood rush in my ears, and instead of teeth closing over my flesh, I felt a pair of strong hands take hold of me.

I yelped as I was turned over to look up into the face of the dark-haired boy. He gave me a swift assessing glance and turned to yell some more at the pit bulls. The dogs had retreated a few yards, their barking fading to peevish snarls.

"Go on, damn it," the boy snapped at them. "Get your hindquarters back home and stop scaring people, you sorry pair of sh—" He checked himself and darted a quick glance at me.

The pit bulls quieted and slunk backward in a startling change of mood, pink tongues dangling like the half-curled ribbons of party balloons.

My rescuer viewed them with disgust and spoke to the boy in the tank top. "Pete, take the dogs back to Miss Marva's."

"They'll git home by theirselves," the boy protested, reluctant to part company with the blond girl in the bikini top.

"Take 'em back," came the authoritative reply, "and tell Marva to stop leaving the damn gate open."

While this conversation was taking place, I glanced down at my knees and saw they were oozing and peppered with gravel dust. My descent into the pit of soul-shriveling embarrassment was complete as the shock wore off and I started to cry. The harder I gulped against the tightness of my throat, the worse it became. Tears runneled from beneath my big plastic-framed glasses.

"For God's sake . . ." I heard the boy in the tank top mutter. Heaving a sigh, he went to the dogs and grabbed them by the collars. "Come on, troublemakers." They went with him willingly, trotting smartly on either side as if they were auditioning for the 4H state dog show.

The dark-haired boy's attention returned to me, and his voice gentled. "Here, now . . . you're okay. No need to cry, honey." He plucked a red handkerchief from his back pocket and began to mop at my face. Deftly he wiped my eyes and nose and told me to blow. The handkerchief held the sharp bite of male sweat as it clamped firmly over my nose. Back then men of every age had a red handkerchief tucked in the back pocket of their jeans. I'd seen kerchiefs used as a sieve, a coffee filter, a dust mask, and once as a makeshift baby diaper.

"Don't ever run from dogs like that." The boy tucked the kerchief in his back pocket. "No matter how scared you are. You just look to the side and walk away real slow, understand? And shout 'No' in a loud voice like you mean it."

I sniffled and nodded, staring into his shadowed face. His wide mouth held the curve of a smile that sent a quiver down to the pit of my stomach and knotted my toes inside my sneakers.

True handsomeness had escaped him by millimeters. His features were too blunt and bold, and his nose had a crook near the bridge from having been broken once. But he had a slow burn of a smile, and blue-on-blue eyes that seemed even brighter against the sun-glazed color of his skin, and a tumble of dark brown hair as shiny as mink fur.

"You got nothing to fear from those dogs," he said. "They're full of mischief, but as far as I know they've never bitten anyone. Here, take my hand."

As he pulled me up and set me on my feet, my knees felt like they'd been set on fire. I hardly noticed the pain, I was so occupied with the fury of my heartbeat. The grip of his hand was strong around mine, his fingers dry and warm.

"Where do you live?" the boy asked. "Are you moving into the new trailer on the loop?"

"Uh-huh." I wiped a stray tear off my chin.

"Hardy . . ." The blond girl's voice was sweetly cajoling. "She's all right now. Come walk me back. I got somethin' in my room to show you."

Hardy. So that was his name. He remained facing me, his vivid gaze shifting to the ground. It was probably just as well the girl couldn't see the wry smile secreted in the corners of his mouth. He seemed to have a pretty good idea of what she wanted to show him.

"Can't," he said cheerfully. "I have to take care of this little one."

The disgruntlement I felt at being referred to as if I were a toddler was promptly replaced by the triumph of being chosen over the blond girl. Although I couldn't figure out why in the world he wasn't leaping at the chance to go with her.

I wasn't a homely child, but neither was I the kind people made much of. From my Mexican father I had inherited dark hair, heavy eyebrows, and a mouth I thought was twice the size it needed to be. From Mama I had gotten a skinny build and light-colored eyes, but they weren't a clear sea-green like hers, they were hazel. I had often longed to have Mama's ivory skin and blond hair, but Daddy's darkness had won out.

It didn't help matters that I was shy and wore glasses. I was never one to stand out in the crowd. I liked to stay in corners. And I was happiest when I was alone reading. That and the good grades I got in school had doomed any chance of being popular with my peers. So it was a foregone conclusion that boys like Hardy were never going to take notice of me.

"Come on," he urged, leading the way to a tan single-wide with concrete steps at the back. A hint of a strut livened Hardy's walk, giving him the jauntiness of a junkyard dog.

I followed cautiously, wondering how mad Mama would be if she found out I'd wandered off with a stranger. "Is this yours?" I asked, my feet sinking into the crackling beige grass as we went toward the trailer.

Hardy replied over his shoulder. "I live here with my mom, two brothers, and a sister."

"That's a lot of people for a single-wide," I commented.

"Yeah, it is. I've got to move soon—there's no room for me in there. Mom says I'm growing so fast I'm like to bust the walls of the trailer out."

The notion that this creature still had some growing to do was almost alarming. "How big are you going to get?" I asked.

He chuckled and went to a spigot attached to a dusty gray garden hose. Turning it with a few deft twists, he started the flow of water and went to find the end of the hose. "Don't know. I'm already taller than most of my kin. Sit on that bottom step and stretch your legs out."

I obeyed, looking down at my scrawny calves, the skin covered with childish dark fuzz. I had experimented a few times with shaving my legs, but it hadn't yet become an established routine. I couldn't help comparing them to the smooth tanned legs of the blond girl, and the heat of embarrassment rose inside me.

Approaching me with the hose, Hardy sank to his haunches and warned, "This'll probably sting a little, Liberty."

"That's all right, I—" I stopped, my eyes widening in amazement. "How did you know my name?"

A smile lurked in one corner of his mouth. "It's written on the back of your belt."

Name belts had been popular that year. I had begged Mama to order one for me. We'd chosen pale pink leather with my name tooled in red letters.

I inhaled sharply as Hardy rinsed my knees with a stream of tepid water, washing off the blood and grit. It hurt more than I expected, especially when he passed his thumb over a few stubborn particles of rock to loosen them from my swollen skin.

He made a soothing sound as I flinched, and talked to distract me. "How old are you? Twelve?"

"Fourteen and three quarters."

His blue eyes sparkled. "You're kind of little for fourteen and three quarters."

"Am not," I replied indignantly. "I'm a sophomore this year. How old are you?"

"Seventeen and two fifths."

I stiffened at the gentle mockery, but as I met his gaze, I saw a flicker of playfulness. I had never felt the allure of another human being this strongly, warmth and curiosity mixing to form an unspoken question in the air.

A couple of times in your life, it happens like that. You meet a stranger, and all you know is that you need to know everything about him.

"How many brothers and sisters do you have?" he asked.

"None. It's just me and Mama and her boyfriend."

"Tomorrow if I get a chance, I'll bring my sister, Hannah, to meet you. She can introduce you to some of the kids around here and point out the ones to stay clear of." Hardy took the water off my raw knees, which were now pink and clean.

"What about the one you were just talking to? Is she someone I should stay clear of?"

A flash of a smile. "That's Tamryn. Yeah, stay away from her. She doesn't like other girls much." He went to turn the water off and came back to stand over me as I sat on the doorstep, his dark brown hair spilling over his forehead. I wanted to push it back. I wanted to touch him, not with sensuality but in wonder.

"Are you going home now?" Hardy asked, reaching down for me. Our palms locked. He pulled me to my feet and made certain I was steady before letting go.

"Not yet. I have an errand. A check for Mr. Sadlek." I felt for my back pocket to make sure it was still there.

The name caused a frown to tug between his straight dark brows. "I'll go with you."

"You don't have to," I said, although I felt a surge of shy delight at the offer.

"Yes I do. Your mama should know better than to send you to the front office by yourself."

"I don't understand."

"You will after you meet him." Hardy took my shoulders in his hands and said firmly, "If you ever need to visit Louis Sadlek for any reason, you come get me first."

The grip of his hands was electrifying. My voice sounded breathless as I said, "I wouldn't want to put you to trouble."

"No trouble." He looked down at me for a moment longer and fell back a half step.

"That's real nice of you," I said.

"Hell." He shook his head and replied with a smile, "I'm not nice. But between Miss Marva's pit bulls and Sadlek, someone's got to watch out for you."

We walked along the main drive, Hardy shortening his long stride to correspond with mine. When the pace of our feet matched perfectly, I felt a deep inner pang of satisfaction. I could have gone on walking like that forever, side by side with him. There had been few times in my life I had ever inhabited a moment so fully, with no loneliness lurking at the edges.

When I spoke, my voice sounded languid to my own ears, as if we were lying in lush grass beneath a shade tree. "Why do you say you're not nice?"

A low, rueful-sounding chuckle. "Because I'm an unrepentant sinner."

"So am I." It wasn't true, of course, but if this boy was an unrepentant sinner, I wanted to be one too.

"No you're not," he said with lazy certainty.

"How can you say that when you don't know me?"

"I can tell by looking."

I darted a covert glance at him. I was tempted to ask what else he read from my appearance, but I was afraid I already knew. The unkempt tangle of my ponytail, the modest length of my cutoffs, the big glasses and unplucked brows . . . it didn't exactly add up to the picture of a boy's wildest fantasies. I decided to change the conversation. "Is Mr. Sadlek mean?" I asked. "Is that why I shouldn't visit him alone?"

"He inherited the trailer park from his parents about five years ago, and ever since then he's harassed every woman who crosses his path. He tried it with my mother a time or two until I told him if he did it again I'd make sure he was nothing but a smear on the ground from here to Sugar Land."

I didn't doubt the claim for a minute. Despite Hardy's youth, he was big enough to inflict quite a lot of damage on someone.

We reached the redbrick ranch house, which clung to the flat arid land like a deer tick. A large black-and-white sign proclaiming BLUE-BONNET RANCH MOBILE HOME ESTATES had been planted on the side of the house closest to the main drive, with clusters of faded plastic bluebonnets tacked to the corners. Just beyond the sign a parade of pink yard flamingos riddled with bullet holes had been arranged precisely along the roadside.

I was to find out later it was the habit of some residents from the trailer park, including Mr. Sadlek, to visit a neighbor's field for target practice. They shot at a row of yard flamingos that bobbed and sprang back whenever they were shot. When a flamingo was too full of holes to be useful, it was strategically placed at the front entrance of the trailer park as an advertisement of the residents' shooting skills.

An OPEN sign hung in the little side window by the front door. Reassured by Hardy's solid presence beside me, I went to the front door, knocked tentatively and pushed it open.

A Latina cleaning lady was busy mopping the entranceway. In the corner, a cassette player spat out the cheerful polka rhythm of tejano music. Glancing upward, the girl spoke in rapid-fire Spanish. *"Cuidado, el piso es mojado."*

I only knew a few words of Spanish. Having no idea what she had meant, I shook my head apologetically. But Hardy replied without missing a beat, *"Gracias, tendremos cuidados."* He put a hand on the center of my back. "Careful. The floor's wet."

"You speak Spanish?" I asked him in mild surprise.

His dark brows lifted. "You don't?"

I shook my head, abashed. It had always been a source of vague embarrassment that despite my heritage I couldn't speak my father's language.

A tall, heavy figure appeared in the doorway of the front office. At first glance Louis Sadlek was a good-looking man. But it was a ruined handsomeness, his face and body showing the decay of habitual self-indulgence. His striped Western shirt had been left untucked in an effort to hide the billow of his waist. Although the fabric of his pants looked like cheap polyester, his boots were made of blue-dyed snakeskin. His even, regular features were marred by the florid bloat around his neck and cheeks.

Sadlek stared at me with casual interest, his lips pulling back in a dirty joke of a smile. He spoke to Hardy first. "Who's the little wetback?"

Out of the corner of my eye, I saw the cleaning lady stiffen and pause in her scrubbing. It seemed she had been exposed to the word often enough to know its meaning.

Seeing the instant tension in Hardy's jaw, and the clenching of the fist at his side, I broke in hastily. "Mr. Sadlek, I'm—"

"Don't call her that," Hardy said in a tone that made the hairs rise on the back of my neck.

They stared at each other with palpable animosity, their gazes level. A man well past his prime, and a boy who hadn't yet entered it. But there was no doubt in my mind how it would have ended if there had been a fight.

"I'm Liberty Jones," I said, trying to smooth the moment over. "My mother and I are moving into the new trailer." I dug the envelope from my back pocket and extended it to him. "She told me to give you this."

Sadlek took the envelope and tucked it into his shirt pocket, letting his gaze slide over me from head to toe. "Diana Jones is *your* mama?"

"Yes, sir."

"How'd a woman like that get a little dark-skinned girl like you? Your daddy musta been a Mexican."

"Yes, sir."

He gave a scornful snicker and shook his head. Another grin eased across his mouth. "You tell your mama to drop off the rent check herself next time. Tell her I got stuff I want to talk about."

"All right." Eager to be out of his presence, I tugged at Hardy's rigid arm. After a last warning glance at Louis Sadlek, Hardy followed me to the door.

"You'd best not run with white trash like the Cateses, little girl," Sadlek called out after us. "They're trouble. And Hardy's the worst of the lot."

After a scant minute in his presence, I felt as if I'd been wading through chest-high garbage. I turned to glance at Hardy in amazement.

"What a jerk," I said.

"You could say that."

"Does he have a wife and kids?"

Hardy shook his head. "Far as I know, he's been divorced twice. Some women in town seem to think he's a catch. You wouldn't know it to look at him, but he's got some money."

"From the trailer park?"

"That and a side business or two."

"What kind of side business?"

He let out a humorless laugh. "You don't want to know."

We walked to the loop intersection in contemplative silence. Now that evening was settling there were signs of life at the trailer park . . . cars turning in, voices and televisions filtering through the thin walls, smells of frying food. The white sun was resting on the horizon, bleeding out color until the sky was drenched in purple and orange and crimson.

"Is this it?" Hardy asked, stopping in front of my white trailer with its neat girdle of aluminum siding.

I nodded even before I saw the outline of my mother's profile in the window of the kitchenette. "Yes, it is," I exclaimed with relief. "Thank you."

As I stood there peering up at him through my brown-framed glasses, Hardy reached out to push back a piece of hair that had straggled loose from my ponytail. The callused tip of his finger was gently abrasive against my hairline, like the tickle of a cat's tongue. "You know what you remind me of?" he asked, studying me. "An elf owl."

"There's no such thing," I said.

"Yes there is. They mostly live to the south in the Rio Grande Valley and beyond. But every now and then an elf owl makes its way up here. I've seen one." He used his thumb and forefinger to indicate a distance of five inches. "They're only about this big. Cute little bird."

"I'm not little," I protested.

Hardy smiled. His shadow settled over me, blocking the light of sunset from my dazzled eyes. There was an unfamiliar stirring inside me. I wanted to step deeper into the shadow until I met his body, to feel his arms go around me. "Sadlek was right, you know," he said.

"About what?"

"I am trouble."

I knew that. My rioting heart knew it, and so did my weak knees, and so did my heat-prickling stomach. "I like trouble," I managed to say, and his laugh curled through the air.

He walked away in a graceful long-legged stride, a dark and solitary figure. I thought of the strength in his hands as he had picked me up from the ground. I watched him until he had disappeared from sight, and my throat felt thick and tingly like I'd just swallowed a spoonful of warm honey.

The sunset finished with a long crack of light rimming the horizon, as if the sky were a big door and God was taking one last peek. Good night, Welcome, I thought, and went into the trailer.

CHAPTER 9

My new home smelled agreeably of fresh-molded plastic and new carpeting. It was a two-bedroom single-wide with a concrete patio pad in the back. I'd been allowed to pick out the wallpaper in my room, white with bunches of pink roses and a narrow blue ribbon woven throughout. We had never lived in a trailer before, having occupied a rent house in Houston before we moved east to Welcome.

Like the trailer, Mama's boyfriend, Flip, was a new acquisition. He'd gotten his name from his habit of constantly flipping through TV channels, which hadn't been so bad at first but after a while it drove me crazy. When Flip was around, no one could watch more than five minutes of any one show.

I was never sure why Mama invited him to live with us—he seemed no better or different than any of her other boyfriends. Flip was like a friendly, oversized dog, good-looking and lazy, with the hint of a beer belly, a shaggy mullet, and an easy grin. Mama had to support him financially from day one, with her salary as a receptionist at the local title company. Flip, on the other hand, was perpetually unemployed. Although Flip had no objection to having a job, he was strongly opposed to the concept of actually looking for one. It was a common redneck paradox.

But I liked Flip because he made Mama laugh. The sound of those elusive laughs was so precious to me, I wished I could capture one in a Mason jar and keep it forever.

As I walked into the trailer, I saw Flip stretched out on the sofa with a beer in hand while Mama stacked cans in a kitchen cabinet.

"Hey, Liberty," he said easily.

"Hey, Flip." I went into the kitchenette to help my mother. The fluorescent ceiling light shone on the glasslike smoothness of her blond hair. My mother was fine-featured and fair, with mysterious green eyes and a vulnerable mouth. The only clue to her monumental stubbornness was the sharp, clean line of her jaw, vee-shaped like the prow of an ancient sailing ship.

"Did you give the check to Mr. Sadlek, Liberty?"

"Yes." I reached for sacks of flour, sugar, and cornmeal, and stowed them in the pantry. "He's a real jerk, Mama. He called me a wetback."

She whipped around to face me, her eyes blazing. A flush covered her face in delicate red patches. "That bastard," she exclaimed. "I can't believe— Flip, did you hear what Liberty just said?"

"Nope."

"He called my daughter a wetback."

"Who?"

"Louis Sadlek. The property manager. Flip, get off your ass and go talk to him. Right now! You tell him if he ever does that again—"

"Now, honey, that word don't mean nothing," Flip protested. "Everyone says it. They don't mean no harm."

"Don't you dare try to justify it!" Mama reached out and pulled me close, her arms wrapping protectively around my back and shoulders. Surprised by the strength of her reaction—after all, it wasn't the first time the word had been applied to me and certainly wouldn't be the last—I let her hold me for a moment before wriggling free.

"I'm okay, Mama," I said.

"Anyone who uses that word is showing you he's ignorant trash," she said curtly. "There's nothing wrong with being Mexican. You know that." She was more upset for my sake than I was.

I had always been acutely aware that I was different from Mama. We garnered curious glances when we went anywhere together. Mama, as fair as an angel, and me, dark-haired and obviously Hispanic. I had learned to accept it with resignation. Being half-Mexican was no different than being all-Mexican. That meant I would sometimes be called a wetback even though I was a natural-born American and had never set so much as a toe in the Rio Grande.

"Flip," Mama persisted, "are you going to talk to him?"

"He doesn't have to," I said, regretting having told her anything. I couldn't imagine Flip going to any trouble for something he plainly considered to be a minor issue.

"Honey," Flip protested, "I don't see no point in making trouble with the landlord on our first day—"

"The point is you should be man enough to stand up for my daughter." Mama glared at him. "I'll do it, damn it."

A long-suffering groan from the sofa, but there was no movement save the flick of his thumb on the remote control.

Anxiously I protested, "Mama, don't. Flip's right, it didn't mean anything." I knew in every cell of my body that my mother must be kept away from Louis Sadlek.

"I won't be long," she said stonily, looking for her purse.

"*Please,* Mama." I searched frantically for a way to dissuade her. "It's time for dinner. I'm hungry. *Really* hungry. Can we go out to eat? Let's try out the town cafeteria." Every adult I knew, including Mama, liked going to the cafeteria.

Mama paused and glanced at me, her face softening. "You hate cafeteria food."

"It's grown on me," I insisted. "I've started to like eating out of trays with compartments." Seeing the beginnings of a smile on her lips, I added, "If we're lucky it'll be senior citizens' night and we can get you in for half-price."

"You brat," she exclaimed, laughing suddenly. "I *feel* like a senior citizen after all this moving." Striding into the main room, she turned off the TV and stood in front of the fading screen. "Up, Flip."

"I'm gonna miss *WrestleMania*," he protested, sitting up. One side of his shaggy head was flattened from lying on a cushion.

"You won't watch the whole thing anyway," Mama said. "*Now,* Flip . . . or I'll hide the remote for an entire month."

Flip heaved a sigh and got to his feet.

The next day I met Hardy's sister, Hannah, who was a year younger than me but almost a head taller. She was striking rather than pretty, with a long-limbed athleticism that was common to the Cateses. They were physical people, competitive and prankish and completely opposite of everything I was. As the only girl in the family, Hannah had been taught never to back down from a dare, and to rush headlong into every challenge no matter how impossible it seemed. I admired such recklessness even if I didn't share it. It was a curse,

Hannah informed me, to be adventurous in a place where there was no adventure to be found.

Hannah was crazy about her older brother and loved to talk about him nearly as much as I loved to hear about him. According to Hannah, Hardy had graduated last year but was dating a senior named Amanda Tatum. He'd had girls throwing themselves at him since the age of twelve. Hardy spent his days building and repairing barbed-wire fencing for local ranchers, and had made the down payment on his mama's pickup. He'd been a fullback on the football team before he'd torn some ligaments in his knee, and he had run the forty-yard dash in 4.5 seconds. He could imitate the song of nearly any Texas bird you could name, from a chickadee to a wild turkey. And he was kind to Hannah and their two young brothers, Rick and Kevin.

I thought Hannah was the luckiest girl in the world to have Hardy for a brother. As poor as her family was, I envied her. I'd never liked being an only child. Whenever I was invited to a friend's house for dinner, I felt like a visitor to a foreign land, absorbing how things were done, what was said. I especially liked families that made a lot of commotion. Mama and I were quiet-living, and even though she assured me two people could be a family, ours didn't seem complete.

I had always hungered for family. Everyone else I knew was familiar with their grandparents and great-uncles and second and third cousins and all the distant relations that met up for reunions once every year or two. I never knew my relatives. Daddy had been an only child like me, and his parents were dead. The rest of his people were scattered around the state. His family, the Jimenezes, had lived for generations in Liberty County. That was how I got my name, actually. I was born in the town of Liberty, a little northeast of Houston. The Jimenezes had settled there way back in the eighteen hundreds, when Mexico opened the area to colonists. Eventually the Jimenezes had re-named themselves the Joneses, and they either died off or sold their land and moved away.

That left only Mama's side of the family. Whenever I asked her about them, she turned cold and quiet, or snapped at me to go play outside. One time I saw her crying afterward, sitting on the bed with her shoulders hunched over as if they were laden with invisible weights. After that I never asked her about her family again. But I knew her maiden name. Truitt. I wondered if the Truitts even knew I existed.

But most of all I wondered, what had Mama done that was so bad her own family didn't want her anymore?

Despite my worries Hannah insisted on taking me to meet Miss Marva and her pit bulls even after I protested they'd scared the wits out of me.

"You better go make friends with 'em," Hannah had warned. "Someday they'll get past the gate and run loose again, but they won't bother you if they know you."

"You mean they just eat strangers?"

I didn't think my cowardice was unreasonable under the circumstances, but Hannah rolled her eyes. "Don't be a scaredy-cat, Liberty."

"Do you know what happens to people who get dog-bitten?" I asked indignantly.

"No."

"Blood loss, nerve damage, tetanus, rabies, infection, amputation . . ."

"Gross," Hannah said admiringly.

We were walking along the main drive of the trailer park, our sneakers kicking up pebbles and dust clouds. The sunlight bore down on our uncovered heads and burned the thin lines of our parted hair. As we neared the Cateses' lot I saw Hardy washing his old blue truck, his bare back and shoulders gleaming like a new-minted penny. He wore denim shorts, flip-flops, and a pair of aviator sunglasses. His teeth flashed white in his tanned face as he smiled, and something pleasurable caught in my midsection.

"Hey, there," he said, rinsing swirls of foam from the pickup, his thumb partially capping the end of the hose to increase the pressure of the spray. "What are you up to?"

Hannah answered for both of us. "I want Liberty to make friends with Miss Marva's pit bulls, but she's scared."

"I'm not," I said, which was not at all true, but I didn't want Hardy thinking I was a coward.

"You were just telling me all the stuff that could happen if you get bitten," Hannah pointed out.

"That doesn't mean I'm scared," I said defensively. "It means I'm well informed."

Hardy gave his sister a warning glance. "Hannah, you can't push someone to do something like that before they're ready. You let Liberty deal with it in her own time."

"I want to," I insisted, abandoning all common sense in favor of pride.

Hardy went to turn off the hose, pulled a white T-shirt from a nearby umbrella-shaped laundry rack, and tugged it over his lean torso. "I'll come with you. Miss Marva has been after me to carry some of her paintings to the art gallery."

"She's an artist?" I asked.

"Oh, yes," Hannah said. "Miss Marva does bluebonnet paintings. Her stuff is real pretty, isn't it, Hardy?"

"It is," he said, coming to tug gently on one of his sister's braids.

As I watched Hardy, I felt the same puzzling yearning I had before. I wanted to draw closer to him, to investigate the scent of his skin beneath the layer of bleached cotton.

Hardy's voice seemed to change a little when he spoke to me. "How your knees doing, Liberty? Are they still sore?"

I shook my head mutely, nearly quivering like a plucked guitar string at his interest.

He began to reach out to me, hesitated, then gently pulled the brown-framed glasses from my upturned face. As usual, the lenses were covered with smears and fingerprints.

"How do you see out of these?" he asked.

I shrugged and smiled at the intriguing blur of his face above mine.

Hardy polished the glasses on the hem of his shirt and viewed them critically before handing them back. "Come on, you two, I'll walk you to Miss Marva's. I'll be interested to see what she makes of Liberty."

"Is she nice?" I fell into step by his right side, while Hannah walked on his left.

"She's nice if she likes you," he said.

"Is she old?" I asked, recalling the crotchety lady in our Houston neighborhood who had chased me with a stick if I ever stepped on her carefully cultivated front yard. I didn't especially like old people. The few I had been acquainted with had been either cranky, sluggish, or interested in detailed discussions of bodily discomforts.

The question made Hardy laugh. "I'm not exactly sure. She's been fifty-nine ever since I was born."

A quarter mile down the road, we approached Miss Marva's trailer, which I could have identified even without the help of my companions. The barking of the two hell spawn behind the chain-link fence in the back yard gave it away. They could tell I was coming. I felt instantly sick, my skin covered with chills and sweat, my heart pounding until I could feel its beat even in my scabby knees.

I stopped in my tracks, and Hardy paused to smile quizzically. "Liberty, what is it about you that gets those dogs so riled?"

"They can smell fear," I said, my gaze glued to the corner of the fenced-in yard, where I could see the pit bulls lunging and frothing.

"You said you weren't scared of dogs," Hannah said.

"Not the regular kind. But I draw the line at vicious, rabies-infested pit bulls."

Hardy laughed. He fitted a warm hand around the nape of my neck and squeezed comfortingly. "Let's go on in to meet Miss Marva. You'll like her." Taking his sunglasses off, he stared down at me with smiling blue eyes. "I promise."

The trailer smelled strongly of cigarettes and bluebonnet water, and something good baking in the oven. It seemed every square inch of the place was covered in art and handicrafts. Hand-painted bird-houses, tissue box covers made of acrylic yarn, Christmas ornaments, crocheted place mats, and unframed bluebonnet canvases of every size and shape.

In the middle of the chaos sat a plump little woman with hair that had been moussed and teased into a perfect hive. It was dyed a shade of red I had never seen duplicated in nature. Her skin was webbed and furrowed, constantly shifting to accommodate her animated expressions. Her gaze was as alert as a hawk's. Although Miss Marva might have been old, she wasn't the least bit sluggish.

"Hardy Cates," she rasped in a nicotine-stained voice, "I expected you to pick up my paintings two days ago."

"Yes, ma'am," he said humbly.

"Well, boy, what's your excuse?"

"I got too busy."

"If you show up late, Hardy, it's only decent to come up with a colorful excuse." Her attention turned to Hannah and me. "Hannah, who is that girl with you?"

"This is Liberty Jones, Miss Marva. She and her mama just moved into the new trailer on the loop."

"*Just* you and your mama?" Miss Marva asked, her mouth pursing like she'd just eaten a handful of fried pickles.

"No, ma'am. Mama's boyfriend lives with us too." Prodded by

Miss Marva's interrogation, I proceeded to explain all about Flip and his channel-changing, and how Mama was a widow and answered the phone at the local title company, and how I was here to make peace with the pit bulls after they'd run up and scared me.

"Those rascals," Miss Marva exclaimed without heat. "More trouble than they're worth most of the time. But I need 'em for company."

"What's wrong with cats?" I asked.

Miss Marva shook her head decisively. "I gave up on cats a long time ago. Cats attach to places, dogs attach to people."

Miss Marva steered the three of us into the kitchen and gave us plates heaped with red velvet cake. Between mouthfuls of cake Hardy told me Miss Marva was the best cook in Welcome. According to Hardy, her cakes and pies won the tricolored ribbon at the county fair every year until the officials had begged her not to enter so someone else could have a chance.

Miss Marva's red velvet cake was the best I had ever tasted, made with buttermilk and cocoa, and enough red food coloring to make it glow like a stoplight, the whole of it covered with an inch-thick layer of cream cheese frosting.

We ate like ravenous wolves, nearly scraping layers off the yellow Fiesta ware with our aggressive forks, until every bright crumb had vanished. My tonsils were still tingling from the sweetness of the frosting as Miss Marva directed me to the jar of dog biscuits on the end of the Formica counter. "You take two of those for the dogs," she instructed, "and hand 'em through the fence. They'll warm up to you right quick, soon as you feed 'em."

I swallowed hard. Abruptly the cake turned into a brick in my stomach. Seeing my expression, Hardy murmured, "You don't have to."

I wasn't eager to confront the pit bulls, but if it allowed me a few more minutes of Hardy's company, I'd have faced down a herd of rampaging longhorns. Reaching into the jar, I closed my hand around two bone-shaped biscuits, their surfaces turning tacky against my damp palm. Hannah stayed inside the trailer to help Miss Marva pile more handicrafts into a liquor-store box.

Angry barking littered the air as Hardy took me to the gate. The dogs' ears were flattened against their bullet-shaped heads as they pulled their lips back to sneer and snarl. The male was black and white, the female light tan. I wondered why they thought harassing me was worth leaving the shade of the trailer overhang.

"Will the fence keep them in?" I asked, staying so close to Hardy's side that I nearly tripped him. The dogs were full of coiled energy, straining as if to leap over the top of the gate.

"Absolutely," Hardy said with comforting firmness. "I built it myself."

I regarded the irritable dogs warily. "What are their names? Psycho and Killer?"

He shook his head. "Cupcake and Twinkie."

My mouth dropped open. "You're kidding."

A grin flitted across his lips. "Afraid not."

If naming them after dessert snacks had been Miss Marva's attempt to make them seem cute, it wasn't working. They slavered and snapped at me as if I were a string of sausages.

Hardy spoke to them in a no-nonsense tone, telling them to hush up and act nice if they knew what was good for them. He also commanded them to sit, with mixed success. Cupcake's rump lowered reluctantly to the ground, while Twinkie's remained defiantly aloft. Panting and openmouthed, the pair regarded us with eyes like flat black buttons.

"Now," Hardy coached, "offer a biscuit to the black one with your hand open, palm up. Don't look him directly in the eyes. And don't make any jerky movements."

I switched the biscuit to my left palm.

"Are you a lefty?" he asked with amiable interest.

"No. But if this hand gets bitten off, I'll still have my good one to write with."

A low chuckle. "You won't get bitten. Go on."

I pinned my gaze to the flea collar that encircled Cupcake's neck, and began to extend the dog cookie toward the metal web that separated us. I saw the animal's body tense expectantly as he saw the treat in my palm. Unfortunately, it seemed in question as to whether the attraction was the biscuit or my hand. Losing my nerve at the last moment, I pulled back.

A whine whistled in Cupcake's throat, while Twinkie reacted with a series of truncated barks. I darted a shamed glance at Hardy, expecting him to make fun of me. Wordlessly he slid a solid arm around my shoulders, and his free hand sought mine. He cradled it as if he held a hummingbird in the cup of his palm. Together we offered the biscuit to the waiting dog, who gobbled it with a gigantic slurp and wagged a pencil-straight tail. His tongue left a film of saliva on my upturned palm, and I wiped it on my shorts. Hardy kept an arm on my shoulders as I gave the other biscuit to Twinkie.

"Good girl," came Hardy's quiet praise. He gave a brief squeeze and let go. The pressure of his arm seemed to linger across my shoulders even after it was withdrawn. The place where our sides had pressed together was very warm. My heart had lurched into a new rhythm, and every breath I drew fed a sweet ache in my lungs.

"I'm still scared of them," I said, watching the two beasts return to the side of the trailer and flop down heavily in the shade.

Still facing me, Hardy rested his hand on top of the fence and lent some of his weight to it. He looked at me as if he were fascinated by something he saw in my face. "Being afraid's not always bad," he said gently. "It can keep you moving forward. It can help you get things done."

The silence between us was different than any silence I'd known before, full and warm and waiting. "What are you afraid of?" I dared to ask.

There was a flicker of surprise in his eyes, as if it were something he'd never been asked before. For a moment I thought he wouldn't answer. But he let out a slow breath, and his gaze left mine to sweep across the trailer park. "Staying here," he finally said. "Staying until I'm not fit to belong anywhere else."

"Where do you want to belong?" I half whispered.

His expression changed with quicksilver speed, amusement dancing in his eyes. "Anywhere they don't want me."

CHAPTER 3

I spent most of the summer in Hannah's company, falling in with her schemes and plans, which never amounted to anything but were enjoyable nonetheless. We rode our bikes into town, went out to explore ravines and fields and cave entrances, or sat together in Hannah's room listening to Nirvana. To my disappointment I seldom saw Hardy, who was always working. Or raising hell, as Hannah's mother, Miss Judie, said sourly.

Wondering how much hell-raising could be done in a town like Welcome, I culled as much information as I could from Hannah. It seemed to be a matter of general agreement that Hardy Cates was born for trouble, and sooner or later he would find it. So far his crimes had been minor ones, misdeeds and small acts of mischief that broadcast a frustrated voltage beneath his good-natured exterior. Breathlessly Hannah related that Hardy had been seen with girls much older than himself, and there had even been rumors of a dalliance with an older woman in town.

"Has he ever been in love?" I couldn't resist asking, and Hannah said no, according to Hardy falling in love was the last thing he needed. It would get in the way of his plans, which were to leave Welcome as soon as Hannah and her brothers were old enough to be of some help to their mother, Miss Judie.

It was hard to understand how a woman like Miss Judie could have produced such an untamed brood. She was a self-disciplined woman who seemed suspicious of pleasure in any form. Her angular features were like one of those old-time prospector scales upon which were balanced equal amounts of meekness and brittle pride. She was a tall, frail-looking woman whose wrists you could snap like cottonwood twigs. And she was living proof you should never trust a skinny cook. Her notion of fixing dinner was to open cans and ferret out scraps in the vegetable drawer. No wilted carrot or petrified celery stalk was safe from her reach.

After one meal of leftover bologna mixed with canned green beans and served on warmed-over biscuits, and a dessert of canned frosting on toast, I learned to take my leave whenever I heard the rattling of pans in the kitchen. The strange thing was, the Cates children didn't seem to notice or care how terrible the food was. Every fluorescent curl of macaroni, every morsel of something suspended in Jell-O, every particle of fat and gristle disappeared from their plates within five minutes of being served.

On Saturdays the Cateses went out to eat, but not at the local

Mexican restaurant or the cafeteria. They went to Earl's meat market, where the butcher dumped all the scraps and cuts he hadn't been able to sell that day—sausages, tails, ribs, innards, pigs' ears—into a big metal tub. "Everything but the oink," Earl used to say with a grin. He was a huge man with hands the size of catcher mitts and a face that glowed as red as fresh ham.

After collecting the day's leftovers, Earl would fill the tub with water and boil it all together. For twenty-five cents you could pick out whatever you wanted, and Earl would set it on a piece of butcher paper along with a slice of Mrs. Baird's bread, and you would eat at the linoleum table in the corner. Nothing was wasted at the meat market. After people were through with the tub, Earl took what was left, ground it up, added bright yellow cornmeal, and sold it as dog food.

The Cateses were dirt poor, but they were never referred to as white trash. Miss Judie was a respectable God-fearing woman, which elevated the family to the level of "poor white." It seems a minor distinction, but many doors in Welcome were open to you if you were poor white and closed if you were white trash.

As a file clerk to the only CPA in Welcome, Miss Judie earned barely enough to put a roof over her children's heads, with Hardy's income supplementing her meager earnings. When I asked Hannah where her daddy was, she told me he was in the Texarkana State Penitentiary, although she'd never been able to find out what he'd done to get himself there.

Maybe the family's troubled past was the reason Miss Judie had established a spotless record of church attendance. She went every Sunday morning and Wednesday night and was always to be found in the first three pews, where the Lord's presence was the strongest. Like most people in Welcome, Miss Judie drew conclusions about a person based on his or her religion. It confounded her when I said Mama and I didn't go to church. "Well, what *are* you?" she pressed, until I said I thought I was a lapsed Baptist.

This led to another tricky question. "Progressive Baptist or Re-formed Baptist?"

Since I wasn't sure of the difference, I said I thought we were pro-gressive. A frown appeared on Miss Judie's forehead as she said in that case we should probably go to First Baptist on Main, although from what she understood, their main Sunday service featured rock bands and a line of chorus girls.

When I told Miss Marva about the conversation later, and protested that "lapsed" meant I didn't have to go to church, Miss Marva replied there was no such thing as lapsed in Welcome, and I might as well go with her and her gentleman friend Bobby Ray to the nondenomina-tional Lamb of God on South Street, because for all that they had a guitarist instead of an organist and held open communion, they also had the best potluck in town.

Mama had no objection to my attending church with Miss Marva and Bobby Ray, although she said it suited her to remain lapsed for the time being. It soon became my habit on Sundays to arrive at Miss Marva's trailer at eight o'clock sharp, eat a breakfast of Bisquick sausage squares or pecan pancakes, and ride to the Lamb of God with Miss Marva and Bobby Ray.

Having no children or grandchildren of her own, Miss Marva had decided to take me under her wing. Discovering my only good dress was too short and small, she offered to make me a new one. I spent an hour happily sorting through the stacks of discount fabric she kept in her sewing room, until I found a bolt of red cloth printed with tiny yellow and white daisies. In a mere two hours Miss Marva had run up a simple sleeveless dress with a boatneck top. I tried it on and looked at myself in the long mirror on the back of her bedroom door. To my delight, it flattered my adolescent curves and made me look a little older.

"Oh, Miss Marva," I said with glee, throwing my arms around her stalwart form, "you are the best! Thank you a million times. A zillion times."

"It was nothing," she said. "I can't take a girl in pants to church, can I?"

Naïvely I thought when I brought the dress home that Mama would be pleased by the gift. Instead it set off her temper and launched her on a tirade about charity and interfering neighbors. She trembled with anger and hollered until I was in tears and Flip had left the trailer to go get more beer. I protested that it had been a present and I didn't have any dresses, and I was going to keep it no matter what she said. But Mama snatched the dress from me, stuffed it in a plastic grocery sack, and left the trailer, marching to Miss Marva's in high dudgeon.

I cried myself sick, thinking I wouldn't be allowed to visit Miss Marva anymore, and wondering why I had the most selfish mother in the world whose pride meant more than her own daughter's spiritual welfare. Everyone knew girls couldn't go to church in pants, which meant I would continue to be a heathen and live outside the Lord, and worst of all I would miss the best potluck in town.

But something happened in the time that Mama was gone to Miss Marva's. When she returned, her face was relaxed and her voice was peaceful, and she had my new dress in hand. Her eyes were red as if she'd been crying. "Here, Liberty," she said absently, placing the crackling plastic bag into my arms. "You can keep the dress. Go put it in the washer. And add a spoonful of baking soda to get rid of the cigarette smell."

"Did you . . . did you talk with Miss Marva?" I ventured.

"Yes, I did. She's a nice woman, Liberty." A wry smile tipped the corners of her mouth. "Colorful, but nice."

"Then I can go to church with her?"

Mama gathered her long blond hair at the nape of her neck and secured it with a scrunchie. Turning to lean her back against the edge of the counter, she stared at me thoughtfully. "It's certainly not going to hurt you any."

"No, ma'am," I agreed.

Her arms opened, and I obeyed the motion at once, speeding to her until my body was crowded tightly against hers. There was nothing better in the world than being held by my mother. I felt the press of her mouth at the top of my head, and the tender shift of her cheek as she smiled. "You've got your daddy's hair," she murmured, smoothing the inky tangles.

"I wish I had yours," I said, my voice muffled against her fragile softness. I breathed in the delicious scent of her, tea and skin and some powdery perfume.

"No. Your hair is beautiful, Liberty."

I stood quietly against her, willing the moment to last. Her voice was a low, pleasant hum, her chest rising and falling beneath my ear. "Baby, I know you don't understand why I was so mad about the dress. It's just . . . we don't want anyone to think you need things I can't get for you."

But I did need it, I was tempted to say. Instead I kept my mouth shut and nodded.

"I thought Marva gave it to you because she felt sorry for you," Mama said. "Now I realize it was meant as a gift between friends."

"I don't see why it was such a big deal," I mumbled.

Mama eased me away a little, and stared into my eyes without blinking. "Pity goes hand in hand with contempt. Don't ever forget that, Liberty. You can't take handouts or help from anyone, because that gives people the right to look down on you."

"What if I need help?"

She shook her head immediately. "No matter what trouble you're in, you can get yourself out of it. You just work hard, and use your mind. You've got such a good mind—" She paused to clasp my face in her hands, my cheeks compressed in the warm framework of her fingers. "When you grow up I want you to be self-reliant. Because most women aren't, and it puts them at everyone's mercy."

"Are you self-reliant, Mama?"

The question brought a wash of uncomfortable color to her face, and her hands fell away from my face. She took a long time about answering. "I try," she half whispered, with a bitter smile that made the flesh prickle on my arms.

As Mama started to make dinner, I went out for a walk. By the time I reached Miss Marva's trailer, the afternoon, fierce and kiln-hot, had drained all the energy out of me.

Knocking at the door, I heard Miss Marva call me to come in. An ancient air conditioner rattled from its berth on the window frame, spurting cold air toward the sofa where Miss Marva sat with a needle-point frame.

"Hey, Miss Marva." I viewed her with new respect in light of her mysterious influence over my stormy-natured parent.

She motioned me to sit beside her. Our combined weights caused the sofa cushion to compress with a squeak.

The TV was on; a lady reporter with neat bobbed hair stood in front of a map of a foreign country. I listened with only half an ear, having no interest in what was happening in a place so far away from Texas. " '. . . heaviest fighting so far occurred at the emir's palace, where the royal guard held off Iraqi invaders long enough for members of the royal family to escape . . . concern over thousands of Western visitors who have so far been detained from leaving Kuwait . . .' "

I focused on the circular frame in Miss Marva's hands. She was making a seat cushion that, when finished, would resemble a giant tomato slice. Noticing my interest, Miss Marva asked, "Do you know how to needlepoint, Liberty?"

"No, ma'am."

"Well, you should. Nothing settles your nerves like working on needlepoint."

"I don't have nerves," I told her, and she said I would when I was older. She put the canvas in my lap, and showed me the way to push the needle through the little squares. Her vein-corrugated hands were warm on mine, and she smelled like cookies and tobacco.

"A good needlepointer," Miss Marva said, "makes the back side look as good as the front side." Together we bent over the big tomato slice, and I managed to put in a few bright red stitches. "Good work," she praised. "Look how nice you pulled the thread—not too tight, not too loose."

I continued to work on the needlepoint. Miss Marva watched patiently and didn't fuss even when I got a few stitches wrong. I tried to pull the strand of pale green wool through all the little squares that had been dyed a matching color. As I stared closely at the needlepoint, it appeared as if the dots and splashes of color had been strewn randomly across the surface. But when I pulled back and looked at it as a whole, the pattern suddenly made sense and formed a complete picture.

"Miss Marva?" I asked, scooting back in the corner of the springy sofa and hooking my arms around my knees.

"Take your shoes off if you're going to put your feet up."

"Yes, ma'am. Miss Marva . . . what happened when my mother came to visit you today?"

One of the things I liked about Miss Marva was that she always answered my questions frankly. "Your mama came here breathing fire, all riled about that dress I made you. So I told her I meant no offense and I'd take it back. Then I poured some iced tea and we got to talking, and I figured out right quick she wasn't really mad about the dress."

"She wasn't?" I asked dubiously.

"No, Liberty. She just needed someone to talk to. Someone to sympathize about the load she's carrying."

That was the first time I'd ever discussed my mother with another adult. "What load?"

"She's a single working mother. That's about the hardest thing there is."

"She's not single. She's got Flip."

Amused, Miss Marva gave a little cackle. "Tell me, how much help does he give your mama?"

I pondered Flip's responsibilities, which centered primarily around the procurement of beer and the disposal of the cans. Flip also spent a lot of time cleaning his guns, in between the occasions he went to the flamingo range with other men from the trailer park. Basically Flip's function in our house was ornamental.

"Not very much," I admitted. "But why are we keeping Flip if he's so useless?"

"For the same reason I keep Bobby Ray. Sometimes a woman needs a man for company, no matter how useless he is."

From what I knew of Bobby Ray, I liked him pretty well. He was an amiable old man, smelling of drugstore cologne and WD-40. Although Bobby Ray didn't officially reside in Miss Marva's trailer, he could be found there most of the time. They seemed so much like an old married couple that I had assumed they were in love.

"Do you love Bobby Ray, Miss Marva?"

The question made her smile. "Sometimes I do. When he takes me to the cafeteria, or rubs my feet while we watch our Sunday-night programs. I guess I love him at least ten minutes a day."

"That's all?"

"Well, it's a good ten minutes, child."

Not long after that, Mama kicked Flip out of our trailer. It was a surprise to no one. Although there was a high tolerance for shiftless males at the trailer park, Flip had distinguished himself as a major league underachiever, and everyone knew a woman like Mama could do better. It was just a question of what the last straw would be.

I don't think anyone could have predicted the emu.

Emus aren't native Texas birds, although from the number of them to be found, both wild and domestic, you'd have been excused for thinking otherwise. In fact, Texas is still known as the emu capital of the world. It started around '87 when some farmers brought some of the big flightless birds to the state with the ambition to replace beef as a cash crop. They must have been slick talkers, because they convinced just about everybody that the public would soon be clamoring for emu oil, leather, and meat. So emu producers raised birds to sell to other people to raise birds, and at one point a breeding pair cost about thirty-five thousand dollars.

Later on when a contrary public didn't take to the idea of replacing a Big Mac with a Big Bird, the bottom dropped out of the market and dozens of emu ranchers turned their worthless birds loose. At the height of the emu craze, there were plenty of birds to be found in fenced pastures, and like any animal in a restricted area, they occasionally found a way to get past the fence.

As best I could make out, Flip's emu encounter happened on one of those narrow country roads in the middle of nowhere, while he was driving back from a dove lease someone had let him in on. Dove season lasts from the beginning of September to the end of October. If you don't have your own acreage, you can pay someone else for the privilege of hunting their land. The best leases are covered with sunflowers or corn and feature a water tank, which brings the doves in fast and low, wings flashing.

Flip's share of the lease had been seventy-five dollars, which Mama had paid just to get him out of the trailer for a few days. We hoped Flip might be lucky enough to hit some doves we could grill with some bacon and jalapeños. Unfortunately, while Flip's aim was dead-on when an object was holding still, he couldn't get the knack of hitting a target in motion.

Heading back home empty-handed, his gun barrel still hot from the day's shooting, Flip was forced to stop his truck when the road was blocked by a six-foot-tall blue-necked emu. He honked the horn and shouted at the creature to move away, but the emu wouldn't budge. It just stood there looking at him with beady yellow eyes. It wouldn't move even when Flip got his shotgun from the back of the truck and fired in the air. The emu was either too mean or too puny-brained to scare.

It must have occurred to Flip as he waited in a standoff with the emu that it looked a lot like a giant chicken with long legs. It also must have occurred to him that there was a lot of eating on that bird, about a thousand times more than a handful of tiny dove breasts. Better yet, unlike the doves, the emu was holding still. So in a bid to restore his injured masculinity, his aim fine-tuned by hours of flamingo practice, Flip hefted the gun to his shoulder and blew the emu's head clean off.

He returned home with the huge carcass in the back of the truck, expecting to be hailed as a conquering hero.

I was on the patio reading when I heard the familiar putter of Flip's truck and the sound of the engine being cut. Skirting around the trailer, I went to ask if Flip had caught any doves or not. Instead I saw a big dark-feathered body in the pickup bed, and bloodstains all over Flip's camo shirt and jeans like he'd been slaughtering cattle instead of dove hunting.

"Looky here," he told me with a big grin, tipping the bill of his cap back on his head.

"What's that?" I asked in amazement, inching closer to view the thing.

He postured a little. "Shot me an ostrich."

I wrinkled my nose at the smell of fresh blood that wafted thick and sweet in the air. "I don't think that's an ostrich, Flip. I think it's an emu."

"No difference." Flip shrugged, his grin broadening as Mama came to the door of the trailer. "Hey, honey pie . . . look what Daddy brung home."

I'd never seen my mother's eyes turn so big. *"Holy shit,"* she said. "Flip, where the hell did you get that emu?"

"Shot it on the road," he replied proudly, mistaking her shock for admiration. "Gonna be mighty good eating tonight. Tastes just like beef, they say."

"That thing must be worth at least fifteen thousand dollars," Mama exclaimed, putting a hand on her heart as if to keep it from leaping out of her chest.

"Not anymore," I couldn't resist saying.

Mama glared at Flip. "You've destroyed someone's private property."

"No one'll find out," he said. "Come on, honey, hold the door open so I can bring it inside and butcher it."

"You're not about to bring that into my trailer, you crazy dumbass! Take it away. Take it away *now*! You're going to get us both arrested for this."

Flip was plainly bewildered that his gift was so unappreciated. Seeing the storm about to come, I mumbled something about returning to the patio and retreated to a spot behind the corner of the trailer. In the minutes that followed it was likely most of Bluebonnet Ranch heard Mama screaming that she'd had it, there was no way she was going to put up with him another minute. Disappearing into the trailer, she rummaged around for a short time, then came back with an armload of denim and boots and men's underwear. She flung the lot of it onto the ground. "Take your stuff and get out of here now!"

"You call me crazy?" Flip shouted back. "You're out of your gourd, woman! Quit throwing my things like— Hey, stop that!" It began to rain T-shirts and hunting magazines and foam beer can holders, the effluvia of Flip's life of leisure. Swearing and huffing indignantly, Flip gathered the objects from the ground and hurled them into his truck.

In less than ten minutes Flip had driven away from the trailer, his wheels spinning, gravel flying behind him. All that remained was the hulk of a headless emu, deposited right in front of our door.

Mama was breathing heavily, her face crimson. "That useless jackass," she muttered. "Should have gotten rid of him a long time ago . . . an *emu*, for Christ's sake . . ."

"Mama," I asked, coming to stand beside her. "Is Flip gone for good?"

"*Yes*," she said vehemently.

I stared at the mountainous carcass. "What are we going to do with it?"

"I have no idea." Mama scrubbed her hands through her pale, rumpled hair. "But we've got to dispose of the evidence. That bird was worth a lot to somebody . . . and I'm not paying for it."

"Somebody should eat it," I said.

Mama shook her head and groaned. "That thing is one step up from road kill."

I thought for a moment, and inspiration struck. "The Cateses," I said.

Mama's gaze met mine, and gradually the scowl on her face was replaced by reluctant humor. "You're right. Go get Hardy."

To hear the Cateses tell it later, there had never been such a feast. And it went on for days. Emu steaks, emu stew, emu sandwiches, and chili con emu. Hardy had taken the bird to Earl's Meat Market, where the butcher, after promising strict confidentiality, had a high time processing it into fans, fillets, and ground meat.

Miss Judie even sent over an emu casserole for Mama and me, made with Tater Tots and Hamburger Helper. I tried it and thought it was one of Miss Judie's better efforts. But Mama, who was watching me with a doubtful gaze, suddenly turned green and fled the kitchenette, and I heard her getting sick in the bathroom.

"I'm sorry, Mama," I said anxiously through the door. "I won't eat the casserole anymore if it makes you sick. I'll throw it out. I'll—"

"It's not the casserole," she said in a guttural voice. I heard the sounds of her spitting, and the gurgle of the toilet flush. The water spigot was turned on as Mama began to brush her teeth.

"What is it, Mama? Did you get a virus?"

"Uh-uh."

"Then—"

"We'll talk about it later, honey. Right now I need some—" She stopped for another spit. *Pt! Pt!* "Privacy."

"Yes, ma'am."

It puzzled me that Mama should have told Miss Marva she was pregnant before she told anyone else, including me. They had become friends in no time, despite the fact that they were so different. Seeing them together was like watching a swan keeping company with a red-headed woodpecker. But they shared a certain steeliness underneath their dissimilar exteriors. They were both strong women who were willing to pay the price for their independence.

I figured out Mama's secret one evening when she was talking in our kitchenette with Miss Marva, who had brought over a delicious peach cobbler with layers of sopping juice-soaked crust inside. Sitting in front of the TV with a dish and a spoon in my lap, I caught a few whispered words between them.

". . . don't see why he should ever be told . . ." Mama said to Miss Marva.

"But he owes you some help . . ."

"Oh no . . ." Mama lowered her voice again, so I could only hear a little here and there. ". . . mine, has nothing to do with him . . ."

"It won't be easy."

"I know. But I have someone to go to if things get bad enough."

I realized what they were talking about. There had been signs, including Mama's queasy stomach and the fact that she'd made two doctor visits in the space of a week. All my wishing and longing for someone to love, for family, had finally been answered. I felt a pinch in the back of my throat, something like tears. I wanted to jump up to my feet, I was so filled with happiness.

I stayed quiet, straining to hear more, and the intensity of my feelings must have reached Mama somehow. Her gaze fell on me, and she broke the conversation with Miss Marva long enough to say casually, "Liberty, go and start your bath now."

I couldn't believe how normal my voice sounded, just as normal as hers. "I don't need a bath."

"Then go read something. Go on, now."

"Yes, ma'am." I made my way reluctantly to the bathroom, questions darting through my mind. Someone to go to . . . An old boyfriend? One of the relatives she never talked about? I knew it had something to do with Mama's secret life, the one she had led before I was born. When I was a grown-up, I vowed silently, I would go and find out everything I could about her.

I waited impatiently for Mama to break the news to me, but after six weeks had passed and still no word, I decided to ask her directly. We were driving to Piggly Wiggly for groceries in the silver Honda Civic we'd had ever since I could remember. Recently Mama had gotten it all fixed up, all the dents and dings pushed out, new paint, new brake pads, so it was good as new. She had also bought new clothes for me, an umbrella table and chair set for the patio, and a brand-new TV. She had gotten a bonus from the title company, she explained.

Our life had always been like that . . . sometimes we would have to count every penny, but then little windfalls would come. Bonuses or small lottery winnings, or something left to Mama in some distant relative's will. I never dared to question her about the pockets of money that came our way. But as I got older I noticed they always happened right after one of her mysterious disappearances. Every few months, maybe twice a year, she would have me stay overnight at a neighbor's house, and she would be gone for a day and sometimes wouldn't come back until the next morning. When she returned, she restocked the pantry and the freezer, and there were new clothes, and things were paid off, and we could go out to eat again.

"Mama," I asked, staring at the delicately stern lines of her profile, "you're going to have a baby, aren't you?"

The car swerved slightly as Mama shot me an astonished glance. She returned her attention to the road, her hands gripping the steering wheel. "Good Lord, you almost made me wreck the car."

"Are you?" I persisted.

She was quiet for a moment. When she replied, her voice was a little unsteady. "Yes, Liberty."

"A boy or a girl?"

"I don't know yet."

"Are we going to share it with Flip?"

"No, Liberty, it's not Flip's baby, or any man's. Just ours."

I relaxed back in the seat while Mama's quick-stolen glance darted through the silence. "Liberty . . ." she said with effort. "There are going to be some adjustments for both of us. Sacrifices we'll both have to make. I'm sorry. I didn't plan on this."

"I understand, Mama."

"Do you?" A humorless chuckle. "I'm not sure I understand it."

"What are we going to name it?" I asked.

"I haven't even started thinking about that."

"We need to get one of those baby name books." I was going to read every name there was. This baby was going to have a long, important-sounding name. Something from Shakespeare. Something that would make everyone aware of how special he or she was.

"I didn't expect you would take the news this well," Mama said.

"I'm happy about it," I said. "Really happy."

"Why?"

"Because now I won't be alone anymore."

The car turned into a parking space in one of the rows of super-heated vehicles, and Mama turned the key in the ignition. I was sorry I'd answered that way, because it had brought a stricken look to her eyes. Slowly she reached out and smoothed back the front of my hair. I wanted to nudge against her hand like a cat being petted. Mama was a believer in personal space, her own and everyone else's, and she was not given to casual invasions of it.

"You're not alone," she said.

"Oh, I know, Mama. But everyone has brothers and sisters. I've always wanted someone to play with and take care of. I'll be a good babysitter. You won't even have to pay me."

That earned one more hair-smoothing, and then we got out of the car.

CHAPTER 4

As soon as school started, I discovered my polo shirts and baggy jeans qualified me as a fashion emergency. The style was grunge, everything shredded and stained and wrinkled. Trash-can chic, Mama said in distaste. But I was desperate to fit in with the other girls in my class, and I begged her to take me to the nearest department store. We bought thin gauzy blouses and long tank tops, a crocheted vest and an ankle-length skirt, and clunky Doc Martens shoes. The price tag on a pair of distressed jeans nearly sent Mama into shock—"Sixty dollars and they already have holes in them?"—but she bought them anyway.

The high school in Welcome had no more than a hundred students in the entire ninth-grade class. Football was everything. The whole town turned out every Friday night for the game, or shut down so fans could follow the Panthers for the away games. Mothers, sisters, and girlfriends barely flinched as their warriors engaged in battles that, had they occurred outside the stadium, would have counted as attempted murder. For most of the players, this was their place in the sun, their one shot at glory. The boys were recognized like celebrities as they walked down the street, and the coach was ostentatiously told to put away his driver's license whenever he wrote a check—no ID was needed.

Since the athletic-supplies budget outstripped that of every other department, the school library was adequate at best. That was where I spent most of my free time. I had no thought of trying out for cheerleading, not only because it looked silly to me, but because it took money and string-pulling by frantic parents to assure their daughter's place on the squad.

I was lucky to find friends quickly, a circle of three other girls who hadn't made it into any of the popular cliques. We visited each other's houses, experimented with makeup, vogued in front of the mirror, and saved our money for ceramic flattening irons. For my fifteenth-birthday present, Mama finally allowed me to have contact lenses. It was a strange but delicious feeling to look at the world without the weight of thick glasses on my face. To celebrate my liberation, my best friend, Lucy Reyes, announced she was going to pluck my eyebrows. Lucy was a dark, slim-hipped Portuguese girl who devoured fashion magazines between classes and kept up with all the latest styles.

"My eyebrows aren't that bad," I protested as Lucy advanced on me with witch hazel, tweezers, and to my alarm, a tube of Anbesol. "Are they?"

"Do you really want me to answer that?" Lucy asked.

"I guess not."

Lucy pushed me toward the vanity chair in her bedroom. "Sit." I gazed into the mirror with concern, focusing on the hair between my brows, which Lucy had said constituted a linking section. Since it was a well-known fact that no girl with a monobrow could ever have a happy life, I had no choice but to put myself in Lucy's capable hands.

Maybe it was just a coincidence, but the next day I had an unexpected encounter with Hardy Cates that seemed to prove Lucy's claim about the power of brow-shaping. I was practicing alone at the communal basketball hoop at the back of the subdivision, because earlier at gym class I had revealed I couldn't make a free throw to save my life. The girls had been divided into two teams, and there had actually been an argument over who would have to take me. I didn't blame them—I wouldn't have wanted me on my team either. Since the season wouldn't end until late November, I was doomed to more public embarrassment unless I could improve my skills.

The autumn sun was strong. It had been good melon weather, the hot days and cool nights bringing the local crops of casabas and muskmelons to full-slip sugar. After five minutes of shooting practice, I was streaked with sweat and dust. Plumes of powdered fire rose from the paved ground with each impact of the basketball.

No dirt on earth sticks to you like East Texas red clay. The wind blows it over you and it tastes sweet in your mouth. As the clay lurks under a foot of light tan topsoil, it expands and shrinks so drastically that in the driest months Martian-colored cracks run across the ground. You can soak your socks in bleach for a week, and you won't get that red out.

As I puffed and struggled to get my arms and legs working together, I heard a lazy voice behind me.

"You've got the worst free-throw form I've ever seen."

Panting, I tucked the basketball against my hip and turned to face him. A hank of hair escaped my ponytail and dangled over one eye.

There are few men who can turn a friendly insult into a good opening line, but Hardy was one of them. His grin held a wicked charm that robbed the words of any sting. He was rumpled and as dusty as I was, dressed in jeans and a white shirt with the sleeves ripped off. And he wore a Resistol hat that had once been white but had turned the olive-gray of ancient straw. Standing with relaxed looseness, he stared at me in a way that made my insides do somersaults.

"You got any pointers?" I asked.

As soon as I spoke Hardy looked sharply at my face, and his eyes widened. "Liberty? Is that you?"

He hadn't recognized me. Amazing, what removing half your eyebrows could accomplish. Suddenly I had to clamp my teeth on my inner cheeks to keep from laughing. Pushing the loose hair back from my face, I said calmly, "Of course it's me. Who'd you think it was?"

"Damned if I know. I . . ." He tipped his hat back on his head and approached me cautiously, as if I were some volatile substance that might explode at any moment. That was certainly how I felt. "What happened to your glasses?"

"I got contacts."

Hardy came to stand in front of me, his broad shoulders creating a shadowed lee from the sunlight. "Your eyes are green." He sounded distracted. Disgruntled, even.

I stared at the front of his throat, where the skin was tanned and smooth and dappled with a glitter of moisture. He was close enough that I could smell the intimate salt of his sweat. The crescents of my fingernails dug into the pebbled surface of the basketball. As Hardy Cates stood there looking at me, really seeing me for the first time, it felt like the whole world had been snatched up in a great unseen hand, its motion arrested.

"I'm the worst basketball player in school," I told him. "Maybe all of Texas. I·can't make the ball go in that thing."

"The hoop?"

"Yeah, that."

Hardy studied me for another long moment. A smile curled one corner of his mouth. "I can give you some pointers. Lord knows you couldn't get any worse."

"Mexicans can't play basketball," I said. "I should be given a waiver because of my heritage."

Without taking his eyes from mine, he reached for the ball and dribbled a few times. Smoothly he turned and executed a perfect jump shot. It was a show-off move, looking all the better for being done in a cowboy hat, and I had to laugh as Hardy glanced at me with an expectant grin.

"Am I supposed to praise you now?" I asked.

He retrieved the ball and dribbled slowly around me. "Yeah, now would be a good time."

"That was awesome."

Hardy managed the ball with one hand while using the other to remove his battered hat and send it sailing to the side. He came to me, catching up the ball in his palm. "What do you want to learn first?"

Dangerous question, I thought.

Being near Hardy brought back the feeling of heavy sweetness that robbed me of any inclination to move. I felt like I had to breathe twice as fast as normal to get the necessary amount of oxygen into my lungs. "Free throw," I managed to say.

"All right, then." Hardy motioned me to the white line that had been painted fifteen feet from the backboard. It seemed an enormous distance.

"I'll never make it," I said, taking the ball from him. "I don't have the upper-body strength."

"You're going to use your legs more than your arms. Square up, honey . . . spread your feet about as wide apart as your shoulders. Now show me how you've been— Well, hell, if that's how you hold the ball, no wonder you can't shoot straight."

"No one ever showed me how," I protested as he arranged my shooting hand on the ball. His tanned fingers covered mine briefly, and I felt the strength in them, and the roughened skin. His nails were clipped short and bleached white from the sun. A working man's hand.

"I'm showing you how," he said. "Hold it like this. Now bend your knees, and aim for the square on the backboard. As you straighten up, release the ball and let the energy come up from your knees. Try to shoot in one smooth motion. Got it?"

"Got it." I aimed and threw with all my might. The ball went crazily off course, frightening the wits out of an armadillo that had unwisely ventured out of its hole to investigate Hardy's discarded hat. The armadillo squeaked as the ball bounced too close for comfort. Its long toenails scored the baked ground as it scuttled back into its hiding place.

"You're trying too hard." Hardy trotted after the ball. "Relax."

I shook my arms out and grabbed the ball from the air as he passed it to me.

"Square up." Hardy stood beside me as I took up position at the line again. "Your left hand is the support, and your right hand is—" He broke off and began to chuckle. "No, damn it, not like that."

I scowled at him. "Look, I know you're trying to help, but—"

"Okay. Okay." Manfully he wiped the grin from his face. "Hold still. I'm going to stand behind you. I'm not making a move on you, all right? I'm just going to put my hands over yours."

I went still as I felt his body behind mine, the solid pressure of his chest against my back. His arms were on either side of me, and the feel of being surrounded in his warm strength drew a shiver from deep between my shoulder blades. "Easy," came his quiet murmur, and I closed my eyes as I felt the rush of his breath in my hair.

His hands coaxed mine into position. "Your palm goes here. Rest these three fingertips against the seam. Now, when you push against the ball, you're going to let it roll over your fingertips, and then you'll flick 'em down in the follow-through. Like this. That's how you give the ball a backspin."

His hands covered mine completely. The color of our skin was almost identical, except that his came from the sun and mine came from within. "We're going to throw it together now so you can get a feel of the motion. Bend your knees and look at the backboard."

The moment his arms had gone around me, I stopped thinking entirely. I was a creature of instinct and feeling, every heartbeat and breath and movement attuned to his. With Hardy at my back I threw the ball, and it rose in the air in a sure arc. Instead of the hoped-for swish, it bounced off the rim. But considering I hadn't even gotten close to the backboard before, it was a big improvement.

"Better," Hardy said, a smile in his voice. "Nice going, kid."

"I'm not a kid. I'm only a couple of years younger than you."

"You're a baby. You've never even been kissed."

The word "baby" rankled. "How would you know? And don't try to claim you can tell by looking. If I say I've been kissed by a hundred boys, you'd have no way to prove otherwise."

"If you've been kissed even once, I'd be amazed."

A great all-consuming wish burned inside me, that Hardy would have been wrong. If only I had the experience and the confidence to say something like "Prepare to be amazed, then," and walk up to him and give him the kiss of all time, one that would blow the top of his head off.

But this scenario wasn't going to work. First, Hardy was so much taller, I'd have to climb halfway up his body before I could reach his lips. Second, I had no clue about the technicalities of kissing, whether you started with the lips parted or closed, what to do with your tongue, when to close your eyes . . . and although I didn't mind Hardy laughing about my klutzy basketball moves—well, not much—I would die if he laughed at my attempt to kiss him.

So I settled for a muttered, "You don't know as much as you think you do," and went to get the ball.

Lucy Reyes asked me if I wanted to get my hair cut at Bowie's, the fancy Houston salon where she and her mom got their hair cut. It would cost a lot, she warned, but after Bowie started me off with a good cut, maybe I could find a hairdresser in Welcome who could maintain it. After Mama gave her approval, and I had collected every cent I had saved from babysitting the neighbors' kids, I told Lucy to go ahead and make the call. Three weeks later Lucy's mom drove us to Houston in a white Cadillac with tan upholstery and a cassette player, and windows that rolled down at the touch of a button.

The Reyes family was well-off by Welcome standards, due to the prosperity of their shop, which they had named Trickle-Down Pawn. I had always thought pawn shops were visited by derelicts and desperate people, but Lucy assured me that perfectly nice folks went to get loans from such places. One day after school she had taken me to Trickle-Down, which was run by her older brother, uncle, and father. The shop was filled with rows of shiny guns and pistols, big scary knives, microwave ovens, and television sets. To my delight, Lucy's mom had let me try on some of the gold rings in the velvet-lined glass cases . . . there were hundreds of them sparkling with every stone imaginable.

"We do a big business in bust-up engagements," Lucy's mom had said brightly, pulling out a velvet tray pebbled with diamond solitaires. I loved her thick Portuguese accent, which made it sound like she'd said "beeg beesiness."

"Oh, that's sad," I said.

"No, not at all." Lucy's mom had gone on to explain how it was empowering for women to pawn the engagement rings and take the money after their no-good fiancés had cheated on them. "He scroo her, you scroo heem," she said authoritatively.

Trickle-Down's prosperity had given Lucy and her family the means to go to the uptown area of Houston for their clothes, manicures, and haircuts. I had never been to the upscale Galleria area, where restaurants and shops straddled the city's main loop. Bowie's was located in a luxurious cluster of stores at the intersection of the loop and Westheimer. It was hard to conceal my astonishment when Lucy's mom drove up to a parking attendant's station and gave him the keys. Valet parking for a haircut!

Bowie's was filled with mirrors and chrome and exotic styling equipment, the biting scent of perm activator hanging thick in the air. The owner of the shop was a man in his mid-thirties, with long wavy blond hair that hung down his back. It was a rare sight in South Texas, and it led me to assume Bowie must have been tough as hell. He was certainly in great shape, lean and muscular as he prowled through the shop dressed in black jeans, black boots, a white Western shirt and a bolo tie made of suede cord and a chunk of unpolished turquoise.

"Come on," Lucy urged, "let's go look at the new nail polish."

I shook my head, remaining seated in one of the deep black leather chairs in the waiting area. I was too dumbstruck to say a word. I knew Bowie's was the most wonderful place I had ever been to. Later I would explore, but for the time being I wanted to sit still and take it all in. I watched the stylists at work, razor-cutting, blow-drying, deftly wrapping tiny portions of hair around pastel-colored perm rods. Tall wood-and-chrome display racks contained intriguing pots and tubes of cosmetics, and medicinal-looking bottles of soap, lotion, balms, and perfumes.

It seemed every woman in the place was being transformed right before my eyes, submitting to the combing, painting, filing, processing, until they had achieved a well-tended glossiness I had never seen except in magazines. While Lucy's mom sat at a manicure table and had her acrylic nails filled, and Lucy dabbled in the cosmetics area, a woman dressed in black and white came to show me to Bowie's station. "First you'll have a consultation," she told me. "My advice is to let Bowie do whatever he wants. He's a genius."

"My mother said not to let anyone cut it all off . . ." I began, but she had already walked away.

Then Bowie appeared before me, charismatic and handsome and a little artificial-looking. As we shook hands, I felt the clatter of multiple rings, his fingers loaded with stacks of silver and gold bands adorned with turquoise and diamonds.

An assistant draped me in a shiny black robe and washed my hair with expensive-smelling potions. I was rinsed, combed out, and led back to the cutting station, where I was greeted with the vaguely unnerving sight of Bowie standing there with a straight razor. For the next half hour I let him position my head at every imaginable angle, while he exerted tension on strategic locks and sheared off inches at a time with the razor. He was quiet as he worked, frowning in concentration. By the time he finished, my head had been pushed back and forth so many times, I felt like a Pez dispenser. And long swirls of hair were heaped on the floor.

The hair was quickly swept away, and then Bowie did the blow-dry in an exercise of dazzling showmanship. He lifted pieces of hair over the long tip of the blow-dryer and twirled them around a round brush as if he were collecting strands of cotton candy. He showed me how to apply a few spritzes of hair spray at the roots, and then he pushed my chair around to face the mirror.

I couldn't believe it. Instead of a frizzy skein of black hair, I had long bangs and shoulder-length layers, shining and bouncing with every movement of my head. "Oh," was all I could say.

Bowie wore the smile of a Cheshire cat. "Beautiful," he said, scrubbing his fingers over the back of my head, flicking the layers upward. "It's a transformation, isn't it? I'll have Shirlene show you how to do your makeup. I usually charge for that, but it's my present to you."

Before I could find the words to thank him, Shirlene appeared and guided me to a tall chrome stool beside the glass-fronted makeup counter. "You've got good skin, lucky girl," she pronounced after taking one look at my face. "I'll teach you the five-minute face."

When I asked her how to make my lips look smaller, she reacted with shocked concern. "Oh, *honey,* you don't want your lips to look smaller. Ethnic is in now. Like Kimora."

"Who's Kimora?"

A dog-eared fashion magazine was tossed into my lap. The cover featured a gorgeous honey-skinned young woman, long limbs arranged in an artless jumble. Her eyes were dark and tip-tilted, and her lips were even fuller than mine. "The new Chanel model," Shirlene said. "Fourteen years old—can you believe that? They say she's going to be the face of the nineties."

This was a new concept, that an ethnic-looking girl with jet-black hair and a real nose and big lips could be chosen as a model for a design house I had always associated with skinny white women. I studied the photo while Shirlene lined my lips with a rosy-brown pencil. She applied a matte pink lipstick, dusted my cheeks with powdered blush, and applied two coats of mascara to my lashes.

A hand mirror was pressed into my palm, and I inspected the final results. I had to admit, I was startled by the difference the new hair and makeup had made. It wasn't the kind of beauty I had wished for—I would never be the classic American blue-eyed blonde. But this was my own look, a glimpse of what I might someday become, and for the first time in my life I felt a stirring of pride in my own appearance.

Lucy and her mother appeared beside me. They studied me with an intensity that made me duck my head in embarrassment.

"Oh . . . my . . . God," Lucy exclaimed. "No, don't hide your face, let me see. You're so . . ." She shook her head as if the right word eluded her. "You're going to be the most beautiful girl in school."

"Don't go overboard," I said mildly, but I could feel a flush rising to my hairline. This was a vision of myself I had never dared to imagine, but I felt awkward rather than excited. I touched Lucy's wrist, and looked into her glowing eyes. "Thank you," I whispered.

"Enjoy it," she said fondly, while her mother chattered to Shirlene. "Don't look so nervous. It's still you, dummy. It's just you."

CHAPTER 5

The surprising thing about a makeover is not how you feel afterward but how differently other people treat you. I was accustomed to walking through the school hallways without being noticed. It threw me off balance when I walked through those same hallways and boys stared at me, remembered my name, fell into step beside me. They stood at my locker while I fiddled with the combination lock, and took the chair beside mine in open-seating classes or during lunch. The banter that came so easily to my lips when I was with my girlfriends seemed to dry up when I was in the company of those eager boys. My shyness should have discouraged them from asking me out, but it didn't.

I accepted a date with the least threatening of them all, a freckled boy named Gill Mincey, a fellow sophomore who wasn't much taller than me. We were in earth science together. When we were assigned as partners to write a paper on phytoextraction—the use of plants to remove metal contamination from soils—Gill invited me over to his house to study. The Minceys' house was a cool old tin-roof Victorian, freshly painted and refurbished, with all kinds of interesting-shaped rooms.

As we sat surrounded by piles of books on gardening, chemistry, and bioengineering, Gill leaned over and kissed me, his lips warm and light. Drawing back, he waited to see if I would object. "An experiment," he said as if to explain, and when I laughed, he kissed me again. Lured by the undemanding kisses, I pushed aside the science books and put my arms around his narrow shoulders.

More study dates ensued, involving pizza, conversation, and more kissing. I knew right off I was never going to fall in love with him. Gill must have sensed it, because he never tried to push it further. I wished I could have felt passionately about him. I wished this shy, friendly boy could be the one to reach inside the part of my heart that was held so tightly in reserve.

Later that year, I discovered life sometimes has a way of giving you what you need, but not in the form you expect.

If Mama's pregnancy was an example of what I might go through one day, I decided having children wasn't worth it. She swore when she'd carried me, she'd never felt better in her life. This one must be a boy, she said, because it was an entirely different experience. Or maybe it was just that she was so much older. Whatever the reason, her body seemed to revolt against the child in her belly as if it were some toxic growth. She felt sick all the time. She could hardly force herself to eat, and when she did, she retained water until the lightest touch of your finger would leave a visible depression in her skin.

Feeling so bad all the time and having great washes of hormones in her system made Mama peevish. It seemed nearly everything I did was an unholy irritation. In an effort to reassure her, I checked out a number of pregnancy books from the library and read helpful quotes to her. "According to the *Journal of Obstetrics and Gynecology,* morning sickness is good for the baby. Are you listening, Mama? Morning sickness helps regulate insulin levels and slows your fat metabolism, which ensures more nutrients for the baby. Isn't that great?"

Mama said if I didn't stop reading helpful quotes, she was going to come after me with a switch. I said I'd have to help her up from the sofa first.

She returned from each doctor visit with worrisome words like "preeclampsia" and "hypertension." There was no anticipation in her tone when she spoke about the baby, when it would come, the May due date, the maternity leave from work. The revelation that the baby was a girl sent me over the moon, but my excitement felt inappropriate in light of Mama's resignation.

The only times Mama seemed like her old self were when Miss Marva came to visit. The doctor had commanded Miss Marva to stop smoking or she would eventually drop dead from lung cancer, and his warnings worried her so much, she actually obeyed. Dotted with nicotine patches, her pockets filled with teaberry gum, Miss Marva walked around in a constant low-level temper, saying most of the time she felt like skinning small animals.

"I'm not fit for company," Miss Marva pronounced, walking in with a pie or plate of something good, and sitting next to Mama on the couch. And she and Mama would bitch to each other about anyone and anything that had stepped on their last nerves that day, until they both started laughing.

In the evenings after I'd finished my homework, I would sit with Mama and rub her feet, and bring her cups of soda water. We watched TV together, mostly evening soaps about rich people with interesting problems, like being approached by the long-lost son they never knew they had, or getting amnesia and sleeping with the wrong person, or going to a fancy party and falling into the swimming pool in an evening gown. I would steal glances at Mama's absorbed face, and her mouth always looked a little sad, and I comprehended she was lonely in a way I could never ease. She was going through this experience by herself, no matter how much I wanted to be a part of it.

I returned a glass pie plate to Miss Marva on a cold November day. There was a frosty snap in the air. My cheeks stung from the occasional whip of a breeze unimpeded by walls, buildings, or trees of appreciable size. Winter often brought rain and flash floods that were referred to as "turd-floaters" by exasperated residents of Welcome, who had long protested the town's badly managed drainage system. Today was a dry day, however, and I made a game of avoiding the cracks in the parched pavement.

As I neared Miss Marva's trailer I saw the Cates pickup parked alongside it. Hardy was loading boxes of artwork into the truck bed, to cart it to the gallery in town. Miss Marva had been doing brisk business of late, which was proof that Texans' appetite for bluebonnet paraphernalia should never be underestimated.

I savored the strong lines of Hardy's profile, the tilt of his dark head. A flush of desire and adoration swept over me. It was that way every time our paths crossed. For me, at least. My tentative experiments with Gill Mincey had brought to life a sexual awareness I had no idea how to satisfy. All I knew was that I didn't want Gill, or any of the other boys I knew. I wanted Hardy. I wanted him more than air and food and water.

"Hey, you," he said easily.

"Hey yourself."

I passed him without stopping, carrying the pie plate up to Miss Marva's door. Marva was busy cooking and greeted me with an unintelligible grunt, too involved in her task to bother with conversation.

I went back outside and found Hardy waiting for me. His eyes were such a fathomless blue I could have drowned in them. "How's basketball?" he asked.

I shrugged. "Still terrible."

"You need more practice?"

"With you?" I asked stupidly, caught off guard.

He smiled. "Yeah, with me."

"When?"

"Now. Right after I change clothes."

"What about Miss Marva's artwork?"

"I'm going to take it to town later. I'm meeting someone."

Someone. A girlfriend?

I hesitated, smarting with jealousy and uncertainty. I wondered what had prompted him to offer to practice with me, if he had some misbegotten idea we could be friends. Some shadow of despair must have crossed my expression. Hardy took a step closer, his forehead scored with a frown beneath the rumpled silk of his hair.

"What is it?" he asked.

"Nothing, I . . . I was just trying to remember if I had any homework." I filled my lungs with the biting air. "Yes, I need more practice."

Hardy gave a businesslike nod. "Bring the ball. I'll meet you in ten minutes."

He was already there by the time I made it to the basketball hoop. We were both dressed in sweatpants, long-sleeved tees, and ragged sneakers. I dribbled the ball and passed it to him, and he executed a flawless free throw. Jogging to the basket, he retrieved the ball and passed it to me. "Don't let it bounce so high," he advised. "And try not to watch the ball while you're dribbling. You're supposed to keep an eye on the guys around you."

"If I don't watch the ball while I dribble, I'll lose it."

"Try it anyway."

I did, and the basketball bounced out of my control. "See?"

Hardy was patient and relaxed as he taught me the basics, moving like a big cat across the pavement. My size allowed me to move around him easily, but he used his height and long reach to block most of my shots. Breathing fast from exertion, he grinned at my frustrated exclamation when he obstructed yet another jump shot.

"Take a break for a minute," he said, "and then I'll teach you a pump fake."

"A what?"

"It'll throw your opponent off long enough to give you a clear shot."

"Great." Although the air was chilled by the approach of nightfall, the exercise had made me warm and damp. I pushed up the sleeves of my tee and pressed a palm against a stitch in my side.

"Heard you were going out with someone," Hardy said casually, working the ball into a spin on the blunt tip of his forefinger.

I shot a glance at him. "Who told you that?"

"Bob Mincey. He says you're going with his little brother Gill. Nice family, the Minceys. You could do a lot worse."

"I'm not 'going out' with Gill." I made little quotation marks in the air with my fingers. "Not officially. We're just sort of . . ." I paused, at a loss to explain my relationship with Gill.

"You like him, though?" he asked with the kindly concern of a big older brother. His tone made me feel as irritable as a cat being dragged backward through a hedge.

"I can't imagine anyone not liking Gill," I said shortly. "He's real nice. I've got my breath back. Show me the pump fake."

"Yes, ma'am." Hardy motioned me to stand beside him, and he dribbled the ball in a semicrouch. "Say I've got a defender standing over me, ready to block my shot. I have to fake him out. Make him think I'm taking a shot, and when he takes the bait, it throws him off position, and then I've got my chance." He raised the ball to his sternum, sold the move, and made a smooth jump shot. "All right, you try it."

We faced each other while I dribbled. As he had instructed, I kept my eyes on his instead of focusing on the ball. "He kisses me," I said, still dribbling steadily.

I had the satisfaction of seeing Hardy's eyes widen. "What?"

"Gill Mincey. When we study together. He's kissed me a lot, in fact." I moved from side to side, trying to get around him, and Hardy stayed with me.

"That's great," he said, a new edge to his tone. "Are you going to take a shot?"

"I think he's pretty good at it too," I continued, increasing the pace of my dribbling. "But there's a problem."

Hardy's alert gaze found mine. "What is it?"

"I don't feel anything." I raised the ball, faked the move, and took the shot. To my amazement the ball went through the hoop with a silky swish. It bounced in diminishing strikes on the ground, unheeded by either of us. I went still, cold air searing my superheated throat. "It's boring. During the kissing, I mean. Is that normal? I don't think

so. Gill doesn't seem bored. I don't know if something's wrong with
me or—"

"Liberty." Hardy approached and paced slowly around me as if
a ring of fire separated us. His face gleamed with perspiration. It seemed
difficult to wring the words from his own throat. "There's nothing
wrong with you. If there's no chemistry between you, that's not your
fault. Or his. It just means . . . someone else would suit you better."

"Do you have chemistry with a lot of girls?"

He didn't look at me, just rubbed his nape to ease a pinch of tension in his neck muscles. "That's not something you and I are going to
talk about."

Now that I had started along this line, I couldn't stop. "If I was
older, would you feel that way about me?"

His face was averted. "Liberty," I heard him mutter. "Don't do this
to me."

"I'm just asking, is all."

"Don't. Some questions change everything." He released an unsteady breath. "Do your practicing with Gill Mincey. I'm too old
for you, in more ways than one. And you're not the kind of girl I
want."

Surely he couldn't mean the fact that I was Mexican. From what I
knew of Hardy, there wasn't a bit of prejudice in him. He never used
racist words, never looked down on someone for things they couldn't
help.

"What kind do you want?" I asked with difficulty.

"Someone I can leave without looking back."

That was Hardy, offering the brutal truth without apology. But I
heard the submerged admission in his statement, that I wouldn't be the
kind he could leave easily. I couldn't keep from taking it as encouragement, even though that wasn't what he intended.

He looked at me then. "Nothing and no one is going to keep me
here, do you understand?"

"I understand."

He took a ragged breath. "This place, this life . . . Lately I've started to understand what made my dad so mean and crazy he ended up in jail. It'll happen to me too."

"No," I protested softly.

"Yes it will. You don't know me, Liberty."

I couldn't stop him from wanting to leave. But neither could I stop myself from wanting him.

I crossed the invisible barrier between us.

His hands lifted in a defensive gesture, which was comical in light of the difference between our sizes. I touched his palms, and the taut wrists where his pulse rampaged, and I thought, *If I never have anything from him except this one moment I am going to take it.* Take it now, or drown in regret later.

Hardy moved suddenly, catching my wrists, his fingers forming tight manacles that kept me from moving forward. I stared at his mouth, the lips that looked so soft. "Let go," I said, my voice thick. "Let go."

His breath had quickened, and he gave a slight shake of his head. Nerves were jumping in every part of my body. We both knew what I was going to do if he released me.

Suddenly his hands opened. I moved forward and pressed my body against his, length to length. I gripped the back of his neck, discovering the embedded toughness of his muscles. I tugged his head down until his lips caught mine, his hands remaining half-suspended in the air. His resistance lasted for a matter of seconds before he gave in with a rough sigh, putting his arms around me.

It was so unlike what I had experienced with Gill. Hardy was infinitely more powerful, and yet so much gentler. One of his hands slid into my hair, his fingers cradling my head. His shoulders hunched over and around me, his free arm clamping across my back as if he wanted to pull me inside himself. He kissed me over and over, trying to discover every way our mouths could fit together. A gust of wind chilled my back, but heat surged wherever I touched against him.

He tasted the inside of my mouth, his breath coming in scalding rushes against my cheek. The intimate flavor of him confounded me with desire. I clung to him tightly, shaken and aroused and wanting it never to end, desperately gathering every sensation to hoard as long as possible.

Hardy pried away my clinging arms and urged me back with a forceful push. "Oh, damn," he whispered, shivering. He moved from me and grasped the pole of the backstop, resting his forehead against it as if relishing the feel of chilled metal. "Damn," he muttered again.

I felt sleepy and dazed, my balance wavering in the sudden absence of Hardy's support. I scrubbed the heels of my hands over my eyes.

"That won't happen again," he said gruffly, still facing away from me. "I mean it, Liberty."

"I know. I'm sorry." I wasn't, actually. And I must not have sounded too sorry, because Hardy threw a sardonic glance over his shoulder.

"No more practicing," he said.

"You mean basketball practice or . . . what we just did?"

"Both," he snapped.

"Are you mad at me?"

"No, I'm mad as hell at myself."

"You shouldn't be. You didn't do anything wrong. I wanted you to kiss me. I was the one who—"

"Liberty," he interrupted, turning toward me. Suddenly he looked weary and frustrated. He rubbed his eyes the same way I had rubbed mine. "Shut up, honey. The more you talk, the worse I'll feel. Just go home."

I absorbed his words, the inexorable set of his face. "Do you . . . do you want to walk me back?" I hated the thread of timidity in my own voice.

He threw me a wretched glance. "No. I don't trust myself with you."

Glumness settled over me, smothering the sparks of desire and elation. I wasn't sure how to explain any of it, Hardy's attraction to me, his unwillingness to pursue it, the intensity of my response . . . and the knowledge that I was never going to kiss Gill Mincey again.

CHAPTER 6

Mama was about a week overdue when she finally went into labor in late May.

Springtime in Southeast Texas is a mean season. There are some pretty sights, the dazzling fields of bluebonnets, the flowering of Mexican buckeyes and redbuds, the greening of dry meadows. But spring is also a time when fire ants begin to mound after lying idle all winter, and the gulf whips up storms that spit out hail and lightning and twisters. Our region was scored by tornadoes that would double back in surprise attacks, jigsawing across rivers and down main streets, and other places tornadoes weren't supposed to go. We got white tornadoes too, a deadly rotating froth that occurred in sunlight well after people thought the storm was over.

Tornadoes were always a threat to Bluebonnet Ranch because of a law of nature that says tornadoes are irresistibly attracted to trailer parks. Scientists say it's a myth, tornadoes are no more drawn to trailer parks than anywhere else. But you couldn't fool the residents of Welcome. Whenever a twister appeared in or around town, it headed either to Bluebonnet Ranch or another Welcome subdivision called Happy Hills. How Happy Hills got its name was a mystery, because the landscape was as flat as a tortilla and barely two feet over sea level.

Anyway, Happy Hills was a neighborhood of new two-story residences referred to as "big hair houses" by everyone else in Welcome who had to make do with one-level ranch dwellings. The subdivision had undergone just as many tornado strikes as Bluebonnet Ranch, which some people cited as an example of how tornadoes would just as likely strike a wealthy neighborhood as a trailer park.

But one Happy Hills resident, Mr. Clem Cottle, was so alarmed by a white tornado that cut right across his front yard that he did some research on the property and discovered a dirty secret: Happy Hills had been built on the remains of an old trailer park. It was a rotten trick in Clem's opinion, because he would never have knowingly bought a house in a place where a trailer park once stood. It was an invitation to disaster. It was just as bad as building on an Indian graveyard.

Stuck with residences that had been exposed as tornado magnets, the homeowners of Happy Hills made the best of the situation by pooling their resources to build a communal storm shelter. It was a concrete room that had been half-sunk in the ground and banked with soil on all sides, with the result that there was finally a hill in Happy Hills.

Bluebonnet Ranch, however, didn't have anything remotely resembling a storm shelter. If a tornado cut through the trailer park, we were all goners. The knowledge gave us a more or less fatalistic attitude about natural disasters. As with so many other aspects of our lives, we were never prepared for trouble.

We just tried like hell to get out of the way when it came.

Mama's pains had started in the middle of the night. At about three in the morning, I realized she was up and moving around, and I got up with her. I'd found it nearly impossible to sleep anyway, because it was raining. Until we'd moved to Bluebonnet Ranch, I'd always thought rain was a soothing sound, but when it rains on the tin roof of a single-wide, the noise rivals the decibel level of an airplane hangar.

I used the oven timer to measure Mama's contractions, and when they were eight minutes apart, we called the ob-gyn. Then I called Miss Marva to come take us to the family clinic, a local outreach of a Houston hospital.

I had just gotten my license, and although I thought I was a pretty good driver, Mama had said she would feel more comfortable if Miss Marva drove us. Privately I thought we would have been a lot safer with me behind the wheel, since Miss Marva's driving technique was at best creative, and at worst she was an accident waiting to happen. Miss Marva drifted, turned from the wrong lanes, sped up and slowed down according to the pace of her conversation, and pushed the gas pedal flush to the floor whenever she saw a yellow light. I would have preferred Bobby Ray to drive, but he and Miss Marva had broken up a month earlier on suspicion of infidelity. She said he could come back when he figured out which shed to put his tools in. Since their separation, Miss Marva and I had gone to church by ourselves, her driving with me praying all the way there and back.

Mama was calm but chatty, wanting to reminisce about the day I was born. "Your daddy was such a nervous wreck when I was having you, he tripped over the suitcase and nearly broke his leg. And then he drove the car so fast, I yelled at him to slow down or I'd drive myself to the hospital. He didn't stay in the delivery room with me—I think he was nervous he'd get in the way. And when he saw you, Liberty, he cried and said you were the love of his life. I'd never seen him cry before. . . ."

"That's real sweet, Mama," I said, pulling out my checklist to make certain we had everything we needed in the duffel bag. I had packed it a month earlier, and I'd checked it a hundred times, but I was still worried I might have forgotten something.

The storm had worsened, thunder vibrating the entire trailer. Although it was seven in the morning, it was black as midnight. "Shit," I said, thinking that getting into a car with Miss Marva in this kind of weather was risking our lives. There would be flash-flooding, and her low-slung Pinto wagon wasn't going to make it to the family clinic.

"Liberty," Mama said in surprised disapproval, "I've never heard you swear before. I hope your friends at school aren't influencing you."

"Sorry," I said, trying to peer through the streaming window.

We both jumped at the sudden roar of hail on the roof, a battering shower of hard white ice. It sounded like someone was dumping coins onto our house. I ran to the door and opened it, surveying the bouncing balls on the ground. "Marble-sized," I said. "And a few golf balls."

"Shit," Mama said, wrapping her arms around her tightening stomach.

The phone rang, and Mama picked it up. "Yes? Hey, Marva, I— You what? Just now?" She listened for a moment. "All right. Yes, you're probably right. Okay, we'll see you there."

"What?" I asked wildly as she hung up. "What did she say?"

"She says the main road is probably flooded by now, and the Pinto won't make it. So she called Hardy, and he's coming to get us in the pickup. Since there's only room for three of us, he'll drop us off and come back to get Marva."

"Thank God," I said, instantly relieved. Hardy's pickup would plow through anything.

I waited at the door and watched through the crack. The hail had stopped falling but the rain held steady, sometimes coming in cold sideways sheets through the narrow opening of the door. Every now and then I glanced back at Mama, who had subsided in the corner of the sofa. I could tell the pains were getting worse—her chatter had died away and she had drawn inward to focus on the inexorable process that had overtaken her body.

I heard her breathe my father's name softly. A needle of pain went through the back of my throat. My father's name, when she was giving birth to another man's child.

It's a shock the first time you see your parent in a helpless condition, to feel the reverse of your situations. Mama was my responsibility now. Daddy wasn't here to take care of her, but I knew he would have wanted me to. I wouldn't fail either of them.

The Cateses' blue truck stopped in front, and Hardy strode to the door. He was wearing a fleece-lined windbreaker with the school panther logo on the back. Looking large and capable, he entered the trailer and closed the door firmly. His assessing glance swept over my face. I blinked in surprise as he kissed my cheek. He went to my mother, sank to his haunches before her and asked gently, "How does a ride in a pickup sound, Mrs. Jones?"

She mustered a faint laugh. "I think I might take you up on that, Hardy."

Standing, he looked back at me. "Anything I should bring out to the truck? I've got the cover on the back, so it should stay pretty dry."

I ran to get the duffel, and handed it to him. He headed for the door. "No, wait," I said, continuing to load objects into his arms. "We need this tape player. And this—" I gave him a large cylinder with an attachment that looked like a screwdriver.

Hardy looked at it with genuine alarm. "What is it?"

"A hand pump."

"For what? No, never mind, don't tell me."

"It's for the birth ball." I went to my bedroom and brought back a huge half-inflated rubber ball. "Take this out too." Seeing his bewilderment, I said, "We're going to inflate it all the way when we get to the clinic. It uses gravity to help the labor along, and when you sit on it, it puts pressure on the—"

"I get it," Hardy interrupted hastily. "No need to explain." He went out to stow the objects in the truck, and returned at once. "The storm's at a lull," he said. "We need to get going before another band hits us. Mrs. Jones, do you have a raincoat?"

Mama shook her head. As pregnant as she was, there was no way her old raincoat was going to fit. Wordlessly Hardy removed his panther jacket and guided her arms through the sleeves as if she were a child. It didn't quite zip over her stomach, but it covered most of her.

While Hardy guided Mama out to the truck, I followed with an armload of towels. Since the water hadn't broken yet, I thought it was best to be prepared. "What are those for?" Hardy asked after loading my mother into the front seat. We had to raise our voices to be heard above the din of the storm.

"You never know when you might need some towels," I replied, figuring it would cause him unnecessary distress if I explained further.

"When my mother had Hannah and the boys, she never took more than a paper sack, a toothbrush, and a nightgown."

"What was the paper sack for?" I asked in instant worry. "Should I run in and get one?"

He laughed and lifted me up to the front seat beside Mama. "It was to put the toothbrush and nightgown in. Let's go, honey."

The flooding had already turned Welcome into a chain of little islands. The trick of going from one place to another was to know the roads well enough that you could judge which flowing streams were passable. All it takes is two feet of water to float virtually any car. Hardy was a master at negotiating Welcome, taking a circuitous route to avoid low ground. He followed farm roads, cut through parking lots, and guided the pickup through currents until fountains of water spewed from the trenching tires.

I was amazed by Hardy's presence of mind, the lack of visible tension, the way he made small talk with Mama to distract her. The only sign of effort was the notch between his brows. There is nothing a Texan loves more than to pit himself against the elements. Texans take a kind of ornery pride in the state's raucous weather. Epic storms, killing heat, winds that threaten to strip a layer of skin off, the endless variety of twisters and hurricanes. No matter how bad the weather gets, or what level of hardship is imposed, Texans receive it with variations on a single question . . . "Hot enough for you?" . . . "Wet enough for you?" . . . "Dry enough for you?" . . . and so forth.

I watched Hardy's hands on the wheel, the light capable grip, the water spots on his sleeves. I loved him so much, loved his fearlessness, his strength, even the ambition that would someday take him away from me.

"A few more minutes," Hardy murmured, feeling my gaze on him. "I'll get you both there, safe and sound."

"I know you will," I said, while the windshield wipers flailed helplessly at the flats of rain that pounded the glass.

As soon as we arrived at the family clinic, Mama was taken in a wheelchair to be prepped, while Hardy and I took our belongings to the labor room. It was filled with machines and monitors, and a neonatal open care warmer that looked like a baby spaceship. But the room's appearance was softened by ruffled curtains, a wallpaper border featuring geese and baby ducks, and a gingham-cushioned rocking chair.

A stout gray-haired nurse moved around the room, checking the equipment and adjusting the level of the bed. As Hardy and I came in, she said sternly, "Only mothers-to-be and their husbands are allowed in the labor room. You'll have to go to the waiting area down the hall."

"There's no husband," I said, feeling a little defensive as I saw her brows inching up toward her hairline. "I'm staying to help my mother."

"I see. But your boyfriend will have to leave."

Hot color rushed over my face. "He's not my—"

"No problem," Hardy interrupted easily. "Believe me, ma'am, I don't want to get in anyone's way."

The nurse's stern face relaxed into a smile. Hardy had that effect on women.

Pulling a colored folder from the duffel bag, I gave it to the nurse. "Ma'am, I'd appreciate it if you'd read this."

She looked suspiciously at the bright yellow folder. I had printed the words "BIRTH PLAN" on the front and decorated it with stickers of baby bottles and storks. "What is this?"

"I've written out our preferences for the labor experience," I explained. "We want dim lighting and as much peace and quiet as possible, and we're going to play nature sounds. And we want to maintain my mother's mobility until it's time for the epidural. About pain relief—she's fine with Demorol but we wanted to ask the doctor about Nubain. And please don't forget to read the notes about the episiotomy."

Looking harassed, the nurse took the birth plan and disappeared.

I gave the hand pump to Hardy and plugged in the tape player. "Hardy, before you go, would you inflate the birth ball? Not all the way. Eighty percent would be best."

"Sure," he said. "Anything else?"

I nodded. "There's a tube sock filled with rice in the duffel. I'd appreciate it if you'd find a microwave oven somewhere and heat it for two minutes."

"Absolutely." As Hardy bent to inflate the birth ball, I saw the line of his cheek tauten with a smile.

"What's so funny?" I asked, but he shook his head and didn't answer, only continued to smile as he obeyed my instructions.

By the time Mama was brought into the room, the lighting had been adjusted to my satisfaction, and the air was filled with the sounds of the Amazon rain forest. It was a soothing patter of rain punctuated with the chirping of tree frogs and the occasional cry of a macaw.

"What are those sounds?" Mama asked, glancing around the room in bemusement.

"A rain forest tape," I replied. "Do you like it? Is it soothing?"

"I guess so," she said. "Although if I start to hear elephants and howler monkeys, you'll have to turn it off."

I did a subdued version of a Tarzan cry, and it made her laugh.

The gray-haired nurse went to help Mama from the wheelchair. "Is your daughter going to stay in here the whole time?" she asked Mama. Something in her tone gave me the impression she was hoping the answer would be "no."

"The whole time," Mama said firmly. "I couldn't do without her."

At seven o'clock in the evening, Carrington was born. I had picked the name from one of the soaps Mama and I liked to watch. The nurse had washed and wrapped her like a miniature mummy, and placed her in my arms while the doctor took care of Mama and stitched the places the baby had torn. "Seven pounds, seven ounces," the nurse said, smiling at my expression. We had gotten to like each other a little more during the birth process. Not only had I been less of an annoyance than she had anticipated, but it was difficult not to feel connected, if only temporarily, by the miracle of new life.

Lucky seven, I thought, staring at my little sister. I'd never had much to do with babies before, and I had never held a newborn. Carrington's face was bright pink and crumpled-looking, her eyes grayish-blue and perfectly round. Hair covered her head like the pale feathers of a wet chick. The weight of her felt about the same as a large sack of sugar, but she was fragile and floppy. I tried to make her comfortable, shifting her awkwardly until she was on my shoulder. The round ball of her head fit perfectly against my neck. I felt her back heave with a kitten-sigh, and she went still.

"I'll need to take her in a minute," the nurse said, smiling at my expression. "They'll have to check her out and clean her up."

I didn't want to let her go. A thrill of possessiveness went through me. She felt like my baby, part of my body, knotted to my soul. Impassioned to the verge of tears, I turned to the side and whispered to her. "You are the love of my life, Carrington. The love of my life."

Miss Marva brought a bouquet of pink roses and a box of chocolate-covered cherries for Mama, and a baby blanket she had made for Carrington, soft yellow fleece with hand-crocheted edges. After admiring and cuddling the baby for a few minutes, Miss Marva handed her back to me. She focused all her attention on Mama, fetching her a cup of ice chips when the nurse was too slow, adjusting the controls on her bed, helping her walk to the bathroom and back.

To my relief, Hardy appeared to drive us home the next day in a big sedan he had borrowed from a neighbor. While Mama signed papers and took a folder of postpartum instructions from the nurse, I dressed the baby in her going-home outfit, a little blue dress with long sleeves. Hardy stood beside the hospital bed and watched as I struggled to capture the tiny starfish hands and push them gently through the sleeves. Her fingertips kept catching and gripping the fabric, making it difficult to inch the dress over her arms.

"It's like trying to feed cooked spaghetti through a straw," Hardy observed.

Carrington grunted and complained as I managed to tug her hand through the sleeve. I started on the other arm, and the first hand pulled right out of the dress again. I let out an exasperated puff. Hardy snickered.

"Maybe she doesn't like the dress," he said.

"Would you like to give it a try?" I asked.

"Hell, no. I'm good at getting girls *out* of their clothes, not putting them on."

He had never made that kind of remark around me before, and I didn't like it.

"Don't swear in front of the baby," I said sternly.

"Yes, ma'am."

The touch of vexation made me less tentative with the baby, and I managed to finish dressing her. Gathering the curls at the top of her head, I fastened a Velcro bow around them. Tactfully Hardy turned his back while I changed her diapers, which were the size of a cocktail napkin.

"I'm ready," came Mama's voice behind me, and I picked Carrington up.

Mama was in a wheelchair, dressed in a new blue robe and matching slippers. She held the flowers from Marva in her lap.

"Do you want to take the baby and I'll carry the flowers?" I asked reluctantly.

She shook her head. "You carry her, sweetheart."

The baby car seat was webbed with enough buckled straps to restrain a fighter pilot in an F-15. Gingerly I settled the squirming baby into the seat. She began to squall as I tried to fasten the straps around her. "It's a five-point safety system," I told her. "*Consumer Reports* said it was the best one available."

"I guess the baby didn't read that issue," Hardy said, climbing in on the other side of the car seat to help.

I was tempted to tell him not to be such a smart-ass, but remembering my rule about no swearing in front of Carrington, I kept silent. Hardy grinned at me.

"Here we go," he said, deftly untwisting a strap. "Put this buckle over there and cross the other one over."

Together we managed to fasten Carrington securely in the seat. She was revving up, shrieking in objection to the indignity of being strapped in. I put my hand on her, my fingers curving over her heaving chest. "It's okay," I murmured. "It's okay, Carrington. Don't cry."

"Try singing to her," Hardy suggested.

"I can't sing," I said, rubbing circles on her chest. "You do it."

He shook his head. "Not a chance. My singing sounds like a cat being run over by a steamroller."

I tried a rendition of the opening song from *Mister Rogers' Neighborhood,* which I had watched every day as a child. By the time I reached the last "won't you be my neighbor?" Carrington had stopped crying and was staring at me in myopic wonder.

Hardy laughed softly. His fingers slid over mine, and for a moment we stayed like that, our hands resting lightly on the baby. Staring at his hand, I reflected that you could never mistake it for someone else's. His work-roughened fingers dotted with tiny star-shaped scars from encounters with hammers, nails, and barbed wire. There was enough strength in those fingers to bend a sixteen-penny nail with ease.

I raised my head and saw that Hardy's lashes had lowered to conceal his thoughts. He seemed to be absorbing the feel of my fingers beneath his.

Suddenly he withdrew and pulled out of the car, going to help Mama into the passenger seat. Leaving me to grapple with the eternal fascination that seemed to have become a part of me as surely as a hand or foot. But if Hardy didn't want me, or wouldn't allow himself to, I now had someone else to lavish with all my affection. I kept my hand on the baby all the way home, learning the rhythm of her breathing.

CHAPTER 7

During the first six weeks of Carrington's life, we developed habits that later proved impossible to break. Some would last a lifetime.

Mama was slow to heal, both spiritually and physically. The baby's birth had depleted her in ways I didn't understand. She still laughed and smiled, still hugged me and asked how my day at school was. Her weight receded until she looked almost the same as she had before. But something was wrong. I couldn't put my finger on it; it was a subtle erasure of something that had been there before.

Miss Marva said it was just that Mama was tired. When you were pregnant, your body went through nine months of change, and it took at least that long to get back to normal. The main thing, she said, was to give Mama lots of understanding and help.

I wanted to help, not just for Mama's sake, but because I loved Carrington so passionately. I loved everything about her, the silky baby skin and platinum curls, the way she splashed in the bath like a baby mermaid. Her eyes had turned the exact blue-green shade of Aquafresh toothpaste. Her gaze followed me everywhere, her mind filled with thoughts she couldn't yet express.

My friends and my social life didn't interest me nearly as much as the baby. I pushed Carrington in her stroller, fed and played with her, and put her down for naps. That wasn't always easy. Carrington was a fussy baby, just shy of being colicky.

The pediatrician had said that for an official diagnosis of colic, the baby had to cry three hours a day. Carrington cried about two hours and fifty-five minutes, and the rest of the day she fretted. The pharmacist mixed up a batch of something he called "gripe water," a milky-looking liquid that smelled like licorice. Giving Carrington a few drops before and after her bottle seemed to help a little.

Since her crib was in my room, I usually heard her first at night and I ended up being the one to comfort her. Carrington woke three or four times a night. I soon learned to fix her bottles and line them up in the refrigerator before I went to bed. I began to sleep lightly, one ear pressed to the pillow, the other waiting for a signal from Carrington. As soon as I heard her snuffling and grunting, I leaped out of bed, ran to warm a bottle in the microwave, and rushed back. It was best to catch her early. Once she started crying in earnest, it took a while to settle her down.

I would sit back in the slider rocker, tilting the bottle to keep

Carrington from sucking down air, while her little fingers patted mine. I was so tired I was nearly delirious, and the baby was too, both of us intent on getting formula into her tummy quickly so we could go back to sleep. After she had taken about four ounces I sat her up in my lap, her body folded over my supporting hand like a beanbag toy. As soon as she burped, I put her back in the crib and crawled into bed like a wounded animal. I had never suspected I could reach a level of exhaustion that actually hurt, or that sleep could become so precious I'd have sold my soul for another hour.

Not surprisingly, after school started, my grades were not impressive. I was still okay in the subjects that had always been easy for me, English and history and social science. But math was impossible. Every day I slipped farther behind. Each gap in my understanding made the next lessons that much more difficult, until I went to math class with a sick stomach and the pulse rate of a Chihuahua. A big mid-semester test was the make-or-break point at which I would get such a bad grade that I would be doomed to fail the rest of the semester.

The day before the test, I was a wreck. My anxiety spread to Carrington, who cried when I held her and screamed when I put her down. It happened to be a day when Mama's friends from work had invited her out to dinner, which meant she wouldn't be home until eight or nine. Although I had planned to ask Miss Marva if she would look after Carrington an extra couple of hours, she had greeted me at the door with an ice bag clasped to her head. She had a migraine, she said, and as soon as I took the baby she was going to take some medicine and go to bed.

There was no way to save myself. Even if I'd had time to study, it wouldn't have made a difference. Filled with hopelessness and unendurable frustration, I held Carrington against my chest while she screeched in my ear. I wanted to make her stop. I was tempted to cover her mouth with my hand, anything to make the noise go away. "Stop it," I said furiously, my own eyes stinging and welling. *"Stop crying now.*" The rage in my voice caused Carrington to scream until she choked. I was certain anyone outside the trailer could hear and would assume someone was being murdered.

There was a knock on the door. Stumbling toward it blindly, I prayed it was Mama, that her dinner had been canceled and she was back early. I opened the door with the writhing baby in my arms, and saw Hardy Cates's tall form through a blur of tears. Oh, God. I couldn't decide if he was the person I most wanted to see, or the absolute last person I wanted to see.

"Liberty . . ." He gave me a baffled glance as he came in. "What's going on? Is the baby okay? Have you been hurt?"

I shook my head and tried to talk, but suddenly I was crying as hard as Carrington. I gasped with relief as the baby was lifted from my arms. Hardy propped her over his shoulder, and she began to calm down instantly.

"I thought I'd stop by to see how you were doing," he said.

"Oh, I'm just great," I said, dragging my sleeve across my streaming eyes.

With his free arm, Hardy reached out and drew me against him. "Tell me," he murmured into my hair. "You tell me what's wrong, honey." Between sobs I babbled about math and babies and lack of sleep, while Hardy's hand coasted slowly over my back. He didn't seem at all disconcerted at having two wailing females in his arms, just held us both until the trailer had quieted.

"There's a handkerchief in my back pocket," he said, his lips brushing my wet cheek. I fumbled for it, flushing as my fingers brushed against the hard surface of his backside. Raising the kerchief to my nose, I blew it with a gusty snort. Right after that, Carrington burped loudly. I shook my head in defeat, too tired to feel shame at the fact that my sister and I were disgusting and troublesome and completely out of control.

Hardy chuckled. Easing my head back, he looked into my reddened eyes. "You look like hell," he said frankly. "Are you sick or just tired?"

"Tired," I croaked.

He smoothed my hair back. "Go lie down," he said.

It sounded so good, and so impossible, that I had to set my jaw against another flurry of sobs. "I can't . . . the baby . . . the math test . . ."

"Go lie down," he repeated gently. "I'll wake you in an hour."

"But—"

"Don't argue." He nudged me in the direction of the bedroom. "Go on."

The feeling of relinquishing responsibility to someone else, letting him take control, was a relief beyond words. I found myself trudging to my bedroom as if wading through quicksand, and collapsed to the bed. My bruised mind insisted I shouldn't have dumped my burden on Hardy. At the very least I should have explained about how to fill the formula bottles and where the diapers and wipes were. But as soon as my head sank into the pillow, I fell asleep.

It seemed that scarcely five minutes had passed before I felt Hardy's hand on my shoulder. Groaning, I shifted to look at him with a bleary stare. Every nerve in my body screamed in protest at the necessity of waking up.

"It's been an hour," he whispered.

He looked so fresh and self-possessed, radiating vitality as he bent over me. He seemed to have such inexhaustible strength, and I wished I could have just a little of it. "I'm going to help you study," he said. "I'm great at math."

I replied with the surliness of a punished child. "Don't bother. I'm beyond help."

"No you're not," he said. "By the time I'm finished with you, you'll know everything you need to know."

Realizing the trailer was quiet—too quiet—I raised my head. "Where's the baby?"

"She's with Hannah and my mother. They're looking after her for a couple of hours."

"They . . . they . . . but they can't!" The thought of my fractious baby sister in the care of Miss Judie "spare the rod, spoil the child" Cates was enough to give me a heart attack. I lurched to a sitting position.

"Sure they can," Hardy said. "I dropped Carrington off with the diaper bag and two bottles of formula. She'll be fine." He grinned at my expression. "Don't worry, Liberty. One afternoon with my mother is not going to kill her."

I'm ashamed to admit it took some coaxing and even a threat or two before Hardy could get me to leave the bed. No doubt, I thought sourly, he was far more accustomed to talking girls *into* bed rather than getting them out. Staggering to the table, I plonked down on the chair. A pile of books, a stack of graph paper, and three freshly sharpened pencils were laid out neatly before me. Hardy went into the kitchenette and returned with a cup of heavily creamed and sugared coffee. My mother was a coffee drinker, but I couldn't stand the stuff.

"I don't like coffee," I said crabbily.

"You do tonight," he said. "Start drinking."

The combination of caffeine, quiet, and Hardy's ruthless patience began to work magic on me. He went down the study list methodically, unraveling problems so I could understand how they worked, answering the same questions over and over. I learned more in one afternoon than I had in weeks of math class. Gradually the mass of concepts I had found so overwhelming became more understandable.

Midway through, Hardy took a break to make a couple of phone calls. The first was for a large pepperoni pizza that would be delivered within forty-five minutes. The second call was a lot more interesting. I huddled over a book and a piece of graph paper, pretending to be absorbed in a logarithm while Hardy wandered to the main room and spoke in low tones.

". . . can't make it tonight. No, I'm sure." He paused, while the person on the other end of the line replied. "No, I can't explain," he said. "It's important . . . have to take my word for it . . ." There must have been some complaints, because he said a few more things that sounded soothing, and said "sweetheart" a couple of times.

Finishing the call, Hardy returned to me with a carefully blank expression. I knew I should have felt guilty for interrupting his plans for the evening, especially since they had involved a girlfriend. But I didn't. I acknowledged privately that I was a low and petty person, because I couldn't have been more delighted with how things were turning out.

As the math study continued we sat with our heads close together. We were coccooned in the trailer while darkness unfolded outside. It seemed odd not to have the baby nearby, but it was a relief too.

When the pizza arrived we ate it quickly, folding the steaming triangles to contain the gooey strings of cheese. "So . . ." Hardy said a little too casually, "you still going out with Gill Mincey?"

I hadn't spoken to Gill in months, not because of any animosity, but because our fragile connection had dissolved as soon as summer had started. I shook my head in answer. "No, he's just a friend now. What about you? Are you going with someone?"

"No one special." Hardy took a swallow of iced tea and stared at me thoughtfully. "Liberty . . . have you talked to your mom about the amount of time you're spending with the baby?"

"What do you mean?"

He gave me a chiding glance. "You know what I mean. All this babysitting. Waking up with her every night. She seems more like your baby than your baby sister. It's a lot for you to handle. You need time

for yourself . . . have fun . . . go out with friends. And boyfriends."
He reached out and touched the side of my face, his thumb brushing
the pinkening crest of my cheek. "You look so tired," he whispered.
"It makes me want to—" He stopped and bit back the words.

A groundswell of silence moved between us. Trouble on the surface
and even deeper currents beneath. There was so much I wanted to confide to him . . . Mama's troubling distance from the baby, and the
guilty question of whether I had somehow taken Carrington from her
or if I had just stepped in to fill a vacancy. I wanted to tell him about
my own longings, and the fear that I would never find anyone I loved
as much as him.

"It's time to get the baby," Hardy said.

"Okay." I watched as he went to the door. "Hardy . . ."

"Yes?" He stopped without looking back.

"I—" My voice wobbled, and I had to take a deep breath before I
went on. "I'm not always going to be too young for you."

He still didn't look at me. "By the time you're old enough, I'll be
gone."

"I'll wait for you."

"I don't want you to." The door closed with a quiet click.

I threw away the empty pizza box and plastic cups and wiped off
the table and counters. The weariness was coming back again, but this
time I had reason to hope I might survive the next day.

Hardy returned with Carrington, who was quiet and yawning, and
I rushed to take her. "Sweet baby, sweet little Carrington," I crooned.
She settled into her usual position on my shoulder, her head a warm
weight against my neck.

"She's fine," Hardy said. "She probably needed a break from you
as much as you did from her. Mom and Hannah gave her a bath and a
bottle, and now she's ready to sleep."

"Hallelujah," I said feelingly.

"You need sleep too." He touched my face, his thumb smoothing the wing of my eyebrow. "You'll do fine on the test, honey. Just don't let yourself panic. Take it step by step, and you'll make it through."

"Thank you," I said. "You didn't have to do any of this. I don't know why you did. I really—"

His fingertips came to my lips with feather-light pressure. "Liberty," he whispered. "Don't you know I'd do anything for you?"

I swallowed painfully. "But . . . you're staying away from me."

He knew what I meant. "I'm doing that for you too." Slowly he lowered his forehead to mine, with the baby cradled between us.

I closed my eyes, thinking, *Let me love you, Hardy, just let me.* "Call me if you ever need help," he murmured. "I can be there for you that way. As a friend."

I turned my face until my mouth touched the shaven smoothness of his skin. His breath caught, and he didn't move. I nuzzled into the pliancy of his cheek, the hardness of his jaw, loving the texture of him. We stayed like that for a few seconds, not quite kissing, suffused with each other's nearness. It had never been like this with Gill or any other boy, my bones turning liquid, my body shaken with cravings that had no previous reference point. Wanting Hardy was different from wanting anyone else.

Lost in the moment, I was slow to respond when I heard the door open with a rattle. My mother had come back. Hardy pulled back from me, his face wiped clean of expression, but the air was weighted with emotion.

Mama entered the trailer, her arms filled with a jacket, keys, and a take-out box from the restaurant. She took in the scene with a single glance and shaped her mouth into a smile. "Hi, Hardy. What are you doing here?"

I jumped in before he could reply. "He helped me study for a math test. How was your dinner, Mama?"

"Just fine." She set her things on the kitchenette counter, and came to take the baby from me. Carrington protested the change of arms, her head bobbing, her face flooding with color. "Shhh," Mama soothed, bouncing her in gentle repetition until she subsided.

Hardy murmured goodbye and went to the door. Mama spoke in a carefully calibrated tone. "Hardy. I appreciate you coming here to help Liberty study. But I don't think you should spend any more time alone with my daughter."

I drew in a hissing breath. To deliberately drive a wedge between me and Hardy, when we had done nothing wrong, seemed an ugly hypocrisy coming from a woman who'd just had a fatherless baby. I wanted to say that, and worse things.

Hardy spoke before I could, his bleak gaze locked with my mother's. "I think you're right."

He left the trailer.

I wanted to scream at my mother, to hurl words at her like a shower of darts. She was selfish. She wanted me to pay for Carrington's childhood with my own. She was jealous that someone might care for me when there was no man in her life. And it wasn't fair of her to go out with her friends so often, when she should want to stay at home with her newborn. I wanted to say those things so badly, I nearly suffocated beneath the weight of unspoken words. But it has always been my nature to turn my anger inward, like a Texas skink eating its own tail.

"Liberty—" Mama began gently.

"I'm going to bed," I said. I didn't want to hear her opinion of what was best for me. "I've got a test tomorrow." I went to my room with swift strides and closed the door in a cowardly half-slam, when I should have had the guts to do it full-out. But at least I had the mean, fleeting satisfaction of hearing the baby cry.

CHAPTER 8

As the year went on I had begun to measure the passage of time not by the signposts of my own development, but by Carrington's. The first time she rolled over, the first time she sat on her own, ate applesauce mixed with powdered rice, the first haircut, the first tooth. I was the one she always raised her arms to first, giving me a wet gummy grin. It amused and disconcerted Mama at first, and then it became something everyone accepted matter-of-factly.

The bond between Carrington and me was closer than that of sisters; it was more

like that of parent and child. Not as a result of intention or choice . . .
it simply *was*. It seemed natural that I would go with Mama and the
baby to her pediatrician's visits. I was more intimately acquainted
with the baby's problems and patterns than anyone else. When it was
time for vaccinations, Mama retreated to the corner of the room while
I pinned the baby's arms and legs down on the doctor's table. "You do
it, Liberty," Mama said. "She won't hold it against you like she would
someone else."

I stared into Carrington's pooling eyes, flinching at her incredulous
scream as the nurse injected the vaccines into her plump little thighs. I
ducked my head beside hers. "I wish it could be me," I whispered to
her scarlet ear. "I would take it for you. I would take a hundred of
them." Afterward I comforted her, holding her tightly until her sob-
bing stopped. I made a ceremony of placing the I WAS A GOOD PATIENT
sticker on the center of her T-shirt.

No one, including me, could say that Mama wasn't a good parent
to Carrington. She was affectionate and attentive to the baby. She made
certain Carrington was well dressed and had everything she needed.
But the puzzling distance remained. It troubled me that she didn't seem
to feel as intensely for the baby as I did.

I went to Miss Marva with my concerns, and her answer surprised
me. "There's nothing strange about that, Liberty."

"There isn't?"

She stirred a big pot of scented wax on the stove, getting it ready to
pour into a row of glass apothecary jars. "It's a lie when they say you
love all your children equally," she said placidly. "You don't. There's
always a favorite. And you're your mother's favorite."

"I want Carrington to be her favorite."

"Your mama will take to her in time. It's not always love at first
sight." She dipped a stainless steel ladle into the pot and brought it up
brimming with light blue wax. "Sometimes you have to get to know
each other."

"It shouldn't take this long," I protested.

Miss Marva's cheeks jiggled as she chuckled. "Liberty, it could take a lifetime."

For once her laugh was not a happy sound. I knew without asking that she was thinking about her own daughter, a woman named Marisol who lived in Dallas and never came to visit. Miss Marva had once described Marisol, the product of a brief and long-ago marriage, as a troubled soul, given to addictions and obsessions and relationships with men of low character.

"What made her that way?" I had asked Miss Marva when she told me about Marisol, expecting her to lay out logical reasons as neatly as balls of cookie dough on a baking sheet.

"God did," Miss Marva had replied, simply and without bitterness. From that and other conversations, I gathered that on questions of nature versus nurture, she was firmly on the side of the former. Me, I wasn't so sure.

Whenever I took Carrington out people assumed she was mine, despite the fact that I was black haired and amber skinned, and she was as fair as a white-petaled daisy. "How young they have them," I heard a woman say behind me, as I pushed Carrington's stroller through the mall. And a masculine voice replied in patent disgust, "Mexicans. She'll have a dozen by the time she's twenty. And they'll all be living off our tax money."

"Shhh, not so loud," the woman admonished.

I quickened my pace and turned into the next store I could reach, my face burning with shame and anger. That was the stereotype—Mexican girls were supposed to have sex early and often, breed like rabbits, have volcanic tempers, and love to cook. Every now and then a circular would appear on the racks near the supermarket entrance, containing pictures and descriptions of Mexican mail-order brides.

"These lovely ladies enjoy being women," the circular said. *"They're not interested in competing with men. A Mexican wife, with her traditional values, will put you and your career first. Unlike their American counterparts, Mexican women are satisfied with a modest lifestyle, as long as they are not mistreated."*

Living so close to the border, Tex-Mex women were often subject to the same expectations. I hoped no man would ever make the mistake of thinking *I* would be happy to put him and his career first.

My junior year seemed to go quickly. Mama's disposition had improved considerably, thanks to the antidepressants the doctor had prescribed. She regained her figure and her sense of humor, and the phone rang often. Mama seldom brought her dates to the trailer, and she hardly ever spent a full night away from Carrington and me. But there were still those odd disappearances when she would be gone for a day and come back without a word of explanation. After these episodes she was always calm and strangely peaceful, as if she'd gone through a period of prayer and fasting. I didn't mind her leaving. It always seemed to do her good, and I had no problem taking care of Carrington by myself.

I tried to rely on Hardy as little as possible, because seeing each other seemed to bring us more frustration and unhappiness than pleasure. Hardy was determined to treat me as if I were a younger sister, and I tried to comply, but the pretense was awkward and ill-fitting.

Hardy was busy with land clearing and other brutal labor that toughened him in body and spirit. The mischievous twinkle of his eyes had cooled into a flat, rebellious stare. His lack of prospects, the fact that other boys his age were going to college while he seemed to be going nowhere, was eating away at him. Boys in Hardy's position had few choices after high school other than to take a petrochem job with Sterling or Valero, or go into road construction.

When I graduated, my choices weren't going to be any better. I had no special talents that would afford me a scholarship anywhere, and so far I hadn't even taken any summer jobs that would have given me experience to put on a résumé. "You're good with babies," my friend Lucy had pointed out. "You could work at a day care, or maybe as a teacher's assistant at the elementary school."

"I'm only good with Carrington," I said. "I don't think I'd like to take care of other people's children."

Lucy had pondered my possible future careers, and had decided I should get a cosmetology degree. "You love doing makeup and hair," she pointed out. That was true. But beauty school would be expensive, though. I wondered what Mama's reaction would be if I asked her for thousands of dollars of tuition money. And then I wondered what other plans or ideas she might have for my future, if any. It was pretty likely she didn't. Mama chose to live in the moment. So I stored the idea away, saving it for a time when I thought Mama would be open to it.

Winter came, and I began to go out with a boy named Luke Bishop, whose father owned a car dealership. Luke was on the football team—in fact, he had taken the fullback position after Hardy's knee had gone out the previous year—but Luke wasn't considering a sports career. His family's financial status would allow him to go to any college he could get into. He was a good-looking boy with dark hair and blue eyes, and he bore enough of a physical resemblance to Hardy that I was drawn to him.

I met Luke at a Blue Santa party just before Christmas. It was the local law enforcement's annual toy drive to collect presents for poor families with needy children. For most of December toys were donated, gathered and sorted, and on the twenty-first, the presents were wrapped at a party at the police station. Anyone could volunteer to help. The football coach had ordered all his players to participate in some capacity, whether it was to collect toys, attend the wrapping party, or deliver them the day before Christmas.

I went to the party with my friend Moody and her boyfriend Earl Jr., the butcher's son. There must have been at least a hundred people at the party, and a mountain of toys stacked around and beside the long tables. Christmas music was playing in the background. A makeshift coffee station in the corner featured big stainless steel carafes, and boxes of cookies plastered with white icing. Standing in a row of present-wrappers, wearing a Santa Claus hat someone had put on my head, I felt like a Christmas elf.

With so many people cutting paper and curling ribbons, there was a shortage of scissors. As soon as a pair was set down, they were immediately snatched up by someone who had been waiting for his or her turn. Standing at the table with a pile of unwrapped toys, and a roll of red and white striped paper, I watched impatiently for my chance. A pair of scissors clattered on the table, and I reached for them. But someone else was too fast for me. My fingers inadvertently clamped over a male hand that had already grasped the scissors. I looked up into a pair of smiling blue eyes.

"Dibs," the boy said. With his other hand, he flipped the tail of my Santa hat away from my eyes and over my shoulder.

We spent the rest of the night side by side, talking, laughing, and pointing out presents we thought the other would like. He chose a Cabbage Patch doll with curly brown hair for me, and I picked out a model kit of a Star Wars X-wing fighter for him. By the end of the evening, Luke had asked me out on a date.

There were many things to like about Luke. He was average in all the right ways, intelligent but not a geek, athletic but not musclebound. He had a nice smile, although it wasn't Hardy's smile. His deep blue eyes didn't have the ice-and-fire brightness of Hardy's, and his dark hair was crisp and wiry, instead of thick and soft like mink fur. Luke also didn't have Hardy's outsized presence or restless spirit. But in other ways they were similar, both tall and physically self-possessed, both uncompromisingly masculine.

It was a time in my life when I was especially vulnerable to male attention. Everyone else in the small world of Welcome seemed to be paired up. My own mother had been dating more than I had. And here was a boy who resembled Hardy, without the complexity, and he was available.

As Luke and I began to see more of each other, we were accepted as a couple and other boys stopped asking me out. I liked the security of being half of a pair. I liked having someone to walk through the halls with, someone to eat lunch with, someone to take me out for pizza after the Friday-night game.

The first time Luke kissed me, I was disappointed to discover it wasn't anything like Hardy's kisses. He had just brought me back home from a date. Before getting out of the car, he leaned over and pressed his mouth to mine. I returned the pressure, trying to summon a response, but there was no heat or excitement, just the alien moisture of another person's mouth, the slippery probing of a tongue. My brain remained uninvolved from what was happening to my body. Feeling guilty and embarrassed by my own coldness, I tried to make up for it by wrapping my arms around his neck and kissing him harder.

As we continued to date, there were more kisses, embraces, tentative explorations. Gradually I learned to stop comparing Luke to Hardy. There was no mysterious magic, no invisible circuitry of sensation and thought between us. Luke was not the kind who thought deeply about things, and he had no interest in the secretive territory of my heart.

At first Mama hadn't approved of my dating a senior, but when she met Luke, she'd been charmed by him. "He seems like a nice boy," she told me afterward. "If you want to date him, I'll allow it as long as you keep to an eleven-thirty curfew."

"Thank you, Mama." I was grateful that she had given her permission, but some inner devil prompted me to say, "He's only one year younger than Hardy, you know."

She understood my unspoken question. "It's not the same."

I knew why she'd said that.

At nineteen, Hardy had already become more of a man than some men ever were. In the absence of a father he'd learned to shoulder the responsibility of a family, providing for his mother and sisters. He'd worked hard to ensure their survival, and his own. Luke, by contrast, was sheltered and coddled, secure in the belief that things would always come easily to him.

If I hadn't known Hardy, it was possible I would have come to care more about Luke. But it was too late for that. My emotions had bent around Hardy like wet-molded leather left to dry and harden in the sun, until any attempt to alter its shape would break it.

One night Luke brought me to a party held at someone's house while their parents were away for the weekend. The place was filled with seniors, and I looked in vain for a familiar face.

The hard blues rock of Stevie Ray Vaughan blasted from outside patio speakers, while plastic cups of orange liquid were handed out to the crowd. Luke brought some to me, advising me with a laugh not to drink it too fast. It tasted like flavored rubbing alcohol. I took the tiniest sips possible, the caustic liquor stinging my lips. While Luke stood talking with his friends, I excused myself by asking where the restroom was.

Gripping the plastic cup, I went into the house and pretended not to notice the couples making out in shadows and corners. I found the guest bathroom, which was miraculously unoccupied, and I poured the drink into the commode.

When I emerged from the bathroom, I decided to take a different route outside. It would be easier, not to mention less embarrassing, to go out the front door and around the side of the house rather than return through the gauntlet of amorous couples. But as I passed the big staircase in the entranceway, I caught sight of a pair of entwined bodies in a shadow.

I felt as if I'd been stabbed through the heart as I recognized Hardy, his arms around a long-limbed blond girl. She was riding one of his thighs, her upper back and shoulders revealed by a black velvet bustier top. One of his fists was closed in her hair, holding it back as he dragged his mouth slowly along the side of her throat.

Pain, desire, jealousy . . . I hadn't known it was possible to feel so many things so strongly, all at once. It took every ounce of will I possessed to ignore them and keep going. My steps faltered, but I didn't stop. Out of the corner of my eye, I saw Hardy's head lift. I wanted to die as I realized he'd seen me. My hand shook as I grasped the cold brass doorknob and let myself outside.

I knew he wouldn't come after me, but my pace quickened until I was half running to the patio. The breath shot from my lungs in hard bursts. I longed to forget what I had just seen, but the image of Hardy with the blond girl was permanently seared in my memory. It shocked me, the fury I felt toward him, the white heat of betrayal. It didn't matter that he'd promised nothing, owed nothing to me. He was *mine*. I felt it in every cell of my body.

Somehow I managed to find Luke in the crowd on the patio, and he looked at me with a questioning smile. He could hardly fail to notice the burning color of my cheeks. "What's the matter, baby doll?"

"I dropped my drink," I said thickly.

He laughed and laid a heavy arm around my shoulders. "I'll get you another one."

"No, I . . ." I stood on my toes to whisper in his ear. "Would you mind if we left now?"

"Now? We just got here."

"I want to be alone with you," I whispered desperately. "Please, Luke. Take me somewhere. Anywhere."

His expression changed. I knew he was wondering if my sudden desire to be alone with him could mean what he thought it meant.

And the answer was yes. I wanted to kiss him, hold him, do everything Hardy was doing at that exact moment with another girl. Not out of desire, but furious grief. There was no one I could go to. My mother would dismiss my feelings as childish. Maybe they were, but I didn't care. I had never felt this kind of consuming anger before. My only anchor was the weight of Luke's arm.

Luke took me to the public park, which contained a man-made lake and several wooded copses. At the side of the lake there was a ramshackle open-sided gazebo lined with splintery wood benches. Families went there to picnic in the daytime. Now the gazebo was empty and dark. The air rustled with night sounds, an orchestra of frogs croaking among the cattails, a mockingbird's song, the flap of herons' wings.

Just before we had left the party, I had chugged the rest of Luke's tequila sunrise. My head was spinning, and I reeled between waves of giddiness and nausea. Luke laid his jacket on the gazebo bench and pulled me onto his lap. He kissed me, his mouth wet and searching. I tasted the purpose in his kiss, the message that tonight he would go as far as I would let him.

His smooth-skinned hand slipped beneath my shirt, over my back, plucking at the clasp of my bra. The underwire garment loosened across my chest. Immediately he reached around to my front, finding the tender curve of a breast, capturing it in a rough squeeze. I winced, and he loosened his grip a little, saying with a shaky laugh, "Sorry, baby doll. It just . . . you're so beautiful, you make me crazy . . ." His thumb rubbed over the hardening tip of my breast. He pinched and chafed my nipples insistently, while our mouths moved together in long unbroken kisses. Soon my breasts were raw and sore. I gave up any hope of feeling pleasure and tried instead to simulate it. If something was wrong, it was my fault, because Luke was experienced.

It must have been the tequila that gave me the sense of being an outside observer as Luke pushed me off his lap and onto the jacket-covered bench. The impact of the wood against my shoulders struck a flare of panic in my midsection, but I ignored it and lay back.

Luke tugged at the fastenings of my jeans and pushed them down over my hips and off one leg. I saw a section of sky from beneath the gazebo roof. It was a misty night with no stars or moon. The only light came from the distant blue glow of a street lamp, flickering from a moth storm.

Like any average teenage boy, Luke understood next to nothing about the more subtle erogenous areas on a woman's body. I knew even less than he, and being too timid to volunteer what I did or didn't like, I passively let him do what he would. I had no idea where to put my hands. I felt him reach beneath my panties, where the hair was warm and flattened. More rubbing, a few times roughly grazing the sensitive place that made me jump. He gave an excited half-laugh, mistaking my discomfort for enjoyment.

Luke's body was broad and heavy as he lowered himself until my legs stiffly bracketed his. He groped between us, unzipping his jeans, using both hands to accomplish some hurried task. I heard the sound of crackling plastic, and felt him pulling at something, arranging it, and then there was the unfamiliar taut, bobbing length of him against my inner thigh.

He pushed my shirt and bra up higher, bunching them beneath my chin. His mouth was at my breast, pulling tightly. I thought we had probably gone too far to stop, that I had no right to say no at this point. I wished it was over, that he would finish soon. Even as that thought crossed my mind, the pressure between my legs became bruising. I tensed and gritted my teeth, and looked up at Luke's face. He didn't look back at me. He was focused on the act itself, not on me. I had become nothing more than the instrument by which he would gain relief. He shoved harder, harder into my resistant flesh, and a pained sound broke from my lips.

It only took a few searing thrusts, the condom turning slick from blood, and then he was shuddering against me, groaning in his throat.

"Oh, baby, that was so good."

I kept my arms around him. A ripple of revulsion ran through me as I felt him kiss my neck, his breath like steam on my skin. It was enough—he'd had enough of me—I needed to belong to myself again. I was relieved beyond measure when he lifted away, my flesh raw and hurting.

We dressed ourselves silently. I had held all my muscles so tightly that when I finally relaxed, they began to tremble from the strain. I trembled all over until even my teeth chattered.

Luke drew me against him, patting my back. "Are you sorry?" he asked, his voice low.

He didn't expect me to say yes, and I wouldn't. It seemed bad manners somehow, and it wouldn't change anything. What was done was done. But I wanted to go home. I wanted to be alone. Only then could I start to catalog the changes that had occurred in me.

"No," I mumbled against his shoulder.

He patted my back some more. "It'll be better for you the next time. I promise. My last girlfriend was a virgin, and it took a few times before she started to like it."

I stiffened a little. No girl wanted to hear about a previous girlfriend at such a time. And although I wasn't surprised that Luke had had sex with a virgin before, it rankled. It seemed to lessen the value of what I'd given him. As if being someone's first lover was a commonplace occurrence for him, Luke, the kind of boy virgins threw themselves at.

"Please," I said, "take me home. I'm so tired . . ."

"Of course, baby."

On the way back to Bluebonnet Ranch, Luke drove with one hand and held mine with the other, often giving it a small squeeze. I wasn't sure whether he was offering reassurance or asking for it, but I squeezed back every time. He asked if I wanted to go out to eat tomorrow night, and I automatically said yes.

We made some conversation. I was too dazed to know what I was saying. Random thoughts went through my mind in the darting, irregular patterns of mourning doves. I was worried about how bad I was going to feel when the numbness wore off, and trying silently to convince myself there was no reason to feel bad. Other girls my age slept with their boyfriends . . . Lucy had, and Moody was seriously considering it. So what if I had? I was still me. I kept repeating that to myself. Still me.

Now that we had done it once, was it going to happen all the time? Would Luke expect every date to end with sex? I literally cringed at the thought. I felt stings and twitches in unexpected places, and the pinch of strained muscles in my thighs. It would have been no different with Hardy, I told myself. The pain, the smells, the physical functions would have been the same.

We pulled up to the trailer, and Luke walked me to the front steps. He seemed inclined to linger. Desperate to get rid of him, I put on a show of affection, hugging him hard, kissing his lips and chin and cheek. The display seemed to restore his confidence. He grinned and let me go inside.

"Bye, baby doll."

"Bye, Luke."

A lamp in the main room had been left on, but Mama and the baby were asleep. Thankfully I went to get my pajamas, carried them to the bathroom, and ran the hottest shower I could tolerate. Standing in the near-scalding water, I scrubbed hard at the rusty smears on my legs. The heat eased the clustering aches, water pouring over me until my skin no longer seemed imprinted with the feel of Luke. By the time I stepped from the shower, I was parboiled.

I dressed in my pajamas and went to my room, where Carrington was beginning to wriggle in her crib. Wincing at the soreness between my legs, I hurried to get a bottle ready. She was awake by the time I came back to her, but for once she wasn't screaming. She was waiting patiently, as if she knew I needed some forbearance. She reached for me with chubby arms and clung to my neck as I brought her to the rocker.

Carrington smelled like baby shampoo and diaper cream. She smelled like innocence. Her small body conformed to mine exactly, and she patted my hand as I held the bottle for her. Her blue-green eyes stared into mine. I rocked in the languid motion she liked best. With each soft forward pitch, the tightness in my chest and throat and head disintegrated until tears began to leak from the outward corners of my eyes. No one on earth, not Mama, not even Hardy, could have consoled me as Carrington did. Grateful for the relief of tears, I continued to cry silently as I fed and burped the baby.

Instead of putting Carrington back in her crib, I took her in bed with me, putting her on the side against the wall. It was something Miss Marva had advised me never to do. She had said the baby would never willingly go back in her crib alone again.

As usual, Miss Marva was right. From that night on Carrington insisted on sleeping with me, erupting in coyote howls if I ever tried to ignore her upraised arms. And the truth was, I loved sleeping with her, the two of us snuggled together beneath the rose-patterned duvet. I figured if I needed her, and she needed me, it was our right as sisters to comfort each other.

CHAPTER 9

Luke and I did not sleep together often, both from lack of opportunity—neither of us had our own place—and because it was obvious that no matter how I pretended to enjoy it, I didn't. We never discussed the situation directly. Whenever we did go to bed together, Luke would try this or that, but nothing he did seemed to matter. I couldn't explain to him or myself why I was a failure in bed.

"Funny," Luke commented one afternoon, lying with me in his bedroom after school. His parents had gone to San Antonio for the day, and the house was empty. "You're the most beautiful girl I've ever been with, and the sexiest. I don't understand why you can't . . ." He paused, cupping his hand over my naked hip.

I knew what he meant.

"That's what you get for dating a Mexican Baptist," I said. His chest moved beneath my ear as he chuckled.

I had confided my problem to Lucy, who had recently broken up with her boyfriend and was now going with the assistant manager at the cafeteria. "You need to date older boys," she had told me authoritatively. "High school boys have no idea what they're doing. You know why I broke up with Tommy? . . . He always twirled my nipples like he was trying to find a good radio station. Talk about bad in bed! Tell Luke you want to start seeing other people."

"I won't have to. He's leaving for Baylor in two weeks." Luke and I had both agreed that it would be impractical to continue dating exclusively while he was at college. It wasn't a breakup exactly—we had agreed that he could come see me when he was home on break.

I had mixed feelings about Luke's departure. Part of me looked forward to the freedom I would regain. The weekends would belong to me again, and there would be no more necessity of sleeping with him. But I would be lonely without him too.

I decided I was going to pour all my attention and energy into Carrington, and into my schoolwork. I was going to be the best sister, daughter, friend, student, the perfect example of a responsible young woman.

Labor Day was humid, the afternoon sky pale with visible steam rising from the broiled earth. But the heat didn't hinder the turnout at the annual Redneck Roundup, the county rodeo and livestock show. The fairgrounds were filled to capacity, with a kaleidoscope of arts and crafts booths and tables of guns and knives for sale. There were pony rides, horse pulls, tractor exhibits, and endless rows of food stalls. The rodeo would be held at eight in an open arena.

Mama and Carrington and I arrived at seven. We planned to have dinner and visit Miss Marva, who had rented a booth to sell her work. As I pushed the stroller across the dusty broken ground, I laughed at the way Carrington's head swiveled from side to side, her gaze following the strings of colored lights that webbed the interior of the central food court.

The fairgoers were dressed in jeans and heavy belts, and Western shirts with barrel cuffs, flap pockets, and plackets of mother-of-pearl snaps running down the front. At least half the men wore hats of white or black straw, beautiful Stetsons and Millers and Resistols. Women wore tight-fitting denim, or crinkly broomstick skirts, and embroidered boots. Mama and I had both opted for jeans. We had dressed Carrington in a pair of denim shorts that snapped down the insides of the legs. I had found her a little pink felt cowgirl hat with a ribbon that tied under the chin, but she kept pulling it off so she could clamp her gums on the brim.

Interesting smells floated through the air, the flurry of bodily odors and cologne, cigarette smoke, beer, hot fried food, animals, damp hay, dust, and machinery.

Pushing the stroller through the food court, Mama and I decided on deep-fried corn, pork-chop-on-a-stick, and fried potato shavings. Other booths offered deep-fried pickles, deep-fried jalapeños, and even strips of battered deep-fried bacon. It does not occur to Texans that some things just aren't meant to be put on a stick and deep-fried.

I fed Carrington applesauce from a jar I had packed in the diaper bag. For dessert, Mama bought a deep-fried Twinkie, which was made by dipping a frozen cake in tempura batter and dropping it in crackling-hot oil until the inside was soft and melting.

"This must be a million calories," Mama said, biting into the golden crust. She laughed as the filling squished out, and lifted a napkin to her chin.

After we finished, we scrubbed our hands with baby wipes and went to find Miss Marva. Her crimson hair was as bright as a torch in the gathering evening. She was doing a slow but steady business in bluebonnet candles and hand-painted birdhouses. We waited, in no hurry, for her to finish making change for a customer.

A voice came from behind us. "Hey, there."

Mama and I both turned, and my face froze as I saw Louis Sadlek, the owner of Bluebonnet Ranch. He was tricked out in snakeskin boots and denim, with a silver arrowhead-shaped bolo tie. I had always kept my distance from him, which turned out to be easy because he usually left the front office empty. He had no sense of regular work hours, spending his time drinking and tomcatting around town. If one of the trailer park residents went to ask him about fixing things like a clogged septic line or a pothole on the main drive, he promised to take care of it but never did a thing. Complaining to Sadlek was a waste of air.

Sadlek was well groomed but puffy, with broken capillaries spreading across the tops of his cheeks like the mesh of hairline cracks at the bottom of antique china cups. He had enough good looks left to make you sorry for his ruined handsomeness.

It struck me that Sadlek was an older version of the same boys I had met at the parties Luke had taken me to. In fact, he reminded me a little of Luke himself, the same sense of unearned privilege.

"Hi yourself, Louis," Mama replied. She had picked Carrington up and was trying to pry the baby's tweezerlike grip from a long curl of her light hair. She looked so pretty with her bright green eyes and her wide smile . . . it gave me a jolt of unease to see Sadlek's reaction to her.

"Who's this little dumplin'?" he asked, his accent so thick it was nearly devoid of consonants. He reached out to tickle Carrington's plump chin, and she gave him a wet baby-grin. The sight of his finger against the baby's pristine skin made me want to grab

Carrington and run without stopping. "You already eaten?" Sadlek asked Mama.

She continued to smile. "Yes, have you?"

"Tight as a tick," he replied, patting the belted jut of his stomach.

Although there wasn't anything remotely clever about what he'd said, Mama astonished me by laughing. She looked at him in a way that sent a creeping sensation down the back of my neck. Her gaze, her posture, the way she tucked a stray lock of hair behind her ear, all of it conveyed an invitation.

I couldn't believe it. Mama knew about his reputation just as I did. She had even made fun of him to me and Miss Marva, saying he was a small-town redneck who thought he was a big shot. She couldn't possibly have been attracted to Sadlek—it was obvious he wasn't good enough for her. But neither was Flip, or any of the other men I had ever seen her with. I puzzled over the common denominator between all of them, the mysterious thing that drew Mama to the wrong men.

In the piney woods of East Texas, pitcher plants attract bugs with an advertisement of bright yellow trumpets and red veins. The trumpets are filled with sweet-smelling juice that insects can't resist. But once a bug crawls into the pitcher, it can't get back out. Sealed in the crisp interior of the pitcher plant, it drowns in sugar water and is consumed. As I looked at Mama and Louis Sadlek, I saw the same alchemy at work, the false advertising, the attraction, the danger ahead.

"Bull-riding's gonna start soon," Sadlek remarked. "I've got a reserved box in the front. Why don't y'all come join me?"

"No, thank you," I said instantly. Mama gave me a warning glance. I knew I was being rude, but I didn't care.

"We'd love to," Mama said. "If you don't mind the baby."

"Hell no, how could I mind a sugar pie like this?" He played with Carrington, flicking the lobe of her ear, making her gurgle and coo.

And Mama, who was usually so critical of people's language, didn't say one word about swearing in front of the baby.

"I don't want to watch the bull-riding," I snapped.

Mama gave an exasperated sigh. "Liberty . . . if you're in a bad mood, don't take it out on everyone else. Why don't you go see if some of your friends are here?"

"Fine. I'll take the baby." I knew at once I shouldn't have said it that way, with a possessive edge to my tone. Had I asked Mama differently, she would have said yes.

As it was, however, she narrowed her eyes and said, "Carrington's fine with me. You go on. I'll see you back here in an hour."

Fuming, I slunk away down the row of stalls. The air was filled with the agreeable twangs and drumbeats of a country band warming up to play at the big canopy-covered dance floor nearby. It was a fine night for dancing. I scowled at the couples who headed toward the tent, their arms slung around each other's waists or shoulders.

I lingered at the vendors' tables, examining jars of preserves, salsas, and barbecue sauces, and T-shirts decorated with embroidery and sequins. I progressed to a jewelry stall, where felt trays were littered with silver charms and glittering silver chains.

The only jewelry I owned was a pair of pearl studs from Mama, and a delicate gold link bracelet Luke had given me for Christmas. Brooding over the selection of charms, I picked up a little figure of a bird inset with turquoise . . . a shape of Texas . . . a steer head . . . a cowboy boot. My attention was caught by a silver armadillo.

Armadillos have always been my favorite animals. They're awful pests, digging trenches through people's yards and burrowing under foundations. They're also as dumb as rocks. The best thing you can say about their appearance is that they're so ugly, they're cute. An armadillo is prehistoric in design, armored with that hard ribbed shell, his tiny head poking out the front as if someone stuck it on as an afterthought. Evolution just plain forgot to do anything about armadillos.

But no matter how armadillos are scorned or hounded, no matter how often people try to trap or shoot them, they persist in coming out night after night to do their work, searching for grubs and worms. If there are no grubs or worms to be had, they make do with berries and plants. They're the perfect example of persistence in the face of adversity.

There's no meanness in armadillos—their teeth are all molars, and they would never think of running up to bite someone even if they could. Some old people still call them Hoover Hogs for the days when the public had been promised a chicken in every pot and instead had to settle for whatever they could find to eat. Armadillos taste like pork, I've been told, although I never intend to test the claim.

I picked up the armadillo, and asked the seller what it would cost along with a sixteen-inch rope chain. She said it was twenty dollars. Before I could reach into my purse for the money, someone behind me handed over a twenty-dollar bill.

"I'll take care of that," came a familiar voice.

I spun to face him so quickly that he put his hands on my elbows to secure my balance. "Hardy!"

Most men, even those of average appearance, look like the Marlboro man when they wear boots, a white straw Resistol hat, and well-fitted jeans. The combination has the same transformative ability as a tuxedo. On someone like Hardy, it can knock out your breath like a blow to the chest.

"You don't have to buy me that," I protested.

"I haven't seen you for a while," Hardy said, taking the armadillo necklace from the lady behind the counter. He shook his head when she asked if he needed a receipt, and motioned me to turn around. Obeying, I lifted my hair out of the way. The backs of his fingers brushed against my nape, sending pleasure-chills across my skin.

Thanks to Luke, I'd been sexually initiated, if not awakened. I had traded my innocence in the hopes of gaining comfort, affection, knowledge . . . but as I stood there with Hardy, I understood the folly of trying to substitute someone else for him. Luke wasn't like Hardy in any way other than a passing physical resemblance. Bitterly I wondered if Hardy was going to overshadow every relationship for the rest of my life, haunting me like a ghost. I didn't know how to let him go. I'd never even had him.

"Hannah said you're living in town now," I commented. I touched the little silver armadillo as it hung at the hollow of my clavicle.

He nodded. "I've got a one-bedroom apartment. It's not much, but for the first time in my life I've got some privacy."

"Are you here with someone?"

He nodded. "Hannah and the boys. They're off watching the horse pull."

"I came with Mama and Carrington." I was tempted to tell him about Louis Sadlek too, and how outraged I was that Mama would even give him the time of day. But it seemed I laid my problems at Hardy's feet every time I was with him. For once I wasn't going to do that.

The sky had darkened from lavender to violet, the sun sinking so fast I half expected it to bounce on the horizon. The dance canopy was lit with strands of big white lightbulbs, while the band let loose with a fast two-stepping song.

"Hey, Hardy!" Hannah appeared at his side along with their two younger brothers, Rick and Kevin. The little boys were grimy and sticky-faced, wearing big grins as they jumped and squealed about wanting to go to the calf scramble.

The calf scramble was always held just before the rodeo. Children crowded into the ring and chased three agile calves that had yellow ribbons tied to their tails. Each child who managed to get a ribbon would receive a five-dollar bill. "Hi, Liberty," Hannah exclaimed, turning to her brother before I could answer. "Hardy, they're dying to go to the calf scramble. It's just about to start. Can I take 'em?"

He shook his head, regarding the trio with a reluctant grin. "You might as well. Just mind where you step, boys."

The children whooped with joy and took off at a dead run with Hannah chasing after them. Hardy chuckled as he watched them disappear. "My mother's gonna tear a strip off my hide for bringing them back smelling like cow patties."

"Children are supposed to get good and dirty every now and then."

Hardy's smile turned rueful. "That's what I tell my mother. Sometimes I have to get her to loosen up on them, let 'em run around and be boys. I wish . . ."

He hesitated, a frown weaving across his forehead.

"What?" I asked softly. The phrase "I wish," which came so naturally and frequently to my lips, was something I had never heard from Hardy before.

We began to walk aimlessly, Hardy shortening his stride to match mine. "I wish she'd brought herself to marry someone after Dad got put away for good," he said. "She has every right to divorce him. And if she'd found a decent man to be with, she might have had an easier time of it."

Having never known the nature of the crime his father had committed to get put away for life, I was hesitant to ask about it. I tried to look wise and concerned. "Does she still love him?"

"No, she's scared to death of him. He's as mean as a sack of snakes when he drinks. And he drinks most of the time. Ever since I could remember, he went in and out of jail . . . come back every year or two, knock my mother around, get her pregnant, and leave with every cent we had. I tried to stop him once when I was eleven—that's how my nose got broken. But the next time he came back, I'd gotten big enough to beat the tar out of him. He never bothered us again."

I flinched at the mental image of Miss Judie, so tall and skinny, being knocked around by anyone.

"Why doesn't she divorce him?" I asked.

Hardy smiled grimly. "The minister of our church told my mother that divorcing her husband, no matter how abusive, would be giving up on her chance to serve Christ. He said she shouldn't put her own happiness before her devotion to Jesus."

"He wouldn't believe that if *he* was the one getting beat up."

"I went to lay him out about it. He wouldn't budge though. I had to leave before I wrung his neck."

"Oh, Hardy," I said, my chest aching with compassion. I couldn't help thinking of Luke, and the easy life he'd had so far, and how different it was from Hardy's. "Why is life so difficult for some people and not for others? Why do some people have to struggle so much?"

He shrugged. "No one has it easy forever. Sooner or later God makes you pay for your sins."

"You should come to the Lamb of God on South Street," I advised. "He's a lot nicer over there. He'll overlook a few sins as long as you bring fried chicken to the Sunday potluck."

Hardy grinned. "You little blasphemer." We stopped in front of the covered dance floor. "I suppose the Lamb of God congregation believes in dancing too?"

I hung my head guiltily. "Afraid so."

"Lord Almighty, you're practically a Methodist. Come on." He took my hand and led me to the edge of the dance floor, where shadowed couples glided in rhythm, two steps slow, two steps fast. It was a circumspect dance with a careful distance maintained between your body and your partner's, unless he slid his hand to your waist and spun you in a tight circle that brought you flush against him. And then it became something else entirely. Especially if the music was slow.

Following Hardy's deliberate movements, my hand lightly caught in his, I felt my heart thump with dizzying force. I was surprised that he would want to dance with me, when in the past he had taken every opportunity to make it clear that he would allow nothing more than friendship. I was tempted to ask why, but I didn't say a word. I wanted this too badly.

I was nearly sick with giddy apprehension as he eased me closer. "This is a bad idea, isn't it?" I asked.

"Yeah. Put your hand on me."

My palm settled on the hard ascent of his shoulder. His chest rose and fell in an uneven rhythm. As I looked into the beautiful severity of his face, I realized he was giving in to a rare moment of self-indulgence. His eyes were alert but resigned, like a thief who knew he was about to get caught.

I was dimly aware of the bittersweet song once played by Randy Travis, desolate and angular and wounded as only a sad country song could be. The pressure of Hardy's hands guided me, our denim-clad legs brushing together. It seemed we didn't dance so much as simply cut ourselves adrift. We followed the current, keeping pace with other couples in a slow, seemly glide that was more intensely sexual than anything I had ever done with Luke. I didn't have to think about where I would step or which way I would turn.

Hardy's skin smelled like smoke and sun. I wanted to push beneath his shirt and explore every secret place of his body, every variation of skin and texture. I wanted things I didn't know how to name.

The band took the pace even slower, the two-step fading into another song that curtailed the dancing into a standing, swaying embrace. I felt him all against me now, and it filled me with agitation. I laid my head against his shoulder and felt the touch of his mouth on the apple of my cheek. His lips were dry and smooth. Transfixed, I didn't make a sound. He crowded me closer against him, one of his hands sliding low on my hips and imparting a gentle pressure. As I felt how aroused he was, my thighs and hips settled against him hungrily.

The span of three or four minutes is pretty insignificant in the scheme of things. People lose hundreds of minutes every day, squandering them on trivial things. But sometimes in those fragments of time, something can happen you'll remember the rest of your life. Being held by Hardy, suffused in his nearness, was an act of far greater intimacy than sex. Even now as I look back on it I can feel that moment of absolute connection, and the blood still rises to my face.

When the music snapped into a new rhythm, Hardy led me away from the dance canopy. His hand cupped my left elbow, and he murmured a warning as we crossed bulky electrical cables that crossed the ground like uncoiled snakes. I had no idea where we were going, only that we were headed away from the concession stands. We reached the boundary of a red cedar rail fence. Hardy fitted his hands around my waist and lifted me up with astonishing ease. I sat on the top rail, so that we were face-to-face, my closed knees pressed between us.

"Don't let me fall," I said.

"You won't fall." He grasped my hips securely, the heat of his palms sinking through my summer-weight denim. I was seized by a nearly uncontrollable urge to part my thighs and pull him forward until he stood between them. Instead I sat there with my knees primly cinched and my heart hammering. The dusty glow of the fair lights fanned out behind Hardy, making it difficult to see his expression.

He shook his head slowly, as if confronted with a problem he couldn't begin to solve. "Liberty, I have to tell you . . . I'm leaving soon."

"Leaving Welcome?" I could hardly speak.

"Yes."

"When? Where?"

"In a couple of days. One of the jobs I applied for came through, and . . . I won't be coming back for a while."

"What are you doing to do?"

"I'll be welding for a drilling company. I'm starting on an offshore rig in the Gulf. But they move the welders around a lot, wherever the company has a contract." He paused as he saw my expression. He knew my father had died on a platform rig. Jobs on offshore rigs were high-paying but dangerous. You have to be crazy or suicidal to work on an oil rig with a blowtorch in hand. Hardy seemed to read my thoughts. "I'll try not to cause too many explosions."

If he was trying to make me smile, the effort flopped. It was pretty obvious this was the last I'd be seeing of Hardy Cates. There was no use in asking if he'd ever come back for me. I had to let go of him. But I knew that as long as I lived, I would feel the phantom-pain of his absence.

I thought about his future, the oceans and continents he would cross, far away from everyone who knew and loved him. Far outside the sphere of his mother's prayers. Among the women in his future, there was one who would know his secrets and bear his children, and witness the changes the years worked on him. And it wouldn't be me.

"Good luck," I said thickly. "You'll do fine. I think you'll end up with everything you want. I think you'll be more successful than anyone could begin to guess."

His voice was quiet. "What are you doing, Liberty?"

"I'm trying to tell you what you want to hear. Good luck. Have a nice life." I pushed at him with my knees. "Let me down."

"Not yet. First you're going to tell me why you're mad when at every turn I've tried to keep from hurting you."

"Because it hurts anyway." I couldn't control the words that burst from me. "And if you'd ever asked what I wanted, I would rather have had as much of you as I could and taken the hurt that came with it. But instead I've gotten nothing except these stupid—" I paused, trying in vain to think of a better word. "*Stupid* excuses about not wanting to hurt me when the truth is *you're* the one afraid of being hurt. You're afraid you might love someone too much to leave, and then you'd have to give up all your dreams and live in Welcome for the rest of your life. You're afraid—"

I broke off with a gasp as I felt him grab my shoulders and give me a little shake. Abbreviated as the motion was, it sent reverberations through every part of me.

"Stop it," he said hoarsely.

"Do you know why I went with Luke Bishop?" I asked in reckless despair. "Because I wanted you and couldn't have you, and he was the nearest thing I could find to you. And every time I slept with him I wished it was you, and I hate you for that, even worse than I hate myself."

As the words left my lips, a sense of bitter isolation made me shrink from him. My head ducked, and I wrapped my arms around myself in an effort to take up as little physical space as possible.

"It's your fault," I said, words that would cause me infinite shame later, but I was too worked up to care.

Hardy's grip tightened until my muscles registered the beginnings of pain. "I made no promises to you."

"It's still your fault."

"Damn it." He took a ragged breath as he saw the slide of a tear on my cheek. "Damn it, Liberty. That's not fair."

"Nothing is fair."

"What do you want from me?"

"I want you to admit just once what you feel for me. I want to know if you'll miss me even a little. If you'll remember me. If you're sorry for anything."

I felt his fingers clench in my hair, tugging until my head tilted back. "Christ," he whispered. "You want to make this as hard as possible, don't you? I can't stay, and I can't take you with me. And you want to know if I'm sorry for anything." I felt the hot strikes of his breath on my cheek. His arms wrapped around me, stifling all movement. His heart pounded against my flattened breasts. "I'd sell my soul to have you. In my whole life, you'll always be what I wanted most. But I've got nothing to give you. And I won't stay here and turn into my father. I would take everything out on you—I would hurt you."

"You wouldn't. You could never be like your father."

"Do you think so? Then you have a hell of a lot more faith in me than I do." Hardy caught my head in both hands, his long fingers curving around the back of my skull. "I wanted to kill Luke Bishop for touching you. And you for letting him." I felt a tremor run through him. "You're mine," he said. "And you're right about one thing—all that's ever stopped me from taking you is knowing I could never leave once I did."

I hated him for regarding me as part of a trap he had to escape from. He bent his head to kiss me, the salt taste of my tears vanishing between our lips. I stiffened, but he urged my mouth open and kissed me more deeply, and I was lost.

He found every weakness with diabolical gentleness, gathering sensation as if it were honey to be lapped up with his tongue. His hand coasted over the seam of my thighs and urged them apart, and before I could close them again his body was there. Murmuring softly, he helped me to wrap my arms around his neck, and his lips returned to mine, ravishing slowly. No matter how I squirmed and strained, I couldn't get close enough. I wanted nothing less than the full weight of him on me, full possession, full surrender. I pushed the hat from his head and sank my fingers into his hair, pulling his mouth harder, harder against mine.

"Easy," Hardy whispered, lifting his head, gripping my shivering body against his. "Take it easy, honey."

I fought for breath and sat there with the wooden rail digging into my backside, my knees clamped on his hips. He wouldn't give me his mouth again until I quieted, and then his kisses were soothing, his lips absorbing the sounds that climbed in my throat. His hand moved up and down my spine in repeated strokes. Slowly he brought his palm to the undercurve of my breast, caressing me over the fabric of my shirt, and his thumb swirled gently until he found the hardening tip. My arms became weak, too heavy to lift, and I lent more of my weight to him, resting on him like a Friday-night drunk.

I understood how it would be with him, how different from the times I'd slept with Luke. Hardy seemed to drink in every nuance of my response, every sound and shiver and respiration. He held me as if the weight of me were precious in his arms. I lost track of how long he kissed me, his mouth alternately gentle and demanding. The tension built until low whimpers broke from my throat, and my fingertips scrabbled over the surface of his shirt, desperate for the feel of his skin. He took his mouth from mine and buried his face in my hair, struggling to control his breathing.

"No," I protested. "Don't stop, don't—"

"Hush. Hush, darlin'."

I couldn't stop shaking, rebelling against being left high and dry. Hardy folded me against his chest and rubbed my back, trying to ease me into stillness. "It's okay," he whispered. "Sweet girl, sweet . . . it's all right."

But nothing was all right. I thought when Hardy left me, I would never be able to take pleasure in anything again. I waited until I thought my legs would support my own weight, and then I half slid, half fell to the ground. Hardy reached out to steady me, and I pulled away from him. I could hardly see him, my eyes were so blurred.

"Don't say goodbye," I said. "Please."

Perhaps understanding it was the last thing he could do for me, Hardy kept silent.

I knew I would replay the scene countless times in the years before me, each time thinking of different things I should have said and done.

But all I did was walk away without looking back.

Many times in my life I've regretted the things I've said without thinking.

But I've never regretted the things I said nearly as much as the words I left unspoken.

CHAPTER 10

The sight of a sullen teenager is common no matter where you go. Teenagers want things so powerfully and can never seem to get them, and to add insult to injury, people make light of your feelings because you're a teenager. They say time will mend a broken heart and they're often right. But not where my feelings for Hardy were concerned. For months, all through the winter holidays and beyond, I just went through the motions, distracted and gloomy and of no use to anyone including myself.

The other thing feeding my sullenness

was Mama's flourishing relationship with Louis Sadlek. Their pairing caused me no end of confusion and resentment. If there was ever a moment of peace between them, I never saw it. Most of the time they got along like two cats in a sack.

Louis brought out Mama's worst tendencies. She drank when she was around him, and my mother had never been a drinker. She was physical with him in a way I had never seen before, pushing, slapping, poking, she who had always insisted on her personal space. Sadlek appealed to a wild streak in her, and mothers weren't supposed to have a wild streak. I wished she wasn't pretty and blond, that she would be the kind of mother who wore aprons and went to church socials.

What bothered me as much as anything was the vague understanding that Mama and Louis's arguing and tussling and jealousies, the small damages they did to each other, were a kind of foreplay. Louis rarely visited our trailer, thank God, but I and everyone else at Bluebonnet Ranch knew that Mama was spending nights at his red-brick house. Sometimes she came back with bruises on her arms, her face worn from lack of sleep, her throat and jaw scraped red from unshaven bristle. Mothers weren't supposed to do that either.

I don't know how much of Mama's relationship with Louis Sadlek was pleasure and how much was self-punishment. I think she regarded Louis as a strong man. Lord knows she wouldn't have been the first to mistake brutishness for strength. Maybe when a woman had been fending for herself as long as Mama did, it was a relief to submit to someone else, even if he wasn't kind. I've felt like that more than a few times, aching under the weight of responsibility and wishing anyone was in charge of me except me.

I'll admit Louis could be charming. Even the worst of Texas men have that amiable veneer, the soft-spokenness that appeals to women and the flair for storytelling. He seemed to genuinely like young children—they were so ready to believe anything he told them. Car-

rington giggled and grinned whenever Louis was near, thereby dis-
proving the notion that children instinctively know who to trust.

But Louis didn't like me at all. I was the only holdout in our house-
hold. I couldn't stand the very things that impressed Mama so, the
masculine posturing, the endless gestures meant to convey how little
things meant to him because he had so much. He had a closet full of
custom-made boots, the kind the bootmaker starts by asking you to
stand in your sock feet on a piece of butcher paper and trace around
the edges. Louis had a pair of eight-hundred-dollar boots made of elephant hide from "Zimbab-way." They were the talk of Welcome,
those boots.

But when Louis and Mama and two other couples went dancing at
a place in Houston, the men at the door wouldn't let him bring his silver liquor flask inside. So Louis went to the side and drew out his
Dozier folding hunter knife and cut a long slit right through the top of
that boot, so he could wedge the flask inside. When Mama told me
about it later, she said it had been a stupid gesture and a ridiculous
waste of money. But she mentioned it so many times in the months afterward that I realized she admired the flamboyance of it.

That was Louis, doing whatever it took to keep up the appearance
of wealth, when in reality he was no better off than anyone else. All
hat, no cattle. No one seemed to know how Louis got his spending
money, which surely amounted to more than the income from the
trailer park. There were rumors of casual drug-dealing. Since we were
located so close to the border, that was fairly easy for anyone who
wanted to take the risk. I don't believe Louis ever smoked or snorted.
Alcohol was his drug of choice. But I don't think he had any scruples
about siphoning poison to college students who were home on break,
or locals who wanted a more potent escape than could be found in a
bottle of Johnnie Walker.

When I wasn't preoccupied with Mama and Louis, I was absorbed in Carrington, who had lurched into toddlerhood and had begun staggering around like a miniature drunken linebacker. She tried to stick her tiny wet fingers in electric sockets, pencil sharpeners, and Coke cans. She tweezed bugs and cigarette butts from the grass, and petrified Cheerios from the carpet, and everything went into her mouth. When she started feeding herself with a bent-handled spoon, she made such an unholy mess I sometimes had to take her outside to hose her down. I kept an oversized plastic dishpan from Wal-Mart on the back patio, and watched over Carrington as she played and splashed in it.

When she started to talk, the closest she could get to pronouncing my name was "BeeBee," and she said it whenever she wanted anything. She loved Mama, twinkled like a lightning bug when they were together, but when she was sick or cantankerous or afraid, she reached for me and I reached for her. It was nothing Mama and I ever talked about, or even thought much about, we all just took it for granted. Carrington was my baby.

Miss Marva encouraged us to visit often, saying her days were too quiet otherwise. She had never taken Bobby Ray back. There would probably be no more boyfriends for her, she said, since all the men her age were getting to be sorry-looking or feebleminded or both. Every Wednesday afternoon I drove her to the Lamb of God, because she was a volunteer cook for their Meals-on-Wheels program and the church had a commercial-rated kitchen. With Carrington balanced on my hip, I would measure out ingredients and stir bowls and pots, while Miss Marva taught me the basics of Texas cooking.

Under her direction I scraped milky sweet corn off fresh cobs, seared it in bacon drippings and added half-and-half, stirring until the aroma caused tickles of saliva on the insides of my cheeks. I learned how to make chicken-fried steak topped with white cream gravy, and okra dusted with cornmeal and skillet-fried in hot grease, and pinto beans boiled with a ham bone, and turnip greens with pepper sauce. I even learned the secrets of Miss Marva's red velvet cake, which she warned me never to make for a man unless I wanted him to propose to me.

The hardest thing to learn was how to make Miss Marva's chicken and dumplings, which she didn't have a recipe for. They were so good, so rich and gummy and melting, they could almost make you cry. She started with a little hill of flour on the counter, added salt and eggs and butter, and mixed it all up with her fingers. She rolled it out into a flat sheet, cut the dough into long strips, and added it to a boiling pot of homemade chicken stock. There is hardly an illness that chicken and dumplings can't cure. Miss Marva made a pot of them for me right after Hardy Cates had left Welcome, and they almost provided a temporary relief from heartache.

I helped deliver the Meals-on-Wheels containers, while Miss Marva looked after Carrington. "Ain't you got homework, Liberty?" she would ask, and I always shook my head. I hardly ever did homework. I went to the bare minimum of classes to avoid truancy, and I didn't give a thought to my prospects beyond high school. I figured if Mama had stopped caring about my good mind and my education, I wasn't going to care either.

For a while Luke Bishop asked me out when he came home from Baylor, but when I kept refusing him, he gradually stopped calling. I felt as if something in me had been shut off after Hardy left, and I didn't know how or when it would turn back on. I had experienced sex without love, and love without sex, and now I wanted nothing to do with either of them. Miss Marva advised me to start living by my own lights, a phrase I didn't understand.

Coming up on one year since Mama and Louis had started dating, Mama broke up with him. She had a high tolerance for fireworks, but even she had her limits. It happened at a honky-tonk where they went two-stepping on occasion. While Louis was off in the men's room, some drunken cowboy—a real cowboy who worked on a small ten-thousand-acre ranch outside of town—bought Mama a tequila shot.

Texas men are more territorial than most. This is a culture in which they put up fences to defend their land, and sleep with shotguns propped against the nightstands to defend their homes. Making a move on someone's woman is considered grounds for justifiable homicide. So the cowboy should have known better even if he was drunk, and many said Louis was justified in beating the crap out of him. But Louis lit into him with singular viciousness, walloping him to a bloody pulp in the parking lot and kicking him half to death with his two-inch boot heels. And then Louis went to his truck to get his gun, presumably to finish him off. Only the intervention of a couple of friends kept Louis from committing outright murder. As Mama told me later, the odd thing was how much bigger the cowboy had been. There was no way Louis should have beaten him. But sometimes meanness wins out over muscle. Having seen what Louis was capable of, Mama broke up with him. It was the happiest day I'd known since before Hardy had left.

It didn't last long though. Louis wouldn't leave her—or us—alone. He started calling at all hours of the day and night until our ears rang from the sound of the phone, and Carrington was cranky from constantly interrupted sleep. Louis followed Mama in his car, dogging her on her way to work or out to eat or shop. Often he would park his truck right outside our house and watch us. One time I went into the bedroom to change, and just before I pulled my shirt off I saw him staring at me through the window in back that faced the neighboring farmer's field.

It's funny how many people still think stalking is a phase of courtship. Some people told Mama it wasn't stalking unless you were a celebrity. When she finally went to the police, they were reluctant to do anything. To them the situation looked like two people who just couldn't get along. She was embarrassed by it, ashamed, as if she were somehow to blame.

The worst part is, Louis's tactics worked. He wore her down until going back to him seemed like the easiest thing to do. She even tried to convince herself she wanted to be with him. To my mind it wasn't dating, it was hostage-taking.

Their relationship had undergone a sea change though. Louis may have had Mama back physically, but she wasn't his like she had been before. He and everyone else knew that if she'd been free to leave, if there had been some assurance he wouldn't bother her anymore, she might have bolted. I say "might have" instead of "would have" because it seemed there was a terrible fracture in her that still wanted him, was caught by him, just as a lock tumbler is engaged by the bit of a key.

One night, I'd just put Carrington in her crib when I heard a knock at the door. Mama was out with Louis to a dinner and a show in Houston.

I don't know why a policeman's knock is different from other people knocking, why the sound of their knuckles striking the door tightens all the vertebrae in your spine. The grim authority in that sound told me immediately something was wrong. I opened the door and found two policemen standing there. To this day I can't remember their faces. Just their uniforms, light blue shirts and navy pants, and shield-shaped patches embroidered with a little planet earth crossed with two red bands.

My mind shot to the last moment I had seen Mama that night. I had been quiet but irritable, watching her walk to the door in jeans and high heels. There were a few meaningless remarks, Mama telling me she might not be home before morning, and me shrugging and saying "whatever." I have always been haunted by the ordinariness of that conversation. You figure the last time you ever see somebody, something of significance should be said. But Mama exited my life with a quick smile and a reminder to lock the door behind her so I would be safe while she was gone.

The police said the accident happened on the east freeway—this was back before I-10 was finished—where eighteen-wheelers went as fast as they wanted. At any given time at least a quarter of all vehicles on the freeway were trucks, carrying loads to and from breweries and chemical plants. It didn't help matters that the lanes were narrow, and the sight lines were almost nonexistent.

Louis ran a red light on a feeder road just off the freeway and collided with an oncoming truck. The driver of the truck had minor injuries. Louis had to be cut out of the car before he was taken to the hospital, where he died an hour later of massive internal bleeding.

Mama was killed on impact.

She never knew what hit her, the policemen said, and that would have comforted me, except . . . just for one second, she would have had to know, wouldn't she? There must have been a blur, a sense of the world exploding, a flashpoint of receiving more damage than a human body could endure. I wondered if she hovered over the scene afterward, looking down on what had become of her. I wanted to believe an escort of angels came for her, that the promise of heaven replaced the grief of leaving me and Carrington, and that whenever Mama wanted, she could peek through the clouds to see how we were. But faith has never been my strong suit. All I knew for certain was my mother had gone somewhere I couldn't follow.

And I finally understood what Miss Marva had said about living by your own lights. When you're walking through the darkness, you can't depend on anything or anyone else to light your way. You have to rely on whatever sparks you've got inside you. Or you're going to get lost. That was what had happened to Mama.

And I knew if I let it happen to me, there would be no one for Carrington.

CHAPTER 11

Mama had no life insurance and hardly any savings. That left me with a trailer, some furniture, a car, and a two-year-old sister. I would have to maintain all that on a high school education with no past work experience. I had spent my summers and afternoons with Carrington, which meant the only employment references I had were from someone who until recently had been riding backward in the car.

Shock is a merciful condition. It allows you to get through disaster with a necessary distance between you and your feelings, so you can get things done. The first thing I had to do was arrange the funeral. I'd never set foot in a funeral home before. I had always imagined such places were creepy and sad. Miss Marva went with me even though I told her I didn't need help. She said she used to date the funeral director, Mr. Ferguson, who was a widower now, and she wanted to see how much hair he'd kept over the years.

Not much, as it turned out. But Mr. Ferguson was about the nicest man I'd ever met, and the funeral home—tan brick with white columns—was bright and clean and done up like a comfortable living room. The sitting area featured blue tweed sofas, and coffee tables with big scrapbooks, and landscape pictures on the walls. We had cookies from a china plate, and coffee from a big silver carafe. As we started to talk, I appreciated the way Mr. Ferguson discreetly nudged the Kleenex box across the coffee table. I wasn't crying, my emotions were still suspended in ice, but Miss Marva went through half the box.

Mr. Ferguson had the wise, kind, gently droopy face of a basset hound, with brown eyes like melted chocolate. He gave me a brochure titled "The Ten Rules of Grief," and tactfully asked if Mama had ever mentioned having preplanned a funeral. "No, sir," I said earnestly. "She wasn't the planning-ahead type. It took her forever just to order from the cafeteria menu."

The creases in the outside corners of his eyes deepened. "My wife was like that," he said. "There's people who like to plan and those who take life as it comes. Nothing wrong with either way. I'm a planner, myself."

"So am I," I said, although that wasn't at all true. I had always followed Mama's example, taking life as it came. But now I wanted to be different, I had to be.

Opening a book of laminated price sheets, Mr. Ferguson led me into the subject of the funeral budget.

There was a long list of things that needed to be paid for, cemetery fees, taxes, the obituary notice, prices for embalming, hair and cosmetics, a concrete grave liner, hearse rental, music, a headstone.

Lord, it was expensive to die.

It was going to take most of the cash Mama had left, unless I wanted to put it on credit. But I was suspicious of debt. I'd seen what happened to people who started down that plastic slide to disaster. Most of the time they were never able to climb out. This being Texas, there were no shelters or programs that would afford us a decent life. The only safety net was people's kin. And I was too proud to consider tracking down unknown relatives, all strangers, so I could beg for money. I realized Mama's funeral would have to be done on a shoestring, a thought that brought a pinching sensation in my throat and hot pressure behind my eyes.

My mother had not been a churchgoer, I told Mr. Ferguson, and therefore we wanted a nonreligious ceremony.

"You can't have a nonreligious funeral," Miss Marva protested, shocked out of a weepy spell by the very idea. "There's no such thing in Welcome."

"You'd be surprised, Marva," Mr. Ferguson informed her. "We have a few humanists in town. They just don't care to admit it publicly, or they know they'd find their doorsteps occupied with Bible-bangers carrying potted begonias and Bundt cakes."

"Have you turned into a heathen, Arthur?" Miss Marva demanded, and he smiled.

"No, ma'am. But I've come to accept that some folks are happier not being saved."

After discussing some ideas for Mama's humanist funeral, we went to the casket room, which had at least thirty of them set up in rows. I hadn't realized there would be so many choices. Not only could you pick out the outside materials, you could choose linings of velvet or satin in just about any color. It unnerved me to learn you could also decide on the firmness of the mattress on the interior bed, as if it would make a difference to the deceased person's comfort.

Some of the more elegant coffins, like the one made of oak with a French Provincial hand-rubbed finish, or the steel in brushed bronze with the embroidered interior head panel, were four or five thousand dollars. And the casket in the farthest corner of the room was gaudier than anything I could have imagined, hand-painted like a Monet landscape with water, flowers, and a bridge, all yellows, blues, greens, and pinks. It had a tufted blue satin interior and pillow, and a matching throw.

"Something to look at, isn't it?" Mr. Ferguson asked, his smile a touch sheepish. "One of our suppliers was pushing these art caskets this year, but I'm afraid it's a little fancy for small-town tastes."

I wanted it for my mother. I didn't care that it was god-awful tacky and ostentatious and that once it was six feet under, no one would ever see it. If you were going to sleep someplace forever, it should be on blue satin pillows in a secret garden concealed beneath the ground. "How much is it?" I asked.

Mr. Ferguson took a long time to answer, and when he did, his voice was very quiet. "Sixty-five hundred, Miss Jones."

I could afford maybe a tenth of that.

Poor people have few choices in life, and most of the time you don't think much about it. You get the best you can, and do without when necessary, and hope to God you won't be wiped out by something you can't control. But there are moments it hurts, where there is something you want in the very marrow of your bones and you know there's no way you can have it. I felt like that about Mama's casket. And I realized this was an augury of things to come. A house, braces and clothes for Carrington, education, things that would help us climb across the deep trench between white trash and middle class . . . these things would require more money than my ability to earn. I didn't know why I had never grasped the urgency of my situation before, even when Mama was alive. Why had I been so careless and unthinking? I felt sick to my stomach.

Stiffly I followed Mr. Ferguson to the side of the room featuring the econocaskets, and found a lacquered pine model lined with white taffeta for six hundred dollars. We went out back to a row of headstones and markers, and chose a bronze rectangular plate to lay over Mama's grave. Someday, I vowed silently, I would replace it with a big marble headstone.

As soon as news of the accident got out, ovens all over town were turned on. Even people we didn't know, or were only casually acquainted with, brought a casserole, pie, or cake to the trailer. Foil-wrapped parcels were piled on every available surface; the counters, tables, the fridge and stove. Bereavement in Texas is a time to pull out your best recipes. Many people taped them to the plastic wrap or foil that covered their offerings, which wasn't usually done, but I guess there was a general agreement that I needed all the help I could get. None of the recipes had more than four or five ingredients, and they were the kind of food you'd often find at bake sales or potlucks. Tamale pie, ugly cake, King Ranch casserole, Coca-Cola brisket, Jell-O salad.

I was truly sorry so much food was given to us at a time when I couldn't have felt less like eating. I pulled off the recipe cards and tucked them in a manila envelope for safekeeping, and took most of the food to the Cateses. For once I was grateful for Miss Judie's reserve—I knew that no matter how sympathetic she was, she wasn't going to discuss anything emotional.

It was difficult to see Hardy's family, when I wanted him so badly. I needed Hardy to come back and rescue me, and take care of me. I wanted him to hold me tight, and let me cry in his arms. But when I asked if Miss Judie had heard from him, she said not yet, he'd be too busy to write or call for a while.

The relief of tears came the second night after Mama had died, when I had crawled into bed next to Carrington's robust little body.

She snuggled against me in her sleep, and let out a baby sigh, and that sound cracked the seal around my heart.

At two, Carrington had no understanding of death. The finality of it escaped her. She kept asking when Mama was coming back, and when I had tried to explain about heaven, she had listened without comprehension and interrupted me by asking for a Popsicle. I lay there holding her, worrying about what would happen to us, if some social worker would show up to take her away, or what I would do if Carrington became seriously ill, and how to prepare her for life when I knew so damn little.

I had never paid a bill before. I didn't know where either of our Social Security cards were. And I worried if Carrington would remember Mama at all. Realizing there was no one for me to share my memories of my mother with, I felt tears begin to leak out of my eyes in a continuous stream. That went on for a while until I began to cry so hard that I finally went to the bathroom and filled the tub and sat upright like a child, crying into my bathwater until a great dull calmness had settled over me.

Do you need money?" my friend Lucy asked bluntly as she watched me dress for the funeral. She was going to look after Carrington until I came back from the service. "My family can loan you some. And Daddy says there's a part-time job available at the shop."

I couldn't have made it without Lucy in the days following Mama's accident. She had asked if there was anything she could do for me, and when I said no, she went ahead and did things anyway. She insisted on taking Carrington to her house for an afternoon so I could have some quiet time to make calls and clean the trailer.

Another day Lucy brought her mother, and the two of them packed away Mama's belongings in cardboard boxes. I couldn't have done it by myself. Mama's favorite jacket, her white wrap dress with the daisies, the blue blouse, the gauzy pink scarf she had tied around her hair, these and other things were littered with memories in every fold and pleat. At night I had taken to wearing a T-shirt that hadn't been washed yet. It still held the smells of Mama's skin and Estee Lauder Youth Dew. I didn't know how to make the scent last. One day long after it was gone, I would wish for one more breath of mother-smell, and it would exist only in my memory.

Lucy and her mother carried the clothes off to a storage place, and gave me the key. The pawnshop would take care of the monthly fee, Mrs. Reyes said, and I could leave everything there indefinitely.

"You could work whenever you wanted," Lucy pressed.

I shook my head in answer to Lucy's mention of the part-time job. I was pretty certain they didn't need any help at the pawnshop, and they had made the offer out of sympathy. And although I appreciated their kindness more than they would ever know, it's a fact that friends last longer the less you use them.

"Tell your parents thank you," I said, "but I'll probably need something full-time. I haven't figured out what to do yet."

"I've always said you should go to beauty school. You would be such a great hairstylist. I can see you with your own shop someday." Lucy knew me too well—the idea of working in a salon, all aspects of it, appealed to me more than any other kind of job. But . . .

"It would take about nine months to a year, full-time, to get my license," I said regretfully. "And there's no way I could afford the tuition."

"You could borrow—"

"No." I pulled on a black sleeveless acrylic top and tucked it into the top of my skirt. "I can't start by borrowing, Luce, or I'll just keep going on that way. If I don't have the means for it, I'll have to wait until I've saved enough."

"You may never save enough." She regarded me with patent exasperation. "Girlfriend, if you're waiting for a fairy godmother to show up with a dress and a ride, you're not going to make it to the party."

I picked up a brush from my dresser and began to fix my hair in a low ponytail. "I'm not waiting for anyone. I can do it by myself."

"All I'm saying is, take help where you can get it. You don't have to do everything the hard way."

"I know that." Swallowing back the irritation, I managed to haul the corners of my mouth up into a smile. Lucy was a concerned friend, and knowing that made her bossiness a little easier to take. "And I'm not as stubborn as you make it sound—I let Mr. Ferguson upgrade the casket, didn't I?"

The day before the funeral, Mr. Ferguson had called and said he had a deal for me if I was interested. Seeming to choose his words carefully, he told me that the casket manufacturer had just put its art models on sale, and the Monet casket had been discounted. Since the starting price had been sixty-five hundred, I said I doubted I could afford it even on sale.

"They're nearly giving them away," Mr. Ferguson had pressed. "In fact, the Monet is now the exact same price as the pine coffin you purchased. I can switch them out for you at no extra expense."

I had almost been too stunned to speak. "Are you sure?"

"Yes, ma'am."

Suspecting that Mr. Ferguson's generosity might have had something to do with the fact that he had taken Miss Marva out to dinner a couple of nights before, I went to ask her exactly what had happened on their date.

"Liberty Jones," she had said indignantly, "are you suggesting I slept with that man to get you a discounted coffin?"

Abashed, I replied that I'd meant no disrespect, and of course I didn't think such a thing.

Still indignant, Miss Marva had informed me that if she *had* slept with Arthur Ferguson, there was no doubt he would have given me the dadgum coffin for free.

The graveside service was beautiful, if a little scandalous by Welcome standards. Mr. Ferguson conducted the service, talking a little about Mama and her life, and how much she would be missed by her friends and two daughters. There was no mention at all of Louis. His kin had taken his body off to Mesquite, where he'd been born and many of the Sadleks still lived. They'd hired a manager for Bluebonnet Ranch, a shiftless young man named Mike Mendeke.

One of Mama's closest friends at work, a plump woman with tea-colored hair, read a poem:

Do not stand at my grave and weep
I am not there, I do not sleep.
I am a thousand winds that blow,
I am the diamond glints on snow,
I am the sun on ripened grain,
I am the gentle autumn rain.
When you awaken in the morning's hush
I am the swift uplifting rush
Of quiet birds in circled flight.
I am the soft stars that shine at night.
Do not stand at my grave and cry,
I am not there; I did not die.

It may not have been a religious poem, but by the time Deb had finished, there were tears in many eyes.

I laid two yellow roses, one from Carrington and one from me, on top of the coffin. Red may be the preferred color of roses everywhere else, but in Texas it's yellow. Mr. Ferguson had promised me the flowers would be buried with Mama when it was lowered into the ground.

At the end of the service, we played "Imagine" by John Lennon, which elicited smiles from a few faces, and disapproving frowns from many more. Forty-two white balloons—one for each year of Mama's age—were released in the warm blue sky.

It was the perfect funeral for Diana Truitt Jones. I think my mother would have loved it. When the service was over, I felt a sudden fierce need to rush back to Carrington. I wanted to hug her for a long time, and stroke the pale blond curls that reminded me so much of Mama's. Carrington had never seemed so fragile to me, so vulnerable to every kind of harm.

As I turned to glance at the row of cars, I saw a black limo with tinted windows parked in the distance. Welcome is not what you'd call limo country, so this was a mildly startling sight. The design of the vehicle was modern, its doors and windows sealed, its shape as streamlined and perfect as a shark's.

No other funeral was being held that day. Whoever was sitting in that limo had known my mother, had wanted to watch her service from a distance. I stood very still, staring at the vehicle. My feet moved, and I suppose I was going over to ask if he—or she—wanted to come to the graveside. But just as I started toward it, the limo pulled away in a slow glide.

It bothered me, the thought that I would never find out who it was.

Soon after the funeral Carrington and I were visited by a guardian ad litem, or GAL, who had been appointed to assess whether I was fit to be her legal guardian. The GAL's fee was one hundred and fifty dollars, which I thought was pretty steep considering she stayed less than an hour. Thank God the court had waived the fee—I didn't think my checking account would cover it.

Carrington seemed to know it was important for her to behave well. Under the GAL's observation, she built a block tower, dressed her favorite doll, and sang the ABC song from start to finish. While the GAL asked me questions about the baby's upbringing and my plans for the future, Carrington climbed into my lap and pressed a few impassioned kisses on my cheek. After each kiss, she glanced significantly at the GAL to make certain her actions were being duly noted.

The next phase of the process was surprisingly easy. I went to Family Court and gave the judge letters from Miss Marva, the pediatrician, and the pastor of the Lamb of God, all offering good opinions as to my character and my parenting abilities. The judge expressed concern over my lack of a job, advised me to get something right away, and warned me to expect the occasional visit from Social Services.

When the hearing was over, the court clerk told me to write out a check for seventy-five dollars, which I did with a purple glitter pen I found at the bottom of my purse. They gave me a folder with copies of the petition and information release forms I'd filled out, and the certificate of guardianship. I couldn't help feeling like I'd just bought Carrington and been handed the receipt.

I went outside the courthouse and found Lucy waiting for me at the bottom of the steps, with Carrington in her stroller. For the first time in days, I laughed as I saw Carrington's chubby hands clutching a cardboard sign Lucy had made for her: *PROPERTY OF LIBERTY JONES.*

CHAPTER 19

Fly High with TexWest!

Are you ready for a rewarding and people-oriented job in the skies? Travel, learn, expand your horizons as a flight attendant for TexWest, the fastest-growing commuter airline service in the nation. Must be willing to locate to our domiciles in CA, UT, NM, AZ, TX. High school diploma required, height requirement of 5'0" to 5'8", no exceptions. Come to our open house and discover more about the exciting possibilities at TexWest.

I have always hated flying. The idea of it is an affront to nature. People are meant to stay on the ground.

I put down the classifieds and glanced at Carrington, who was sitting in her high chair and feeding long strands of spaghetti into her mouth. Most of her hair was fastened into a sprig of hair at the top of her head and clipped with a big red bow. She was dressed in her diapers and nothing else. We had discovered that cleanup after dinner was a lot easier if she ate topless.

Carrington regarded me solemnly, with a big orange smear of spaghetti sauce across her mouth and chin.

"How would you like to relocate to Oregon?" I asked her.

Her small round face split into a grin, displaying a set of widely spaced white teeth. "Okeydokey."

It was her latest favorite phrase, the other being "No way."

"You could stay in day care," I continued, "while I go up in a plane and serve little bottles of Jack Daniel's to cranky businessmen. How does that sound?"

"Okeydokey."

I watched Carrington meticulously pick out a shred of cooked carrot that I had sneaked into her spaghetti sauce. After divesting the strand of pasta of as much nutritional value as possible, she put the end in her mouth and sucked it up.

"Quit picking off those vegetables," I told her, "or I'll make you some broccoli."

"No way," she said, her mouth full of spaghetti, and I laughed.

I pored over the notes I had made on the jobs available to a girl with a high school diploma and no work experience. So far it seemed I was qualified to be a Quick-Stop cashier, a sanitation pump driver, a nanny, a cleaning lady for Happy Helpers, or a cat groomer at a pet clinic. They all paid about what I had expected, which was next to nothing. The job I wanted least was to be a nanny, because it meant I would be taking care of someone else's kids instead of Carrington.

I sat there with my limited options spread around me in the form of newspaper pages. I felt small and powerless, and I didn't want to get used to that feeling. I needed a job I was going to keep for a while. It wouldn't be good for me or Carrington if I hopped from place to place. And I suspected there wasn't going to be much rising through the ranks at a Quick-Stop store.

Seeing that Carrington was depositing her carrot bits onto the newspaper in front of her, I muttered, "Quit doing that, Carrington." I pulled the paper away and began to crumple it up, and stopped as I saw the orange-speckled ad on the side.

A new career in under a year!
A well-trained beauty technician is always in demand, in good times or bad. Every day millions of people go to their favorite stylists for cuts, coloring, chemical treatments, and other necessary cosmetic services. The knowledge and abilities you acquire at East Houston Academy of Cosmetology will prepare you for a successful career in any aspect of the beauty business you choose. Apply for a place at EHAC, and let your future begin.
Financial aid available to those who qualify.

You often hear the word "job" in a trailer park. At Bluebonnet Ranch, people were always losing jobs, hunting for jobs, avoiding jobs, nagging someone else to get jobs. But no one I knew had ever had a career.

I wanted a cosmetology license so badly I could hardly stand it. There were so many places I could work at, so much I wanted to learn. I thought I had the right temperament to be a hairstylist, and I knew I had the drive. I had everything but money.

There was no point in applying. But I watched my hands as if they belonged to someone else, wiping off the carrots and ripping out the ad.

———

The director of the academy, Mrs. Maria Vasquez, sat behind a kidney-shaped oak desk in a room with pale aqua walls. Metallic-framed photos of beautiful women were hung at measured intervals. The smell of the studio and workshop rooms drifted into the administrative area, a mixture of hair spray and shampoo, and the tang of perming chemicals. A beauty shop smell. I loved it.

I concealed my surprise at the discovery that the director was Hispanic. She was a slim woman with highlighted hair and angular shoulders, and a stern, strong-boned face.

She explained that the academy had accepted my application, but they had only so many students they could provide with financial aid each semester. If I couldn't afford to attend the school without a scholarship, then did I want to go on a waiting list and reapply next year?

"Yes, ma'am," I said, my face gone stiff with disappointment, my smile a thin fracture. I gave myself an instant lecture. A waiting list wasn't the end of the world. It wasn't as if I didn't have a lot to do in the meantime.

Mrs. Vasquez's eyes were kind. She said she would call me when it was time to fill out a new application, and she hoped to see me again.

On the way back to Bluebonnet Ranch, I tried to envision myself in a green Happy Helpers shirt. Not so bad, I told myself. Organizing and cleaning other people's houses was always easier than cleaning your own. I would do my best. I would be the hardest-working Happy Helper on the planet.

While I was talking to myself, I didn't pay attention to where I was going. My mind was so busy, I had taken the long way instead of the shortcut. I was on the road that passed the cemetery. My car slowed and turned onto the cemetery drive, heading past the cemetery office. I parked and wandered among the headstones, a granite and marble garden that seemed to have sprung from the earth.

Mama's grave was the newest, a spartan mound of raw earth that interrupted the orderly corridors of grass. I stood at the foot of my mother's grave, somehow needing proof it had really happened. I could hardly believe my mother's body was down there in that Monet coffin with the matching blue satin pillow and throw. It made me feel claustrophobic. I pulled at the buttoned collar of my blouse, and blotted my damp forehead on my sleeve.

The stirrings of panic faded as I noticed something beside the bronze marker, a liberal splash of yellow. Skirting around the edge of the grave, I went to investigate. It was a bouquet of yellow roses. The flowers were in an inverted bronze holder that had been buried so the top rim was flush with the ground. I had noticed vases like that in the catalog at Mr. Ferguson's funeral home, but at three hundred and fifty dollars apiece, I hadn't even considered buying one. As nice as Mr. Ferguson had been, I didn't think he would have thrown in the expensive addition, especially without having mentioned something.

I pulled one of the yellow roses from the bouquet, and brought it, stem dripping, to my face. The heat of the day had brought it to its strongest essence, and the half-open blossom was spilling out perfume. Many varieties of yellow rose have no scent, but this kind, whatever it was, had an intense, almost pineapple fragrance.

I used my thumbnail to peel off the thorns as I walked to the cemetery office. A middle-aged woman with reddish-brown hair shaped into a helmet was seated behind the welcome desk. I asked her who had put the bronze vase at my mother's grave, and she said she couldn't release that information, it was private.

"But it's my mother," I said, more bewildered than annoyed. "Can someone just do that? . . . Put something on someone else's grave?"

"Are you askin' if we should take it off?"

"Well, no . . ." I wanted the bronze vase to stay right where it was. Had I been able to afford one, I would have gotten it myself. "But I do want to know who gave it to her."

"I can't tell you that." After a minute or two of debate, the receptionist allowed she could give me the name of the florist who delivered the roses. It was a Houston shop named Flower Power.

The next couple of days were taken up with going on errands, and filling out the application for Happy Helpers and going for the interview. I didn't get a chance until later in the week to call the florist. The girl who answered the phone said, "Please hold," and before I could say anything, I found myself listening to Hank Williams crooning "I Just Don't Like This Kind of Livin'."

I sat on the lid of the closed toilet seat, the phone loosely cupped to my ear, and watched Carrington play in her bathwater. She concentrated on pouring water from one plastic Dixie cup to another, and then adding liquid soap and stirring with her finger.

"What are you doing, Carrington?" I asked.

"Making somethin'."

"Making what?"

She poured the soap mixture over her tummy and rubbed it. "People polish."

"Rinse that off—" I began, when the girl's voice came through the receiver.

"Flower Power, can I help you?"

I explained the situation and asked if she could tell me who had sent the yellow roses to my mother's grave. As I had expected, she told me she wasn't authorized to divulge the sender's name. "It says on my computer there's a standing order to send the same arrangement to the cemetery every week."

"What?" I asked faintly. "A dozen yellow roses every week?"

"Yes, that's what it says."

"For how long?"

"There's no stop date. It could go on for a while."

My jaw dropped like it was on hinges. "And there's no way you could tell me—"

"No," the girl said firmly. "Is there anything else I can help you with?"

"I guess not. I—" Before I could say "thank you" or "goodbye," there was another ring in the background, and the girl hung up.

I went through a list in my mind of every possible person who would have arranged such a thing.

No one I knew had the money.

The roses had come from Mama's secret life, the past she had never talked about.

Frowning, I picked up a folded towel and shook it out. "Stand up, Carrington. Time to get out."

She grumbled and obeyed reluctantly. I lifted her from the tub and dried her, my gaze admiring the dimpled knees and rounded tummy of a healthy toddler. She was perfect in every way, I thought.

It was our game to make a tent out of the towel after Carrington was dry. I pulled it over our heads and we giggled together beneath the damp terry cloth, kissing each other's noses.

The phone ringing interrupted our play, and I quickly wrapped Carrington in the towel.

I pressed the receiver button. "Hello?"

"Liberty Jones?"

"Yes?"

"This is Maria Vasquez."

Since she was the last person I had expected to hear from, I was temporarily speechless.

She filled the silence smoothly. "From the Academy of Cosmetology—"

"Yes. Yes, I'm sorry, I . . . how are you, Mrs. Vasquez?"

"I'm fine, Liberty, thank you. I have some good news for you, if you're still interested in attending the academy this year?"

"Yes," I managed to whisper, sudden excitement clutching at my throat.

"It turns out that another place in our scholarship program has just become available for the fall term. I can give you a full financial aid package. If you would like, I can put all your registration materials in the mail, or you can stop by the office to pick them up."

I shut my eyes tightly, gripping the phone so tightly I was surprised it didn't crack from the pressure. I felt Carrington's fingers investigating my face, playing with my eyelashes. "Thank you. Thank you. I'll come by tomorrow. *Thank you.*"

I heard the director chuckle. "You're welcome, Liberty. We're pleased to have you in our program."

After I hung up, I hugged Carrington and squealed. "I'm in! I'm in!" She squirmed and shrieked happily, sharing my excitement even though she didn't understand the reason for it. "I'm going to school, I'm going to be a hairstylist. Not a Happy Helper. I don't believe it. Oh, baby, we were due for some good luck."

I didn't expect it was going to be easy. But hard work is a lot easier to tolerate when it's something you want to do instead of something you have no choice about.

Rednecks have a saying, "Always skin your own deer." The deer I had to skin was school. I had never felt as smart as Mama had thought I was, but I figured if I wanted something badly enough, I would find a way to wrap my brain around it.

I'm sure a lot of people think it's easy going to beauty school, that there isn't much to it. But there's a lot to learn before you ever get near a pair of scissors.

The curriculum had descriptions of courses like "Sterilization Bacteriology," which required lab work and theory courses . . . "Chemical Rearranging," which would teach us about the procedures, materials, and implements used for permanents and relaxers . . . and "Hair Coloring," which included lessons on anatomy, physiology, chemistry, procedures, special effects, and problem solving. And that was just the beginning. Looking over the booklet, I understood why it would take nine months to get a degree.

I ended up taking the part-time job at the pawnshop, working evenings and weekends and leaving Carrington in day care. Carrington and I lived on next to nothing, surviving on peanut butter and white bread, microwaveable burritos, Oodles of Noodles soup, and discount vegetables and fruit from dented cans. We shopped at consignment stores for clothes and shoes. Since Carrington was under five, we were still eligible for the WIC program, which helped with vaccinations. But we had no health insurance, which meant we couldn't afford to get sick. I watered down Carrington's fruit juice and brushed her teeth like a maniac because we couldn't afford cavities. Every strange new rattle of our car warned of some expensive problem lurking beneath the battered hood. Every utility bill had to be scrutinized, every mysterious extra fee from the phone company had to be questioned.

There is no peace in poverty.

The Reyes family helped a lot, however. They let me bring Carrington to the shop, where she sat in the back with her coloring books and plastic animals and sewing cards while I worked. We were often invited to dinner, and Lucy's mom always insisted on giving us the leftovers. I adored Mrs. Reyes, who had a Portuguese saying for just about everything, like "Beauty doesn't feed the pigs." (Her criticism of Lucy's handsome but shiftless boyfriend, Matt.)

I didn't see much of Lucy, who was going to junior college and dating a boy she had met in a botany class. Every now and then Lucy would come into the shop with Matt, and we would talk across the counter for a few minutes before they left to go out to eat. I can't say I didn't have a few moments of envy. Lucy had a loving family, a boyfriend, money, a normal life with a good future. Whereas I had no family, I was tired all the time, I had to count every penny, and even if I were looking for a boyfriend, it would have been impossible to attract one while I was pushing a stroller everywhere. Men in their twenties are not turned on by the sight of diaper bags.

But none of that mattered when I was with Carrington. Whenever I picked her up from day care or Miss Marva's, and she came running toward me with her arms outstretched, life couldn't have been sweeter. She had begun to acquire words faster than a TV preacher sells blessings, and she and I talked all the time. We still slept together every night, our legs tangled together as Carrington chattered. She would tell me about her day-care friends, and complain about the one whose artwork was "just scribble-scrabble," and report on who got to be the mother when they played house at recess.

"Your legs are scratchy," she complained one night. "I like 'em smooth."

That struck me as funny. I was exhausted, worried about an exam the next day, I had about ten dollars in my checking account, and now I had to deal with a toddler criticizing my grooming habits. "Carrington, one of the benefits of not having a boyfriend is that I can go a few days without shaving my legs."

"What does that mean?"

"It means deal with it," I told her.

"Okay." She snuggled deeper into her pillow. "Liberty?"

"What?"

"When are you gonna get a boyfriend?"

"I don't know, baby. It might be a while."

"Maybe if you shave your legs, you'd get one."

A huff of laughter escaped me. "Good point. Go to sleep."

In the winter Carrington had a cold that wouldn't go away, and it turned into a hacking cough that seemed to rattle her bones. We went through a whole bottle of over-the-counter medicine, but it seemed to have little effect. One night I woke up from what sounded like dog barks, and I realized Carrington's throat had swollen until she could only breathe in shallow pants. In a terror worse than anything I had ever known, I drove her to the hospital, where they admitted us without insurance.

My sister was diagnosed with croup, and they brought out a plastic mask attached to a nebulizer machine that pumped out medicine in a gray-white mist. Frightened by the noise the machine made, not to mention the mask, Carrington shrank into my lap and cried pitifully. No matter how I reassured her that it wouldn't hurt, it would make her better, she refused until her body spasmed with coughing.

"Can I put it on?" I asked the RN desperately. "Just to show her it's okay? Please?"

He shook his head and looked at me as if I were crazy.

I turned my wailing sister around in my lap so we were face-to-face. "Carrington, listen to me. Carrington. It's just like a game. We'll pretend you're an astronaut. Let me put the mask on you for just a minute. You're an astronaut—what planet do you want to visit?"

"Planet H-h-*home,*" she sobbed.

After another few minutes of her crying and my insisting, we played Carrington-the-space-explorer until the RN was satisfied that she had inhaled enough of the Vaponefrin.

I carried my sister back out to the car in the cold dark of midnight. By then she had exhausted herself and was sleep-heavy. Her head dropped on my shoulder and her legs wrapped around my midriff. I relished the solid, vulnerable heft of her in my arms.

As Carrington slept in her car seat, I cried all the way home, feeling inadequate, anguished, filled with love and relief and worry.

Feeling like a parent.

As time passed, Miss Marva and Mr. Ferguson's relationship acquired the knotty tenderness of two independent people who had no reason to fall in love but did anyway. They were a good match, Miss Marva's peppery nature balanced by Mr. Ferguson's stubborn tranquility.

Miss Marva proclaimed to anyone who would listen that she had no intention of getting married. No one believed her. I think what finally did Marva in was that despite his comfortable financial situation, Arthur Ferguson was clearly a man who needed taking care of. He had missing buttons on his shirt cuffs. He sometimes skipped meals because he simply forgot to eat. His socks weren't always matched. Some men just thrive on a little nagging, and Miss Marva came to acknowledge that she probably needed someone to nag.

So after they had been dating for about eight months, Miss Marva fixed Arthur Ferguson his favorite meal, beer pot roast and green beans and a big skillet of cornbread. And red velvet cake for dessert, after which, naturally, he proposed.

Miss Marva told me the news sheepishly, and claimed Arthur must have tricked her somehow, because there was no reason a woman with her own business should get married. But I could see how happy she was. I was glad that after all the ups and downs of her life, Miss Marva had found herself a good man. They were going to Las Vegas, she said, to get married by Elvis, and after that they would see a Wayne Newton show and maybe the fellas with the tigers. When they returned, Miss Marva was going to leave Bluebonnet Ranch and move into Mr. Ferguson's brick house in town, which he had given her leave to redecorate from top to bottom.

It was less than five miles from Miss Marva's single-wide to her new residence. But she was traveling a greater distance than you could measure with an odometer. She was moving into a different world, acquiring a new status. The thought that I would no longer be able to run down the street to visit her was unsettling and depressing.

With Miss Marva gone, there was nothing keeping me and Carrington at Bluebonnet Ranch. We were living in an old mobile home worth nothing, sitting on a rented lot. Since my sister was going into preschool next year, I needed to find an apartment in a good school district. I would find a job in Houston, I decided, if I was lucky enough to pass the upcoming Cosmetology Commission exams.

I wanted to get out of the trailer park—I wanted it even more for my sister than I did for myself. But at the same time it would be cutting off the last link I had with Mama. And Hardy.

My mother's absence was driven home every time I wanted to tell her about something that had happened to me or Carrington. Long after she was gone there were moments when the child in me who wanted comfort still cried for her. And then as the grief was weathered by time, Mama slipped farther away from me. I couldn't remember the exact sound of her voice, the shape of her front teeth, the color of her cheeks. I struggled to hold the details of her like water cupped in my hands.

The loss of Hardy was nearly as acute, in a different way. If a man ever looked at me with interest, spoke to me, smiled, I found myself helplessly searching for hints of Hardy. I didn't know how to stop wanting him. It wasn't that I had any hope—I knew I'd never see him again. But that didn't stop me from comparing every other man to Hardy and finding them all lacking. I had exhausted myself loving him, like a blackbird fighting its own reflection in a plate-glass window.

Why was love so easy for some people and so hard for others? Most of my high school friends were already married. Lucy was engaged to her boyfriend, Matt, and she claimed to have no doubts at all. I thought of how wonderful it would be to have someone to lean on. To my shame, I fantasized about Hardy coming back for me, telling me he'd been wrong to leave, we'd find a way to make it because nothing was worth being apart from each other.

If loneliness was a choice, what was the other option? To settle for second-best and try to be happy with that? And was that fair to the person you settled for? There had to be someone out there, some man who could help me get over Hardy. I had to find him, not only for my own sake, but for my little sister's. Carrington had no masculine influence in her life. All she'd had so far was Mama, Miss Marva, and me. I didn't know psychology, but I was aware that fathers, or father figures, had a big impact on how children turned out. I wondered if I'd had some more time with my own father, how different my own choices might have been.

The truth was, I wasn't comfortable around men. They were alien creatures, with their hard handshakes and love of red sports cars and power tools, and their seeming inability to replace the toilet paper roll when it was empty. I envied girls who understood men and were at ease with them.

I realized I wasn't going to find a man until I was willing to expose myself to possible harm, to assume the risks of rejection and betrayal and heartbreak that came along with caring about someone. Someday, I promised myself, I would be ready for that kind of risk.

CHAPTER 13

Mrs. Vasquez said she wasn't a bit surprised that I'd passed the written and practical exams with near-perfect scores. She beamed and bracketed my face in her firm, narrow hands as if I were a favorite daughter. "Congratulations, Liberty. You've worked very hard. You should be very proud of yourself."

"Thank you." I was breathless with excitement. Passing the exam was a huge boost to my confidence; it made me feel I could do anything. As Lucy's mom had said, if you can make one basket, you can make a hundred baskets.

The academy director motioned me to sit. "Will you be looking for an apprenticeship now, or do you plan to rent an operator's booth?"

Renting an operator's booth was like being self-employed, requiring you to lease a little part of a beauty shop for a monthly fee. I wasn't crazy about the idea of no guaranteed salary.

"I'm leaning toward the apprenticeship," I said. "I'd rather have regular pay . . . my little sister and I—"

"Of course," she interrupted before I had to explain. "I think a young woman with your skills and beauty should be able to find a paying position at a good salon."

Unused to praise, I smiled and hitched my shoulders in a shrug. "Do looks have anything to do with it?"

"The most upscale salons have an image they prefer. If you happen to fit in, so much the better for you." Her considering stare made me straighten self-consciously in my chair. Thanks to the incessant styling practice the cosmetology students had done on each other, I'd had a lifetime's worth of manicures, pedicures, skin treatments, and hair-coloring. I had never looked so polished. My dark hair was artfully highlighted with shades of caramel and honey, and after what had felt like about a thousand facials, my skin was so clear I had no need of foundation makeup. I looked a little like one of Barbie's ethno-friends, all fresh and shiny behind a clear plastic dome and a hot-pink label.

"There is a very exclusive salon in the Galleria area," Mrs. Vasquez continued. "Salon One . . . have you heard of it? Yes? I am well acquainted with the manager. If you are interested, I will recommend you to her."

"Would you?" I could hardly believe my luck. "Oh, Mrs. Vasquez, I don't know how to thank you."

"They are very particular," she warned. "You may not make it past the first interview. But. . . ." She paused and gave me a curious glance. "Something tells me you will do well there, Liberty."

Houston is a long-legged city laid out akimbo like a wicked woman after a night of sin. Big problems and big pleasures—that's Houston. But in a state of generally friendly people, Houstonians are the nicest, as long as you don't mess with their property. They have a high regard for property, that is to say land, and they have a particular understanding of it.

As the only major American city with no zoning code to speak of, Houston is an ongoing experiment in the influence of free market forces on land use. You're likely to see strip clubs and triple-X stores cozying up to circumspect office buildings and condos, and shade-tree mechanics and shotgun houses sidled against concrete plazas studded with glass skyscrapers. That's because Houstonians have always preferred real ownership of their land over letting the government have control over how things ought to be arranged. They'll gladly pay the price for that freedom, even if it results in undesirable businesses springing up like mesquite trees.

In Houston, new money is just as good as old. No matter who you are or where you came from, you're welcome to the dance as long as you can afford the ticket. There are tales of legendary Houston society hostesses who came from relatively humble backgrounds, including one who was once a furniture salesman's daughter and another who had gotten her start in party-planning. If you have money and you value quiet good taste, you'll be appreciated in Dallas. But if you have money and you like to throw it around like fire-ant bait, you belong in Houston.

On the surface it's a lazy city filled with slow-talking, slow-moving people. Most of the time it's too hot to get stirred up about anything. But power in Houston is wielded with an economy of motion, just like good bass fishing. The city is built on energy, you can see it in the skyline, all those buildings reaching up as if they intend to keep on growing.

I found an apartment for Carrington and me inside the 610 loop, not far from my job at Salon One. People who live inside 610 are regarded as somewhat cosmopolitan, the kind who might sometimes see an art house movie or drink lattes. Outside the loop, latte-drinking is seen as suspicious evidence of possible liberal leanings.

The apartment was in an older complex, with a swimming pool and a jogging trail. "Are we rich now?" Carrington had asked in wonder, awed by the size of the main building and the fact that we rode up to our apartment in an elevator.

As an apprentice at Salon One, I would earn about eighteen thousand dollars a year. After taxes and a monthly rent of five hundred dollars, there wasn't much left over, especially since the cost of living was much higher in the city than in Welcome. However, after the first year of training I would be promoted to junior stylist, and my salary would be bumped up to the low twenties.

For the first time in my life I was filled with a sense of possibility. I had a degree and a license, and a job that might turn into a career. I had a six-hundred-and-fourteen-square-foot apartment with beige carpeting and a used Honda that still ran. And most of all I had a piece of paper that said Carrington was mine, and no one could take her away from me.

I enrolled Carrington in preschool and bought her a Little Mermaid lunch box and sneakers with flashing lights embedded in the sides. The first day of school I walked her to her classroom and fought to hold back my own tears as my sister sobbed and clutched at me and begged me not to leave her. Withdrawing to the side of the doorway, away from the gaze of the sympathetic teacher, I crouched on the floor and wiped Carrington's streaming face with a tissue. "Baby, it's just for a little while. Just a few hours. You're going to play and make new friends—"

"I don't wanna make friends!"

"You're going to do artwork and paint and draw—"

"I don't wanna paint!" She buried her face in my chest. Her voice was muffled in my shirt. "I wanna go home with you."

I cupped the back of her small head, holding her securely against my damp shirt. "I'm not going home, baby. We both have our jobs, remember? Mine is to go fix people's hair, and yours is to go to school."

"I don't like my job!"

I eased her head back and applied a tissue to her runny nose. "Carrington, I have an idea. Here, look—" I took her arm and gently turned it wrist up. "I'm going to give you a kiss you can carry with you all day. Watch." Bending my head, I pressed my lips to the pale skin right below her elbow. My lipstick left a perfect imprint. "There. Now if you start to miss me, that will remind you that I love you and I'm coming soon to pick you up."

Carrington regarded the waxy pink mark dubiously, but I was relieved to see her tears had stopped. "I wish it was a red kiss," she said after a long moment.

"Tomorrow I'll wear red lipstick," I promised. I stood and took her hand. "Come on, baby. Go make some new friends and draw me a picture. The day will be over before you know it."

Carrington approached preschool in a soldierly manner, regarding it as a duty that had to be performed. The ritual of the goodbye kiss persisted, however. The first day I forgot about it, I received a call at the salon from the teacher, who said apologetically that Carrington was so distraught she was disrupting the class. I raced to the school on my break and met my swollen-eyed sister at the classroom door.

I was rattled and out of breath, and thoroughly exasperated. "Carrington, did you have to make such a fuss? Can't you go one day without a kiss on your arm?"

"No." She extended her arm stubbornly, her face tear-streaked and mulish.

I sighed and made the lipstick mark on her skin. "Are you going to behave now?"

"Okay!" She bounced and skipped back into the classroom while I hurried back to work.

People always noticed Carrington when we went out. They stopped to admire her and asked questions, and said what a pretty little girl she was. No one ever guessed I was related to her—they assumed I was the nanny, and they said things like "How long have you been taking care of her?" or "Her parents must be so proud." Even the receptionist in our new pediatrician's office insisted I would have to bring Carrington's forms home to be signed by a parent or legal guardian, and she treated me with open skepticism when I said I was Carrington's sister. I understood why our link seemed questionable; our coloring was too dissimilar. We were like a brown hen with a white egg.

Not long after Carrington turned four, I got a glimpse of what dating was going to be like—and it wasn't pretty. One of the stylists at the salon, Angie Keeney, arranged a blind date for me with her brother Mike. He had been divorced recently, two years after marrying his college sweetheart. According to Angie, Mike wanted to find someone completely different from his wife.

"What does he do?" I asked her.

"Oh, Mike does real well. He's the top appliance salesman for Price Paradise." Angie gave me a significant glance. "Mike's a provider."

In Texas the code word for a man with a steady job is "provider," and the one for a man who doesn't have or want a job is the all-purpose "bubba." And it's a well-known fact that while providers sometimes turn into bubbas, it seldom goes the other way.

I wrote down my phone number for Angie to give to her brother. Mike called the next night, and I liked his pleasant voice and easy laugh. We agreed he would take me out for Japanese food since I'd never had it before.

"I'll try anything except the raw fish," I said.

"You'll like it the way they fix it."

"Okay." I figured if millions of people ate sushi and lived to tell about it, I might as well give it a try. "When do you want to pick me up?"

"Eight o'clock."

I wondered if I could find a babysitter who'd be willing to stay until midnight. I had no idea what a babysitter would charge. I wondered how Carrington would react to being left alone with a stranger. I wondered how I was going to react to it. Carrington, at some stranger's mercy . . .

"Great," I said. "I'll see if I can get a sitter, and if there's any problem, I'll call you b—"

"A sitter," he interrupted sharply. "A sitter for what?"

"For my little sister."

"Oh. She's spending the night with you?"

I hesitated. "Yes."

I hadn't discussed my personal life with anyone at Salon One. No one, not even Angie, was aware that I was the permanent guardian of a four-year-old. And although I knew I should have revealed it to Mike right away, the truth was I wanted to go out on a date. I'd been living like a nun for what seemed like forever. And Angie had warned me that her brother didn't want to date anyone with baggage, he wanted a fresh start.

"Define 'baggage,' " I had said to her.

"Have you ever lived with anyone, been engaged or married?"

"No."

"Do you have any incurable diseases?"

"No."

"Ever gone to rehab or signed up for a twelve-step program?"

"No."

"Ever been convicted of a felony or misdemeanor?"

"No."

"Psychiatric medication?"

"No."

"Dysfunctional family?"

"I don't have a family, really. I'm sort of an orphan. Except I—"

Before I could explain about Carrington, Angie had interrupted with a gushing, "My God, you're *perfect*! Mike's going to love you."

Technically I hadn't lied. But withholding information is often the same as a lie, and most people would say Carrington was definitely baggage. In my opinion, they would have been dead wrong. Carrington wasn't baggage, and she didn't deserve to be lumped in with incurable diseases and felonies. Besides, if I wasn't going to hold it against Mike that he'd had a divorce, he shouldn't hold it against me that I was raising my little sister.

The first part of the date went well. Mike was a handsome man with a full head of blond hair and a nice smile. We ate at a Japanese restaurant with a name I couldn't pronounce. To my surprise, the waitress led us to a table no higher than my kneecaps, and we sat on cushions on the floor. Unfortunately I had worn my least favorite pants because my best black ones were at the cleaners. The pair I'd had to settle for, also black, were too short in the stride, with the result that sitting on the floor gave me a wedgie for the entire meal. And even though the sushi was beautifully made, if I closed my eyes I would have sworn I was eating out of a bait bucket. Still, it was nice to be out on a Saturday night at an elegant restaurant instead of the kind where they handed out crayons along with the menus.

For all that Mike was in his mid-twenties, there was something unformed about him. Not physically . . . he was nice-looking and appeared to be in good shape. But I knew five minutes after meeting him that he was still trapped in the end of his marriage, even though the divorce was final.

It had been a bad divorce, he told me, but he'd put one over on his ex because she had thought winning the dog was a major concession, when Mike had secretly never liked it. He went on to tell me how they had split up their belongings, even breaking up pairs of lamps to achieve strict equality.

After dinner I asked Mike if he wanted to go back to my apartment and watch a movie, and he said yes. I was overwhelmed with relief when we reached the apartment. Since this was the first time I had ever left Carrington alone with a sitter in Houston, I'd worried about her all during dinner.

The babysitter, Brittany, was a twelve-year-old whose family lived in the apartment building. She had been recommended by the woman in the front office. Brittany had assured me that she babysat for lots of children in the building, and if there were any problems, her mother was only two floors down.

I paid Brittany, asked how things had gone, and she said she and Carrington had gotten along great. They had made popcorn and watched a Disney movie, and Carrington had had a bath. The only problem had been getting Carrington to stay in bed. "She keeps getting up," Brittany said with a helpless shrug. "She won't fall asleep. I'm sorry, Mrs. . . . Miss . . ."

"Liberty," I said. "That's just fine, Brittany. You did a great job. I hope you can come back and help us out again sometime."

"I sure will." Pocketing the fifteen dollars I had given her, Brittany went out, giving a little wave over her shoulder.

At the same time, the bedroom door burst open, and Carrington came flying into the main room in her pajamas. "Liberty!" She flung her arms around my hips and hugged me as if we hadn't seen each other in a year. "I missed you. Where did you go? Why did you stay out so long? Who's that yellow-haired man?"

I glanced quickly at Mike. Although he had forced a smile, it was obviously not the time for introductions. His gaze traveled slowly around the room, adhering briefly to the worn-out sofa, the places on the coffee table where the wood-grain veneer had chipped. It surprised me that I felt a sting of defensiveness, that it felt so uncomfortable to see myself from his perspective.

I hunched over my little sister and kissed her hair. "That's my new friend. He and I are going to watch a show. You're supposed to be in bed. Asleep. Go on, Carrington."

"I want you to come with me," she protested.

"No, it's not my bedtime, it's yours. Go on."

"But I'm not tired."

"I don't care. Go lie down and close your eyes."

"Will you tuck me in?"

"No."

"But you *always* tuck me in."

"Carrington—"

"It's all right," Mike said. "Tuck her in, Liberty. I'll look through the videos."

I flashed him a grateful smile. "It'll only take a minute. Thanks, Mike."

I took Carrington into the bedroom and closed the door. Carrington, like most children, was ruthless when she had a tactical advantage. Usually I had no problem letting her cry and holler if she didn't like it. But we both knew I didn't want her making a scene in front of my visitor.

"I'll be quiet if you let me keep the light on," she wheedled.

I hoisted her into the bed and pulled the covers up to her chest, and gave her a picture book from the nightstand. "All right. Stay in bed and—I mean this, Carrington—I don't want to hear a peep out of you."

She opened the book. "I can't read the words by myself."

"You know all the words. We've read that story a hundred times. Stay here and be good. Or else."

"What's the 'or else'?"

I gave her an ominous stare. "Four words, Carrington. Hush and stay put."

"Okay." She subsided behind the book until all that was visible of her was a pair of small hands clamped on either side of the cover.

I went back into the living room, where Mike was sitting stiffly on the sofa.

At some point in the process of dating someone, whether you've gone out one time or a hundred times, a moment occurs when you know exactly how much significance that person will have in your life. You know this person will be an important part of your future, or you know he's only someone to pass the time with. Or you wouldn't care if you never saw him again. I regretted having invited Mike into the apartment. I wished he was gone so I could have a bath and get in bed. I smiled at him.

"Find anything you want to watch?" I asked.

He shook his head, gesturing to the trio of rented movies on the coffee table. "I've already seen those." He gave me a sort of cardboard-looking smile. "You've got a ton of kids' movies. I guess your sister stays with you a lot?"

"All the time." I sat next to him. "I'm Carrington's guardian."

He looked bewildered. "Then she's not going back?"

"Back to where?" I asked, my confusion mirroring his. "Our parents are both gone."

"Oh." He looked away from me. "Liberty . . . are you sure she's your sister and not your daughter?"

What did he mean, was I sure? "Are you asking if I had a baby and somehow forgot about it?" I asked, more stunned than angry. "Or are you asking if I'm lying? She's my sister, Mike."

"Sorry. Sorry." Chagrin corrugated his forehead. He spoke rapidly. "I guess there's not much resemblance between you. But it doesn't really matter if you're her mom or not. The result is the same, isn't it?"

Before I could reply the bedroom door burst open. Carrington ventured into the room, her face wreathed in anxiety. "Liberty, something happened."

I stood from the sofa like I'd just sat on a hot stove-plate. "What do you mean, something happened? What? What?"

"Something went down my throat without my permission."

Shit.

Fear wrapped around my heart like barbed wire. "What went down your throat, Carrington?"

Her face crumpled and turned red. "My lucky penny," she said, and began to cry.

Trying to think above the panic, I recalled the stray brown penny we'd found on the carpeted elevator floor. Carrington had been keeping it in the dish on our nightstand. I rushed over and picked her up. "How did you swallow it? What were you doing with that dirty penny in your mouth?"

"I don't know," she wailed. "I just put it in there and then it jumped down my throat."

I was dimly aware of Mike in the background, mumbling something about how this wasn't a good time, maybe he should go. We both ignored him.

I grabbed the phone and dialed the pediatrician, sitting with Carrington in my lap. "You could have choked on it," I scolded. "Carrington, don't put pennies or nickels or dimes or anything like that in your mouth ever again. Did it hurt your throat? Did it go all the way down when you swallowed?"

She stopped crying as she considered my questions solemnly. "I think I feel it in my zorax," she said. "It's stuck."

"There's no such thing as a zorax." My pulse was hammering. The answering service put me on hold. I wondered if swallowing a penny would give you metal poisoning. Were pennies still made of copper? Was the penny going to lodge somewhere in Carrington's esophagus and require an operation for its removal? How much would that kind of operation cost?

The woman at the other end of the phone was annoyingly calm as I described the emergency. She took down the information and said the pediatrician would call back within ten minutes. Hanging up the phone, I continued to hold Carrington in my lap, her bare feet dangling.

Mike approached us both. I saw from his expression that this would be forever engraved in his mind as the date from hell. He wanted to leave almost as badly as I wanted him to go.

"Look," he said awkwardly, "you're a gorgeous girl, and you're sweet as all get-out, but . . . I don't need this in my life right now. I need someone with no baggage. It's just . . . I can't help you pick up the pieces. I've got too many of my own pieces to pick up. You probably don't understand."

I understood. Mike wanted a girl with no problems and no past experiences, someone who came with a guarantee that she would never make mistakes or disappoint or hurt him.

Later I would feel sorry for him. I knew there was a lot of disappointment in store for Mike, in his search for the woman with no baggage. But for the moment I felt only annoyance at him. I thought of how Hardy had always come to the rescue at times like this, the way he would stride into a room and take charge, and the incredible relief I felt at knowing he was there. But Hardy wasn't coming. All I had was a useless male who didn't even think to ask if he could do something to help.

"That's fine." I tried to sound casual. I wanted to throw something, like you would to get rid of a stray dog. "Thank you for the date, Mike. We'll be fine. If you wouldn't mind seeing yourself to the door—"

"Sure," he said hastily. "Sure."

He vanished.

"Am I gonna die?" Carrington inquired, sounding interested and mildly concerned.

"Only if I catch you with another penny in your mouth," I said.

The pediatrician called, and he interrupted my frantic chatter. "Miss Jones, is your sister wheezing or choking?"

"She's not choking." I looked into Carrington's face. "Let me hear you breathe, baby."

She complied enthusiastically, hyperventilating like a phone pervert. "No wheezing," I told the doctor, and turned back to my sister. "That's enough, Carrington."

I heard the doctor chuckle. "Carrington's going to be just fine. What I need you to do is check her stools for the next couple of days to make certain the coin passes. If you can't find it, we may have to take an X-ray to make certain it hasn't lodged somewhere. But I can almost guarantee you'll see that penny in the commode."

"Can I have a hundred-percent guarantee?" I asked. " 'Almost' is just not working for me today."

He chuckled again. "I don't usually give out hundred-percent guarantees, Miss Jones. But for you I'll make an exception. One full-out guarantee for a penny in the commode within forty-eight hours."

For the next two days I had to poke around in the toilet with a wire hanger every time Carrington reported progress. The penny was eventually found. In the months afterward, however, Carrington told everyone who would listen she had a lucky penny in her tummy. It was only a matter of time, she assured me, until something big happened to us.

CHAPTER 14

Hair is serious business in Houston. It amazed me how much people were willing to pay for the services at Salon One. Being blond, in particular, was a serious investment of time and money, and Salon One gave women the best color of their lives. The salon was known for a tricolor blond that was so good, women would fly in from out of state for it. There was always a waiting list for any of the stylists, but for the head stylist and part-owner, Zenko, the wait was three months minimum.

Zenko was a small man with a powerful

presence and the electric grace of a dancer. Although Zenko had been born and raised in Katy, he'd gone to England for an apprenticeship. When he returned, he had lost his first name and had gained an authentic-sounding British accent. Everyone loved that accent. We loved it even when he was yelling at one of us behind the scenes.

Zenko yelled a lot. He was a perfectionist, not to mention a genius. And when something wasn't just the way he liked it, there were fireworks. But oh, what a business he had created. It had won Salon of the Year from magazines like *Texas Monthly, Elle,* and *Glamour.* Zenko himself had appeared in a documentary film about a famous actress. He'd been busy straightening her long red hair with a flat iron while she answered an interviewer's questions. That documentary had boosted Zenko's career, already thriving, into a white glare of fame known by few stylists. Now he had his own line of products, all packaged in glittering silver cans and bottles with star-shaped tops.

To me, the interior of Salon One looked like an English manor house, appointed with polished oak floors, antiques, and ceilings with medallions and hand-painted designs. When a client wanted coffee, it was served in bone china cups on a silver tray. If she wanted diet Coke, it was poured into tall glasses over Evian-water ice cubes. There was a large room with styling stations, and a few private rooms for celebrities and megawealthy clients, and a shampoo room filled with candlelight and classical music.

As an apprentice, I didn't actually get to cut anyone's hair for a year. I watched and learned, I did errands for Zenko, I brought refreshments to customers who wanted them, and sometimes I applied deep conditioning treatments with hot towels and swaths of foil. I gave manicures and hand massages to some clients while they waited for Zenko. The most fun was being enlisted to give pedicures to ladies who were having a spa day together. While the women chatted, the other pedicurist and I worked silently on their feet, and we got to hear the best and newest gossip.

They talked first about who'd had what done lately, and what needed to be done on themselves, and whether having Botox injected in your cheeks was worth giving up your smile. They talked about husbands briefly, and then it turned to the children, their private schools, their friends, their achievements and disorders. Many of the children were sent to psychotherapists to catalog all the little damages it does to a soul to have whatever you want whenever you want it. These things were so far removed from my life, it seemed we were from different planets. But then there were more familiar-sounding stories that reminded me of Carrington, and sometimes it was all I could do to keep from exclaiming, "Yes, that happened to my little sister too," or "I know exactly what you're talking about."

I kept my mouth shut, however, because Zenko had instructed all of us sternly that we must never, ever volunteer anything about our personal lives. Clients didn't want to hear our opinions, he had warned, and they didn't want to become friends. They came to Salon One to relax and be treated with absolute professionalism.

I heard a lot though. I knew which relatives were having arguments over who was monopolizing the family jet, who was suing whom over the management of trusts and estates, whose husband liked to go on canned hunts to shoot exotic game, where to go for the best custom-made chairs. I heard about scandals and successes, about the best parties, the favorite charities, and all the intricacies of leading a full-time social life.

I liked Houston women, who were funny and frank, and always interested in what was new and fashionable. Of course there were a few grand old ladies who insisted on having their hair permed, cut, and ratted into a big round ball, a style Zenko loathed and privately referred to as "the Drain Clog." However, even Zenko wasn't going to refuse these wives of multimillionaires who wore ashtray-sized diamonds on their fingers and could wear their hair any way they wanted.

The salon was also frequented by men of all shapes and sizes. Most were well dressed, with scrupulously maintained hair and skin and nails. Cowboy images to the contrary, Texan men are pretty fastidious about their appearance, everything scrubbed and clipped and strictly controlled. Before long I had assembled a clientele of regulars who came for lunch-hour manicures or neck and eyebrow trims. There were a few attempts at flirtation, especially from the younger ones, but Zenko had rules about that. And that was fine with me. At that time in my life I wasn't interested in flirtation or romance. I wanted steady work and tip money.

A couple of the girls, including Angie, managed to keep part-time sugar daddies on the side. The arrangements were discreet enough that Zenko either didn't notice or deliberately looked the other way. The agreement between an older, wealthier man and a younger woman didn't appeal to me, but at the same time I was fascinated by it.

There is a subculture of sugar daddies and sugar babies in most big cities. The arrangement is by its very nature temporary. But both parties seem to like its impermanence, and there is a kind of safety in its unspoken rules. The relationship starts out with something casual like drinks or dinner, but if the girl plays it right, she can coax a sugar daddy into paying for things like tuition, vacations, clothes, even plastic surgery. According to Angie, the arrangement rarely involved the direct transfer of money. Cash scrubs the romantic veneer off the relationship. Sugar daddies prefer to think of it as a special friendship in which they provide gifts and help to a deserving young woman. And sugar babies convince themselves that a nice boyfriend should want to help out his girlfriend, and in return she would naturally want to show her appreciation by spending time with him.

"But what if you don't want to sleep with him one night, and he's just bought you a car?" I asked Angie skeptically. "You still sort of have to, don't you? How is that different from being a—"

I caught myself as I saw the warning twitch of her mouth.

"It's not all about sex," Angie said tautly. "It's about friendship. If you can't understand that, I'm not going to waste my time trying to explain."

I apologized immediately and said I was from a small town and didn't always have a sophisticated understanding of things. Mollified, Angie forgave me. And she added that if I was smart, I'd get a generous boyfriend too, and it would help me achieve my goals a lot faster.

But I didn't want trips to Cabo or Rio, or designer clothes, or the trappings of a luxe life. All I wanted was to honor the promises I had made to myself and Carrington. My modest ambitions included a good home, and the means to keep us both clothed and fed, and health insurance with a dental plan. I didn't want any of that to come from a sugar daddy. The obligation of it, the gift-giving and sex dressed in the trappings of friendship . . . it was a road I knew I wouldn't be able to negotiate well.

Too many potholes.

Among the important people who came to Salon One was Mr. Churchill Travis. If you've ever subscribed to *Fortune* magazine, or *Forbes,* or a similar publication, you know something about him. Unfortunately I had no clue who he was, since I had no interest in finance and never reached for *Forbes* unless I needed fly-swatting material.

One of the first things you noticed upon meeting Churchill was his voice, so low and gravelly you could almost feel it underfoot. He wasn't a big man, medium height at most, and when he slouched you could have called him short. Except if Churchill Travis slouched, everyone else in the room did too. His build was lean but for a barrel chest and arms that were capable of straightening a horseshoe. Churchill was a man's man, able to hold his liquor and shoot straight and negotiate like a gentleman. He'd worked hard for his money, paid just about every kind of dues there were.

Churchill was most comfortable around old-fashioned types like himself. He knew which areas of housework were men's territory, and he knew which were women's. The only time he ever went into a kitchen was to pour himself coffee. He was genuinely perplexed by men who took an interest in china patterns or ate alfalfa sprouts or sometimes contemplated their feminine sides. Churchill had no feminine side, and he would have taken a swing at anyone would might have dared to suggest otherwise.

Churchill's first visit to Salon One happened around the time I started working there. One day the serenity of the salon was interrupted by a flurry of excitement, stylists murmuring, clients' heads turning. I caught a glimpse of him—a thick ruff of steel-colored hair, dark gray suit—as he was guided to one of Zenko's VIP rooms. He paused in the doorway, his gaze crossing the main room. His eyes were dark, the kind of brown that makes the irises nearly indistinguishable from the pupils. He was a good-looking old coot, but there was something offbeat about him, a hint of the eccentric.

Our gazes caught. He went still, his eyes narrowing as he stared at me intently. And then I had the curious feeling, nearly impossible to describe . . . a sort of pleasant catch deep in my chest, in a place words couldn't reach. I felt soothed and relaxed and expectant, I could actually feel the tiny muscles in my forehead and jaw softening. I wanted to smile at him but before I could he had gone into the room with Zenko.

"Who was that?" I asked Angie, who was standing with me.

"Advanced-level sugar daddy," she replied in an awed tone. "Don't tell me you've never heard of Churchill Travis."

"I've heard of the Travises," I replied. "They're like the Basses in Fort Worth, right? Money people?"

"Honey, in the investment world Churchill Travis is Elvis. He's on CNN all the time. He's written books. He owns half of Houston, and he has yachts, jets, mansions . . ."

Even knowing Angie's tendency toward hyperbole, I was impressed.

". . . and the best part of all is, he's a widower," Angie finished. "His wife died not too long ago. Oh, I'm going to find a way to get in that room with him and Zenko. I've got to meet him! Did you see the way he just looked at me?"

That provoked a self-conscious laugh. I'd thought he was looking at me, but it had been Angie, it must have been, because she was blond and sexy and men adored her.

"Yes," I said. "But would you really go after him? I thought you were happy with George." George was Angie's current sugar daddy, who had just given her a Cadillac Escalade. It was a loaner, but he'd said she could drive it as long as she wanted.

"Liberty, a smart sugar baby never misses an opportunity to trade up." Angie sped to the makeup station to reapply eyeliner and lipstick, freshening her face in preparation to meet Churchill Travis.

I went to the cleaning closet and got out a broom to sweep up some hair clippings from the floor. Just as I got started, a stylist named Alan hurried over to me. He was trying to look calm, but his eyes were as big as silver dollars.

"Liberty," he said in an urgent undertone, "Zenko wants you to bring a glass of iced tea for Mr. Travis. Strong tea, lots of ice, no lemon, two packets of sweetener. The blue packets. Bring it on a tray. Don't fuck it up, or Zenko will kill us all."

I was instantly alarmed. "Why me? Angie should bring it to him. He was looking at her. I'm sure she wants to do it. She—"

"He asked for you. 'The dark-haired little girl,' he said. *Hurry,* Liberty. Blue packets, *blue.*"

I went to prepare the tea as directed, stirring carefully to make certain every grain of sweetener was dissolved. I had filled the glass to the top with the most symmetrical ice cubes available. When I approached the VIP room, I had to balance the tray on one hand while I opened the door with the other. The ice jiggled dangerously in the glass. I wondered in desperation if a few drops had spilled.

Assuming an implacable smile, I entered the VIP room. Mr. Travis was seated in the chair, facing a huge gold-framed mirror. Zenko was describing possible variations on Mr. Travis's current hairstyle, which was the standard businessman's cut. I gathered Zenko was gently hinting that Mr. Travis should try something a little different, maybe allow him to texture and gel it at the top to update his look to something edgier.

I tried to deliver the tea as unobtrusively as possible, but those shrewd dark eyes locked onto me, and Travis turned in his chair to face me as he took the glass from the tray. "What's your opinion?" he demanded. "Do you think I need updating?"

Considering my reply, I noticed that his teeth were slightly snaggled on the bottom row. As he smiled, it gave him the appearance of a fierce old lion inviting a cub to play. His eyes were warm in his craggy face, an umber glaze permanently seared into the top few layers of skin. Holding his gaze, I felt a small knot of delight form in my throat, and I swallowed it back.

I told him the truth. I couldn't help it. "I think you're edgy enough as it is," I said. "Any more and you'd scare people."

Zenko's face went blank, and I was certain he was going to fire me on the spot.

Travis's laugh sounded like a bag of rocks being shaken. "I'll go by this young lady's opinion," he told Zenko. "Just take a half-inch off the top and taper the back and sides." He continued to look at me. "What's your name?"

"Liberty Jones."

"Where'd you get that name? What part of Texas are you from? You one of the shampoo girls?"

I learned later that Churchill was in the habit of throwing questions out in twos and threes, and if you missed any of them, he repeated them.

"I was born in Liberty County, lived in Houston for a while, then grew up in Welcome. I'm not allowed to do shampoos yet, I've just started here and I'm apprenticing."

"Not allowed to do shampoos," Travis repeated, his heavy brows rising as if such a thing were absurd. "What in Sam Hill does an apprentice do?"

"I bring people iced tea." I gave him my prettiest smile and began to leave.

"Stay right there," came his command. "You can practice your shampooing on me."

Zenko broke in, his expression hypercalm. His accent was more pronounced than usual, as if he'd just done lunch with Camilla and Charles. "Mr. Travis, this girl hasn't finished her training. She isn't qualified to shampoo anyone. However, we have highly trained stylists who will be helping you today, and—"

"How much training does it take to wash hair?" Travis asked incredulously. You could tell he wasn't used to being denied anything, from anyone, for any reason. "You do your best, Miss Jones, and I won't complain."

"Liberty," I said, returning to him. "And I can't."

"Why not?"

"Because if I do and you never come back to Salon One, everyone will assume I screwed up, and I don't want that on my record."

Travis scowled. I should have had the sense to be afraid of him. But the air between us was alive with a sense of playfulness. And a smile kept bobbing to my lips no matter how hard I tried to push it back.

"What else can you do besides bring tea?" Travis demanded.

"I could give you a manicure."

He scoffed at the word. "Never had a manicure in my life. Why any man would need one I don't know. Damn female thing to do."

"I manicure lots of men." I began to reach for his hand and hesitated. In the next moment I found his hand resting on mine, his palm down, my palm up. It was a strong, broad hand, one you could easily imagine gripping a horse's reins or a shovel handle. The nails were clipped almost to the quick, the skin of his fingers nicked and pale-rusted. One of his thumbnails was permanently ridged from some long-ago injury. Gently turning his hand over in mine, I saw his palm was webbed with so many lines, it would have made a fortune-teller stutter. "You could use some work, Mr. Travis. Especially on the cuticles."

"Call me Churchill." He pronounced it without the *i,* so it sounded like "Church'll." "Go get your stuff."

Since keeping Churchill Travis happy had become the modus operandi of the day, I had to ask Angie to take over my duties, which included floor-sweeping and a ten-thirty pedicure.

Angie would have liked to stab me with the nearest pair of scissors, but at the same time she couldn't keep from offering advice as I stocked my manicure supplies. "Do *not* talk too much. In fact, say as little as possible. Smile, but don't do that big smile you do sometimes. Get him to talk about himself. Men love that. Try to get his business card. And no matter what, *don't* mention your little sister. Men are turned off by women with responsibilities."

"Angie," I muttered back, "I'm not looking for a sugar daddy. And even if I was, he's too old."

Angie shook her head. "Honey, there's no such thing as too old. I can tell just by looking, that man hasn't lost his juice yet."

"I'm not interested in his juice," I said. "Or his money."

After Churchill Travis's hair was cut and styled, I met him in another private room. We sat facing each other across the manicure table in the white light of a large swing-arm lamp. "Your cut looks good," I commented, taking one of his hands and placing it gently in a bowl of softening solution.

"It should, for what Zenko charges." Travis stared dubiously at the array of tools and bottles of colored liquid on the manicure table. "You like working for him?"

"Yes, sir, I do. I'm learning a lot from Zenko. I'm lucky to have this job."

We talked as I tended his hands, sloughing off dead skin, trimming and pushing back cuticles, filing and buffing his nails to a glassy sheen. Travis watched the procedure with great interest, having never submitted to such a thing in his life.

"What made you decide to work in a beauty shop?" he asked.

"When I was younger, I used to do my friends' hair and makeup. I've always liked making people look good. And I like it that when I'm done, they feel better about themselves." I uncapped a small bottle, and Travis regarded it with something close to alarm.

"I don't need that," he said firmly. "You can do the other stuff, but I draw the line at polish."

"This isn't polish, it's cuticle oil. And you need plenty of it." Ignoring his flinching, I used a tiny brush to apply the oil to his cuticles. "Funny," I commented, "you don't have a businessman's hands. You must do something besides push paper across a desk."

He shrugged. "Some ranching work now and then. Lot of riding. And I work in the garden from time to time, although not as much as I did before my wife died. That woman had a passion for growing things."

I slicked some cream between my palms and began a hand and wrist massage. It was hard to get him to relax, his fingers unwilling to give up their knotty tension. "I heard she died pretty recently," I said, glancing at his rough-cast face, where grief had left signs of obvious weathering. "I'm sorry."

Travis gave a slight nod. "Ava was a good woman," he said gruffly. "The best woman I ever knew. She had breast cancer—we caught it too late."

In spite of Zenko's adamance that employees refrain from discussing their personal lives, I was nearly overcome with the urge to tell Churchill that I, too, had lost someone dear to me. Instead I commented, "They say it's easier when you've had time to prepare for someone's death. But I don't believe that."

"Neither do I." Churchill's hand tightened over mine so briefly that I barely had time to register its pressure. Startled, I looked up and saw the kindness and muted sadness in his face. Somehow I knew that no matter what I chose to tell or to keep secret, he would understand.

As it turned out, my relationship with Churchill became something far more complex than a romantic one. It would have been more understandable and straightforward had it involved romance or sex, but Churchill was never interested in me that way. As an attractive and insanely wealthy widower just past sixty, he had his pick of women. I got into the habit of looking for mentions of him in newspapers and magazines. I was highly entertained by photos of him with glamorous society women and B-movie actresses, and even occasionally with foreign royalty. Churchill moved in fast circles.

When he was too busy to come to Salon One for a haircut, he'd summon Zenko to his mansion. Sometimes he would drop by for a neck and eyebrow trim, or a manicure from me. Churchill was always a little sheepish about the manicures. But after the first time I filed, trimmed, scraped, and moisturized his hands, and buffed his nails to a subtle sheen, he liked the look and feel of them so much that he said he guessed he'd just added a new time-waster to his routine. And he admitted, after some goading from me, that his lady friends appreciated the results of his manicures too.

Churchill's friendship, the chats we had across the manicure table, made me the target of both envy and admiration at the salon. I understood the nature of the speculation about our friendship, the general consensus being that he certainly wasn't seeking out my company to ask my opinions about the stock market. I think everyone assumed something had happened between us, or happened every so often, or was inevitably going to happen. Zenko certainly assumed so, and treated me with a courtesy he showed to no other employees of my level. I guess he figured even if I weren't the exclusive reason Churchill came to Salon One, my presence certainly didn't hurt.

Finally one day I asked, "Are you planning to make a move on me sometime, Churchill?"

He looked startled. "Hell, no. You're too young for me. I like my women seasoned." A pause, and then an almost comical expression of dismay. "You don't want me to, do you?"

"No."

Had he ever tried, I'm not sure what I would have done. I had no idea how to define my feelings toward Churchill—I hadn't had enough relationships with men to put this one in context. "But I don't understand why you've been paying attention to me," I continued, "if you're not planning to . . . you know."

"Someday I'll let you know why," he said. "But not now."

I admired Churchill more than anyone I had ever met. He wasn't always easy to deal with, of course. His mood could turn ornery in a flash. He was not a restful man. I don't think there were many moments in Churchill's life when he was a hundred percent happy. A lot of that had to do with his having lost two wives, the first, Joanna, right after the birth of their son . . . and Ava, his wife of twenty-six years. Churchill was not one to accept the whims of fate passively, and the losses of people he loved had hit him hard. I understood about that.

It was almost two years before I could bring myself to talk to Churchill about my mother, or anything but the barest facts about my past. Somehow Churchill had found out when my birthday was, and he had one of his secretaries call in the morning to tell me we were going out to lunch. I wore a neat black knee-length skirt and a white top, and my silver armadillo necklace. Churchill arrived at noon in an elegant British-made suit, looking like a prosperous old European hit man. He escorted me to a white Bentley waiting curbside, with a driver who opened the back door.

We went to the fanciest restaurant I had ever seen, with French décor and white tablecloths and beautiful paintings on the walls. The menus were written in calligraphy on textured cream-colored paper, and the food was described in such intricate terms—roulades and rissoles and complex sauces—I had no idea what to order. The prices nearly gave me a heart attack. The cheapest item on the menu was a ten-dollar appetizer, and it consisted of a single shrimp prepared in ways I couldn't begin to pronounce. Near the bottom of the menu I saw a description of a hamburger served with sweet potato fries, and nearly spewed a mouthful of diet Coke when I saw the price.

"Churchill," I said in disbelief, "there's a hundred-dollar hamburger on the menu."

He frowned, not out of shared incredulity but because my menu had prices on it. One twitch of his finger summoned a waiter, who apologized profusely. The menu was whipped out of my hands and replaced by another, almost identical one, except this one had no dollar amounts.

"Why shouldn't mine have prices on it?" I asked.

"Because you're the woman," Churchill said, still annoyed by the waiter's mistake. "I'm taking you to lunch, and you're not supposed to think about how much it costs."

"That hamburger was *one hundred dollars.*" I couldn't stop obsessing over it. "What could they possibly do to that hamburger to make it worth a hundred dollars?"

My expression seemed to amuse him. "Let's ask."

A waiter was enlisted to answer questions about the menu. When asked how the hamburger was prepared and what made it so special, he explained the ingredients were all organic, including those in the homemade parmesan bun, and it contained smoked buffalo mozzarella, hydroponic butterhead lettuce, vine-ripened tomato, and chile compote layered atop a burger made of organic beef and ground emu.

The word "emu" set me off.

I felt a laugh break from my lips, and then another, and then there was no stopping the helpless giggles that made my eyes water and my shoulders tremble. I clamped a hand over my mouth to hold them back, but that only made it worse. I began to seriously worry if I could stop. I was making a spectacle of myself in the fanciest restaurant I'd ever been in.

The waiter tactfully disappeared. I tried to gasp out an apology to Churchill, who watched me with concern and shook his head slightly, as if to say *No, don't apologize.* He put his hand on my wrist in a reassuring grip. Somehow the pressure on my wrist quieted the wild laughter. I was able to take a long breath, and my chest relaxed.

I told him about moving to the trailer in Welcome, and Mama's boyfriend named Flip who had shot the emu. I couldn't seem to talk fast enough, so many details tumbled out. Churchill caught every word, his eyes crinkling at the corners, and when I finally reached the part about giving the dead emu to the Cateses, he was chuckling.

Although I hadn't been aware of ordering wine, the waiter brought a bottle of pinot noir. The liquid glittered richly in tall-stemmed crystal glasses. "I shouldn't," I said. "I'm going back to work after lunch."

"You're not going back to work."

"Of course I am. My afternoon is booked." But I felt weary at the thought of it, not just the work, but summoning the appropriate charm and cheerfulness my clients expected.

Churchill reached inside his jacket, extracted a cell phone no larger than a domino, and dialed Salon One. As I watched, openmouthed, he asked for Zenko, informed him that I would be taking the afternoon off, and asked if that would be all right. According to Churchill,

Zenko said of course it would be all right and he would rearrange the schedule. No problem.

As Churchill closed the cell phone with a self-satisfied click, I said darkly, "I'm going to catch hell for this later. And if anyone else but you had made that call, Zenko would have asked if you have your head up your *culo*."

Churchill grinned. One of his flaws was that he enjoyed people's inability to tell him off.

I talked through the entire lunch, prodded by Churchill's questions, his warm interest, the wineglass that somehow never emptied no matter how much I drank. The freedom of saying anything to him, telling all, relieved a burden I hadn't even realized I'd been carrying. In my relentless push to keep moving forward, there had been so many emotions I hadn't let myself inhabit fully, so many things I hadn't talked about. Now I couldn't quite catch up to myself. I fumbled in my purse for my wallet and got out Carrington's school picture. She had a gap-toothed smile, and one of her ponytails was a little higher than the other.

Churchill looked at the photo for a long time, even reached in his pocket for a pair of reading glasses so he could see every detail. He drank some wine before commenting. "Happy child, looks like."

"Yes, she is." I tucked the photo back into my wallet with care.

"You've done well, Liberty," he said. "It was the right thing to keep her."

"I had to. She's all I've got. And I knew no one would take care of her like I would." I was surprised by the words that slipped out so easily, the need to confess everything.

This was what it would have been like, I thought with a small, painful thrill. This was a glimpse of what I might have had with Daddy. A man so much older and wiser, who seemed to understand everything, even the things I hadn't said. It had bothered me for years that

Carrington didn't have a father. What I hadn't realized was how much I still needed one for myself.

Still buzzed from the wine, I told Churchill about Carrington's upcoming Thanksgiving pageant at school. Her class, which would perform two songs, was divided into Pilgrims and Native Americans, and Carrington had balked at being part of either group. She wanted to be a cowgirl. She'd been so stubborn about it that her teacher, Miss Hansen, had called me at home. I'd explained to Carrington that there had been no cowgirls in 1621. There hadn't even been a Texas then, I told her. It turned out my sister didn't care about historical accuracy.

The argument had finally been resolved by Miss Hansen's suggestion that Carrington be allowed to wear the cowgirl costume and walk out on stage at the very beginning of the pageant. She would carry a cardboard sign shaped like our state, printed with the words A TEXAS THANKSGIVING.

Churchill roared with laughter at the story, seeming to think my sister's muleheadedness was a virtue.

"You're missing the point," I told him. "If this is a sign of things to come, I'm going to have a terrible time when she hits adolescence."

"Ava had two rules about dealing with adolescents," Churchill said. "First, the more you try to control them, the more they rebel. And second, you can always reach a compromise as long as they need you to drive them to the mall."

I smiled. "I'll have to remember those rules. Ava must have been a good mother."

"In every way," he said emphatically. "Never complained when she got the short end of the stick. Unlike most people, she knew how to be happy."

I was tempted to point out that most people would be happy if they had a nice family and a big mansion and all the money they needed. I kept my mouth closed, however.

Even so, Churchill seemed to read my mind. "With all you hear at work," he said, "you should have figured out by now rich folks are just as miserable as poor ones. More, in fact."

"I'm trying to work up some sympathy," I said dryly. "But I think there's a difference between real problems and invented problems."

"That's where you're like Ava," he said. "She could tell the difference too."

CHAPTER 15

After four years, I had finally become a full-fledged stylist at Salon One. Most of my work was as a colorist—I had a talent for highlights and corrections. I loved mixing liquids and pastes in a multitude of small bowls like a mad scientist. I enjoyed the myriad small but critical calculations of heat, timing, and application, and the satisfaction of getting everything just right.

Churchill still went to Zenko for his cuts, but I did his neck and eyebrow trims, and I did his manicures whenever he wanted them. And there were the infrequent lunches when one of us had something to celebrate. When we were together, we talked about anything and everything. I knew a lot about Churchill's family, particularly his four children. There was Gage, the oldest at thirty, whom he'd had by his first wife, Joanna. The other three he'd had with Ava: Jack, who was twenty-five, Joe, who was two years younger, and the only daughter, Haven, who was still in college. I knew Gage had become reserved since he had lost his mother at the age of three, and that he had a hard time trusting people, and one of his past girlfriends had said he had commitment phobia. Being unacquainted with psychospeak, Churchill didn't know what that meant.

"It means he won't talk about his feelings," I explained, "or allow himself to be vulnerable. And he's afraid of being tied down."

Churchill looked baffled. "That's not commitment phobia. That's being a man."

We discussed his other children too. Jack was an athlete and a ladies' man. Joe was an information junkie and an adventurer. The youngest, Haven, had insisted on going to college in New England, no matter how much Churchill begged her to consider Rice or UT, or even, God help him, A&M.

I told Churchill the latest news about Carrington, and sometimes about my love life. I had confided in him about Hardy and how he haunted me. Hardy was every loose-limbed cowboy in worn denim, every pair of blue eyes, every battered pickup, every hot cloudless day.

Maybe, Churchill had pointed out, I should stop trying so hard *not* to love Hardy, and accept that some part of me might always want him. "Some things," he said, "you just have to learn to live with."

"But you can't love someone new without getting over the last one."

"Why not?"

"Because then the new relationship is compromised."

Seeming amused, Churchill said that every relationship was compromised in one way or another, and you were better off not picking at the edges of it.

I disagreed. I felt I needed to let Hardy go completely. I just didn't know how. I hoped someday I might meet someone so compelling that I could take the risk of loving again. But I had serious doubts such a man existed.

And that man was certainly not Tom Hudson, whom I'd met while waiting for a parent-teacher conference in a hallway at Carrington's school. He was a divorced father of two, a big teddy bear of a man with brown hair and a neatly trimmed brown beard. I'd gone out with him for just over a year, enjoying the comfortable nature of our relationship.

Since Tom was the owner of a gourmet food shop, my refrigerator was constantly filled with delicacies. Carrington and I feasted on wedges of French and Belgian cheese, jars of tomato-pear chutney, Genovese pesto, and double Devon cream, coral-colored slabs of smoked Alaskan salmon, bottled cream of asparagus soup, jars of marinated peppers or Tunisian green olives.

I liked Tom a lot. I tried my best to fall in love with him. It was obvious he was a good father to his own children, and I felt sure he would be just as good to Carrington. There was so much that was right about Tom, so many reasons I should have loved him. It's one of the frustrations of dating that sometimes you can be with a nice person who is obviously worth loving, but there isn't enough heat between you to light a tea candle.

We made love on the weekends when his ex-wife had the kids and I could get a babysitter for Carrington. Unfortunately the sex was lukewarm. Since I could never come while Tom was inside me—all I felt was the mild inner pressure you feel from the speculum at the gynecologist's office—he would start out by using his fingers to rub me into a climax. It didn't always work, but sometimes I achieved a few gratifying spasms, and when I couldn't and began to feel irritated and chafed, I faked it. Then he would either gently push my head down until I took him into my mouth, or he would lever himself over me and we would do it missionary style. The routine never changed.

I bought a couple of sex books and tried to figure out how to improve things. Tom was amused by my abashed requests to try a couple of positions I had read about, and he told me it was all still just a matter of putting tab A into slot B. But if I wanted to do something new, he said, he was all for it.

I was dismayed to find Tom was right. It felt awkward and silly, and no matter how I tried, I couldn't come while we were arranged in those yogalike tangles. The only new thing Tom wouldn't try was going down on me. I stammered and turned crimson when I asked him for it. I would say that was the most embarrassing moment of my entire life, except it was even worse when Tom replied apologetically he had never liked doing that. It was unhygienic, he said, and he didn't really enjoy how women tasted. If I didn't mind, he would rather not. I said no, of course I didn't mind, I didn't want him to do something he didn't like.

But every time we slept together after that and I felt his hands urging my head down, I started to feel a little resentful. And then I felt guilty, because Tom was generous in so many other ways. It didn't matter, I told myself. There were other things we could do in bed. But the situation bothered me enough—it seemed I was missing some essential understanding—that I told Angie one morning before the salon opened. After making certain everything was set up for the day, the carts well stocked, the styling tools cleaned, we all took a few minutes to primp.

I was spritzing some volumizer in my hair, while Angie reapplied her lip gloss. I can't remember exactly what I asked her, something like had she ever had a boyfriend who didn't want to do certain things in bed.

Angie's gaze met mine in the mirror. "He doesn't want you to blow him?" A few of the other stylists glanced in our direction.

"No, he likes that," I whispered. "It's . . . well, he doesn't want to do it to me."

Her smartly penciled brows twitched upward. "Doesn't like eating tortilla?"

"Nope. He says"—I could feel red flags of color forming on the crests of my cheeks—"it's unhygienic."

She looked outraged. "It's not any more unhygienic than a man's! What a loser. What a selfish— Liberty, most men *love* to do that to a woman."

"They do?"

"It's a turn-on for them."

"It is?" That was welcome news. It made me feel a little less mortified about having asked Tom for it.

"Oh, girl," Angie said, shaking her head. "You've got to dump him."

"But . . . but . . ." I wasn't certain I wanted to take such drastic measures. This was the longest I'd ever dated someone, and I liked the security of it. I remembered all the revolving-door relationships Mama had gone through. Now I understood why.

Dating is like trying to make a meal out of leftovers. Some leftovers, like meat loaf or banana pudding, actually get better when they've had a little time to mature. But others, like doughnuts or pizza, should be thrown out right away. No matter how you try to warm them up, they're never as good as when they were new. I had been hoping Tom would turn out to be a meat loaf instead of a pizza.

"*Dump him,*" Angie insisted.

Heather, a petite blonde from California, couldn't resist breaking in. Everything she said sounded like a question, even when it wasn't. "You having boyfriend problems, Liberty?"

Angie answered before I could. "She's going out with a sixty-eight."

There were a few sympathetic groans from the other stylists.

"What's a sixty-eight?" I asked.

"He wants you to go down on him," Heather replied, "but he won't return the favor. Like, it would be sixty-nine, but he owes you one."

Alan, who was smarter about men than the rest of us put together, pointed at me with a round brush as he spoke. "Get rid of him, Liberty. You can't ever change a sixty-eight."

"But he's nice in other ways," I protested. "He's a good boyfriend."

"No he isn't," Alan said. "You just think he is. But sooner or later a sixty-eight will show his true colors outside the bedroom. Leaving you at home while he goes out with his buddies. Buying himself a new car while you get the used one. A sixty-eight always takes the biggest slice of cake, honey. Don't waste your time with him. Trust me, I know from experience."

"Alan's right," Heather said. "I dated a sixty-eight a couple years ago, and at first he was, like, a total hottie. But he turned out to be the biggest jerk ever. Major bummer."

Until that moment I hadn't seriously considered breaking up with Tom. But the idea was an unexpected relief. I realized what was bothering me had nothing to do with blow jobs. The problem was, our emotional intimacy, like our sex life, had its limits. Tom had no interest in the secret places of my heart, nor I in his. We were more adventurous in our selection of gourmet foods than we were in the hazardous territory of a true relationship. It was beginning to dawn on me how rare it was for two people to find the kind of connection Hardy and I had shared. And Hardy had given it up, given me up, for the wrong reasons. I hoped to hell he wasn't finding it any easier than I was to build a relationship with someone.

"What's the best way to end it?" I asked.

Angie patted my back kindly. "Tell him the relationship isn't going where you hoped it would. Say it's no one's fault, but it's just not working for you."

"And *don't* drop the bomb at your place," Alan added, "because it's always harder to make someone leave. Do it at his place and then you're out the door."

Soon after that I worked up the courage to break up with Tom at his apartment. I told him how much I had enjoyed our time together but it just wasn't working, and it wasn't him, it was me. Tom listened carefully, impassive except for the movement of tiny facial muscles anchored beneath his beard. He had no questions. He didn't offer a single protest. Maybe it was a relief for him too, I thought. Maybe he'd been bothered as I was by the something-missing between us.

Tom walked me to the door, where I stood clutching my purse. I was thankful there was no goodbye kiss. "I . . . I wish you well," I said. It was a quaint, old-fashioned phrase, but nothing else seemed to capture my feeling so exactly.

"Yes," he said. "You too, Liberty. I hope you take some time to work on yourself and your problem."

"My problem?"

"Your commitment phobia," he said with kind concern. "Fear of intimacy. You need to work on it. Good luck."

The door closed gently in my face.

I was late getting to work the next day, so I would have to wait until later to report on what had happened. One of the things you learn about working in a salon is that most stylists love to dissect relationships. Our coffee or smoke breaks often sounded like group therapy sessions.

I felt almost lighthearted about breaking up with Tom, except for that shot he'd taken at the end. I didn't blame him for saying it, since he'd just been dumped. What troubled me was the inner suspicion that he was right. Maybe I did have fear of intimacy. I had never loved any man but Hardy, who was secured in my heart with backward barbs. I still dreamed of him and woke with my blood clamoring, every inch of my skin damp and alive.

I was afraid I should have settled for Tom. Carrington would be ten soon. She had been deprived of so many years of fatherly influence. We needed a man in our life.

As I walked into the salon, which had just opened, Alan approached with the news that Zenko wanted to talk to me right away.

"I'm only a few minutes late—" I began.

"No, no, it's not about that. It's about Mr. Travis."

"Is he coming in today?"

Alan's expression was impossible to interpret. "I don't think so."

I went to the back of the salon, where Zenko stood with a china cup filled with hot tea.

He looked up from a leather-bound appointment book. "Liberty. I've checked your afternoon schedule." He pronounced it the British way, *shedule*. It was one of his favorite words. "It seems to be clear after three-thirty."

"Yes, sir," I said cautiously.

"Mr. Travis wants a trim at his home. Do you know the address?"

I shook my head in bewilderment. "You want me to do it? How come you're not going? You always do his trims."

Zenko explained that a well-known actress was flying in from New York, and he couldn't cancel on her. "Besides," he continued in a careful monotone, "Mr. Travis specifically asked for you. He's had a difficult time since the accident, and he indicated it might do him some good if—"

"What accident?" I felt a nasty sting of adrenaline all over, not unlike the feeling of saving yourself from a fall down the stairs. Even though you avoid the tumble, your body still gets ready for catastrophe.

"I thought you would already know," Zenko said. "Mr. Travis was thrown from a horse two weeks ago."

For a man Churchill's age, horse accidents were never minor. Bones were broken, dislocated, crushed, necks and spines were snapped. I felt my mouth gather in a soundless "oh." My hands shifted in a mosaic of movement, first going to my lips, then crossing over to the upper arms.

"How bad was it?" I managed.

"I'm not aware of the particulars, but I believe a leg was broken, and there was some surgery . . ." Zenko paused as he stared at me. "You look pale. Do you want to sit down?"

"No. I'm fine. I just . . ." I couldn't believe how afraid I was, how much I cared. I wanted to go to Churchill right then. My heartbeat was a painful throb in my chest. My hands came together, fingers laced like those of a praying child. I blinked against the pictures that flashed through my mind, images that had nothing to do with Churchill Travis.

My mother wearing a white dress splashed with daisies. My father, accessible only in a two-dimensional layer of black-and-white silver halide. Tawdry fairground light shivering across Hardy's resolute face. Shadows within shadows. I found it hard to breathe. But then I thought of Carrington. I held on to that image, my sister, my baby, and the panic eddied and washed back.

I heard Zenko asking if I was willing to go to River Oaks to do the trim.

"Sure," I said, trying to sound normal. Matter-of-fact. "Sure I'll go."

After my last appointment Zenko gave me the address and two different security codes. "Sometimes there's a guard at the gate," he said.

"He has a gate?" I asked. "He has a guard?"

"It's called security," Zenko said, his impersonal tone far more withering than sarcasm. "Rich people need it."

I took the slip of paper from him.

My Honda needed a run through the car wash, but I didn't spare the time. I needed to see Churchill as soon as possible. It took only fifteen minutes to get there from Zenko's. In Houston you measure distance by minutes instead of miles, since traffic can turn a short commute into a stop-and-start journey through hell, where road rage is just a driving technique.

I've heard people compare River Oaks to Highland Park in Dallas, but it's bigger and even more expensive. You could call it the Beverly Hills of Texas. River Oaks consists of about a thousand acres located halfway between Downtown and Uptown, with two schools, a country club, upscale restaurants and shops, and esplanades of brilliant flowers. When River Oaks was established in the 1920s, there was what they called a gentleman's agreement to keep out blacks and browns, except for those living in the maids' quarters. Now those so-called gentlemen are gone, and there's more diversity in River Oaks. It's no longer all-white, but it is definitely all-rich, with the cheapest homes starting at a million dollars and going up from there.

I guided my battered Honda along streets of two-story mansions, past Mercedes and BMWs. Some of the homes were designed in the Spanish Revival style, with flagstone terraces, turrets, and ornamental wrought-iron balcony railings. Others had been modeled after New Orleans plantation homes, or New England colonials with white columns, gables, and banded chimneys. They were all large, beautifully landscaped, and shaded by oaks that lined the walks like giant sentinels.

Although I knew Churchill's house was going to be impressive, there was no way I could have been adequately prepared for it. It was an estate, a stone house designed like a European chateau and set back on a three-acre bayou lot. I stopped at the heavy iron gates and entered the code. To my relief, the gates opened with majestic slowness. A broad paved drive led to the house and split into two roads, one encircling the house, the other leading to a separate garage big enough for ten cars.

I pulled up to the garage and parked at the side, trying to find the least conspicuous place. My poor Honda looked like something that had been left out for the garbagemen to collect. The garage doors were made entirely of glass, showcasing a silver Mercedes sedan, the white Bentley, and a yellow Shelby Cobra with Lemans stripes. There were more cars on the other side, but I was too dazed and anxious to look at them.

It was a relatively cool autumn day, and I was grateful for the diffident breeze that cooled my perspiring forehead. Carrying a bag filled with supplies, I walked to the front door.

The plants and hedged sections of lawn around the house looked like they'd been watered with Evian and trimmed with cuticle scissors. I could have sworn the long, silky drifts of Mexican feather grass bordering the front walk had been tended with a Mason Pearson pocket comb. I reached for the doorbell button, which was located beneath an inset video camera just like the ones you see at ATM machines.

As I rang the bell, it caused the video camera to whir and focus on me, and I nearly recoiled. I realized I hadn't brushed my hair or touched up my makeup before leaving the salon. Now it was too late, as I found myself standing in front of a rich people's doorbell that was looking right back at me.

In less than a minute the door opened. I was greeted by a slim elderly woman, elegantly dressed in green pants and beaded mules and a patterned chiffon blouse. She looked about sixty, but she was so well kept I guessed her real age was probably closer to seventy. Her silver hair had been cut and teased into the Drain Clog style, not a hole to be found in the perfect puffy mass. We were nearly of a height, but the hair gave her at least three inches on me. Diamond earrings the size of Christmas ornaments dangled halfway to her shoulders.

She smiled, a genuine smile that made her eyes crinkle into familiar dark slits. Instantly I knew she was Churchill's older sister Gretchen, who had been engaged three times but never married. Churchill had told me all Gretchen's fiancés had died in tragic circumstances, the first in the Korean War, the second in a car accident, the third from a heart defect no one had known about until it killed him without warning. After the last one Gretchen had said it was obvious she was not meant to marry, and she'd stayed single ever since.

I had been so moved by the story I'd almost cried, picturing Churchill's sister as a spinster dressed in black. "Doesn't she find it lonely," I had asked tentatively, "not ever having . . ." I paused as I considered the best way to phrase it. Carnal relations? Physical intimacy? "A man in her life?"

"Hell, no, she doesn't find it lonely," Churchill had said with a snort. "Gretchen kicks up her heels every time she gets a chance. She's had more than her fair share of men—she just won't marry any of 'em."

Staring at this sweet-faced woman, seeing the twinkle in her eyes, I thought, *You are a hot ticket, Miss Gretchen Travis.*

"Liberty. I'm Gretchen Travis." She looked at me as if we were old friends and reached out to take my hands in hers. I set my bag down and awkwardly returned her grip. Her fingers felt warm and fine-boned amid a clatter of chunky jeweled rings. "Churchill told me about you, but he didn't say what a pretty little thing you are. Are you thirsty, honey? Is that bag heavy? Leave it there and we'll have someone carry it up for us. Do you know who you remind me of?"

Like Churchill, she cast out questions in clusters. I hastened to reply. "Thank you, ma'am, but I'm not thirsty. And I can carry this." I picked the bag up.

Gretchen drew me inside the entrance and retained my free hand as if I were too young to be trusted to wander through the house alone. It felt odd but nice to hold the hand of an adult woman. We walked into a marble-floored hall with a ceiling that was two stories high. Niches featuring bronze sculptures were embedded all along the walls. Gretchen's voice echoed slightly as we headed to a pair of elevator doors tucked beneath one side of a horseshoe-shaped staircase.

"Rita Hayworth," she said, answering her own previous question. "Just like she looked in *Gilda,* with that wavy hair and those long eyelashes. Did you ever see that movie?"

"No, ma'am."

"That's all right. I don't recall it ended well." She released my hand and pushed the elevator button. "We could take the stairs. But this is so much easier. Never stand when you can sit and never walk when you can ride."

"Yes, ma'am." I straightened my clothing as discreetly as possible, tugging the hem of my black vee-neck T-shirt over the top of my white jeans. My red-polished toes peeked out from a pair of backless low-heeled sandals. I wished I had chosen a nicer outfit that morning, but I'd had no idea how the day would turn out. "Miss Travis," I said, "please tell me how—"

"Gretchen," she said. "Just Gretchen."

"Gretchen, how is he? I didn't know about his accident until today, or I would have sent flowers or a card—"

"Oh, honey, we don't need flowers. There have been so many deliveries we don't know what to do with them all. And we've tried to keep it quiet about the accident. Churchill says he doesn't want anyone making a fuss over him. I think it embarrasses him to death, what with the cast and the wheelchair—"

"A leg cast?"

"A soft one for now. In two weeks he'll get a hard cast. He had what the doctor said was . . ." She squinted in concentration. "A comminuted fracture of the tibia, and the fibula broke clean through, and one of his ankle bones is busted too. They put eight long screws in his leg, and a rod on the outside they'll take off later, and a metal plate that'll stay in him for good." She chuckled. "He'd never make it through airport security. Good thing he's got his own plane."

I nodded a little but I couldn't speak. I tried an old trick to keep from crying, something Marva's husband, Mr. Ferguson, had once told me about. When you think you're about to cry, rub the tip of your tongue against the roof of your mouth, back where the soft palate is. As long as you do that, he'd said, the tears wouldn't fall. It worked, but barely.

"Oh, Churchill's as tough as they come," Gretchen said, clicking her tongue as she saw my expression. "You don't need to worry about him, honey. It's the rest of us you should be concerned about. He'll be laid up for at least five months. We'll all be crazy by then."

The house was like a museum, with wide hallways and towering ceilings, and paintings with their own little spotlights. The atmosphere was serene, but I was aware of things happening in distant rooms, phones ringing, some kind of tapping or hammering, the unmistakable clank of metal pots and pans. Busy unseen people doing their work.

We went into the largest bedroom I had ever seen. You could have fit my entire apartment inside it and had room to spare. Rows of tall windows were fitted with plantation shutters. The floor, made of hand-planed walnut, was covered in places with artfully faded kilim rugs that each cost the equivalent of a brand-new Pontiac. A king-sized bed with spiral-carved posters was positioned diagonally in one corner of the room. Another area featured a seating arrangement of two love seats and a recliner chair, with a flat-panel plasma TV on the wall.

My gaze immediately found Churchill, who was in a wheelchair with his leg elevated. Churchill, who had always been so well dressed, was wearing cut-up sweatpants and a yellow cotton sweater. He looked like a wounded lion. I reached him in a few strides and wrapped my arms around him. I pressed my lips against the top of his head, feeling the hard curve of his skull beneath the fleece of gray hair. I inhaled his familiar leathery smell and the hint of expensive cologne.

One of his hands came to the back of my shoulder, patting firmly. "No, no," came his gravelly voice. "No need for that. I'll heal up just fine. You stop that, now."

I wiped at my wet cheeks and straightened, and cleared my tear-clotted throat. "So . . . were you trying some kind of Lone Ranger stunt or what?"

He scowled. "I was riding with a friend on his property. A jackrabbit jumped out from a patch of mesquite and the horse spooked. I went head over heels before I could blink."

"Is your back okay? Your neck?"

"Yes, it's all fine. Just the leg." Churchill sighed and grumbled, "I'll be stuck in this chair for months. Nothing but crap on TV. I have to sit on a plastic chair in the shower. Everything brought to me, can't do a damn thing for myself. I'm sick and tired of being treated like an invalid."

"You are an invalid," I said. "Can't you try to relax and enjoy the pampering?"

"Pampering?" Churchill repeated indignantly. "I've been ignored, neglected, and dehydrated. No one brings my meals on time. No one comes when I holler. No one fills my water jug. A lab rat lives better than this."

"Now, Churchill," Gretchen soothed. "We're all doing our best. It's a new routine for everyone. We'll get the way of it."

He ignored her, clearly eager to air his grievances to a sympathetic listener. It was time for his Vicodin, he said, and someone had set it so far back on the bathroom counter, he hadn't been able to reach it. "I'll get it," I said immediately, and went into the bathroom.

The enormous space was lined with terra-cotta tiles and copper-flecked marble, with a half-sunken oval bathtub in the center. The walk-in shower and window were made entirely of glass blocks. It was lucky the bathroom was so big, I thought, in light of Churchill being wheelchair-bound. I found a cluster of brown medicine bottles on one counter, along with an ordinary plastic Dixie cup dispenser that looked out of place in the magazine-perfect surroundings. "One or two?" I called out, opening the Vicodin.

"Two."

I filled a cup with water and brought the pills to Churchill. He took them with a grimace, the corners of his mouth gray with pain. I couldn't imagine how much his leg must be hurting, his bones protesting the new arrangement of metal rods and screws. His system must have been overwhelmed with the prospect of healing so much damage. I asked if he wanted to rest, I could wait for him, or come back some other time. Churchill replied emphatically he'd had enough resting. He wanted some good company, which had been in short supply lately. This with a meaningful glance at Gretchen, who replied serenely that if a person wanted to attract good company, he had to be good company.

After a minute of affectionate squabbling, Gretchen took her leave, reminding Churchill to buzz the intercom button if he needed anything. I pushed his wheelchair into the bathroom and positioned him next to the sink.

"No one answers when I buzz," Churchill told me testily, watching as I unpacked my supplies.

I shook out a black cutting cape and tucked a folded towel around his neck. "You need a set of walkie-talkies. Then you can contact someone directly when you need something."

"Gretchen can't even keep track of her cell phone," he said. "There's no way I'd get her to carry a walkie-talkie."

"Don't you have a personal assistant or secretary?"

"I did," he allowed. "But I fired him last week."

"Why?"

"He couldn't handle being yelled at. And he always had his head up his *culo*."

I grinned. "Well, you should have waited until you hired someone else before you got rid of him." I filled a spray bottle with tap water.

"I have someone else in mind."

"Who's that?"

Churchill made a brief, impatient gesture to indicate it was of no importance, and settled back in his chair. I dampened his hair and combed it carefully. As I cut his hair in careful layers, I saw the moment when the medication took effect. The harsh lines of his face relaxed, and his eyes lost their glazed brightness.

"This is the first actual haircut I've ever given you," I remarked. "Finally I can list you on my résumé."

He chuckled. "How long have you worked at Zenko's? Four years?"

"Almost five."

"What's he paying you?"

Mildly surprised by the question, I considered telling him it was none of his business. But there was hardly any reason to keep it a secret from him. "Twenty-four a year," I said, "not including tips."

"My assistant got fifty a year."

"That's a lot of money. I bet he had to work his tail off for it."

"Not really. He ran some errands, kept my schedule, made phone calls, typed on my book. That kind of stuff."

"You're writing another book?"

He nodded. "Mostly investment strategies. But part of it is autobiographical. I write some pages in longhand, others I dictate into a recorder. My assistant types it all into the computer."

"It would be a lot more efficient if you typed it yourself." I combed his hair back again, searching for the natural line of his part.

"Some things I'm too old to learn. Typing is one of them."

"So hire a temp."

"I don't want a temp. I want someone I know. Someone I trust."

Our gazes met in the mirror, and I realized what he was working up to. *Good Lord,* I thought. A frown of concentration wove across my forehead. I sank to my haunches, hunting for the right angles, my scissors making precise snips around his head. "I'm a hairstylist," I said without looking at him, "not a secretary. And once I leave Zenko, that door is closed for good. I can't go back."

"It's not a short-term offer," Churchill countered in a relaxed manner that gave me an inkling of what a smart business negotiator he must have been. "There's lots of work around here, Liberty. Most of it will challenge you a hell of a lot more than fooling with people's cuticles. Now, settle your feathers—there's nothing wrong with your job, and you do it well—"

"Gee, thanks."

"—but you could learn a lot from me. I'm still a ways out from retirement, and I've got a lot to get done. I need help from someone I can depend on."

I laughed incredulously and picked up the electric clippers. "What makes you think you can depend on me?"

"You're not a quitter," he said. "You stick with things. You meet life head-on. That counts a hell of a lot more than typing skills."

"You say that now. But you haven't seen my typing."

"You'll pick it up."

I shook my head slowly. "So you're too old to learn your way around a keyboard, but I'm not?"

"That's right."

I gave him an exasperated smile and turned on the clippers. Their insistent buzz forestalled further conversation.

It was obvious Churchill needed someone a lot more qualified than me. Minor errands I could do. But making calls on his behalf, helping with his book, interacting even in small ways with the people in his sphere . . . I would be out of my depth.

At the same time I was surprised to discover a stirring of ambition. How many college graduates with their tasseled caps and crisp new diplomas would kill for a chance like this? It was an opportunity that wouldn't come again.

I worked on Churchill's hair, tilting his head down, shaping carefully. Eventually I turned the clippers off and began to brush the shorn hair from his neck. "What if it didn't work out?" I heard myself ask. "Would I get a couple weeks' notice?"

"Plenty of advance notice," he said, "and a good severance package. But it's going to work out."

"What about health insurance?"

"I'll put you and Carrington on the same policy as my own family."

Well, hell.

Except for the WIC vaccinations, I'd had to pay for every medical and health expense Carrington and I had ever had. We'd been lucky, healthwise. But every cough, cold, or ear infection, every minor problem that could turn into a major problem had nearly killed me with worry. I wanted a white plastic card with a group number in my wallet. I wanted it so badly my fists knotted.

"You write out a list of what you want," Churchill said. "I'm not going to peck over the details. You know me. You know I'll be fair. There's only one nonnegotiable."

"What's that?" I still found it difficult to believe we were even having this conversation.

"I want you and Carrington to live here."

There was not one thing I could say. I just stared at him.

"Gretchen and I both need someone at the house," he explained. "I'm in a wheelchair, and even after I'm out of it, I'll have a hitch in my get-along. And Gretchen's been having some problems lately, including memory loss. She claims she's going back to her own house someday, but the truth is she's here for good. I want someone to keep track of her appointments as well as mine. I don't want it to be some stranger." His eyes were shrewd, his voice easy. "You can come and go as you please. Have the run of the place. Treat it like your own home. Send Carrington to River Oaks Elementary. There's eight free guest rooms upstairs—you can each take your pick."

"But I can't just uproot Carrington like that . . . change her home, her school . . . not when I have no idea if this would work out or not."

"If you're asking for a guarantee, I can't give you one. All I can promise is we'll do our best."

"She's not even ten yet. Do you understand what it would be like, having her in the house? Little girls are noisy. Messy. They get into—"

"I've had four children," he said, "including a daughter. I know what eight-year-olds are like." A calculated pause. "Tell you what, we'll hire a language tutor to come here twice a week. And maybe Carrington will want piano lessons. There's a Steinway downstairs no one ever touches. Does she like to swim? . . . I'll have a slide put in at the pool. We'll throw her a big swim party on her birthday."

"Churchill," I muttered, "what the hell are you doing?"

"I'm trying to make you an offer you can't refuse."

I was afraid he had done exactly that.

"Say yes," he said, "and everybody wins."

"What if I say no?"

"We're still friends. And the offer stands." He shrugged slightly and indicated his wheelchair with a sweep of his hands. "Pretty obvious I'm not going nowhere."

"I . . ." I raked my fingers through my hair. "I need to give this some thought."

"Take as long as you need." He gave me an amiable smile. "Before you decide anything, why don't you bring Carrington here to get a look at the place?"

"When?" I asked dazedly.

"Tonight for supper. Go pick her up from her after-school program and bring her here. Gage and Jack are coming. You'll want to meet them."

It had never occurred to me to want to meet Churchill's children. His life and mine had always been strictly separate, and the mingling of their elements made me uneasy. Somewhere along the way I had absorbed the notion that some people belonged in trailer parks and some people belonged in mansions. My concept of upward mobility had its limits.

But did I want to impose those same limits on Carrington? What would happen if I exposed her to a life so different from the one she had always known? It was like bringing Cinderella to the ball in a coach and sending her back in the pumpkin. Cinderella had been a pretty good sport about it, but I wasn't sure Carrington would be so complacent. And actually, I didn't want her to be.

CHAPTER 16

As I might have expected, Carrington had gotten extra dirty that day. She had grass stains on the knees of her jeans and splotches of poster paint down the front of her T-shirt. I picked her up at the door of her classroom and steered her into the nearest girls' room. Quickly I wiped her face and ears with paper towels, and brushed the tangles from her ponytail. When she asked why I was trying to make her look nicer, I explained we were going to dinner at a friend's house, and she'd better be on her best behavior or else.

"What's the 'or else'?" she asked, as always, and I pretended not to hear.

Carrington erupted with squeals of delight when she saw the gated estate. She insisted on climbing out of her seat to push the buttons through my open window while I read the code to her. For some reason it pleased me that Carrington was too young to be intimidated by the lavish surroundings. She rang the doorbell five times before I could stop her, and mugged for the security camera, and bounced on her heels until her light-up sneakers flashed like emergency signals.

This time an elderly housekeeper answered the door. She made Churchill and Gretchen look like teenagers. Her face was so gnarled and grooved she reminded me of one of those dried-up apple dolls with the tufts of white cotton for hair. The bright black buttons of her eyes were set behind glasses with Coke-bottle lenses. She had a Brazos Bottom accent that swallowed up her words as soon as they came out. We introduced ourselves, and she said her name was Cecily or Cissy, I couldn't tell which.

Then Gretchen appeared. Churchill had come downstairs in the elevator, she said, and he was waiting for us in the family room. She looked over Carrington and reached out to cup her face in her hands. "What a beautiful girl, what a treasure," she exclaimed. "You call me Aunt Gretchen, honey."

Carrington giggled and played with the hem of her paint-splotched shirt. "I like your rings," she said, staring at Gretchen's glittering fingers. "Can I try one on?"

"Carrington—" I began to scold.

"Of course you can," Gretchen exclaimed. "But first let's go in to see Uncle Churchill."

The two of them went hand in hand down a hallway, and I followed close behind. "Did Churchill tell you what he and I talked about?" I asked Gretchen.

"Yes, he did," she said over her shoulder.

"What do you think about it?"

"I think it would be a fine thing for all of us. With Ava gone and the children away, the house is too quiet."

We passed rooms with lofty ceilings and tall windows hung with silk and velvet and tea-stained lace. The walnut floors were scattered with Oriental rugs and clusters of antique furniture, everything done in muted shades of red, gold, and cream. Someone in the house loved books— there were built-in bookcases everywhere, filled from top to bottom. It smelled good in the house, like lemon oil and wax and antique vellum.

The family room was big enough to host an auto show, with walk-in fireplaces set on opposite walls. A circular table occupied the center, bearing a massive fresh flower arrangement of white hydrangea, yellow and red roses, and spikes of yellow freesia. Churchill was at a seating cluster on one side of the room, beneath a big sepia-toned picture of a tall-masted sailing ship. A pair of men rose from their chairs as we approached, an old-fashioned courtesy. I didn't look at either of them. My attention was riveted on Carrington as she approached the wheelchair.

They shook hands solemnly. I couldn't see my sister's face, but I saw Churchill's. He fixed her with an unblinking stare. I was puzzled by the emotions that crossed his face: wonder, pleasure, sadness. He looked away and cleared his throat hard. But when his gaze returned to my sister, his expression was clear, and I thought maybe I had imagined the moment.

They began to chat like old friends. Carrington, who was often shy, was describing how fast she could roller-skate down the hallway if roller-skating was allowed in the house, and asking the name of the horse that broke his leg, and telling him about art class and how her best friend, Susan, accidentally spilled blue poster paint on her desk.

While they talked, I dragged my attention to the pair of men standing beside their chairs. After having heard about Churchill's offspring over a period of years, I experienced a mild jolt to have them abruptly made real.

Despite my affection for Churchill, it had not escaped me that he'd been a demanding father. He had admitted to being overzealous in his efforts to make certain his three sons and his daughter did not become the soft, spoiled children of privilege he had seen in other wealthy families. They were brought up to work hard, achieve the goals he set, live up to their obligations. As a parent Churchill had been spare in his rewards, tough in his punishments.

Churchill had wrestled with life, taken some hard blows, and he expected that from his children too. They had been raised to excel in academics and sports, to challenge themselves in every aspect of their lives. Since Churchill had a horror of laziness or a sense of entitlement, any flicker of it had been extinguished beneath his booted foot. He had been the easiest on Haven, the only daughter and the baby of the family. He'd been toughest on the oldest, Gage, the only child by his first wife.

After listening to Churchill's stories about his children, I had found it easy to discern that the greatest pride and highest expectations were reserved for Gage. At age twelve, while attending an elite boarding school, Gage had risked his life to help save other students in his dorm. A fire had broken out in the third-floor lounge one night, and there had been no sprinklers in the building. According to Churchill, Gage had stayed behind to make certain every student had been awakened and got out. He'd been the last to leave and had barely made it out, suffering smoke inhalation and second-degree burns. I found the story telling, and Churchill's comment on it even more so. "He only did what I would have expected of him," Churchill had said. "What anyone in the family would have done." In other words, saving people from a burning building was no big deal for a Travis, barely worthy of notice.

Gage had gone on to graduate from UT and Harvard Business School, and now did double duty working at Churchill's investment firm and also at his own company. The other Travis sons had followed their own pursuits. I had wondered if it had been Gage's choice to work for his father, or whether he had simply stepped into the place he had been expected to fill. And if he nurtured a secret grievance about having to live under the considerable burden of Churchill's expectations.

The younger of the two brothers came forward and introduced himself as Jack. He had a firm grip and an easy smile. His eyes were the color of black coffee, twinkling against the sun-chapped complexion of an avid outdoorsman.

And then I met Gage. He was a full head taller than his father, black haired and big framed and lean. He was about thirty, but he had a seasoned look that could have allowed him to pass for someone older. He rationed out a perfunctory smile as if he didn't have many to spare. There were two things people immediately comprehended about Gage Travis. First, he wasn't the kind who laughed easily. And second, despite his privileged upbringing, he was a tough son of a bitch. A kennel-bred, pedigreed pit bull.

He introduced himself, reaching out to shake my hand.

His eyes were an unusually pale gray, brilliant and black needled. Those eyes allowed a flash of the volatility contained beneath his quiet façade, a sense of tautly restrained energy I had only seen once before, in Hardy. Except Hardy's charisma had been an invitation to draw closer, whereas this man's was a warning to stay back. I was so shaken by him, I had a hard time taking his hand.

"Liberty," I said faintly. My fingers were swallowed in his. A light, burning clasp, and he released me as quickly as possible.

I turned away blindly, wanting to look anywhere other than into those unsettling eyes, and I discovered a woman sitting on a nearby love seat.

She was a beautiful tall waif with a delicate face and puffy pneumatic lips, and a river of highlighted blond hair that streamed down her shoulders and over the arm of the sofa. Churchill had told me Gage was dating a model, and I had no doubt this was her. The woman's arms, no bigger around than Q-tips stems, hung straight from their sockets, and her hipbones protruded beneath her clothes like can-opener blades. Had she been anyone other than a model, she would have been rushed to a clinic for eating disorders.

I have never worried about my weight, which has always been normal. I have a good figure, a woman's shape with a woman's breasts and hips, and probably more of a rear end than I would have wished for. I look good in the right clothes, not so good in the wrong ones. Overall I like my body just fine. But next to this spindly creature I felt like a prizewinning Holstein.

"Hi," I said, forcing a smile as her gaze swept me up and down. "I'm Liberty Jones. I'm . . . a friend of Churchill's."

She gave me a disdainful glance and didn't bother introducing herself.

I thought of the years of deprivation and hunger it would require to maintain such thinnness. No ice cream, no barbecue, never a wedge of lemon pie or a fried chile relleno pepper stuffed with melting white cheese. It would turn anyone mean.

Jack broke in quickly. "So where you from, Liberty?"

"I . . ." I cast a quick glance at Carrington, who was examining a panel of buttons on Churchill's wheelchair. "Don't push any of those, Carrington." I had a sudden cartoonish vision of her triggering a catapult device in the seat cushion.

"I'm not," my sister protested. "I'm just looking."

I returned my attention to Jack. "We live in Houston, near the salon."

"What salon?" Jack asked with an encouraging smile.

"Salon One. Where I work." A short but discomforting silence followed, as if there were nothing anyone could think of to say or ask about a salon job. I was compelled to throw words into the void. "Before Houston, we lived in Welcome."

"I think I've heard of Welcome," Jack said. "Although I can't remember how or why."

"It's just a regular little town," I said. "Got one of everything."

"What do you mean?"

I shrugged awkwardly. "One shoe store, one Mexican restaurant, one dry cleaner's . . ."

These people were used to conversation with their own kind, about people and places and things I had no experience with. I felt like a nobody. Suddenly I was annoyed with Churchill for putting me in this situation, among people who were going to make fun of me the minute I left the room. I tried to keep my mouth shut, but as another mesh of silence settled, I couldn't stop myself from breaking through it.

I looked at Gage Travis again. "You work with your dad, right?" I tried to remember what Churchill had said, that although Gage had a hand in the family investment business, he had also started his own company that developed alternative energy technologies.

"It looks like I'll be stepping in to do Dad's traveling for a while," Gage said. "He was scheduled to speak at a conference in Tokyo next week. I'll be going instead." All lacquered politeness, no hint of a smile.

"When you make a speech for Churchill," I asked, "do you say exactly what he would have said?"

"We don't always share the same opinions."

"That means no, then."

"That means no," he said softly. As he continued to stare at me, I was surprised by a mild, not unpleasant squirming sensation in my abdomen. My face turned hot.

"Do you like to travel?" I asked.

"I've gotten tired of it, actually. What about you?"

"I don't know. I've never been outside the state."

I didn't think it was such a weird thing to say, but the three of them looked at me like I had two heads.

"Churchill hasn't taken you anywhere?" the woman on the love seat asked, toying with a lock of her own hair. "Doesn't he want to be seen with you?" She smiled as if she were making a joke. Her tone could have stripped the fuzz off a kiwi.

"Gage is a homebody," Jack told me. "The rest of the Travises have a big dose of wanderlust."

"But Gage does like Paris," the woman commented, giving him an arch glance. "That's where we met. I was doing the cover for French *Vogue*."

I tried to look impressed. "I'm sorry, I didn't catch your name."

"Dawnelle."

"Dawnelle . . ." I repeated, waiting for her last name.

"*Just* Dawnelle."

"She's just been chosen for a big national ad campaign," Jack told me. "A major cosmetics company is launching a new perfume."

"Fragrance," Dawnelle corrected. "It's called Taunt."

"I'm sure you'll do a great job," I said.

After drinks we had dinner in an oval-shaped dining room with a two-story ceiling and a chandelier with crystals hanging down like strands of raindrops. The arched doorway on one side of the dining room led to the kitchen, while the one on the other side featured a wrought-iron gate. Churchill told me there was a dine-in wine cellar beyond the gate, with a collection of about ten thousand bottles. Heavy chairs upholstered in olive velvet were pulled up to a mahogany table.

The housekeeper and a young Hispanic woman poured inky red wine into large-bowled glasses and brought a flute filled with Seven-Up for Carrington. My sister sat at Churchill's left, and I took her other side. I reminded her in a whisper to put her napkin on her lap and not to set her glass so close to the edge of the table. She behaved beautifully, remembering her pleases and thank-yous.

There was only one worrisome moment when the plates were brought out and I was unable to identify their contents. My sister, although not a picky eater, did not have what anyone would call an adventurous palate.

"What is this stuff?" Carrington whispered, staring dubiously at the collection of strips and balls and chunks on her plate.

"It's meat," I said out of the side of my mouth.

"What kind of meat?" she persisted, poking at one of the balls with the tines of her fork.

"I don't know. Just eat it."

By this time Churchill had noticed Carrington's frown. "What's the matter?" he asked.

Carrington pointed to her plate with her fork. "I'm not gonna eat something if I don't know what it is."

Churchill, Gretchen, and Jack laughed, while Gage regarded us without expression. Dawnelle was in the process of explaining to the housekeeper that she wanted her food taken back to the kitchen and weighed carefully. Three ounces of meat was all she wanted.

"That's a good rule," Churchill said to Carrington. He told her to move her plate closer to his. "All this stuff is what they call mixed grill. Look here—these little things are venison strips. This is elk, and those are moose meatballs, and that's wild turkey sausage." Glancing up at me, he added, "No emu," and winked.

"It's like eating a whole episode of *Wild Kingdom*," I said, entertained by the sight of Churchill trying to talk a reluctant eight-year-old into something.

"I don't like elk," Carrington told him.

"You can't be sure of that until you try some. Go on, take a bite."

Obediently Carrington ate some of the foreign meat, along with some baby vegetables and roasted potatoes. Baskets of bread were passed around, containing rolls and steaming squares of cornbread. To my consternation, I saw Carrington digging through one of the baskets. "Baby, don't do that," I murmured. "Just take the top piece."

"I want the regular kind," she complained.

I looked at Churchill apologetically. "I usually make our corn-bread in a skillet."

"How about that." He grinned at Jack. "That's the way your mama used to make it, wasn't it?"

"Yes, sir," Jack said with a reminiscent smile. "I'd crumble it hot into a glass of milk . . . man, that was good eating."

"Liberty makes the best cornbread," Carrington said earnestly. "You should ask her to make it for you sometime, Uncle Churchill."

Out the corner of my eye, I saw Gage stiffen at the word "uncle."

"I think I just might," Churchill said, giving me a fond smile.

After dinner, Churchill took us on a tour through the mansion, despite my protestations that he must be tired. The others went to a sitting room for coffee, while Churchill, Carrington, and I went off by ourselves.

Our host maneuvered the wheelchair in and out of the elevator, along the hallways, pausing at the doorways of certain rooms he wanted us to see. Ava had decorated the whole place by herself, he said with pride. She had liked European styles, French things, choosing antique pieces with visible wear and tear to balance elegance with comfort.

We peered into bedrooms with their own little balconies, and windows made of diamond-cut glass. Some of the rooms had been decorated like a rustic chateau, the walls aged with hand-sponged glaze, the ceilings crossed with hammerhead beams. There was a library, an exercise room with a sauna and a racquetball court, a music room with furniture upholstered in cream velvet, a theater room with a TV screen that covered an entire wall. There was an indoor pool and an outdoor pool, the latter centered in a landscaped area with a pavilion, a summer kitchen, covered decks, and an outdoor fireplace.

Churchill turned his charm up to full wattage. Several times the crafty old scoundrel gave me a meaningful glance, like when Carrington ran to the Steinway and plunked a few experimental notes, or when she got excited at the sight of the negative-edge pool. *She could have this all the time,* was his unspoken subtext. *You're the only one keeping it from her.* And he laughed when I scowled at him.

His point had been made, however. And there was something else I noticed, something he might not have been fully aware of. I was struck by the way they interacted, the natural ease between them. The small girl with no father or grandfather. The old man who hadn't spent enough time with his own children when they were young. He regretted that, he had told me. Being Churchill, he couldn't have taken any other road. But now that he'd finally gotten to where he'd wanted to go, he could look back and see the distant landmarks of what he'd missed.

I was troubled for both their sakes. I had a lot to think about.

When we were sufficiently dazzled and Churchill had begun to tire, we went to join the others. Seeing the grayish tint of his face, I checked my watch. "It's time for more Vicodin," I murmured. "I'll run up to your room to get it."

He nodded, his jaw set against the oncoming ache. Some kinds of pain you have to catch before it starts, or you never quite get the better of it.

"I'll go with you," Gage said, rising from his chair. "You may not remember the way."

Even though his tone was pleasant, the words bit through the comfortable feeling I'd gotten from being with Churchill.

"Thanks," I said warily, "but I can find it."

He wouldn't back off. "I'll start you off. It's easy to get lost in this place."

"Thanks," I said. "That's real nice of you."

But as we walked together out of the living room, I knew what was coming. He had something to say to me, and it wasn't going to be remotely nice. When we reached the foot of the stairs, reasonably out of earshot of the others, Gage stopped and turned me to face him. His touch made me freeze.

"Look," he said curtly, "I don't give a damn if you're banging the old man. That's not my business."

"You're right," I said.

"But I draw the line when you bring it into this house."

"It's not your house."

"He built it for my mother. This is where the family gets together, where we spend holidays." He looked at me with contempt. "You're on dangerous ground. You set foot on this property again and I'll personally throw you out on your ass. Understand?"

I understood. But I didn't flinch or step back. I had learned a long time ago not to run from pit bulls.

I went from crimson to skull-white. The rush of my blood seemed to scald the insides of my veins. He knew nothing about me, this arrogant bastard, knew nothing about the choices I'd made or the things I'd given up and all the easy ways out I could have taken but didn't, *didn't,* and he was such a complete and unredeemable asshole that if he'd suddenly caught on fire, I wouldn't have bothered to spit on him.

"Your father needs his medicine," I said, stone-faced.

His eyes narrowed. I tried to hold his gaze but I couldn't, the day's events had drawn my emotions too close to the surface. So I stared at a distant point across the room and concentrated on showing nothing, feeling nothing. After an unbearably long time I heard him say, "This better be the last time I lay eyes on you."

"Go to hell," I said, and went upstairs at a measured pace, while my instincts urged me to bolt like a jackrabbit.

I had another private conversation that evening, with Churchill. Jack had long since departed, and mercifully so had Gage, to take his size-zero girlfriend home. Gretchen showed Carrington her collection of antique cast-iron banks, one shaped like Humpty-Dumpty, another like a cow whose back legs kicked a farmer when you dropped a coin in. While they played on the other side of the room, I sat on an ottoman beside Churchill's wheelchair.

"You been thinking?" he asked.

I nodded. "Churchill . . . some people aren't going to be happy if we go ahead with this."

He didn't pretend not to understand. "No one's going to give you a problem, Liberty," he said. "I'm the big dog here."

"I need a day or two to think it over."

"You got it." He knew when to push, and when to let it be.

Together we looked across the room at Carrington, who chortled in delight as a little cast-iron monkey flipped a penny into a box with its tail.

That weekend we went for Sunday dinner at Miss Marva's. The ranch house was filled with the smell of beer pot roast and mashed potatoes. You would have thought Miss Marva and Mr. Ferguson had been married for fifty years, they were so comfortable with each other.

While Miss Marva took Carrington back into her sewing room, I sat in the den with Mr. Ferguson and laid out my dilemma. He listened in silence, his expression mild, his hands templed on his midriff.

"I know what the safe choice is," I told him. "When you get down to it, there's no reason for me to take this kind of risk. I'm doing great at Zenko's. And Carrington likes her school and I'm afraid it would be hard on her to leave her friends. Trying to fit in at a new place where all the other kids are being dropped off in Mercedes. I just . . . I just wish . . ."

There was a smile in Mr. Ferguson's soft brown eyes. "I have the feeling, Liberty, that you're hoping for someone to give you permission to do what you want to do."

I let my head flop back against the back of the recliner. "I'm so not like those people," I said to the ceiling. "Oh, if you'd just seen that house, Mr. Ferguson. It made me feel so . . . oh, I don't know. Like a hundred-dollar hamburger."

"I don't follow you."

"Even if it's served on a china plate in an expensive restaurant, it's still just a hamburger."

"Liberty," Mr. Ferguson said, "there's no reason for you to feel inferior to them. To anyone. When you get to my age, you come to realize all people are the same."

Of course a mortician would say that. Regardless of financial status, race, and all the other things that distinguished people from each other, they all ended up naked on a slab in his basement.

"I can see how it looks that way from your end of things, Mr. Ferguson," I said. "But from where I was looking last night in River Oaks, those people are definitely different from us."

"You remember the Hopsons' oldest boy, Willie? Went off to Texas Christian?"

I wondered what Willie Hopson had to do with my dilemma. But there was usually a point to Mr. Ferguson's stories if you were patient enough to wait for it. "During his junior year," Mr. Ferguson continued, "Willie went to Spain for a study-abroad program. To get an idea of how other people live. Learn something about how they think and their values. It did him a lot of good. I think you ought to consider doing the same."

"You want me to go to Spain?"

He laughed. "You know exactly what I'm saying, Liberty. You could think of the Travis family as your study-abroad program. I don't think it's going to hurt you or Carrington to spend a little time in a place you don't belong. It may benefit you in ways you don't expect."

"Or not," I said.

He smiled. "Only one way to find out, isn't there?"

CHAPTER 17

Every time Gage Travis looked at me, you could tell he wanted to tear me limb from limb. Not in a fury, but in a process of slow and methodical dismemberment.

Jack and Joe dropped by about once a week, but Gage was the one who came to the house on a daily basis. He helped Churchill with things like climbing in and out of the shower and getting dressed, and taking him to doctor's appointments. No matter how much I disliked Gage, I had to admit he was a good son. He could have insisted that Churchill hire a nurse, but instead he showed up to take care of his father himself. Eight o'clock every morning, never one minute early or late. He was good for Churchill, who was cantankerous from the combination of boredom, pain, and constant inconvenience. But no matter how Churchill growled or snapped, I never once saw one sign of impatience from Gage. He was always calm, tolerant, and capable.

Until he was around me, and then he was a first-class jerk. Gage made it clear that in his opinion I was a parasite, a gold digger, and worse. He took no notice of Carrington other than to demonstrate a curt awareness that there was a short person in the house.

The day we moved in, our possessions crammed into cardboard boxes, I thought Gage would throw me out bodily. I had begun to unpack in the bedroom I had chosen, a beautiful space with wide windows and pale moss-green walls, and cream-colored molding. What had decided me on the room was the grouping of black-and-white photographs on one wall. They were Texas images: a cactus, a barbed-wire fence, a horse, and to my delight, a front shot of an armadillo looking straight into the camera. I'd taken that as an auspicious sign. Carrington was going to sleep two doors down, in a small but pretty room with yellow and white striped paper on the walls.

As I opened my suitcase on the king-sized bed, Gage appeared in the doorway. My fingers curled around the edge of the suitcase, my knuckles jutting until you could have shredded carrots on them. Even knowing I was reasonably safe—surely Churchill would keep him from killing me—I was still alarmed. He filled up the doorway, looking big and mean and pitiless.

"What the hell are you doing here?" His soft voice unsettled me far more than shouting would have.

I answered through dry lips. "Churchill said I could choose any room I wanted."

"You can either leave voluntarily, or I'll throw you out. Believe me, you'd rather go on your own."

I didn't move. "You have a problem, you talk to your father. He wants me here."

"I don't give a shit. Get going."

A little trickle of sweat went down the middle of my back. I didn't move.

He reached me in three strides and took my upper arm in a painful grip.

A gasp of surprise was torn from my throat. "Take your hands off me!" I strained and shoved at him, but his chest was as unyielding as the trunk of a live oak.

"I told you before I wasn't going to—" He broke off. I was released with a suddenness that caused me to stagger back a step. Our sharp respirations pierced the silence. He was staring at the dresser, where I had set out a few pictures in stand-up frames. Trembling, I put my hand on the part of my arm he'd gripped. I rubbed the spot as if to erase his touch. But I could still feel an invisible handprint embedded in my skin.

He went to the dresser and picked up one of the photos. "Who is this?"

It was a picture of Mama, taken not long after she'd married my father. She had been impossibly young and blond and beautiful. "Don't touch that," I cried, rushing forward to snatch the photo from him.

"Who is it?" he repeated.

"My mother."

His head bent as he stood over me, looking into my face with a speculative gaze. I was so bewildered by the abrupt halt of our conflict that I couldn't summon the words to ask what in God's name was going through his mind. I was absurdly conscious of the sound of my breathing, and his, the counterpoint gradually evening until the rhythm of our lungs was identical. Light from the plantation shutters made bright stripes across both of us, casting shadow spokes from his lashes down the crests of his cheek. I could see the whisker grain of his close-shaven skin, foretelling a heavy five o'clock shadow.

I dampened my dry lips with my tongue, and his gaze followed the movement. We were standing too close. I could smell the bite of starch in his collar, and a whiff of warm male skin, and I was shocked by my response. In spite of everything, I wanted to lean even closer. I wanted a deep breath of him.

A frown tugged between his brows. "We're not finished," he muttered, and left the room without another word.

I had no doubt he'd gone straight to Churchill, but it would be a long time before I found out what was said between them, or why Gage had decided to abandon that particular battle. All I knew was there was no more interference from Gage as we settled in. He left before supper, while Churchill, Gretchen, Carrington, and I celebrated our first night together. We ate fish steamed in little white paper bags and rice mixed with finely chopped peppers and vegetables that made it look like confetti.

When Gretchen asked if our rooms were all right and did we have everything we needed, Carrington and I both replied enthusiastically. Carrington said her canopy bed made her feel like a princess. I said I loved my room too, the soft green walls were so soothing, and I especially liked the black-and-white photographs.

"You'll have to tell Gage," Gretchen said, beaming. "He took those pictures in college for a photography-class assignment. He had to lie in wait two hours for that armadillo to come out of its burrow."

A horrifying suspicion darted through my mind. "Oh," I said, and swallowed hard. "Gretchen, by any chance . . . does that happen to be . . ." I could barely speak his name. "Gage's room?"

"As a matter of fact, yes," came her placid reply.

Oh, God. Of all the guest rooms on the second floor, I had managed to pick his. For him to walk in and see me there, taking occupation of his territory . . . I was amazed he hadn't tossed me like a bull with a rodeo clown in a barrel. "I didn't know," I said thinly. "Someone should have said something. I'll move to a different—"

"No, no, he never stays here," Gretchen said. "He doesn't live but ten minutes away. The room's been empty for years, Liberty. I'm sure it will please Gage for someone to get some use out of it."

Like hell, I thought, and reached for my wineglass.

Later that evening I emptied my cosmetics bags beside the bathroom sink. As I pulled out the top drawer, I heard something rattling and rolling around. Investigating, I found a few personal items that looked as though they'd been there a while. A used toothbrush, a pocket comb, an ancient tube of hair gel . . . and a box of condoms.

I turned and closed the bathroom door before examining the box more closely. There were three foil packets left out of twelve. It was a brand I had never seen before, British-made. And there was a funny phrase on the side of the box, "kite-marked for your peace of mind." Kite-marked? What the heck did that mean? It sort of looked like a European version of the Good Housekeeping seal of approval. I couldn't help noticing the little yellow sunburst at the corner of the box, printed with the words "Extra Large." This was appropriate, I reflected sourly, in light of the fact that I already thought of Gage Travis as a big prick.

I wondered what I was supposed to do with this stuff. There was no way I was going to return Gage's long-forgotten condoms to him. But I couldn't throw his things away, on the off chance that he might remember someday and ask what I'd done with them. So I pushed them far back in the drawer and put my own things in there. I tried not to think about the fact that Gage Travis and I were sharing a drawer.

For the first few weeks I was busier than I had ever been in my life, and happier than I'd been since before Mama had died. Carrington made new friends quickly, and she was doing well at the new school, which had a nature center, a computer lab, a well-stocked library, and all kinds of enrichment classes. I had braced myself for adjustment problems that so far Carrington didn't seem to be having. Maybe her age made it easier to adapt to the strange new world she found herself living in.

People were usually nice to me, according me the distant friendliness reserved for employees. My status as Churchill's personal assistant ensured I was treated well. I could tell when a former Salon One client recognized me but couldn't figure out where we'd met. The circles the Travises occupied were filled with high-living people, some pedigreed and wealthy, some merely wealthy. But whether they'd earned or inherited their place at the top, they were determined to enjoy it.

Houston high society is blond, tan, and well dressed. It's also toned and slim, despite the city's annual place on the Top Ten Fattest list. The rich people are in great shape. It's the rest of us, the lovers of burritos and Dr Pepper and chicken-fried steak, who inflate the average. If you can't afford a gym membership in Houston, you're going to be fat. You can't jog outside with so many days of triple-degree heat and lethal levels of hydrocarbons in the air. And even if it weren't for the poor air quality, public places like Memorial Park can be crowded and dangerous.

Since Houstonians aren't too proud to take the easy way out, plastic surgery is more popular here than anywhere except California. It seems like everyone has had some kind of work done. If you can't afford it stateside, you can slip across the border and get implants or lipo at a bargain. And if you put it on your credit card, you can earn enough mileage points to pay for Southwest tickets.

Once I accompanied Gretchen to a Botox or Bangs luncheon, where she and her friends chatted and ate and took turns getting injected. Gretchen asked me to drive her, since she tended to get headaches after Botox. It was an all-white meal, and by that I don't mean the color of the guests but the food itself. It started with white soup—cauliflower and Gruyère—a crunchy salad of white jicama and white asparagus with basil dressing, an entrée of white chicken and pears poached in a delicious clear broth, and a dessert of white chocolate coconut trifle.

I was more than happy to eat in the kitchen and watch the caterers. The three of them worked together with the precision of the parts in a watch. It was almost like a dance, the way they moved and turned and never once bumped into each other.

When it was time to leave, each guest received a silk Hermès scarf as a party favor. Gretchen gave me hers as soon as we got into the car. "Here, honey. This is your treat for driving me."

"Oh, no," I protested. I didn't know exactly how much the scarf cost, but I knew anything Hermès had to be insanely expensive. "You don't have to give me that, Gretchen."

"Take it," she insisted. "I have too many of these as it is."

It was hard for me to accept the gift gracefully. Not because I wasn't appreciative, but because after years of penny-pinching I was bewildered by so much extravagance.

I bought a set of two-way radios for me and Churchill, and I wore one clipped to my belt at all times. He must have called me every fifteen minutes the first couple of days. Not only was he delighted with the convenience of it, but it was a relief to him not to feel so isolated in his room.

Carrington pestered me constantly to borrow the walkie-talkie. Whenever I relented and let her have it for ten minutes, she wandered through the house conversing with Churchill, the hallways echoing with "over" and "copy" and "you're breaking up, buddy." Before long they had made a deal that Carrington would be Churchill's go-to girl during the hour before dinner, and she would have her own walkie-talkie. If he didn't come up with enough tasks for her, she would complain until he was forced to invent things to keep her busy. Once I caught him tossing the remote control to the floor, so Carrington could be contacted for a rescue.

Early on I did a lot of shopping for Churchill, trying to find solutions for problems caused by the hard cast. He resented the indignity of being forced to wear sweatpants all the time, but there was no way he could wear regular pants over the bulk of the cast. I found a compromise he could live with, a few pairs of zip-off hiking pants that allowed him to take one leg off to expose the cast, and leave the other long. They were still more casual than he would have preferred, but he admitted they were better than the sweatpants.

I bought yards of cotton tubing to cover Churchill's cast every night, to keep the fiberglass from wearing holes in the eight-hundred-thread-count sheets on his bed. And my best find was at a hardware store, a long aluminum tool with a handle on one end and a pair of jaws on the other, allowing him to grip and pick up things he couldn't otherwise reach.

We fell quickly into a routine. Gage would visit early each morning and return to 1800 Main, where he worked and lived. The Travises owned the entire building, which was located near the Bank of America Center and the blue glass towers that had once been Enron Centers North and South. It had once been the most nondescript building in Houston, a plain gray box. But Churchill had gotten it at a steal, and had redesigned and rebuilt it. It had been stripped, re-covered with a blue skin of Low-E glass, and topped with a glass segmented-pyramid that reminded me of an artichoke.

The building was filled with luxury office space, a couple of upscale restaurants, and four penthouse suites priced at twenty million dollars apiece. There were also a half-dozen condos, relatively cheap at five million each. Gage lived in one of those and Jack in another. Churchill's youngest son, Joe, who didn't like high-rise living, had opted for a house.

When Gage came by to help Churchill shower and dress, he often brought research materials for his book. They would go over the reports, articles, and estimates for a few minutes, debating one issue or another. They both seemed to take great enjoyment in these arguments. I tried to move unobtrusively through the room, taking away Churchill's breakfast tray and bringing him more coffee, and setting out his notepad and recorder. Gage made a point of ignoring me. Understanding that the very fact of my breathing was an irritant to him, I tried to stay out of his way. We didn't speak if we passed each other on the stairs. When Gage left his keys in Churchill's room one morning and I had to chase after him to return them, he could barely bring himself to thank me.

"He's that way with everyone," Churchill had told me. Even though I had never said a word about Gage's coldness, it was obvious. "Always been standoffish—takes a while to warm up to people."

We both knew it wasn't true. I was the focus of a targeted dislike. I assured Churchill it didn't bother me one bit. That wasn't true either. It has always been my curse to be a pleaser. This is bad enough, but when you're a pleaser in the company of someone who is determined to think the worst of you, you're miserable. My only defense was to muster a dislike that equaled Gage's, and to that end, he was being very helpful.

After Gage had left, the best part of the day began. I sat in the corner with a laptop and typed in Churchill's notes and handwritten pages, or worked from his recordings. He encouraged me to ask about anything I didn't understand, and he had a gift for explaining things in terms I could easily grasp.

I made calls and wrote e-mails for him, organized his schedule, took notes when people came to the house for meetings. Churchill usually presented foreign visitors with gifts such as bolo ties or bottles of Jack Daniel's. To Mr. Ichiro Tokegawa, a Japanese businessman Churchill had been friends with for years, we gave a chinchilla-and-beaver Stetson that cost four thousand dollars. As I sat quietly in those meetings, I was fascinated by the insights they shared and the different conclusions they drew from the same information. But even when they disagreed, it was clear that people respected Churchill's opinions.

Everyone remarked how good Churchill looked despite what he had gone through, that obviously nothing could keep him down. But it cost Churchill to maintain that appearance. After his guests left, he seemed to deflate, becoming weary and querulous. The long sedentary periods made him cold, and I was constantly filling up hot water bottles and putting throw blankets on him. When he had muscle cramps, I massaged his feet and his good leg, and helped him with toe and foot exercises to prevent adhesions.

"You need a wife," I told him one morning as I came to take his breakfast tray.

"I had a wife," he said. "Two good ones, as a matter of fact. Trying for another would be like asking fate for a kick in the ass. Besides, I do well enough with my lady friends."

I could see the sense in that. There was no practical reason for Churchill to get married. It wasn't like he had a problem finding female companionship. He got calls and notes from a variety of women, one of them an attractive widow named Vivian who sometimes stayed overnight. I was pretty sure they slept together, despite the logistics of maneuvering around the broken leg. After date night, Churchill was always in a good mood.

"Why don't you get a husband?" Churchill countered. "You shouldn't wait too long or you'll get set in your ways."

"So far I haven't found one worth marrying," I said, making Churchill laugh.

"Take one of my boys," he said. "Healthy young animals. All prime husband material."

I rolled my eyes. "I wouldn't have one of your sons on a silver platter."

"Why not?"

"Joe's too young. Jack is a ladies' man and isn't nearly ready for that kind of responsibility, and Gage . . . well, personality issues aside, he only dates women whose body fat is in the single digits."

A new voice entered the conversation. "That's not actually a requirement."

Glancing over my shoulder, I saw Gage walking into the room. I cringed, fervently wishing I had kept my mouth shut.

I had wondered why Gage would date someone like Dawnelle, who was beautiful but seemed to have no interests other than shopping or reading Hollywood gossip sheets. Jack had summed her up best: "Dawnelle is hot. But ten minutes in her company and you can feel your IQ dropping."

The only possible conclusion was that Dawnelle was going out with Gage because of his money and position, and he was using her as a trophy, and their relationship consisted of nothing more than meaningless sex.

God, I envied them.

I missed sex, even the mediocre sex I'd had with Tom. I was a healthy twenty-four-year-old woman, and I had urges with no means to satisfy them. Alone-sex didn't count. It's like the difference between thinking to yourself or having a good conversation with someone—the pleasure is in the exchange. And it seemed everyone had a love life but me. Even Gretchen.

One night I'd downed a mug of the tension-tamer tea I often made for Churchill to help him sleep. It had done nothing for me. My sleep had been restless, and I woke with the sheets twisted into ropes around my legs, and my head had been filled with erotic images that, for once, had nothing to do with Hardy. I sat bolt upright from a dream in which a man's hands had been playing gently between my thighs, his mouth at my breast, and as I had writhed and begged for more, I had seen his eyes flash silver in the darkness.

Having an erotic dream about Gage Travis was about the stupidest, most embarrassing and confusing thing that had ever happened to me. But the impression of the dream, the heat and darkness and clutch-and-slide, lingered in the corner of my mind. It was the first time I'd ever been sexually attracted to a man I couldn't stand. How was that possible? It was a betrayal of all the memories of Hardy. But here I was, lusting after a cold-faced stranger who couldn't have cared less about me.

Shallow, I scolded myself. Mortified by the direction of my own thoughts, I could hardly stand to look at Gage as he walked into Churchill's room.

"That's good to hear," Churchill said in reference to Gage's earlier comment. "Because I don't see how a woman shaped like a Popsicle stick is going to give me healthy grandchildren."

"If I were you," Gage replied, "I wouldn't worry about grandchildren for a while." He approached the bed. "Your shower's got to be fast today, Dad. I've got a meeting at nine with Ashland."

"You look like hell," Churchill said, giving him an appraising glance. "What's the matter?"

At that, I overcame my self-consciousness long enough to look up at Gage. Churchill was right. Gage did look like hell. He was pale under his tan, his mouth bracketed with harsh lines. He always seemed so inexhaustible, it was startling to see him drained of his usual vitality.

Sighing, Gage dragged his hand through his hair, leaving some of it standing on end. "I've got a headache that won't quit." He rubbed his temples gingerly. "I didn't sleep last night. I feel like I've been hit by an eighteen-wheeler."

"Have you taken something for it?" I asked. I rarely spoke to him directly.

"Yeah." He looked at me with bloodshot eyes.

"Because if not—"

"I'm fine."

I knew he was in considerable pain. A Texan male will say he's fine even if he's just had a limb severed and is bleeding to death in front of you.

"I could get you an ice pack and some painkillers," I said cautiously. "If you—"

"I said I'm fine," Gage snapped, and turned to his father. "Come on, let's get started. I'm running late as it is."

Jerk, I thought, and took Churchill's tray from the room.

We didn't see Gage for two days after that. Jack was enlisted to come in his place. Since Jack had what he called "sleep inertia," I had genuine worries for Churchill's safety in the shower. Even though Jack moved, talked, and gave the appearance of a functioning human being, he wasn't all there until noon. In fact, sleep inertia looked a lot like a hangover to me. Swearing, stumbling, and only half listening to what anyone said, Jack was more of a hindrance than a help. Churchill remarked testily that Jack's sleep inertia would improve a hell of a lot if he didn't go out tomcatting half the night.

Gage, meanwhile, was bedridden with the flu. Since no one could remember the last time he'd been sick enough to take a day off, we all agreed it must have hit him pretty hard. No one heard from him, and when forty-eight hours had passed and Gage still wasn't answering the phone, Churchill began to fret.

"I'm sure he's just resting," I said.

Churchill replied with a noncommittal grunt.

"Dawnelle's probably taking care of him," I said.

That earned me a glance of sour skepticism.

I was tempted to point out that his brothers should visit him. Then I recalled that Joe had gone to St. Simon's Island with his girlfriend for a couple of days. And Jack's caretaking abilities had been pushed to their limits after helping his father shower two mornings in a row.

I was pretty certain he would flat-out refuse to go to any more trouble for ailing family members.

"Do you want me to check on him?" I asked reluctantly. It was my night off, and I had planned to go out to a movie with Angie and some of the girls from Salon One. I hadn't seen them in a while and I was looking forward to catching up with them. "I guess I could stop by Eighteen hundred Main on the way to see my friends—"

"Yes," Churchill said.

I was instantly sorry I had made the offer. "I doubt he'd let me in."

"I'll give you a key," Churchill said. "It's not like Gage to hole up like this. I want to know if he's all right."

To reach the residential elevators of 1800 Main, you had to go through a small lobby with marble flooring and a bronze sculpture that looked like a hunched-over pear. There was a doorman clad in black with gold trim, and two people behind the reception desk. I tried to look like I belonged in a building with multimillion-dollar condos. "I've got a key," I said, pausing to show it to them. "I'm visiting Mr. Travis."

"All right," the woman behind the desk said. "You can go on up, Miss . . ."

"Jones," I said. "His father sent me to check on him."

"That's fine." She motioned me toward a set of automatic sliding doors with etched-glass panels. "The elevators are over there."

I felt like I needed to convince her of something. "Mr. Travis has been sick for a couple of days," I said.

She looked sincerely concerned. "Oh, that's too bad."

"So I'm just going to run up and check on him. I'll only be a few minutes."

"That's fine, Miss Jones."

"Okay, thanks." I held up the key just in case she hadn't seen it the first time.

She responded with a patient smile and nodded toward the elevators again.

I went through the sliding glass doors and into an elevator with wood paneling and a black-and-white tiled floor and a bronze-framed mirror. The elevator whooshed up so swiftly, I barely had time to blink before it reached the eighteenth floor.

The narrow windowless hallways formed a big H. It was unnervingly quiet. My footsteps were muffled by a pale wool carpet, its pile spongy underfoot. I went to the corridor on the right and scrutinized door numbers until I found 18A. I knocked firmly.

No response.

A harder knock produced no results.

Now I was starting to get worried. What if Gage was unconscious? What if he'd gotten dengue fever or mad cow disease or bird flu? What if he was contagious? I wasn't too crazy about the idea of catching some exotic malady. On the other hand, I'd promised Churchill I would check on him.

A rummage through my purse, and I found the key. But just before I inserted it into the lock, the door opened. I was confronted with the sight of Gage Travis à la death-warmed-over. He was barefoot, dressed in a gray T-shirt and plaid flannel pants. His hair hadn't been combed in days. He stared at me through bleary red-rimmed eyes and wrapped his arms around himself. He shook with the tremors of a large animal at slaughter time.

"What do you want?" His voice sounded like the crush of dry leaves.

"Your father sent me to—" I broke off as I saw him tremble again. Against all better judgment I reached up and laid my hand across his forehead. His skin was blazing.

It was a sign of how sick Gage was that he let me touch him. He closed his eyes at the coolness of my fingers. "God, that feels good."

No matter if I might have fantasized about seeing my enemy brought low, I couldn't take pleasure in seeing him reduced to such a pitiful state.

"Why haven't you answered the phone?"

The sound of my voice seemed to recall Gage to himself, and he jerked his head back. "Didn't hear it," he said with a scowl. "I've been sleeping."

"Churchill has been worried half to death." I hunted in my bag again. "I'm going to call him and let him know you're still alive."

"That phone won't work in the hallway." He turned and went back into his condo, leaving the door open.

I followed and closed the door.

The condo was beautifully decorated with hypermodern fixtures and indirect lighting, and a couple of paintings of circles and squares that even my untrained eyes could discern were priceless. There were walls of nothing but windows, revealing wide views of Houston as the sun sank toward a bed of thickening color on the distant flat horizon. The furniture was contemporary, made of precious woods and natural-colored fabrics, no extra ornamentation of any kind. But it was too pristine, too orderly, without a cushion or pillow or any hint of softness. And there was a plasticky staleness in the air as if no one had lived there for a while.

The open kitchen was fitted with gray quartz countertops, black-lacquered cabinets, and stainless steel appliances. It was sterile, unseasoned, a kitchen where cooking was rarely done. I stood beside a counter and dialed Churchill on my cell phone.

"How is he?" Churchill barked when he picked up.

"Not great." My gaze followed Gage's tall form as he staggered to a geometrically perfect sofa and collapsed on it. "He's got a fever, and he's too weak to drag a cat."

"Why the hell," came Gage's disgruntled voice from the sofa, "would I want to drag a cat?"

I was too busy listening to Churchill to answer. I reported, "Your dad wants to know if you're taking any kind of antiviral medication."

Gage shook his head. "Too late. Doctor said if you don't take it within the first forty-eight hours, it won't do any good."

I repeated the information to Churchill, who was highly annoyed and said if Gage had been such a stubborn idiot to wait that long, he damn well deserved to rot. And then he hung up.

A brief, weighty silence.

"What did he say?" Gage asked without much curiosity.

"He said he hopes you feel better soon, and remember to drink lots of liquids."

"Bullshit." He rolled his head on the back of the sofa as if it were too heavy to lift. "You've done your duty. You can go now."

That sounded good to me. It was Saturday night, my friends were waiting, and I could hardly wait to leave this elegantly barren place. But it was so quiet. And as I turned to the door, I knew my evening was already ruined. The thought of Gage sick and alone in a dark apartment was going to nag at me all night.

I turned back and ventured into the living area, with its glass-fronted fireplace and silent television. Gage remained prone on the sofa. I couldn't help noticing the snug fit of his T-shirt against his arms and chest. His body was long, lean, disciplined like an athlete's. So that was what he'd been hiding beneath those dark suits and Armani shirts.

I should have known Gage would approach exercise as he did everything else, no quarter asked, none given. Even at death's door he was strikingly handsome, his features formed with a strong-boned austerity that owed nothing to boyishness. He was the Prada of bachelors. Reluctantly I acknowledged that if Gage had had one teaspoon's worth of charm, I would have thought he was the sexiest man I'd ever met.

He slitted his eyes open as I stood over him. A few locks of black hair had fallen over his forehead, so unlike its usual strict order. I wanted to smooth it back. I wanted to touch him again.

"What?" he asked curtly.

"Have you taken something for the fever?"

"Tylenol."

"Do you have anyone coming to help you?"

"Help me with what?" He closed his eyes. "I don't need anything. I can ride this out alone."

"Ride it out alone," I repeated, gently mocking. "Tell me, cowboy, when was the last time you ate anything?"

No reply. He remained still, the crescents of his lashes heavy against his pale cheeks. Either he had passed out or he was hoping I was a bad dream that would disappear if he kept his eyes closed.

I went to the kitchen and opened the cabinets methodically, finding expensive liquor, modern glassware, black plates shaped like squares instead of circles. Locating the food cabinet, I discovered a box of Wheaties of indeterminate age, a can of lobster consommé, a few jars of exotic spices. The contents of the refrigerator were just as pitiful. A bottle of orange juice, nearly empty. A white baker's box containing two dried-up kolaches. A pint of half-and-half, and a lone brown egg in a foam carton.

"Nothing fit to eat," I said. "I passed a corner grocery store a few streets away. I'll run out and get you—"

"No, I'm fine. I can't eat anything. I . . ." He managed to raise his head. It was clear he was trying desperately to find the magic combination of words that would make me leave. "I appreciate it, Liberty, but I just . . ."—his head dropped back down—"need to sleep."

"Okay." I reached for my purse and hesitated, giving a wistful thought to Angie and my friends and the chick flick we had planned to see. But Gage looked so damn helpless, his big body folded on that hard sofa, his hair messed up like a little boy's. How did the heir to an enormous fortune, a successful businessman in his own right, not to mention a highly eligible bachelor, end up sick and alone in his five-million-dollar condo? I knew he had a thousand friends. Not to mention a girlfriend.

"Where's Dawnelle?" I couldn't resist asking.

"*Cosmo* shoot next week," he muttered. "Doesn't want to catch this stuff."

"I don't blame her. Whatever you've got doesn't look very fun."

A shadow of a smile crossed his dry lips. "Trust me. It's not."

The brief hint of a smile seemed to wedge into some unseen fissure of my heart and widen it. Suddenly my chest felt tight and very warm.

"You need to eat something," I said decisively, "even if it's just a piece of toast. Before rigor mortis sets in." I held up my finger like a stern schoolteacher as he began to say something. "I'll be back in fifteen or twenty minutes."

His mouth turned sullen. "I'm locking the door."

"I've got a key, remember? You can't keep me out." I slung my purse over my shoulder with a nonchalance that I knew would annoy him. "And while I'm gone—I'm trying to put this diplomatically, Gage—it might not be a bad thing if you took a shower."

CHAPTER 18

I called Angie in my car and apologized for bailing on her. "I was really looking forward to this," I said. "But Churchill's son is sick, and I need to run a few errands for him."

"Which son?"

"The oldest one. Gage. He's an asshole, but he's got the worst case of flu I've ever seen. And he's Churchill's favorite. So I've got no choice. I'm so sorry. I—"

"Way to go, Liberty!"

"Huh?"

"You're thinking like a sugar baby."

"I am?"

"Now you've got a Plan B in case your main sugar daddy dumps you. But be careful . . . you don't want to lose Daddy while you're reeling in the son."

"I'm not reeling anyone in," I protested. "This is simple compassion for a fellow human being. Believe me, he's not a Plan B."

"Sure he's not. Call me, sweetie, and let me know what happens."

"Nothing's going to happen," I said. "We can't stand each other."

"You lucky girl. That's the best kind of sex."

"He's half dead, Angie."

"Call me later," she repeated, and hung up.

In about forty-five minutes I returned to the condo with two bags of groceries. Gage was nowhere in sight. As I followed a trail of wadded-up tissues toward the bedroom, I heard the sounds of a shower running, and I grinned as I realized he had taken my suggestion. I went back to the kitchen, picking up tissues along the way, and deposited them in a garbage disposal that looked as if it had never been used. That was about to change. I took the groceries out of the bags, put about half of them away, and rinsed a three-pound chicken in the sink before setting it in a pot to boil.

Finding a cable news channel on TV, I turned up the volume so I could hear while I was cooking. I was making chicken and dumplings, the best cure I knew of. My version was pretty good, although nothing came close to Miss Marva's.

I made a hill of white flour on a cutting board. It felt like silk in my fingers. It seemed like forever since I'd cooked anything. I hadn't realized how much I had missed it. I pinched butter into the flour until it formed tender crumbs. After making a little well in the top of the mound, I broke open an egg and poured its gelatinous contents into the depression. I worked quickly with my fingers, mixing the way

Miss Marva had taught me. Most people use a fork, she had said, but something about the warmth of your hands made the dough better.

The only difficulty came when I hunted around the kitchen for a rolling pin and there was none to be found. I improvised with a cyndrilical highball glass, coating it with flour. It worked perfectly, creating a flat, even sheet that I cut into strips.

Seeing movement out of the corner of my eye, I glanced toward the hallway. Gage stood there looking baffled. He was wearing a fresh white tee and ancient gray sweatpants. His long feet were still bare. His hair, shiny as ribbons, was damp from a recent washing. He was so different from the starched, polished, and buttoned-up Gage I was accustomed to, I think I probably looked as bewildered as he did. For the first time I saw him as an approachable human being instead of some kind of übervillain.

"I didn't think you'd come back," he said.

"And miss my chance to boss you around?"

Gage kept staring at me as he lowered himself carefully to the sofa. He seemed enervated and unsteady.

I filled a glass with water and brought him two ibuprofen tablets. "Take these."

"I've already had Tylenol."

"If you alternate with ibuprofen every four hours, it'll bring the fever down faster."

He took the tablets and washed them down with a big gulp of water. "Where did you hear that?"

"Pediatrician. It's what they tell me every time Carrington has a fever." Noticing the goose bumps on his skin, I went to light the fireplace. A flip of a switch, and real flames spurted out from between sculpted ceramic logs. "More chills?" I asked sympathetically. "Do you have a lap blanket?"

"There's one in the bedroom. But I don't need—"

I was halfway down the hallway before he could finish.

His bedroom was decorated in the same minimalist style as the rest of the condo, the low platform bed covered in cream and navy, with two perfect pillows positioned against the gleaming wood-paneled wall. There was only one picture, an oil painting of a quiet ocean scene.

Finding an ivory cashmere throw on the floor, I brought it back to the living area along with a pillow. "Here you go," I said briskly, covering him with the blanket. I motioned for him to sit up, and I tucked the pillow behind his back. As I leaned over him, I heard a quick hitch in his breathing. I hesitated before pulling back. He smelled so good, so clean and male, and there was the same elusive scent I had noticed before, like amber, something warm and summery. It lured me so strongly that I found it difficult to move away from him. But the closeness was dangerous, it was causing something to unravel inside, something I wasn't ready for. And then the strangest thing happened . . . he deliberately turned his face so a loose lock of my hair slid against his cheek as I drew back.

"Sorry," I said breathlessly, although I didn't know what for.

He gave a brief shake of his head. I was caught by his gaze, those hypnotic light eyes with the charcoal rings around the irises. I touched his forehead with my hand, testing his temperature. Still too hot, a steady fire beneath the skin.

"So . . . you got something against throw pillows?" I asked, withdrawing my hand.

"I don't like clutter."

"Believe me, this is the most *un*cluttery place I've ever been in."

He glanced over my shoulder at the pot on the stove. "What are you making?"

"Chicken and dumplings."

"You're the first person who's ever cooked in that kitchen. Besides me."

"Really?" I reached up to my hair and refastened my ponytail, pulling back the stray pieces that had fallen around my face. "I didn't know you were handy in the kitchen."

One of his shoulders lifted in the barest twitch of a shrug. "I took a class with a girlfriend a couple of years ago. Part of couples counseling."

"You were engaged?"

"No, just going out. But when I wanted to break up, she wanted to try counseling first, and I thought why the hell not."

"So what did the therapist say?" I asked, amused.

"She suggested we find something we could learn together, like ballroom dancing or photography. We decided on fusion cuisine."

"What's that? It sounds like a science experiment."

"A mixture of cooking styles . . . Japanese, French, and Mexican. Like a saki-cilantro salad dressing."

"So did it help?" I asked. "With the girlfriend, I mean?"

Gage shook his head. "We broke up midway through the course. It turned out she hated cooking, and she decided I had an incurable fear of intimacy."

"Do you?"

"Not sure." His slow smile, the first real smile I'd ever gotten from him, caused my heart to thud heavily. "But I can make pan-seared scallops like nobody's business."

"You finished the course without her?"

"Hell, yes. I paid for it."

I laughed. "I have fear of intimacy too, according to my last boyfriend."

"Was he right?"

"Maybe. But I think if it's the right person, you wouldn't have to work so hard at intimacy. I think—hope—it would just happen naturally. Otherwise, opening up to the wrong person . . ." I made a face.

"Like putting ammo in their hands."

"Exactly." Reaching for the TV controller, I handed it to him. "ESPN?" I suggested, and headed back to the kitchen.

"No." Gage left it on the news channel and turned the volume down. "I'm too damn weak to get worked up over a game. The excitement would kill me."

I washed my hands and began to lay the dumpling strips on top of the simmering chicken broth. The air was filled with a homelike smell. Gage shifted on the sofa to watch me. Acutely conscious of his unbroken stare, I murmured, "Drink your water. You're dehydrated."

He obeyed, taking the glass in hand. "You shouldn't be here," he said. "Aren't you worried about catching the flu?"

"I never get sick. Besides, I have this compulsion to take care of ailing Travises."

"You would be the only one. We Travises are bad-tempered as hell when we're sick."

"You're not all that nice when you're well, either."

Gage drowned a grin in the glass of water. "You could open some wine," he said eventually.

"You can't drink when you're sick."

"That doesn't mean you can't." He set his water down and leaned his head against the back of the sofa.

"You're right. After all I'm doing for you, you definitely owe me a glass of wine. What goes with chicken soup?"

"A neutral white. Look in the wine refrigerator for a pinot blanc or a chardonnay."

Since I know nothing about wine, I usually choose according to the label design. I found a bottle of white with some delicate red flowers and French words, and poured myself a glass. Using a big spoon, I pushed the dumplings deeper into the pot and added another layer.

"Did you date him a long time?" I heard Gage ask. "Your last boyfriend."

"Nope." Now that the dumplings were all in, they needed to boil for a while. I walked back into the living area, holding my wine. "I never seem to date anyone for a long time. All my relationships are short and sweet. Well . . . short, anyway."

"Mine too."

I sat in a leather chair near the sofa. It was stylish but uncomfortable, shaped like a cube and encased in a polished chrome frame. "I guess that's bad, isn't it?"

He shook his head. "It shouldn't take a long time to figure out if someone is right for you. If it does, you're either dense or blind."

"Or maybe you're dating an armadillo."

Gage shot me a perplexed glance. "Pardon?"

"I mean someone who's hard to get to know. Shy and heavily armored."

"And ugly?"

"Armadillos aren't ugly," I protested, laughing.

"They're bulletproof lizards."

"I think you're an armadillo."

"I'm not shy."

"But you are heavily armored."

Gage considered that. He conceded the point with a brief nod. "Having learned about projection in couples counseling, I'd venture to say you're an armadillo too."

"What's projection?"

"It means you accuse me of the same things you're guilty of."

"Good Lord," I said, lifting the wineglass to my lips. "No wonder all your relationships are short."

His slow smile caused the fine hairs on my arms to rise. "Tell me why you broke up with your last boyfriend."

I wasn't nearly as heavily armored as I would have liked, because the truth immediately popped into my mind—*He was a sixty-eight*—and I certainly wasn't going to tell him that. I felt my cheeks heat up.

The problem with blushing is the harder you try to stop the worse it gets. So I sat there turning crimson as I tried to think of a nonchalant reply.

And Gage, damn him, seemed to look inside my head and read my thoughts. "Interesting," he said softly.

I scowled and stood up, gesturing with my wineglass. "Drink your water."

"Yes, ma'am."

I cleaned and straightened the kitchen, wishing he would change the channel and find a show. But he kept watching me as if he were fascinated by my technique as I sprayed Windex on the counters.

"By the way," he remarked conversationally, "I figured out you're not sleeping with my father."

"Good for you," I said. "What tipped you off?"

"The fact that he wants me to come over every morning to help him shower. If you were his girlfriend, you'd be in there with him."

The dumplings were ready. Unable to find a ladle, I used a measuring cup to transfer the soup into square-shaped bowls. It didn't look quite right, the wholesome chicken and dumplings in ultramod vessels. But it smelled delicious, and I knew this was one of my better efforts. Deducing that Gage was probably too fatigued to sit up at the dining table, I set his bowl on the beveled-glass coffee table. "It's a pain in the ass for you, going over every morning, isn't it?" I asked. "But you never complain."

"My pain is nothing compared to Dad's," he said. "Besides, I consider it payback. I was a pain in the ass to him when I was younger."

"I'll bet you were." I draped a dry dishtowel over his chest and tucked it into the neck of his tee as if he were an eight-year-old. My touch was impersonal, but as my knuckles brushed his skin I felt points of heat pulsing like fireflies in my stomach. I handed him a half-filled bowl and spoon, along with the advice, "Don't burn your tongue."

He spooned up a steaming dumpling and blew on it gently. "You never complain either," he said. "About having to be a parent to your little sister. And I'm guessing she must have been the reason for at least a few of those short relationships."

"Yes." I got my own bowl of soup. "It's nice, actually. It keeps me from wasting time with the wrong men. If a guy is scared by the responsibility, he's not right for us."

"But you've never known what it's like to be single and childless."

"I've never minded that."

"Really."

"Really. Carrington is . . . she's the best thing about me."

I might have said more, but Gage had downed a spoonful of dumplings and closed his eyes in an expression of what could have been either pain or ecstasy.

"What?" I asked. "Is it okay?"

He got busy with his spoon. "I may live," he said, "if only to have another bowl of this stuff."

Two helpings of chicken and dumplings seemed to bring Gage to life, his waxen paleness replaced by a tinge of color. "My God," he said, "this is amazing. You wouldn't believe how much better I feel."

"Don't push it. You still need to rest." I put all the dishes into the washer and ladled what was left of the soup into a container for the fridge.

"I need more of that," he said. "I have to stock a few gallons in the freezer."

I was tempted to tell him any time he wanted to bribe me with another glass of neutral white wine, I'd be happy to make more soup. But that sounded too much like a proposition, which was the last thing on my mind. Now that Gage no longer looked so glazed and listless, I knew he would soon be back to his old self. There was no guarantee the truce between us was going to last. So I gave him a noncommittal smile.

"It's late," I said. "I've got to head back."

A frown worked across Gage's forehead. "It's midnight. It's not safe for you to be out this late. Not in Houston. Especially not in that rust bucket you drive."

"My car works fine."

"Stay here. There's an extra bedroom."

I let out a surprised laugh. "You're kidding, right?"

Gage looked annoyed. "No, I'm not kidding."

"I appreciate your concern, but I've driven my rust bucket through Houston many times, much later than this. And I've got my cell phone." I walked over to him and reached out to his forehead. It was cool and slightly damp. "No more fever," I said with satisfaction. "It's time for another dose of Tylenol. You'd better take it just to be sure." I made a motion for him to stay on the sofa as he started to rise. "Rest," I said. "I'll see myself out."

Gage ignored that and followed me to the door, reaching it at the same time I did. I saw his hand press flat against the door panel. His forearm was densely muscled and dusted with hair. It was an aggressive gesture, but as I turned to face him, I was reassured by the subtle entreaty in his eyes.

"Cowboy," I said, "you're in no condition to stop me from doing a damn thing. I could wrestle you to the floor in ten seconds flat."

He continued to lean over me. His voice was very soft. "Try me."

I let out a nervous laugh. "I wouldn't want to hurt you. Let me go, Gage."

A moment of electric stillness. I saw the ripple of a swallow in his throat. "You couldn't hurt me."

He wasn't touching me, but I was excruciatingly aware of his body, the heat and solidity of him. And suddenly I knew how it would be if we slept together . . . the rise of my hips against his weight, the hardness of his back beneath my hands. I flushed as I felt a responsive twitch between my thighs, soft-secreted nerves prickling, a shot of heat to the quick.

"Please," I whispered, and was infinitely relieved when he pushed away from the door and stood back to let me pass.

Gage waited in the doorway a little too long as I left. It might have been my imagination, but as I reached the elevator and glanced back, he seemed bereft, as if I had just taken something from him.

It was a relief to everyone, especially Jack, when Gage was able to resume his usual schedule. He showed up at the house on Monday morning, looking so well that Churchill happily accused him of faking his illness.

I hadn't mentioned having stayed with Gage for most of Saturday evening. It was best, I had decided, to let everyone assume I had gone out with my friends as planned. I realized Gage hadn't said anything about it either—if he had, there would have been a comment from Churchill. It made me uneasy, this small secret between Gage and me, even though nothing had happened.

But something had changed. Instead of treating me with his usual reserve, Gage went out of his way to be helpful, fixing my laptop when it froze, taking Churchill's empty breakfast tray downstairs before I could do it. And it seemed to me that he was coming to the house more frequently, dropping by at odd times, always on the pretext of checking on Churchill.

I tried to treat his visits casually, but I couldn't deny that time moved faster when Gage was around, and everything seemed a little more interesting. He wasn't a man you could fit into a neat category. The family, with typically Texan distrust of highbrow pursuits, affectionately mocked him for having more of an intellectual bent than the rest of them.

But Gage had been aptly named after his mother's family, the de-
scendants of warlike Scotch-Irish borderers. According to Gretchen,
who had made a hobby of researching the family genealogy, the
Gages' dour self-reliance and toughness had made them perfect can-
didates to settle the Texas frontier. Isolation, hardship, danger—they
had welcomed all of it, their natures practically demanded it. At
times you could see the echoes of those fiercely disciplined immi-
grants in Gage.

Jack and Joe were far more easygoing and charming, both possessing a boyishness that was completely absent in their older brother.
And then there was Haven, the daughter, whom I met when she came
home on break from school. She was a slim black-haired girl with
Churchill's dark eyes, possessing all the subtlety of a firecracker. She
announced to her father and anyone else in earshot that she had become a second-wave feminist, she had changed her major to women's
studies, and she would no longer tolerate Texas's culture of patriar-
chal repression. She talked so fast I had a hard time following her,
especially when she pulled me aside to express sympathy for the ex-
ploitation and disenfranchisement of my people, and assured me of
her passionate support for the reformation of immigration policies
and guest worker programs. Before I could think of how to reply, she
had bounced away and launched into an enthusiastic argument with
Churchill.

"Don't mind Haven," Gage had said dryly, watching his sister
with a faint smile. "She's never met a cause she didn't like. It was the
biggest disappointment of her life not to be disenfranchised."

Gage was different from his siblings. He worked too hard and
challenged himself compulsively, and seemed to hold nearly everyone
outside his family at arm's length. But he had begun to treat me with
a careful friendliness I couldn't help responding to. And there was his
increasing kindness to my sister. It started in small ways. He fixed the

broken chain of Carrington's pink two-wheeler, and drove her to school one morning when I was running late.

Then there was the bug project. Carrington's class had been studying insects, and every child was required to write a report on a particular bug and make a 3D model. Carrington had decided on a lightning bug. I took Carrington to Hobby Lobby, where we spent forty dollars on paint, Styrofoam, plaster of Paris, and pipe cleaners. I didn't say one word about the cost—my competitive sister was determined to make the best bug in the class, and I had resolved to do whatever was necessary to help.

We made the body of the bug and covered it with wet plaster strips, and painted it black, red, and yellow when it was dry. The entire kitchen had been turned into a disaster zone in the process. The bug was a handsome creation, but to Carrington's disappointment, the glow in the dark paint we had used for the bug's underside was not nearly as effective as we had hoped. It didn't glow hardly at all, Carrington had said glumly, and I had promised to try to find a better quality paint so we could apply another coat.

After spending an afternoon typing a chapter of Churchill's manuscript, I was surprised to discover Gage sitting with my sister in the kitchen, the table piled with tools, wires, small pieces of wood, batteries, glue, a ruler. Cradling the lightning bug model in one hand, he made deep cuts with an X-Acto knife.

"What are you doing?"

Two heads lifted, one dark, one platinum. "Just performing a little surgery," Gage said, deftly extracting a rectangular chunk of foam.

Carrington's eyes were lit with excitement. "He's putting a *real* light inside our bug, Liberty! We're making a 'lectrical circuit with wires and a switch, and when you flip it the lightning bug's going to flash."

"Oh." Nonplussed, I sat at the table. I always appreciated help whenever it was given. But I had never expected Gage, of all people, to get involved in our project. I didn't know whether he'd been recruited by Carrington or if he'd offered on his own, and I wasn't certain why it made me uneasy to see them working together so companionably.

Patiently Gage showed Carrington how to make the wired circuit, how to hold the screwdriver and twist it. He held the pieces of a little switch box together as she glued it. Carrington glowed at his quiet praise, her small face animated as they worked together. Unfortunately the added weight of the bulb and wiring caused the pipe cleaner legs to collapse beneath the model. I had to bite back a sudden grin as Gage and Carrington contemplated the prostrate insect.

"It's a lightning bug with sleep inertia," Carrington said, and the three of us snorted with laughter.

It took Gage another half hour to reinforce the bug's legs with clothes hanger wire. After setting the finished project in the middle of the kitchen table, he turned the kitchen lights off. "All right, Carrington," he said. "Let's give it a test run."

Eagerly Carrington picked up the small wired box and flipped the switch. She crowed in triumph as the lightning bug began to flash in a steady repeated pattern. "Oh, it's so *cool*, look, look at my bug, Liberty!"

"It's great," I said, grinning as I saw how elated she was.

"High five," Gage said to Carrington, holding up his hand.

But to his astonishment, and mine, Carrington ignored the high five. Instead, she threw herself at him and wrapped her arms around his waist.

"You're the best," she said against his shirtfront. "Thanks, Gage."

He didn't move for a second, just looked down at Carrington's small blond head. And then his arms went around her. As she grinned up at him, still hanging around his waist, he ruffled her hair gently. "You did most of the work, shorty. I just helped a little."

I stood outside the moment, marveling at how easily the connection between them had been formed. Carrington had always gotten along with grandfatherly men like Mr. Ferguson or Churchill, but she'd been standoffish with the ones I had dated. I couldn't fathom why she had taken to Gage.

She couldn't become attached to him, when there was no chance of him becoming a permanent fixture in her life. It would only lead to disappointment, even heartbreak, and her heart was too precious for me to let that happen.

When Gage thought to glance at me with a quizzical smile, I couldn't smile back. I turned away on the pretext of cleaning up the kitchen, picking up bits of wire with fingers that clenched until they whitened at the tips.

CHAPTER 19

Churchill told me about strategic inflection points while we wrote the "Why Paranoia Is Good," chapter of his book. A strategic inflection point, he explained, is a huge turning point in the life of a company, a technological advancement or opportunity that changes the way everything is done. Like the breakup of Bell in 1984, or when Apple came out with the iPod. It can boost a business into the stratosphere or sink it beyond any hope of recovery. But no matter what the results are, the rules of the game are changed forever.

The strategic inflection point in my relationship with Gage happened the weekend after Carrington had turned in the lightning bug project. It was late Sunday morning, and Carrington had gone outside to play while I took a long shower. It was a cold day with hard stinging gusts. The flatlands near Houston offered no obstructions, not even a few lonely mesquite trees to hook the hem of the sky, and the long open fetch gave the wind plenty of room to collect momentum.

I dressed in a long-sleeved tee and jeans, and a heavy wool cardigan with a hood. Although I usually flat-ironed my hair to make it shiny and straight, I didn't bother that day, letting it curl crazily over my shoulders and back.

I crossed through the visiting room with its towering ceilings, where Gretchen was busy directing a team of professional Christmas decorators. Angels was the theme she had picked that year, obliging the decorators to perch on high ladders to hang cherubs and seraphim and swags of gold cloth. Christmas music played in the background, Dean Martin singing "Baby, It's Cold Outside" with finger-snapping panache.

My feet bounced to the music as I went outside to the back. I heard Churchill's scuffly laugh, and Carrington squealing in glee. Pulling my hood up, I wandered toward the sounds.

Churchill's wheelchair was at the corner of the patio, facing an incline at the north side of the garden. I stopped short as I saw my sister standing at the end of a zip line, a cable that had been mounted on the incline and hung with a pulley that slid from the higher end to the lower one.

Gage, dressed in jeans and an ancient blue sweatshirt, was tightening the end of the line while Carrington urged him to hurry. "Hold your horses," he told her, grinning at her impatience. "Let me make sure the line will hold you."

"I'm doing it now," she said in determination, grasping the pulley handle.

"Wait," Gage cautioned, giving the cable an experimental yank.

"I can't wait!"

He started laughing. "All right, then. Don't blame me if you fall."

The line was too high, I saw with a jolt of terror. If the line broke, if Carrington couldn't hold on, she would break her neck. "No," I cried out, starting forward. "Carrington, don't!"

She looked toward me with a grin. "Hey, Liberty, watch me! I'm going to fly."

"Wait!"

But she ignored me, the obstinate little mule, grasping the pulley and pushing off the incline. Her slight body sped above the ground, too high, too fast, the legs of her jeans flapping. She let out a shriek of enjoyment. My vision blurred for a moment, my teeth clenching on a pained sound. I half staggered, half ran, reaching Gage almost at the same time she did.

He caught her easily, plucking her from the pulley and swinging her to the ground. The two of them laughed, whooped, neither noticing my approach.

I heard Churchill calling my name from the patio, but I didn't answer him.

"I told you to wait," I shouted at Carrington, dizzy with relief and rage, the remnants of fear still rattling in my throat. She fell silent and blanched, staring at me with round blue eyes.

"I didn't hear you," she said. It was a lie, and we both knew it. I was infuriated as I saw the way she sidled up next to Gage as if seeking his protection. From me.

"Yes you did! And don't think you're going to get off easy, Carrington. I'm ready to ground you for life." I turned on Gage. "That . . . that stupid *thing* is too damn high off the ground! And you have no right to let her try something dangerous without asking me first."

"It's not dangerous," Gage said calmly, his gaze steady on mine. "We had a zip line exactly like this when we were kids."

"I bet you fell off it," I shot back. "I bet you got banged up plenty."

"Sure we did. And we lived to tell about it."

My outrage, salt-flavored and primal, thickened with each second that passed. "You arrogant *jerk*, you don't know anything about eight-year-old girls! She's fragile, she could break her neck—"

"I'm not fragile!" Carrington said indignantly, huddling closer to Gage's side until he put a hand on her shoulder.

"You're not even wearing your helmet. You know better than to do something like this without it."

Gage's face was expressionless. "You want me to take the line down?"

"*No!*" Carrington shouted at me, tears springing to her eyes. "You never let me have any fun. You're not fair. I'm going to play on the zip line and you can't tell me not to. You're not my mom!"

"Hey, hey . . . shorty." Gage's voice had gentled. "Don't talk to your sister like that."

"Great," I snapped. "Now I'm the bad guy. Screw you, Gage. I don't need you to defend me, you—" I raised my hands in a defensive gesture, wrists stiff. A cold wind struck me in the face, needling the inner corners of my eyes, and I realized I was about to cry. I looked at the two of them standing together, and I heard Churchill call my name.

Me against the three of them.

I turned away abruptly, hardly able to see through the bitter slick of tears. Time to retreat. I walked with fast, digging strides. As I passed the man in the wheelchair, I growled, "You're in trouble too, Churchill," without breaking pace.

By the time I reached the warm sanctuary of the kitchen, I was cold to the bone. I sought out the darkest, most sheltered part of the kitchen, the narrow recessed niche of the butler's pantry. The space was lined with glass-fronted china cabinets. I didn't stop until I was hidden at the back of it. I wrapped my arms around myself, shrinking, trying to take up as little physical space as possible.

Every instinct screamed that Carrington was mine, and no one had the right to dispute my judgments. I had taken care of her, sacrificed for her. *You're not my mom.* Ingrate! Traitor! I wanted to stomp outside and tell her how easy it would have been for me to give her away after Mama died, how much better off I might have been. *Mama . . .* oh, I wished I could take back all the hateful things my teenage self had said to her. Now I understood the injustice of parenting. Try to keep them healthy and safe, and you got blame instead of gratitude, rebellion instead of cooperation.

Someone came into the kitchen. I heard the door close. I held still, praying I wouldn't have to talk to anyone. But a dark shadow moved through the unlit kitchen, too substantial to belong to anyone other than Gage.

"Liberty?"

After that I couldn't remain hiding in silence. "I don't want to talk," I said sullenly.

Gage filled the narrow entrance of the butler's pantry. Cornering me. The shadows were so thick, I couldn't see his face.

And then he said the one thing I would never have expected him to say.

"I'm sorry."

Anything else would have bolstered my anger. But those two words caused tears to spill over the wind-stung rims of my eyes. I ducked my head and let out a shuddery sigh. "It's fine. Where's Carrington?"

"Dad's talking to her." Gage came to me in a couple of measured strides. "You were right. About everything. I told Carrington she has to wear a helmet from now on. And I just lowered the line a couple feet." A short pause. "I should have asked you before putting it up. It won't happen again."

He had an absolute gift for surprising me. I would have thought he'd be scathing, argumentative. The tightness left my throat. I lifted my head, the darkness thinning until I could see the outline of his head. The scent of outdoors clung to him, wind laced with ozone, dry grass, something sweet like freshly cut wood.

"I'm overprotective," I said.

"Of course you are," Gage said reasonably. "That's your job. If you weren't—" He broke off with a sharp indrawn breath as he saw a glitter of moisture on my cheek. "Shit. No, no, don't do that." He turned to a set of drawers in the pantry, fumbled until he found a pressed napkin. "Damn it, Liberty, don't. I'm sorry. I'm so sorry I put up that fucking zip line. I'll take it down right away." Gage, usually so deft, was unaccountably clumsy as he blotted my cheeks with the soft folded linen.

"No," I said, sniffling, "I want the line to s-stay up."

"Okay. Okay. Whatever you want. Anything. Just don't cry."

I took the napkin from him and blew my nose and sighed shakily. "I'm sorry I exploded out there. I shouldn't have overreacted."

He hovered, paused, shifted like a restless animal in a cage. "You spend half your life taking care of her, protecting her, and then one day some asshole is shooting her across the yard on a line five feet off the ground with no helmet. Of course you'd be pissed."

"It's just . . . she's all I've got. And if anything ever happened to her—" My throat constricted but I forced myself to continue. "I've known for a long time that Carrington needs a man's influence in her life, but I don't want her to get involved with you and Churchill because this won't last forever, us being here, and that's why—"

"You're afraid for Carrington to get involved," he repeated slowly.

"Emotionally involved, yes. She'll have a hard time when we leave. I . . . I think this was a mistake."

"What was?"

"Everything. All of this. I shouldn't have taken Churchill's offer. We never should have moved here."

Gage was silent. A trick of the light made his eyes gleam as if with their own illumination.

"What?" I asked defensively. "Why aren't you saying anything?"

"We'll talk about it later."

"We can talk about it now. What are you thinking?"

"That you're projecting again."

"About what?"

I stiffened as he reached for me. My thoughts scattered as I felt his hands, the heat of male skin. His legs bracketed mine, the muscles hard beneath thin worn denim. I gasped a little as his hand slid around my neck. His thumb made a slow pass at the side of my throat, and the light stroke aroused me shamefully.

Gage spoke against my hair, the words sinking to my scalp. "Don't pretend this is all about Carrington. You're worried about your own damned emotional involvement."

"Am not," I protested through dry lips.

He eased my head back, bent over me. A mocking whisper tickled my ear. "You're so full of it, darlin'."

He was right. I had been so naïve to think that somehow we were going to visit the Travises' world like a pair of tourists, participating without becoming involved. But somehow connections had been formed, my heart had found purchase in unexpected places. I was involved more than I had ever dreamed possible.

I began to tremble. There was a low tightening in my stomach as Gage's mouth wandered to the edge of my jaw, the corner of my lips. I backed away from him until my shoulders came up hard against the cabinets, causing a delicate rattle of china and crystal. Gage's supporting arm forced an arch at the small of my back. With every breath I took, my chest lifted against his.

"Liberty . . . let me. Let me . . ."

I couldn't talk or move, just waited helplessly as his mouth eased over mine.

I closed my eyes, opening to the taste of him, to slow kisses that explored without demand, while his hand moved to cradle the side of my face. Disarmed by his gentleness, I let my body relax against his. He searched more deeply, nudging, caressing, still with that maddening restraint, until my heart was pumping as if I'd run a marathon.

Closing his hand in the heavy mass of my hair, he held it aside and kissed my neck, taking forever to work his way up to the hollow behind my ear. By the time he had reached it, I was twisting to get closer to him, my fingers gripping the unyielding surface of his upper arms. With a murmur, he took my wrists and drew them around his shoulders. I wobbled on my sneakered toes, straining in every muscle.

He held me firmly, anchoring me against the hard framework of his body, and took my mouth again. This time his kisses were longer, grinding, wet, deeply consuming, and I couldn't catch my breath. I molded all my weight against him until there wasn't a millimeter of space between us. He kissed me as if he were already inside me, greedy kisses with teeth, tongue, lips, kisses of unbearable sweetness that made me want to pass out but instead I clung to his body and moaned into his mouth. His hands slid to my bottom, cupped me snugly against a hard jutting pressure that felt like nothing else in the world, and the desire turned into madness. I wanted him to bear me down to the floor, I wanted him to do anything, everything. His mouth ate at mine, licked deep, and every thought and impulse dissolved into a hum of white noise, raw pleasure rising to the top of my skull.

His hand slipped beneath the hem of my shirt, finding the skin of my back, which was flushed and tender as if I'd been scalded. The cool brush of his fingers was an unspeakable relief. I arched in frantic welcome, while his hand spread like an unfolding fan, traveling up my spine.

The kitchen door burst open.

We sprang apart, and I lurched a few feet away from Gage, throbbing in every part of my body. I fumbled with my shirt, trying to pull it into place. Gage stayed at the back of the pantry, arms braced on the cabinets, head lowered. I saw the muscles bunch beneath his clothes. His body was rigid with frustration; it came off him in waves. I was shocked by my response to him, the pure erotic burn of it.

I heard Carrington's uncertain voice. "Liberty, are you back there?"

I emerged hastily. "Yeah. I was just . . . I needed some privacy . . ."

I went to the far end of the kitchen where my sister was standing. Her small face was tense and anxious, her hair comically wild like a troll doll's. She looked as if she were going to cry. "Liberty . . ."

When you love a child, you forgive her before she can even ask. Basically you've already forgiven her for things she hasn't even done yet. "It's okay," I murmured, reaching for her. "It's okay, baby."

Carrington rushed forward, her skinny arms closing tight around me. "I'm sorry," she said tearfully. "I didn't mean the stuff I said, any of it—"

"I know."

"I just w-wanted to have fun."

" 'Course you did." I folded her in the strongest, warmest embrace I could, pressing my cheek to the top of her head. "But it's my job to make sure you have as little fun as possible." We both chuckled and hugged for a long moment. "Carrington . . . I'm going to try not to be a wet blanket all the time. It's just that you're getting to the age when most of the things you want to do for fun will also be the things that drive me crazy worrying about you."

"I'll do everything you tell me to," Carrington said, a little too quickly.

I smiled. "God. I'm not asking for blind obedience. But we have to find ways of compromising when we disagree on something. You know what compromise is, right?"

"Uh-huh. It's when you don't get to have everything your way and I don't get to have everything my way, and no one's happy. Like when Gage lowered the zip line."

I laughed. "That's right." Being reminded of the zip line, I glanced in the direction of the butler's pantry. From what I could tell it was empty. Gage had left the kitchen without a sound. I had no idea what I was going to say to him the next time I saw him. The way he had kissed me, my response . . .

Some things you're better off not knowing.

"What did you and Churchill talk about?" I asked.

"How did you know Churchill and me were talking?"

"And I," I corrected, thinking fast. "Well, I thought he'd say something to you, since he always has an opinion about things. And since you didn't come inside right away, I assumed you two were having a conversation."

"We were. He said I should know that being a parent isn't near as easy as it looks, and even though you aren't my actual mom, you're the best stand-in he's ever seen."

"He said that?" I was flattered and pleased.

"And," Carrington continued, "he said I shouldn't take you for granted, because lots of girls your age would've put me in foster care when Mama died." She laid her head on my chest. "Did you think about doing that, Liberty?"

"Never," I said firmly. "Not for one second. I loved you too much to give you up. I want you in my life forever." I bent and snuggled her close.

"Liberty?" she asked, her voice muffled.

"Yes, baby?"

"What were you and Gage doing in the butler's pantry?"

I jerked my head back, looking, I was sure, as guilty as hell. "You saw him?"

Carrington nodded innocently. "He left the kitchen a minute ago. It looked like he was sneaking out."

"I—I think he was trying to give us some privacy," I said unsteadily.

"Were you arguing with him about the zip line?"

"Oh, we were just chatting. That's all. Just a chat." Blindly I headed for the refrigerator. "I'm hungry. Let's have a snack."

Gage disappeared for the rest of the day, having suddenly remembered a few urgent errands that would occupy him indefinitely. I was relieved. I needed some time to think about what had happened and how I was going to react to it.

According to Churchill's book, the best way to deal with a strategic inflection point is to move quickly past denial into acceptance of change, and plan your strategy for the future. After considering everything carefully, I decided the kiss with Gage had been a moment of insanity, and he probably regretted it. Therefore, the best strategy was to pretend nothing had happened. I was going to be calm, relaxed, and impersonal.

I was so determined to show Gage how unaffected I had been by the whole thing, to amaze him with my cool sophistication, that it was a letdown when Jack arrived in the morning. Balefully Jack said Gage had given him no advance notice, just called him at the crack of dawn and said to get his ass over to help Dad, he couldn't make it.

"What's so all-fired important he couldn't be bothered to come over here?" Churchill asked testily. As much as Jack didn't want to be there helping him, Churchill didn't want him there even more.

"He's flying up to New York to visit Dawnelle," Jack said. "He's going to take her out after the shoot at Demarchelier."

"Just took off with no notice?" Churchill scowled until his forehead was starred with tiny indentations. "Why the hell's he doing that? He was supposed to meet with the Canadians from Syncrude today." Churchill's eyes narrowed dangerously. "He better not have taken the Gulfstream without one damn word of advance notice or I'll fry his—"

"He didn't take the Gulfstream."

The information mollified Churchill. "Good. Because I told him the last time—"

"He took the Citation," Jack said.

While Churchill growled and reached for his cell phone, I carried the breakfast tray downstairs. It was ridiculous, but the news that Gage had gone to New York to be with his girlfriend had hit me like a gut punch. A great smothering dullness settled over me as I thought of Gage with beautiful whippet-framed Dawnelle, she of the straight blond hair and big perfume contract. Of course he would go to her. I was nothing to him but a momentary impulse. A whim. A mistake.

I was brimming with jealousy, sick with it, over the worst person I could have picked to be jealous of. I couldn't believe it. *Stupid,* I told myself angrily, *stupid, stupid.* But knowing that didn't seem to make things any better.

For the rest of the day I made violent resolutions and promises to myself. I tried to drive thoughts of Gage out of my mind by dwelling on the subject of Hardy, the love of my life, who had meant more to me than Gage Travis ever would . . . Hardy, who was sexy, charming, unreserved, as opposed to Gage, the arrogant, annoying asshole.

But even thinking about Hardy didn't work. So I concentrated on fanning the flames of Churchill's temper by mentioning Gage and the Citation at every possible opportunity. I hoped Churchill would descend on his oldest son like a plague of Egypt.

To my disappointment, Churchill's temper vanished after they talked on the phone. "New development in the works with Dawnelle,"

Churchill reported complacently. I wouldn't have believed it possible, but my mood plummeted further. That could mean only one thing—Gage was asking her to move in with him. Maybe he was even proposing to her.

After working all day and helping Carrington practice her soccer moves outside, I was exhausted. More than that, I was depressed. I was never going to find anyone. I was going to spend the rest of my life sleeping single in a double bed until I was a cranky old woman who did nothing but water the plants, talk about the neighbors, and take care of her ten cats.

I soaked in a long bath, which Carrington had garnished with Barbie bath suds that smelled like bubble gum. Afterward I dragged myself to bed and lay there with my eyes open.

The next day I woke up in a sullen simmer, as if sleep had catalyzed my depression into a general state of pissed-offedness. Churchill raised his brows as I informed him that I didn't feel like running up and down the stairs all day, so I'd appreciate it if he would consolidate his requests into one list. Among the various items was a note to call a newly opened restaurant and make reservations for eight. "One of my friends made a big investment in the place," Churchill told me. "I'm taking the family to eat there tonight. Make sure you and Carrington put on something nice."

"Carrington and I aren't going."

"Yes you are." He counted the guests on his fingers. "It's going to be you two girls, Gretchen, Jack and his girlfriend, Vivian and me, and Gage."

So Gage would be back from New York by tonight. My insides felt as if they'd been coated with lead.

"What about Dawnelle?" I asked curtly. "Is she coming?"

"I don't know. Better make it a party of nine. Just in case."

If Dawnelle was there . . . if the two of them were engaged . . . I was pretty sure I couldn't get through the evening.

"It's going to be a party of seven," I said. "Carrington and I aren't family, so we're not going."

"Yes you are," Churchill said flatly.

"It's a school night. Carrington can't stay out late."

"Make reservations for an early dinner, then."

"You're asking too much," I snapped.

"What the hell am I paying you for, Liberty?" Churchill asked without rancor.

"You're paying me to work for you, not to have dinner with the family."

He met my gaze without blinking. "I aim to talk about work during dinner. Bring your notepad."

CHAPTER 20

I had seldom dreaded anything the way I did that dinner. I fretted about it all day. By five o'clock my stomach felt like it was filled with cement, and I was sure I wasn't going to be able to eat anything.

Pride, however, compelled me to pull out my best dress, a red wool knit with long sleeves and a vee neck that exposed a hint of cleavage. It clung lightly from chest to hips and fell in a gently flared skirt. I spent at least forty-five minutes flat ironing my hair until it was perfectly straight. A careful application of smoky-gray eyeshadow, a slick of sparkly neutral lip gloss, and I was ready to go. Despite my moroseness, I knew I'd never looked better in my life.

I went to my sister's room and discovered the door was locked. "Carrington," I called. "It's six o'clock. Time to go. Come out of there."

Her voice was muffled. "I need another few minutes."

"Carrington, hurry," I said with a touch of exasperation. "Let me in there and I'll help you—"

"I can do it by myself."

"I want you downstairs in the family room, in five minutes."

"Okay!"

Sighing heavily, I went to the elevator. Usually I took the stairs, but not when I was wearing three-inch heels. The house was strangely quiet except for the staccato of my metallic slides across marble flooring, clicks softening on hardwood, disappearing in the pile of wool carpeting.

The family room was empty, a fire winking and snapping in the fireplace. Perplexed, I went to the wet bar and sorted through decanters and bottles. I figured since I wasn't driving, and Churchill was forcing me to go out with the family, he owed me a drink. I poured some cola into a glass, added a shot of Zaya rum, and stirred it with my forefinger. As I took a medicinal gulp, the cold liquid slid down my throat with a sparkling burn. Maybe I'd added a little too much Zaya.

It was my misfortune to turn and catch sight of Gage entering the room while I was still in mid-swallow. I struggled for a second to keep from spewing the drink. After managing to force it down, I started to cough violently, setting aside the glass.

Gage was at my side in an instant. "Went down the wrong way?" he asked sympathetically, rubbing circles on my back.

I nodded and continued to cough, my eyes watering.

He looked concerned and amused. "My fault. I didn't mean to

surprise you." His hand lingered on my back, which did nothing to restore my breathing.

I noticed two things right away—first, Gage was alone, and second, he was outrageously sexy in a black cashmere turtleneck and gray pants and black Prada loafers.

The last cough sputtered away, and I found myself staring helplessly into light crystalline eyes. "Hi," I said lamely.

A smile touched his lips. "Hi."

I was filled with dangerous heat, standing there with Gage. I felt happy just being near him, and miserable for any number of reasons, and humiliated by the desire to throw myself at him, and the turmoil of feeling all those things at once was almost more than I could stand. "Is . . . is Dawnelle with you?"

"No." Gage looked as if he wanted to say more, but he checked himself and glanced around the empty room. "Where is everyone?"

"I don't know. I thought Churchill said six o'clock."

His smile turned wry. "I have no idea why he was so damned impatient to get everyone together tonight. The only reason I came was because I hoped you and I might find a few minutes to talk afterward." A brief pause, and he added, "Alone."

A nervous shiver went down my back. "Okay."

"You look beautiful," Gage said. "But then you always do." He continued before I could respond. "I got a call from Jack on the way over here. He can't make it tonight."

"I hope he's not sick." I tried to sound concerned, when at the moment I couldn't have cared less about Jack.

"No, he's fine. His girlfriend just surprised him with tickets to a Coldplay concert."

"Jack hates Coldplay," I said, having heard him make comments to that effect.

"Yes. But he likes sleeping with his girlfriend."

We both turned as Gretchen and Carrington entered the room.

Gretchen was dressed in a lavender bouclé skirt, a matching silk blouse, and a Hermès scarf knotted around her neck. To my dismay, Carrington was wearing jeans and a pink sweater.

"Carrington," I asked, "you're not dressed yet? I laid out your blue skirt and your—"

"Can't go," my sister said cheerfully. "Got too much homework. So I'm going with Aunt Gretchen to her book club meeting, and I'll do it there."

Gretchen looked regretful. "I just remembered my book club meeting. I can't miss it. The girls are very strict about attendance. Two unexcused absences, and—" She drew her coral-manicured finger across her neck.

"They sound ruthless," I said.

"Oh, honey, you can't imagine. Once you're out, you're out for good. And then I'd have to find something else to do Tuesday nights, and the only thing going on besides the book club is Bunko Group." She looked at Gage apologetically. "You know how I hate Bunko."

"No I didn't."

"Bunko makes you fat," she informed him. "All that snacking. And at my age—"

"Where's Dad?" Gage interrupted.

Carrington answered innocently. "Uncle Churchill said to tell you his leg is bothering him so he's going to stay in tonight and watch a movie with his friend Vivian when she gets here."

"But since you two are dressed up so nice," Gretchen said, "you go on without us and have a good time."

They disappeared like a vaudeville act, leaving us standing there in bemusement.

It was a conspiracy.

Stunned and mortified, I turned to Gage. "I had nothing to do with this, I swear—"

"I know. I know." He looked exasperated, and then he laughed. "As you can see, my family doesn't give a crap about subtlety."

The sight of one of his rare grins sent a rush of delight through me. "There's no need to take me to dinner," I said. "You must be tired after your trip to New York. And I'm guessing Dawnelle wouldn't be too happy about the idea of us going out."

His amusement faded. "Actually . . . Dawnelle and I broke up yesterday."

I thought I hadn't heard right. I was afraid to assume anything from that spare handful of words. I felt my pulse jumping beneath my skin, in my cheeks and throat and the insides of my arms. No doubt I looked pitifully confused, but Gage said nothing else, only waited for me to respond.

"I'm sorry," I eventually managed. "Is that why you went to New York? To . . . to break up with her?"

Gage nodded, tucking a loose strand of hair behind my ear, letting his thumb touch the edge of my jaw. My face burned. I stood tensely, knowing if I relaxed even one muscle, I would wilt entirely. "I realized," he said, "if I'd become so obsessed with a woman I couldn't sleep at night, thinking about her . . . it didn't make sense for me to be going out with someone else, did it?"

I couldn't have said a word to save my life. My gaze fell to his shoulder, and I was overcome with the longing to rest my head against it. His hand played in my hair with electrifying lightness.

"So . . . do we go along with the setup?" I heard him ask after a moment.

I brought myself to look up at him. He was gorgeous. The fire shed hot colors across his skin and lit tiny rushlights in his eyes. The angles of his face were thrown into sharp relief. He needed a haircut. The thick black locks were starting to curl over the tips of his ears and the back of his neck. I remembered the feel of it in my fingers, like coarse silk, and I ached with the desire to touch his head, tug it down to mine. What was his question? Oh, yes . . . the setup. "I'd hate to give them the satisfaction," I said, and he smiled.

"You're right. On the other hand . . . we do have to eat." His gaze swept down my body. "And you're too pretty to stay home tonight." He settled a hand at the small of my back, pressed gently. "Let's get out of here."

His car was parked in the front drive. It was typical of Gage to drive a Maybach. It's a car for rich people who don't like to flaunt it, which is why you don't see many Maybachs in Houston. For about three hundred thousand dollars you get an exterior so understated that parking lot attendants rarely put it in the front along with the BMWs or Lexuses. The interior is fitted with glove leather and glossy amboyna hardwood carried out of an Indonesian jungle on the backs of elephants. Not to mention two video screens, two champagne flute holders, and a built-in minirefrigerator designed to hold a split of Cristal. And all of it can go from zero to sixty in less than five seconds.

Gage helped me into the low-slung car and reached in to buckle my seat belt. I relaxed into the seat, breathing in the smell of polished leather and staring at a front dash that resembled the interior of a small aircraft. The Maybach purred as we pulled away from the house.

Driving with one hand, Gage picked something up from the center console. He held up a cell phone and gave me a brief glance. "All right if I make a quick call?"

"Of course."

We went past the front gate. I looked at the mansions we passed, the bright yellow rectangles of windows, the sight of a couple walking a dog along the quiet street. Just an ordinary night for some people . . . whereas for others, unimaginable things were happening.

Gage speed-dialed a number, and someone picked up the line. He spoke into the phone without even saying hello. "You know, Dad, I just got back from New York two hours ago. I haven't even had time to unpack my luggage. This may be a shocker, but I don't always do things according to your timetable."

A reply from Churchill.

"Yeah," Gage said, "I got that. But I'm warning you—from now on take care of your own damn love life and don't mess with mine." He closed the cell phone with a snap. "Old geezer," he muttered.

"He meddles with everyone," I said, breathless at the implication that I was part of his love life. "It's his way of showing affection."

Gage gave me a sardonic glance. "No kidding."

A thought occurred to me. "Did he know you were going to break up with Dawnelle?"

"Yes, I told him."

Churchill had known, and he hadn't said a word to me. I wanted to kill him. "So that's why he calmed down after he talked to you," I said. "I guess he wasn't a big fan of Dawnelle's."

"I don't think he cared much about Dawnelle one way or the other. But he cares a lot about you."

Delight seemed to be spilling inside me like close-held armfuls of fruit that had become too heavy to carry. "Churchill cares about a lot of people," I said in an offhand tone.

"Not really. He's pretty guarded with most people. I take after him that way."

It was dangerous, this temptation to tell him anything, to relax completely in his presence. But the car was a luxurious dark cocoon, and I was steeped in a feeling of intimacy with this man I barely knew.

"He told me about you for years," I said. "And about your brothers and sister. Whenever he visited the salon, he'd give me an update on the family, and it seemed you and he were always in the middle of some kind of argument. But I could tell he was proudest of you. Even when he was complaining about you, it sounded like bragging."

Gage smiled slightly. "He's not usually that talkative."

"You'd be surprised what people say across the manicure table."

He shook his head, his eyes on the road. "Dad is the last man in the world I'd ever expect to go for a manicure. When I first heard about it, I wondered what kind of woman could get him to do such a thing. As you can guess, it caused more than a little speculation in the family."

I knew it mattered too much, what Gage thought of me. "I never asked him for anything," I said, my voice weighted with anxiety. "I never thought of him as a . . . you know, sugar daddy . . . there were no presents or—"

"Liberty," he interrupted gently, "it's okay. I get it."

"Oh." I let out a long sigh. "Well, I know how it looked."

"I realized right away nothing was going on. I figured any man who slept with you would never let you out of his bed."

Silence.

The deliberately provocative remark split the course of my thoughts into two channels, one of desire, the other profound insecurity. I had seldom, if ever, wanted any man as much as I wanted Gage. But I wasn't going to be enough for him. I wasn't experienced, I had no skills. And during sex I was too easily distracted, I could never block the caprices of a mind that, right in the middle of the action, would summon up worries such as *Did I sign Carrington's form for the school field trip yet?* or *Is the dry cleaner going to be able to take the coffee stain out of my white blouse?* In short, I was bad in bed. And I didn't want this man to find out.

"Are we going to talk about it?" Gage asked, and I knew he meant the kiss.

"About what?" I countered.

He laughed softly. "I guess not." Taking pity, he asked how Carrington was doing in school. Relieved, I told him about the problems my sister was having in math, and the conversation turned to our own memories of school, and soon he was entertaining me with reminiscences of all the trouble he and his brothers had gotten into when they were younger.

Before I knew it we were at the restaurant. A uniformed valet helped me out of the car while another received the keys from Gage. "We can go anywhere," Gage said, taking my elbow. "If you don't like the look of this place, just tell me."

"I'm sure it will be wonderful."

It was a contemporary French restaurant with light-colored walls and tables covered in white linen, and piano music. After Gage explained to the hostess that the Travis party had gone from nine to two, she led us to one of the small tables in the corner, which was partially concealed by a curtainlike panel to allow for privacy.

While Gage looked through a wine list the size of a phone book, a solicitous waiter filled our water glasses and draped a napkin across my lap. After Gage chose the wine, we ordered artichoke soup sprinkled with shreds of caramelized Maine lobster, plates of California abalone, skillet-roasted sole from Dover accompanied by a hot salad of New Zealand eggplant and peppers.

"My dinner is going to be more well traveled than I am," I said.

Gage smiled. "Where would you go, if you could choose any place?"

The question made me animated. I had always fantasized about traveling to places I had seen only in magazines or movies. "Oh, I don't know . . . to start with, Paris, maybe. Or London, or Florence. When Carrington gets a little older I'm going to save enough to take us on one of those bus tours through Europe . . ."

"You don't want to see Europe through a bus window," he said.

"I don't?"

"No. You want to go with someone who knows the right places." He pulled out his cell phone and flipped it open. "Which one?"

I smiled and shook my head in confusion. "What do you mean, which one?"

"Paris or London? I can have the plane ready in two hours."

I decided to play along. "Are we taking the Gulfstream or the Citation?"

"For Europe, definitely the Gulfstream."

Then I realized he was serious. "I don't even own a suitcase," I said, stunned.

"I'll buy whatever you need when we get there."

"You said you were tired of traveling."

"I meant business traveling. Besides, I'd like to see Paris with someone who's never been there before." His voice gentled. "It would be like seeing it for the first time again."

"No, no, no . . . people don't go to Europe on the first date."

"Yes they do."

"Not my kind of people. Besides, it would scare Carrington for me to do something spontaneous like that—"

"Projecting," he murmured.

"All right, it would scare me. I don't know you well enough to take a trip with you."

"That's going to change."

I stared at Gage in amazement. He was more relaxed than I'd ever seen him, a dance of laughter in his eyes. "What's gotten into you?" I asked dazedly.

He shook his head, smiling. "I'm not sure. But I'm going to go with it."

We talked all through dinner. There was so much I wanted to tell him, and even more I wanted to ask. Three hours of conversation wasn't even a scratch on the surface. Gage was a good listener, seeming genuinely interested in the stories about my past, all the details that should have bored him silly. I told him about Mama, how much I missed her and all the problems we'd had with each other. I even told

him about the guilt I had harbored for years, that it was my fault
Mama had never gotten especially close to Carrington.

"I thought at the time I was stepping in to fill a gap," I said. "But
after she died, I wondered if I hadn't . . . well, I loved Carrington so
much right from the start, I just sort of took over. And I've wondered
so often if I was guilty of . . . I don't know the word for it . . ."

"Marginalizing her?"

"What does that mean?"

"Putting her on the sidelines."

"Yes. Yes, that's what I did."

"Bull," Gage said gently. "It doesn't work that way, sweetheart. You
didn't take anything away from your mother by loving Carrington."
He took my hand, wrapping his warm fingers around mine. "It sounds
like Diana was occupied with her own problems. She was probably
grateful you were there to give Carrington the affection she couldn't."

"I hope so," I said, unconvinced. "I . . . how did you know her
name?"

He shrugged. "Dad must have mentioned it."

In the warm silence that followed, I recalled Gage had lost a
mother when he was only three. "Do you remember anything about
your mother?"

Gage shook his head. "Ava was the one who took care of me when
I was sick, read me stories, patched me up after I'd been in a fight and
gave me hell for it later." A reflective sigh. "God, I miss her."

"Your father does too." I paused before daring to ask, "Do you
mind that he has girlfriends?"

"Hell, no." He grinned suddenly. "As long as you're not one
of them."

We got back to River Oaks at about midnight. I was slightly tipsy
from two glasses of wine and a few sips of the port they had brought

out with dessert, which had consisted of French cheese and paper-thin slices of date-nut bread. I felt better than I had in my entire life, maybe even better than those halcyon moments with Hardy so long ago. It almost worried me, feeling that happy. I had a thousand ways of making sure a man could never really get close. Sex was not nearly as difficult, or dangerous, as intimacy.

But the vague worry couldn't quite take root, because something about Gage compelled me to trust him despite my best efforts not to. I wondered how many times in my life I had done something just because I wanted to, without weighing the consequences.

We had both fallen silent as Gage pulled up to the house and stopped the car. The air snapped with unspoken questions. I sat still in my seat, not meeting his gaze. A few raw, coursing seconds, and I fumbled blindly for the buckle of my seat belt. Without hurry, Gage got out of the car and came around to my side.

"It's late," I remarked casually as he helped me out of the car.

"Tired?"

We walked to the front door. The night air was cool and sweet, clouds brooding across the moon in transparent layers.

I nodded to indicate yes, I was tired, although it wasn't true. I was nervous. Now that we were back in familiar territory, I found it difficult not to slip into my old cautions. We stopped by the door, and I turned to face him. My balance was uncertain in the high heels. I must have swayed a little, because he reached out and took my waist in his hands, fingers resting on the upper slope of my hips. My closed hands formed a small barricade between us. Words tumbled from my lips—I thanked him for dinner, tried to express how much I'd enjoyed it . . .

My voice faded as Gage pulled me close and pressed his lips to my forehead.

"I'm in no hurry, Liberty. I can be patient."

He held me carefully, as if I were fragile and in need of shelter.

Tentatively I relaxed against him, nestling, my hands inching up his shoulders. Everywhere we pressed, I felt the pure physical promise of how good it could be, was going to be, and something began to uncoil in all the vulnerable places of my body.

His wide, firm mouth moved to my cheek, touched it in a gentle brand. "I'll see you in the morning."

And then he pulled away.

Dazed, I watched him start down the steps. "Wait," I said lamely. "Gage . . ."

He turned back, his brows lifting in a silent question.

Embarrassed, I mumbled, "Aren't you going to kiss me good night?"

His quiet laugh curled through the air. Slowly he came back to me, bracing one hand on the door. "Liberty, darlin' . . ." His accent was heavier than usual. "I can be patient, but I'm not a saint. One kiss is about all I can handle tonight."

"Okay," I whispered.

My heartbeat turned unruly as his head bent over mine. He touched me with nothing but his mouth, tasting lightly until my lips parted. There was the same elusive flavor that had haunted me for the past two nights, it was in his breath, on his tongue, something sweet and drugging. I tried to draw as much of it in as possible, wrapping my arms around his neck to keep him there. A soft, dark sound came from his throat. His lungs moved in an uneven surge, and he clamped an arm low on my hips and caught me against him.

He kissed me longer, harder, until we were leaning against the door. One of his hands slid upward from my waist, hovered at my breast and snatched back. I put my hand on his and clumsily urged it to where I wanted it, until his fingers were cupped beneath the round weight. His thumb circled, rubbed slowly, until the flesh tightened into an aching bud. He took it in his fingertips, tugged with exquisite gentleness. I wanted his mouth on me, his hands, all his skin against mine.

I needed so much, too much, and the way he touched me, kissed me, made me crave impossible things. "Gage . . ."

He wrapped his arms around me in an effort to still my helpless writhing. His mouth was buried in my hair. "Yes?"

"Please . . . walk me up to my room."

Understanding what I was offering, Gage took his time about replying.

"I can wait."

"No . . ." I wrapped my arms around him as if I were drowning. "I don't want to wait."

CHAPTER 21

Somewhere between the front door and the bedroom, the heat of passion was banked by misgivings. Not that I was going to back out at this point—I wanted Gage too badly. And even if we managed to put it off, I was certain we'd end up in bed eventually. But my mind kept circling around my inadequacies in bed and how to make up for them. I tried to figure out what Gage would want, the things that might please him. By the time we were in my room, my mind was filled with what looked like pages from a football playbook, arrows leading to diagrams of passing routes, blocking strategies, hole assignments, and offensive formations.

As I watched Gage's hand on the doorknob and heard the click of the lock, I felt my stomach swoop. I turned the bedside lamp on low, sending a varnish of yellow light across the floor.

Gage's face softened as he glanced at me. "Hey . . ." He gestured for me to come to him. "You're allowed to have second thoughts."

I felt his arms go around me, and I huddled against him. "No, no second thoughts." My cheek pressed into the soft black cashmere of his sweater. "But . . ."

"But what?" His hand coasted up and down my spine. I argued with myself for a few seconds—if I was going to trust a man enough to go to bed with him, I should trust him enough to say whatever I wanted.

"The thing is . . ." I said with difficulty. No matter how deep a breath I drew, I only seemed to be getting half the air I needed. Gage's hand continued its slow, reassuring motion. "There's something you should know . . ."

"Yes?"

"Well, you see . . ." I closed my eyes and made myself say it. "The thing is, I'm bad in bed."

His hand stopped. He pried my head away from his shoulder and subjected me to a quizzical glance. "No you're not."

"Yes, yes, I'm bad in bed." It was such a relief to admit it, the words tripped over each other as I continued. "I'm not experienced at all. It's so embarrassing at my age. There have only been two—and the last one, oh, it was so *mediocre*. Every time. I have no skills. No focus. I take forever to get in the mood and then I can't hold on to it and I have to fake it. I'm a faker, and I'm not even good at that. I'm—"

"Wait. Hold on. Liberty . . ." Gage hauled me close, stifling the outpouring. I felt a tremor of laughter run through him. I stiffened, and he gripped me more tightly. "No," he said, his voice thick with amusement, "I'm not laughing at you, sweetheart. I just . . . no, I'm taking you seriously. I am."

"You don't sound like it."

"Sweetheart." He smoothed my hair back, nuzzled my temple. "There's nothing mediocre about you. The only problem you've got is that you've led the life of a single working mother since you were . . . what, eighteen, nineteen? I already knew you weren't experienced because . . . to be honest, you throw out all kinds of mixed signals."

"I do?"

"Yes. Which is why I'm fine with taking it slow. Better that than to do something you're not ready for."

"I'm ready," I said earnestly. "I just want to make sure you've lowered your expectations."

Gage looked away from me, and I got the impression he was fighting back another laugh. "Okay. They're low."

"You're just saying that."

He said nothing, his eyes glinting with amusement.

We studied each other, and I wondered if the next move was mine or his. I approached the bed on ramshackle legs, sat on the edge, kicked off the slides. My toes flexed against the pleasant ache of no longer having to endure the forward pitch of my own weight.

Gage watched me, the movement of my bare feet, and his eyes lost their splintered brilliance, looking smoke-hazed, almost drowsy. Encouraged, I reached for the hem of my dress.

"Wait," Gage murmured, sitting beside me on the mattress. "A couple of ground rules."

I nodded, watching the way the fabric of his pants stretched over his thighs, noticing that his feet reached the floor while my legs dangled. I felt one of his hands touch the edge of my jaw, and he turned my face up to his. "First, no faking. You have to be honest with me."

That made me regret having mentioned the faking. I've always hated being the kind of person who says too much out of nervousness. "All right, but just so you know, I usually take too long—"

"I don't care if it takes all damn night. It's not an audition."

"What if I can't manage to . . ." For the first time I realized how much harder it is to talk about sex than actually doing it.

"We'll work at it," Gage said. "Believe me, I'll have no problem helping you practice."

I dared to touch his thigh, which felt like concrete beneath my palm. "What's the other rule?"

"I'm in charge."

I blinked, wondering what he meant. Gage's hand closed on my nape in a light squeeze that sent an erotic shock down my spine. "Just for tonight," he continued evenly. "Trust me to decide when and where and how long. You don't have to do anything except relax. Let go. Let me take care of you." His mouth lowered to my ear, and he whispered, "Can you do that for me, darlin'?"

My toes curled. No one had ever asked me such a thing. I wasn't sure I could. But I nodded, my stomach leaping as his mouth wandered across my cheek to the corner of my lips. He kissed me, searching slow and deep until I was weak and my entire body was draped across his lap. Gage took off his shoes and lay across the bed with me, both of us fully clothed. He pressed a thigh into the folds of the red dress, securing me flat against the mattress. His mouth possessed mine with long kisses, bites and nibbles of kisses, until steam collected between my skin and the wool knit fabric. I slid my fingers into his thick hair, cool on the surface, warm near the scalp, trying to capture him.

Gage resisted my anxious urging, pulling back. In one easy move he sat up and straddled my hips. I took a shaky breath as I felt the intimate pressure of him, rock-hard and rearing. Deftly he tugged off the black sweater and tossed it aside, revealing a torso more powerful than I had imagined, sleek and hard-quilted, his chest lightly covered with dark hair. I wanted to feel his chest against my naked breasts. I wanted to kiss him, explore him, not for his pleasure but my own, he was so damn arousing, so intensely masculine.

Lowering over me, Gage sought my mouth again, and I was smoldering, desperate to be free of my dress, which had begun to prickle and cling like a medieval hair shirt. I reached for the hem, tugging the tormenting fabric upward.

But Gage's mouth left mine abruptly, his hand closing over my wrist. I looked up at him in confusion.

"Liberty." His tone was chiding, his eyes wicked. "Only two rules . . . and you've already broken one."

It took me a moment to understand. With effort, I forced myself to let go of the dress. I tried to lie still, although my hips hitched in a pleading motion. Gage pulled the dress back down to my knees, the sadist, and he spent an eternity fondling me through the layer of wool. I pressed against him harder, closer, gasping at the feel of his aroused body.

The heat climbed until Gage finally peeled the dress upward, away from skin so flushed and sensitive that the waft of air from the overhead fan made me shiver. He unhooked the front clasp of my bra, releasing my breasts from the underwire cups. The teasing brush of his fingers was so exquisite, I could hardly bear it.

"Liberty . . . you're beautiful . . . so beautiful . . ." I felt his ragged murmurs against my throat, my chest, telling me how much he wanted me, how hard I made him, how sweet the taste of my skin was. His lips dragged gently over the cushiony slope of my breast, opened over the peak, pulled it inside the wet fire of his mouth. My hips caught a high arch as he slipped his fingers beneath the top edge of my cotton panties. The place between my thighs was aching, but he didn't seem to understand where I needed him to touch me, he stroked all around without ever quite reaching it. I pushed upward in mute rhythmic pleading, *I want . . . I want . . . I want . . .* and he still didn't respond, and then I realized he was doing it on purpose.

My eyes flew open, my lips parted . . . but Gage stared down into my face with a sort of amused challenge, daring me to complain. Somehow I managed to keep my mouth shut.

"Good girl," he murmured, stripping off my panties.

He settled me firmly into the mattress. I lay exactly as he arranged me, my body heavy as if sensation had acquired the weight of salt water. I was brimming and helpless. He moved over me, around me, until I was wild from stimulation and heat and teasing friction.

He slid lower. I couldn't even lift my head, it had become so heavy. His mouth strayed in a blind search, without design, crossing the small harbor between my thighs. I writhed as I felt his tongue in melting licks that separated and probed until my flesh was open, drenched. He gripped my hips, holding me secure for his mouth, for eager kisses, for slow marauding. My muscles contracted as it all began rolling up to me, I was about to come, I was almost crying in relief, when he pulled away.

Shivering, I begged *don't stop* but Gage said *not yet* and lowered his body over mine. He slipped two fingers inside me, kept them there while he kissed me. Passion had made his features severe in the lamp glow. My body tightened around the gentle thrust of his fingers, I arched to keep them, needing any part of him inside any part of me. His name rose to my lips again and again, I had no way to tell him I would have done anything for him, he was all I wanted, he was too much to be endured.

Gage reached for the nightstand, fumbled with his wallet. I snatched at the flashing foil packet, so frantic to help that I ended up hindering his efforts, and I heard his smothered laugh. I didn't see the humor in anything, I was in a fever, I had been teased into madness.

I felt the temperature of Gage's body, cooler, harder, heavier than mine, rising to match my own internal blaze. He responded to every shiver and sound, his lips stealing secrets from my flesh, his hands gently trespassing until there was no part of me he hadn't claimed. He pushed my legs open and entered me in a deep-rooted thrust, taking my sobs into his mouth, whispering *that's right sweet baby quiet quiet,* and I took all of him, the pleasure thick and sweet, and with every nudge the wet silken hardness guided me closer to the edge. *Oh God there yes please,* I needed it faster but his discipline was absolute, he worked farther into me without altering the terrible slowness of his rhythm. His face nuzzled into the curve of my neck, and the scrape of his bristle was so good, I moaned as if in pain.

Blindly I reached over his flexing back, down to his backside, my fingers clamping over the taut muscle. Without pausing in his measured pace, he pulled my wrists up, one after the other, and deliberately pinned them to the mattress, and covered my mouth with his.

Only one rational thought flickered at the edge of my consciousness—there was something not right about the surrender he demanded—but the relief of it was unspeakable. And so I submitted, and my mind went dark and quiet. The moment I let go, the pleasure rushes started, each one more relentless than the last. My hips nearly lifted him from the bed. He countered with heavier drives, pushing me back down, letting the voluptuous clenching of my flesh draw out his own release. I came, and came, and came. It seemed impossible a person could survive it.

Usually when sex was over, the uncoupling was complete in every sense. Men rolled over and went to sleep, women dashed into the bathroom to freshen up and dispose of the evidence. But Gage held me for a long time, playing with my hair, whispering, brushing kisses on my face and breasts. He washed me with a warm damp cloth. I should have felt drained, but instead I was like a live wire, a circuit of energy running through my body. I stayed in bed as long as I could, and then I jumped up and put my robe on.

"So you're one of those," Gage said, looking amused as I gathered and folded our discarded clothes.

"One of what?" I paused to admire the sight of his long body barely covered by the white sheet, muscles bunching beneath his skin as he propped up on one elbow. I loved the disorder my hands had wrought in his hair, the relaxed curve of his mouth.

"One of those women who gets revved up after sex."

"I've never gotten revved up by it before," I said, placing the folded clothes on a chair. A quick self-evaluation caused me to admit sheepishly, "But right now I feel like I could run ten miles."

Gage smiled. "I've got a few ideas about how to wear you out. Unfortunately, since I didn't know what would happen tonight, I only had one in-case-of-emergency condom."

I half sat on the edge of the bed. "Was I an emergency?"

He pulled me across his chest and rolled back until I sprawled over him. "Since the first moment I saw you."

I grinned and kissed him. "You do have more condoms," I told him. "I found some in the bathroom when I moved in. I hadn't planned on returning them to you, it would have been too embarrassing. So I left them where they were. We've been sharing the drawer."

"We've been sharing a drawer and I didn't even know about it?"

"You can have the condoms back now," I said generously.

His eyes sparkled. "I appreciate that."

As the night unfolded, we established that not only was I *not* bad in bed, I was phenomenal. A prodigy, Gage claimed.

We shared a bottle of wine, showered together, and got back into bed. We kissed voraciously, as if we hadn't already kissed a thousand times. And by morning I had done things with Gage Travis that were illegal in at least nine states. It seemed there was nothing he didn't like, nothing he wasn't willing to do. He was wickedly patient and so thorough that I felt as if I had been taken apart and reassembled in a different way.

Exhausted and sated, I slept curled against his side. I woke as weak morning sunlight pushed through the window. I felt Gage yawn over my head, and his body tensed in a shivering stretch. It all seemed too wonderful to be real, the heavy masculine form beside mine, the subtle stings and aches that reminded me of the night's pleasures. The hand that rested gently on my bare hip. I was afraid he might vanish, this lover who had possessed and explored me with such gentleness, and he would be replaced by the cool-eyed and distant man I had known before.

"Don't go away," I whispered, reaching to cover his hand with mine, pressing it tightly against my skin.

I felt the shape of Gage's smile in the sleep-warmed curve of my neck. "Not going anywhere," he said, and settled me back against him.

Houstonians like to do things in a big way, and a River Oaks mansion debut is no exception. There were many events taking place on Saturday night, but the guest list everyone wanted to be on was for a big charity gala at the home of Peter and Sascha Legrand. The oil company executive and his wife, a city councilwoman, were using the occasion to introduce their brand-new mansion, an Italian-Mediterranean palace with ten antique porticoes imported from Europe and a thirty-six-hundred-square-foot ballroom that covered the entire second floor.

The Travises had been invited, of course, and Gage had asked me to go with him. It wasn't exactly your average second date.

The life section in the *Chronicle* had shown preview pictures of the mansion, including the fourteen-foot-high Chihuly chandelier that hung in the grand foyer. The amazing glass creation looked like a cluster of giant half-open flowers of blue, amber, and orange.

Intended for the benefit of a charitable foundation for the arts, the gala was opera themed, which meant singers from the Houston Opera would entertain. With my limited knowledge of opera, I imagined singers in Viking helmets and long braids who would blow our hair back with their voices.

The four alcoves of the grand foyer had been decorated to represent famous opera houses in Venice and Milan. At the terraced back yard of the mansion, piazzas had been specially built on platforms just for the party, with buffets offering specialties from different regions of Italy. Armies of white-gloved waiters were available to serve the guests' every need.

I had spent the equivalent of two weeks' salary on a white Nicole Miller dress with a halter top that wrapped and twisted neatly down to my hips, then fell in soft folds to the floor. It was a sexy but ladylike dress with a vee neckline. My shoes were Stuart Weitzman, a pair of clear Lucite sandals with crystals on the heels and toe straps. Cinderella shoes, Carrington had said when she saw them. I had scraped my hair back so it was flat and shining against my head, and twisted it into an artfully messy knot in back. After carefully applying sooty eye makeup, delicate pink lip gloss, and subtle blush, I stared at my reflection critically. I had no earrings that went with the dress. But I needed a little something else.

After a few seconds' thought, I went to Carrington's room, looked in her art supplies box, and found a sheet of self-adhesive crystals. I took one of the smallest ones, not much bigger than the head of a pin, and applied it near the outside corner of my eye like a beauty mark.

"Does it look trashy?" I asked Carrington, who couldn't keep from jumping up and down on the bed. Asking an eight-year-old girl if something is a little over-the-top is like asking a Texan if there are too many jalapeños in the salsa. The answer is always no.

"It's perfect!" Carrington was ready to launch herself into orbit.

"No jumping," I reminded her, and she flopped down on her stomach with a grin.

"Are you going to come back here tonight," she asked, "or are you going to have a sleepover at Gage's?"

"I'm not sure." I went to sit on the edge of the bed beside her. "Baby, would it bother you if I slept over at his place tonight?"

"Oh, no," she said cheerfully. "Aunt Gretchen says if you do, I'll get to stay up late and we'll make cookies. And if you want your boyfriend to ask you to marry him, you *have* to sleep at his house. So he can see if you look pretty in the morning."

"What? Carrington, who told you that?"

"I figured it out by myself."

My chin quivered as I held back a laugh. "Gage is not my boyfriend. And I'm not trying to get him to ask me to marry him."

"I think you should," she said. "Don't you like him, Liberty? He's better than any of the other ones you dated. Even better than the one who brang us all those pickles and funny-smelling cheeses."

"Brought us." I stared closely into her small, earnest face. "You seem to like Gage a lot."

"Oh, yes! I think he'd be a good dad for me after I teach him more about kid stuff."

The observations of a child can knock you flat before you even know what's coming. My heart twisted with guilt, pain, and worst of all, hope.

I leaned over her and kissed her very gently. "Don't expect anything, baby," I whispered. "We'll just be patient and see what happens."

Churchill, Vivian, Gretchen, and her date were having cocktails in the family room before they left. We'd had to send Churchill's tuxedo pants to the tailor, to put Velcro seams in on the side he wore the cast. Vivian had been entertained by the idea of the rip-off pants, claiming she felt like she was dating a Chippendale dancer.

As I came downstairs and stepped out of the elevator, I found Gage waiting for me. Magnificent man, all elegance and testosterone contained in a scheme of flawless black and white. Gage wore a tux like he did everything else, looking relaxed and unselfconscious.

He stared at me with a faint smile. "Liberty Jones . . . you look like a princess." Taking my hand carefully, he raised it to his lips and pressed a kiss into the cup of my palm.

This wasn't me. It was far removed from any reality I had ever known. I felt like the young girl I had once been, the one with the frizzy hair and the big glasses, watching a beautifully dressed woman who wanted to be in the moment, to enjoy it, but wasn't quite able. And then I thought, *Damn it all, I don't have to be an outsider.*

I deliberately leaned the front of my body against Gage's, watching his eyes darken. "Are you still aggravated with me?" I asked, making him smile ruefully.

We had argued earlier in the day about Christmas, which was coming soon. It had started when Gage had asked what kind of present I wanted.

"No jewelry," I had said instantly. "Nothing expensive."

"Then what?"

"Take me out for a nice dinner."

"All right. Paris or London?"

"I'm not ready to take a trip with you."

That had produced a frown. "What's the difference between sleeping with me here or sleeping with me in a hotel in Paris?"

"A fortune, to start with."

"This has nothing to do with money."

"To me it does," I'd said apologetically. "It doesn't matter that you're one of those people who never has to think about money. Because I do. So for me to let you spend so much on me . . . it would throw everything off balance. Don't you see?"

Gage had gotten more and more irritated. "Let me get this straight. You're saying you'd go somewhere with me if we both had money, or if neither of us had it."

"That's right."

"That's stupid."

"You can say that because you're the one with the money."

"So if you were dating the UPS guy, he could buy you whatever the hell he wanted. But I can't."

"Well . . . yes." I gave him a cajoling smile. "But I'd never date the UPS guy. Those brown shorts are just not a turn-on for me."

He hadn't smiled back. His calculating gaze had made me uneasy, with good reason. I knew Gage well enough to be certain that when he wanted something, he would find a way over, around, or through all obstacles. Which meant he wouldn't be satisfied until he had found a way to separate my working-class feet from American soil.

"When you think about it," I'd said, "it's actually a good thing, my wanting to take the money out of this . . . this . . ."

"Relationship. And you're not taking the money out of it. You're putting it right in the middle."

I had tried to sound as reasonable as possible. "Look, we've only just started seeing each other. All I'm asking is that you don't buy me extravagant presents or try to arrange some big expensive trip." Seeing his expression, I added reluctantly, "Yet."

The "yet" had seemed to pacify Gage a little. But his mouth had retained a hint of brooding.

Now, as he held me in a light clasp, I saw his usual self-control had returned. "No, I'm not aggravated," he said calmly. "Travises like a challenge."

I didn't know why the touch of arrogance, which used to annoy me, had become so absurdly sexy. I grinned at him. "You can't always have things your way, Gage."

He eased me closer, the heel of his hand brushing the side of my breast. An intimate whisper that kicked my heart into a new, urgent beat. "I will tonight, though."

"Maybe," I said, my breath quickening.

One of his hands ran down my back in a restless stroke, as if he were contemplating ripping the dress off me right there. "I can't wait for this damn party to be over with."

I laughed. "It hasn't even started yet." My eyes half closed as I felt his mouth searching the side of my throat.

"We'll have our own party in the limo."

"Aren't . . ." I caught my breath as he found a sensitive nerve. "Aren't we going to share it with Churchill and the others?"

"No, they've got their own." Gage lifted his head, and I saw the bright, hot flicker in his eyes. "Just you and me," he murmured. "Behind a nice dark privacy screen. And a bottle of chilled Perrier Jouet. Think you can handle it?"

"Bring it on," I said, and took his arm.

Limos were parked three deep on the street outside the Legrand mansion. The building was remarkable in its scale and style; it seemed more a place for people to visit than to actually live in. I started having fun the moment we entered the grand foyer, which seemed like some elaborate European carnival. The crowd of men dressed in black formal wear were a perfect backdrop for the women's colorful evening gowns. Jewels glittered at throats and wrists and fingers and ears, and light scattered like falling jewels from the overhead chandelier. Music from a live orchestra was piped into every part of the house.

Sascha Legrand, a tall, slim woman with frosted hair cut in stylish angles, insisted on taking us through a partial tour of the house. She often paused to plunge us into conversation with one group or another, then withdrew us before the conversation became too involved. I was amazed by the variety of guests . . . a small group of young actors, producers, and directors who had moved to Hollywood and called themselves the "Texas mafia," an Olympic gymnastics gold medalist, a

Rockets guard, the pastor of a nationally known megachurch, some people rich from oil, some people rich from ranching, and even a foreign aristocrat here or there.

Gage was accomplished at this kind of situation, knowing everyone's names, remembering to ask about their golf games or their hunting dogs, or how dove season had gone, or did they still have that place in Andorra or Mazatlán. Even in this high-impact crowd, people were excited and flattered by his interest. With his cool charisma and elusive smile, his aura of breeding and education, Gage was dazzling. And he knew it. I might have been intimidated, except that I still carried in my mind the images of a very different Gage, not nearly so self-possessed, shivering at my touch. The contrast between our formal circumstances and the memory of him in bed caused a hum of arousal inside. Nothing anyone else could perceive, but I became more aware of it every time I felt the brush of Gage's arm against mine, or the heat of his breath as he murmured in my ear.

I found it relatively easy to make small talk, mainly because I didn't know enough to do anything other than ask questions, and that seemed to keep the conversation flowing. We made our way through the sparkling sea of guests, following a current that led to the terraced exterior at the back of the house. A trio of covered wooden pavilions featured cuisines from different regions of Italy. After filling their plates, people sat at tables covered in yellow cloths and lit with Italian glass oil candles, filled with fresh flowers suspended in clear liquid paraffin.

We sat at a table with Jack and his girlfriend, and some of the Texas mafia, who entertained us with accounts of an indie film they were making and talked about going to Sundance in just a couple of weeks. They were so irreverent and funny, and the wine was so good, I felt giddy. It was a magical night. There would be some opera singing soon, and dancing after that, and I would be in Gage's arms until morning.

"My God, you're stunning," said one of the Texas mafia, a dark-haired young woman named Sydney. She was a director. It was said in a tone of observation rather than compliment, her gaze frankly assessing. "You'd look amazing on film—wouldn't she, guys?—you've got one of those transparent faces."

"Transparent?" I held my hands up to my cheeks reflexively.

"Shows everything you're thinking," Sydney said.

Now my face was flaming. "God. I don't want to be transparent."

Gage was laughing quietly, sliding his arm around the back of my chair. "It's okay," he told me. "You're perfect the way you are." He leveled a narrow glance at Sydney. "If I ever catch you trying to put her in front of a camera—"

"Okay, okay," Sydney protested. "No need to get rabid, Gage." She grinned at me. "I guess you two are in pretty deep, huh? I've known Gage since the third grade, and I've never seen him so—"

"Syd," he interrupted, his gaze promising death. Her grin only widened.

Jack's girlfriend, a bubbly blonde named Heidi, steered the conversation in a new direction. "Jaa-aack," she said with a playful pout. "You said you'd buy me something from the silent auction, and I haven't gotten to look at the tables yet." She glanced at me significantly. "They say there's some cool stuff up for bidding . . . a pair of diamond earrings, a week in St. Tropez . . ."

"Shit," Jack said with a good-natured grin. "Whatever she picks out is going to put one hell of a dent in my wallet."

"Don't I deserve a nice present?" Heidi asked, and tugged him up from the table without waiting for an answer.

Gage, who had stood politely when Heidi rose from her chair, saw that I had finished my dessert. "Come on, sweetheart," he told me. "We might as well go look too."

We excused ourselves from the table and followed Jack and Heidi into the mansion. One of the main rooms had been set up for the silent auction, rows of long tables littered with booklets, baskets, and item descriptions. Fascinated, I browsed along the first table. For each numbered item there was a leather folder with a bid list inside. You wrote down your name and the amount of your bid, and if someone wanted to top you, they added their name and a higher number underneath yours. At twelve o'clock, all bidding would be closed.

There was a certificate for a private cooking class given by a famous TV chef . . . a golf lesson from a pro who had once won the masters . . . a rare wine collection . . . a personal song written and recorded for you by a British rock star.

"What looks good?" came Gage's voice over my shoulder, and I had to fight the urge to lean back against him and pull his hands up to my breasts. Right there, in a room full of people.

"Damn." I rested my fingertips lightly on the table, closing my eyes for a second.

"What is it?"

"I'll be glad when we get through this stage and I can think straight again."

He stayed right behind me, sounding amused. "Stage of what?"

My nerves sizzled as I felt his hand settle at my side. "There are five stages of dating," I told him. "The first is attraction . . . you know, the chemistry and the sort of h-hormonal high when you're together. The next stage is exclusivity. And then you settle into reality, when the physical attraction dies down . . ."

His hand moved to the highest curve of my hip. "And you think this"—a subtle stroke that sent my nerves jumping—"is going to die down?"

"Well," I said weakly, "it's supposed to."

"You let me know when we get to the reality stage." His voice was dark velvet. "I'll see what I can do to get your hormonal high going again." He finished the caress with a proprietary pat on my hip. "In the meantime . . . would you mind if I left you just for a few minutes?"

I turned to face him. "Of course not. Why?"

Gage looked apologetic. "I've got to say a quick hello to a friend of the family—I saw him in the other room. I went to high school with his son, who died not long ago in a boating accident."

"Oh, that's so sad. Yes, I'll stay here and wait for you."

"While you're at it, pick out something."

"What kind of something?"

"I don't care. A trip. A painting. Whatever looks good. Anyone who doesn't participate in the auction will get raked over the coals in the paper tomorrow for not giving a crap about the fine arts. It's up to you to save me."

"Gage, I'm not going to be responsible for spending all that money on . . . Gage, are you listening to me?"

"Nope." He smiled and began to walk away.

I looked down at the brochure nearest me. "We're going to Nigeria," I threatened. "I hope you like elephant polo."

He chuckled and left me amid the rows of auction items. I saw Heidi and Jack examining some items several tables away, until more people entered the room and blocked my view. I studied the tables carefully. I couldn't figure out what in the world Gage would want. A fancy limited-edition European motorcycle . . . no way was I going to let him risk losing a limb. A Nascar experience in which you got to drive a six-hundred-horsepower stock car on a super speedway. Ditto. Private chartered yacht trips. Jewels with names. A private lunch with a beautiful soap opera actress . . . *As if,* I thought sardonically.

After a few minutes of dedicated searching, with lively melodic arias in the background, I found something. A high-end massage chair with an intricate control panel promising at least fifteen different kinds of massage. I decided Gage could give it to Churchill for a Christmas present.

Picking up a pen, I began to write Gage's name on the bidding sheet, but the ink wouldn't come out. The pen was a dud. I shook it and tried again with no luck.

"Here," said a man beside me, setting a new pen on the table. He used the flat of his hand to roll it closer. "Try this one."

That hand.

I stared at it dumbly, while the fine hairs on the back of my neck lifted.

A big hand, the nails sun-bleached, the long fingers scattered with tiny star-shaped scars. I knew whose hand it was, I knew it from a place that went deeper than memory. But I couldn't make myself believe it. *Not here. Not now.*

I looked up into a pair of blue eyes that had haunted me for years. Eyes I would remember to the last day of my life.

"Hardy," I whispered.

CHAPTER 22

I was paralyzed as I tried to take him in, this stranger I had loved so dearly. Hardy Cates had grown into all the promise of his younger years. He was a big, bold-looking man. Those eyes, blue upon blue, and the glossy brown hair, and the beginnings of a smile that sent a ripple of wonder through my soul . . . All I could do was stare at him, submerged in fearsome pleasure.

Hardy was still as he looked back at me, but I sensed the vibration of hard-running emotion beneath his exterior.

He took my hand gently, as if I were a small child. "Let's find a place to talk."

I clung to him, not caring that Jack might see us leave, not really aware of anything except the clasp of those callused fingers. Hardy drew me away by the hand, away from the tables, to the waiting darkness of the outside grounds. We skirted the crowd, the noise, the lights, cutting around to the side of the house. It seemed the light tried to follow, stretching weakening tendrils after us, but we headed into the shadows of an empty portico.

We stopped in the lee of a column as thick as an oak trunk. I was winded and trembling. I don't know who moved first, it seemed we reached for each other at the same time. I was seized full-length against him, mouth to mouth, bruising each other's lips with kisses too hard for pleasure. My heart thundered as if I were dying.

Moments of silent ravaging, and then Hardy tore his mouth away, whispering it was all right, he wasn't going to let go. I began to relax in his arms, feeling the heat of his mouth as he followed the tumble of wetness on my cheeks. He kissed me again, slow and easy, the way he had taught me so long ago, and I felt safe and young and suffused with a desire so straightforward it seemed almost wholesome. His kisses tapped into deep mines of memory, and the years that had separated us fell away as if they were nothing.

After a while Hardy cuddled me in the loose sides of his tux jacket, his chest hard beneath the intricately tucked shirt.

"I had forgotten how this feels," I said in an ache of a whisper.

"I never forgot." Hardy touched the shape of my waist and hips through the folds of the white silk gown. "Liberty. I shouldn't have come to you like this. I told myself to wait." A catch of laughter. "I don't even remember crossing the room. You were always beautiful to me, Liberty . . . but now . . . I can't even believe you're real."

"How did you get to be here? Did you know you'd see me? Did you—"

"There's too much to tell you." He rested his cheek on my hair. "I thought you might be here, but I wasn't sure. . . ."

He spoke in the voice I had craved for so long, deeper now than in his youth. He was here at the invitation of a friend, he said, also in the oil business. He told me about starting work on the drilling rig—difficult and dangerous—and the contacts he'd made, the opportunities he'd watched for. Eventually he'd quit the rig and started a small company with two other men, one a geologist, the other an engineer, with the goal of finding new pay zones in mature oil fields. At least half the oil and gas in every field in the world was overlooked, Hardy said, and there was a fortune for those willing to go after bypassed pay. They had raised about a million in financing, and on their first try in a spent Texas field, they'd found a new zone worth an estimated two hundred and fifty thousand barrels of recoverable crude.

Hardy explained enough that I understood he was already rich and going to get a lot richer. He'd bought his mother a house. He had an apartment in Houston, which would be his home base for a while. Knowing of his fierce hunger to succeed, to rise above his circumstances, I was glad for him and I said so.

"It's not enough," Hardy said, taking my face in his hands. "The biggest damn surprise of it all is how little it means once you've got it. For the first time in years I finally had a chance to think, to take a deep breath, and I . . ." A frayed exhalation. "I've never stopped wanting you. I had to find you. I started by going to Marva. She told me where you were, and . . ."

"And that I'm with someone," I said with difficulty.

Hardy nodded. "I wanted to find out if . . ."

If I was happy. If I still needed him. If it wasn't too late for us. If and if . . .

Sometimes life has a cruel sense of humor, giving you the thing you always wanted at the worst time possible. The irony of it split my heart open, setting loose more bitter regret than I could bear.

"Hardy," I said unsteadily, "if only you'd found me a little sooner."

He was quiet, holding me against his chest. One of his hands ran down my bare arm until he reached the tight curl of my fingers. Silently he lifted my left hand, running his thumb over the bareness of my ring finger. "Can you tell me for certain it's too late, honey?"

I thought of Gage, and I was swamped in confusion. "I don't know. I don't know."

"Liberty . . . let me see you tomorrow."

I shook my head. "I promised Carrington I'd spend the day with her. We're going to an ice-skating show at Reliant."

"Carrington." He shook his head. "My God, she must be eight or nine by now."

"Time passes," I whispered.

Hardy held my knuckles up to his cheek, pressed his mouth to them briefly. "What about the day after tomorrow?"

"Yes. Yes." I wanted to leave with Hardy right then. I didn't want to let him go and be left to wonder if I had imagined him. I told him my number. "Hardy, please . . . go back inside first. I need a couple of minutes by myself."

"All right." His arms tightened around me briefly before he let go.

We drew apart and looked at each other. I was confounded by his presence, this man who was so like the boy I had known and yet so unlike him. I didn't know how the connection between us could still be there. But it was. We were the same, Hardy and me, we communicated from the same center, we had come from the same world. But Gage . . . the thought of him wrenched my heart.

Whatever he saw in my face caused Hardy to speak very gently. "Liberty. I'm not going to do anything to hurt you."

I gave a little nod, staring blindly into the darkness as he left.

But he had hurt me in the past, I thought. I had understood his reasons for leaving Welcome. I understood why he'd felt he had no choice.

I didn't blame him. The problem was, I had gone on with my life. And after years of struggle and considerable loneliness, I had finally connected with someone else. My feet ached in my Cinderella shoes. I shifted my weight and wiggled my toes beneath the cutting Lucite straps. My Prince Charming had finally showed up, I thought wretchedly, and he was too damn late.

Not necessarily, my mind insisted. It was still possible for Hardy and me. The old obstacles were gone, and the new ones . . .

There is always a choice. It's a damned uncomfortable thing to know.

I ventured toward the light, fishing in the tiny purse hanging from my arm on a silk loop. I didn't know how I was going to repair the damage done to my makeup. The friction of mouth and skin and fingertips had erased the carefully applied film of color. I powdered my face, and used the tip of my ring finger to wipe smudges of liner from beneath my eyes. I reapplied my lip gloss. The tiny crystal near the corner of my eye was gone. Maybe people wouldn't notice. Everyone was dancing and drinking and eating; surely by now I wasn't the only one with faded makeup.

As soon as I reached the back terrace I saw Gage's dark form, tall and precise as a knife blade. He headed for me in a leisurely stride, catching my chilled upper arm in his hand.

"Hey," he said. "I've been looking for you."

I forced a quick smile. "Just needed a little fresh air. Sorry. Were you waiting long?"

Gage's face was shadowed. "Jack said he saw you leave with someone."

"Yes. I ran into an old friend. Someone from Welcome, if you can believe it." I thought I'd done a pretty good job of sounding casual, but Gage, as always, was terrifyingly perceptive. He turned me toward the light, exposing my face.

"Darlin' . . . I know what you look like when you've been kissed."

I couldn't say anything. The tiny muscles of my face twitched with guilt, my eyes turned wet with a pleading glister.

Gage surveyed me without emotion. In a moment he pulled his cell phone from inside his jacket and said a few words to the limo driver about meeting us out front.

"We're going?" I asked around the spiky ball in my throat.

"Yes."

We went around the side of the house instead of going through it. My Lucite heels sounded brittle on the pavement. Gage made another call as we walked. "Jack. Yeah, it's me. Liberty's got a headache. Too much champagne. We're heading home, so if you could say something to . . . Right. Thanks. And try to keep an eye on Dad." Jack made some comment, and Gage laughed shortly. "Figures. Later." He closed the phone and replaced it in his jacket.

"Is Churchill okay?" I asked.

"He's fine. But Vivian's pissed because of all the women hitting on him."

That almost made me smile. Without thinking I reached for Gage as my heel hit an uneven patch in the pavement. Immediately he took hold of me, his arm fitting across my back as we continued to walk. Even though I knew Gage was furious, he wasn't going to let me fall.

We got into the limo, the plush dark cocoon insulating us from the noise and activity of the party. I was a little worried about being closed away in there with Gage. It hadn't been that long ago that I'd been exposed to the lash of his anger, on the day I'd moved into the mansion. Although I'd managed to stand up to him, it wasn't something I was eager to go through again.

Gage spoke casually to the driver. "Phil, drive us around for a while. I'll let you know when to head downtown."

"Yes, sir."

Gage flicked a few buttons, locking the privacy screen in place, opening the minibar. If he was angry, I couldn't tell. He was relaxed, sort of scary-calm, which was beginning to seem worse than shouting. He took out a highball glass, poured himself a finger of hard liquor, and downed it without seeming to taste it. Silently he poured another shot and offered it to me. I took it gratefully, hoping the alcohol would thaw me out. I was freezing. I tried to down the drink as quickly as Gage had, but it burned my throat and made me sputter.

"Easy," Gage murmured, settling an impersonal hand on my back. Feeling the goose bumps on my skin, he took off his jacket and settled it around me. I was wrapped in the soft silk-lined fabric, warm from his body.

"Thanks," I wheezed.

"No problem." A lengthy pause. The sudden cold-steel impact of his gaze made me flinch. "Who is he?"

In my rambling stories of my childhood, all the details about Mama and my friends, everyone and everything in Welcome, I hadn't once mentioned Hardy. I'd talked to Churchill about him, but I hadn't yet been able to bring myself to do the same with Gage.

Trying to keep my voice steady, I told him about Hardy, that I had known him since I was fourteen . . . that aside from my mother and sister, he'd been the most important person in the world to me. That I'd loved him.

It was so strange, talking to Gage about Hardy. My past and my present colliding. And it made me realize how different the Liberty Jones from the trailer park was from the woman I'd become. I needed to think about that. I needed to think about a lot of things.

"Did you sleep with him?" Gage asked.

"I wanted to," I admitted. "I would have. But he wouldn't. He said it would make it impossible for him to leave me. He had ambitions."

"Ambitions that didn't include you."

"We were both too young. Neither of us had anything. As things turned out, it was for the best. Hardy couldn't have pursued his goals with me hanging like a millstone around his neck. And I could never have left Carrington."

I had no idea how much Gage had read in my expressions, gestures, the razor-thin spaces between my words. All I knew was that as I talked, I felt something cracking, an inflexible mettle breaking like ice over moving water, and Gage trampled through it ruthlessly.

"So you loved him, he left you, and now he wants another shot."

"He didn't say that."

"He didn't have to," Gage said flatly. "Because it's obvious you want another shot."

I felt drained and irritable. My head was a merry-go-round. "I don't know if that's what I want."

Thin shards of light from the minibar broke his face into harsh slats. "You think you're still in love with him."

"I don't know." My eyes watered.

"Don't," Gage said, his calmness vanishing. "I'd do almost anything for you. I think I'd kill for you. But I'm not going to comfort you while you cry in my arms over another man."

I pinched the corners of my eyes with my fingers, swallowing back tears that burned like acid in my throat.

"You're going to see him again," Gage said after a while.

I nodded. "We . . . I . . . need to get things straight."

"Are you going to fuck him?"

The crude word, used to deliberate effect, was like a slap in the face. "I'm not planning to, no," I said stiffly.

"I wasn't asking if you're planning to. I'm asking if you're going to."

Now I was getting mad too. "*No.* I don't fall into bed that easily. You know that."

"Yeah, I know that. I also know you're not the kind who goes to a party with one guy and ends up making out with another one. But you did."

I colored with shame. "I didn't mean to. It was a shock to see him. It just . . . happened."

Gage snorted. "As far as excuses go, sweetheart, that bites the big one."

"I know. I'm sorry. I don't know what else to say. It's just that I loved Hardy a long time before I ever met you. And you and I . . . we've only just started a relationship. I want to be fair to you, but at the same time . . . I have to find out if what I felt for Hardy is still there. Which means . . . I need to put things between you and me on hold until I can figure this out."

Gage was not accustomed to being put on hold. It didn't sit well with him. In fact, it sent him over the edge. I jumped a little as he reached out and hauled me close.

"We slept together, Liberty. There's no backtracking from that. He doesn't get to come in and derail us that easily."

"We only slept together one time," I dared to protest.

He lifted a dark brow, looking sardonic.

"All right, several times," I said. "But it was only one night."

"It was enough. You're mine now. And I want you more than he ever did or ever will. You remember that while you're getting your head straight. While he's telling you whatever the hell it is you want to hear from him, you remember—" Gage stopped abruptly. He wasn't breathing well. His eyes were so hot you could have lit kindling off them. "Remember this," he said in a guttural voice, and reached for me.

His arms were too tight, his mouth punishing. He had never kissed me like that before, with hunger scalded by jealousy. Gage had been driven beyond his limits. His breath came hard as he bore me down to the soft leather upholstery, our bodies stretched full-out, his lips never breaking from mine.

I bucked beneath him, not knowing if I wanted to throw him off or feel more of him. With every movement I made, Gage sank more heavily between my thighs, demanding that I take him, feel him. The hard imprint of his body reminded me of things he had done to me before, the gut-wrenching pleasure, and every thought and emotion was swamped in a rush of desire. I wanted him so badly, I went blind with it, I began to shake from head to toe. I writhed against the pressure of his flesh burgeoning hard and thick beneath the thin black wool. With a low moan, I slid my hands to his hips.

The next few minutes were like a fever dream as we grappled frantically. The fine mesh of my panties caught on the delicate buckled strap of my shoe, resisting Gage's efforts to untangle it until he finally tore the fabric with his fingers. He pulled my dress up to my waist, my skin sticking to the cool leather beneath me, one of my widespread legs dangling wantonly to the floor, and I didn't care, the need was pulsing everywhere.

His fingers gripped the top of my dress, yanking it down until my breasts were freed with a delicate bounce. I groaned at the heat of his mouth at my breast, the edges of his teeth, the flicking tongue. Reaching between us, he tugged at the fastenings of his pants. My eyes widened at the feel of him, hot and ready, demanding entrance . . . then everything blurred as my body yielded to the wet slide, the stunning invasion of hardness within softness. My head fell back over the unyielding bar of his arm and his mouth raked greedily over my exposed throat. He began to thrust in a heavy rhythm that made me squirm and pant.

The car stopped at a red light and all was still except the push and stroke inside me, and then the vehicle was turning, gliding forward with increasing momentum as if we were on a highway. I took him again and again, straining to pull him as close as possible. I clawed at his clothes, I needed his skin, couldn't reach it, needed, needed . . . his lips returned to mine, his tongue plunging into my mouth. He was filling me everywhere, driving deeper until the low sweet spasms started, ricocheting from my body to his. I shuddered, breaking the kiss as I pulled in huge lungfuls of air. Gage caught his breath, let it out like the hiss of a greenwood fire.

Drunk with endorphins, I was as slack as an empty pillowcase as Gage lifted me from the seat. He swore, bracing my head on his arm. I'd never seen him look so upset. The black pupils of his eyes had nearly swallowed the silver irises. "I was rough with you." His voice was ragged. "Damn it. I'm sorry. I just—"

"S'okay," I whispered, the last tremors of delight still echoing through my body.

"It's not okay. I—"

He was silenced abruptly as I pulled up enough to kiss him. He let my mouth move against his, but he didn't respond, only held me and pulled the gown back over my chest and down my naked legs, and wrapped me back up in his tux jacket.

Neither of us spoke after that. I was still on sensation overload, barely registering when Gage pressed a button and spoke to the driver. Still cradling me in one arm, he poured another drink and consumed it slowly. His face gave nothing away, but I felt the ferocious tension in his body.

Held securely in Gage's lap, I drowsed a little, lulled by the car ride and the warmth of his body. It was a rude awakening when the car stopped and the door was opened. I blinked as Gage jostled me awake and helped me out.

Knowing how messed up I was, how obvious the reason for our dishevelment, I shot a quick embarrassed glance at Phil the driver. He made a point of not looking at either of us, his expression strictly marshaled.

We were at 1800 Main. Gage stared at me as if he expected me to object to spending the night at his condo. I tried to weigh the consequences of staying or leaving, but my mind was too addled. In the welter of my thoughts, only one stood out: however I chose to deal with Hardy, this man was not going to stand aside politely.

Wearing Gage's tux jacket over my dress, I went through the lobby and into the elevator with him. The rapid ascent of the elevator caused me to sway on my high heels. Gage reached for me, kissing me until I was red-faced and out of breath. I stumbled a little as he pulled me from the elevator. With an easy motion, he picked me up and carried me—actually carried me—down the hallway to his condo.

We went straight to the waiting silence of the bedroom, where I was undressed in the darkness. Now, after the hasty coupling in the car, the urgency had eased into tenderness. Gage moved over me like a shadow, finding the softest places, the most acute nerves. The more he soothed, the more I ached. Breathing in long sighs, I reached for him, thirsting for the hard planes of muscle, the resilient flesh, the midnight silk of his hair. He coaxed me open, his mouth and fingers harrowing delicately until all my limbs were widespread and my body rose in a shuddering plea to receive him, and I moaned each time he slid inside me. Again, and again, until he had gone past all boundaries, inside me, immersed, possessing and possessed.

As the cowboy saying goes, a horse shouldn't be ridden hard and put away wet. That also applies to girlfriends, especially those who have gone a while without sex and need a little time to get back into the habit of it. I couldn't say how many times Gage reached for me in the night. When I woke up in the morning, muscles I didn't even know I had were aching, and my limbs were strained and stiff. And Gage was being *very* considerate, starting with bringing me coffee in bed.

"Don't bother trying to look remorseful," I said, leaning forward as he tucked an extra pillow behind my back. "It's obviously not a natural expression for you."

"I'm not remorseful." Dressed in a black T-shirt and jeans, Gage sat on the edge of the mattress. "I'm grateful."

I hitched the sheet higher over my naked breasts and took a careful sip of the steaming coffee. "You should be," I said. "Especially after that last time."

Our gazes held, and Gage laid his hand over my knee. The warmth of his palm penetrated the thin fabric of the sheet. "You all right?" he asked gently.

Damn him, he had an unerring ability to disarm me, showing concern just when I expected him to be arrogant or bossy. The nerves in my stomach tautened until my insides felt like a trampoline. Everything was so good with him, I wondered if I could give him up for the man I'd always wanted.

I started to say I was fine, but instead I found myself telling him the truth. "I'm scared of making the biggest mistake of my life. I'm just trying to figure out what the mistake is."

"You mean who the mistake is."

That made me wince. "I know you'll be angry if I see him, but—"

"No I won't. I want you to see him."

My fingers tightened on the heated sides of the cup. "You do?"

"It's obvious I won't have what I want from you until the situation is resolved. You need to find out how he's changed. You need to see if any of the old feelings are still there."

"Yes." I thought it was very evolved of him to show such understanding.

"That's fine with me," Gage continued, "as long as you don't go to bed with him."

Evolved, but still a Texan.

I gave him a quizzical smile. "Does that mean you don't care what I feel for him, just as long as you're the one I'm having sex with?"

"It means," Gage said evenly, "I'll take the sex for now and work on getting the rest later."

CHAPTER 23

From what I gathered, Churchill's evening hadn't been much better than mine. He and Vivian had ended the night with a brawl. She was the jealous type, Churchill said, and it wasn't his fault if other women had been friendly to him.

"How friendly were you to them?" I asked.

Churchill scowled as he used the remote control to flip the channels from his bed. "Let's just say it doesn't matter where I get my appetite, long as I come home for dinner."

"Good Lord, I hope you didn't say that to Vivian."

Silence.

I collected his breakfast tray. "No wonder she didn't stay last night." It was time for his shower—he'd gotten to the point where he could manage solo. "You have any problems getting showered and dressed, just buzz me on the walkie-talkie. I'll get the lawn guy to come in and help you." I started to leave.

"Liberty."

"Yes, sir?"

"I'm not one to poke in other people's business . . ." Churchill smiled at the look I gave him. "But is there anything you might want to talk to me about? Anything new happening in your life?"

"Not a thing. Same old, same old."

"You started up something with my son."

"I'm not going to discuss my love life with you, Churchill."

"Why not? You did before."

"You weren't my boss then. And my love life didn't happen to include your son."

"Fine, we won't talk about my son," he said equably. "Let's talk about an old acquaintance who's started up a nice little bypassed-oil recovery outfit."

I nearly dropped the tray. "You knew Hardy was there last night?"

"Not until someone introduced us. Soon as I heard the name, I knew right off who he was." Churchill gave me a look of such understanding, I wanted to cry.

Instead I set the tray down and made my way to a nearby chair.

"What happened, sugar?" I heard him ask.

I sat, my gaze anchored to the floor. "We just talked for a few minutes. I'm going to see him tomorrow." A long pause. "Gage is not exactly thrilled about the situation."

Churchill gave a dry chuckle. "I imagine not."

I looked at him then, unable to resist asking, "What did you think about Hardy?"

"Got a lot going for him. Smart, nice manners. He'll take a big bite out of the world before he's done. Did you invite him over to the house?"

"God, no. I'm sure we'll go somewhere else to talk."

"Stay if you like. It's your house too."

"Thanks, but . . ." I shook my head.

"Are you sorry you started up with Gage, sugar?"

The question undid me. "No," I said instantly, blinking hard. "I don't know what to be sorry about. It's just . . . Hardy was always the one I was supposed to end up with. He was everything I dreamed of and wanted. But *damn it,* why did he have to show up when I thought I'd finally gotten over him?"

"Some people there's no getting over," Churchill said.

I glanced at him through the salty blur in my eyes. "You mean Ava?"

"I'll miss her for the rest of my life. But no, I didn't mean Ava."

"Your first wife, then?"

"No, someone else."

I blotted the corners of my eyes with my sleeve. It seemed there was something Churchill wanted me to know about. But I'd had just about all the revelations I could handle for the moment. I stood and cleared my throat. "I've got to go downstairs and make breakfast for Carrington." I turned to leave.

"Liberty."

"Huh?"

Churchill appeared to be thinking hard about something, a frown gathering on his face. "Later I'm going to talk to you about this some more. Not as Gage's father. Not as your boss. As your old friend."

"Thanks," I said scratchily. "Something tells me I'm going to need my old friend."

Hardy called later that morning and invited me and Carrington to go riding on Sunday. I was delighted by the prospect, since I hadn't been on a horse in years, but I told him Carrington had only been on carnival ponies, and she didn't know how to ride.

"No problem," Hardy said easily. "She'll pick it up in no time."

In the morning he arrived at the Travis mansion in a huge white SUV. Carrington and I met him at the door, both of us dressed in jeans and boots and heavy jackets. I had told Carrington that Hardy was an old family friend, that he had known her when she was a baby and had in fact driven Mama to the hospital the day she was born.

Gretchen, wildly curious about the mysterious man from my past, was waiting in the entrance with us when the doorbell rang. I went to open it, and I was amused to hear Gretchen murmur, "Oh, my," at the sight of Hardy standing in the sunlight.

With the rangy, developed build of a roughneck, those striking blue eyes, that irresistible grin, Hardy had a larger-than-life quality any woman would find appealing. He swept a quick glance over me, murmured hello, and kissed my cheek before turning to Gretchen.

I introduced them, and Hardy took Gretchen's hand with obvious care, as if he were afraid of crushing it. She fluttered, smiled, and played the part of gracious Southern hostess to the hilt. As soon as Hardy's attention was diverted, Gretchen gave me a significant glance as if to ask, *Where have you been hiding him?*

Hardy, meanwhile, had lowered to his haunches in front of my sister. "Carrington, you're even prettier than your mama was. You probably don't remember me."

"You drove us to the hospital when I was born," Carrington volunteered shyly.

"That's right. In an old blue pickup, through a storm that flooded half of Welcome."

"That's where Miss Marva lives," Carrington exclaimed. "Do you know her?"

"Do I know Miss Marva?" Hardy grinned. "Yes, ma'am, I do. I had more than a few helpings of red velvet cake at Miss Marva's kitchen counter."

Thoroughly charmed, Carrington took Hardy's hand when he stood. "Liberty, you didn't say he knew Miss Marva!"

The sight of them hand in hand caused a tremor of deep emotion inside me. "I never talked about you much," I said to Hardy. My voice sounded odd to my own ears.

Hardy stared into my eyes and nodded, understanding that some things mean too much to be expressed easily.

"Well," Gretchen said brightly, "you all go on and have a good time. You be careful around the horses, Carrington. Remember what I told you about not going near the back hooves."

"I will!"

We went to the Silver Bridle Equestrian Center, where the horses lived better than most people. They were kept in a barn that featured a digital mosquito and fly control system, and piped-in classical music, and the stalls had individual faucets and light fixtures. Outside there was a covered arena, a jumping course, pastures, ponds, paddocks, and fifty acres of land to ride on.

Hardy had arranged for us to ride horses that belonged to a friend. Since the cost of stabling a horse at Silver Bridle rivaled some college tuitions, it was clear Hardy's friend had money to burn. We were brought a palomino and a blue roan, both shining and sleek and well behaved. The quarter horse is a big, muscular breed, known for its calmness and good cow sense.

Before we rode out, Hardy sat Carrington on a sturdy black pony and took her around the corral on a lead. As I expected, he charmed my sister completely, praising her, teasing until she giggled.

It was a gorgeous day to ride, cold but sunny, the air carrying the whiff of pastures and animals and the light earthy fragrance you can never isolate but is really the smell of Texas itself.

Hardy and I were able to talk as we rode side by side, Carrington a little ahead of us on the pony.

"You've done well by her, honey," he told me. "Your mother would have been proud."

"I hope so." I looked at my sister, her hair done in a neat blond braid tied with a white ribbon. "She's wonderful, isn't she?"

"Wonderful." But Hardy was staring at me. "Marva told me some of what you've gone through. You've carried a lot on your shoulders, haven't you?"

I shrugged. It had been difficult at times, but in retrospect my burdens and struggles had been ordinary ones. So many women had to contend with much more. "The hardest part was right after Mama died. I don't think I had a full night's sleep in two years. I was working and taking classes and trying to do my best for Carrington. It seemed like everything was always half-done, we were never on time, I couldn't seem to get anything right. But eventually everything got easier."

"Tell me how you got involved with the Travises."

"Which one?" I asked without thinking, and then my cheeks heated.

Hardy smiled. "Let's start with the old man."

As we talked, I had the sense of uncovering something precious and long-buried, fully formed. Our conversation was a process of removing layers, some of them easily dusted away. Other layers, requiring chisels or axes, were left alone for now. We revealed as much as we dared about what had happened during the years that separated us.

But it wasn't what I had expected, being with Hardy again. There was something in me that remained stubbornly locked away, as if I were afraid to let out the emotion I had harbored for so long.

The afternoon approached and Carrington became tired and hungry. We rode back to the barn and dismounted. I gave Carrington a handful of quarters to get a drink from a vending machine at the main building. She scampered off, leaving me alone with Hardy.

He stood looking at me for a moment. "Come here," he murmured, pulling me into the empty tack room. He kissed me gently, and I tasted dust, sun, skin-salt, and the years dissolved in a slow, sure rush of warmth. I had been waiting for him, for this, and it was just as sweet as I remembered. But as Hardy deepened the kiss, tried to take more, I pulled away with a nervous laugh.

"Sorry," I said breathlessly. "Sorry."

"It's all right." Hardy's eyes were vivid with heat, his voice reassuring. He gave me a quick grin. "Got carried away."

Despite the pleasure I took in Hardy's company, I was relieved when he took us back to River Oaks. I needed to retreat, to think, to let all this settle. Carrington was chattering happily in the back seat, about wanting to ride again, having her own horse someday, speculating on the best horse names.

"You've launched us into a whole new phase," I told Hardy. "Now we've gone from Barbie to horses."

Hardy grinned and spoke to Carrington. "You tell your big sister to call me whenever you want to ride, honey."

"I want to do it again tomorrow!"

"You have school tomorrow," I said, which made Carrington scowl until she remembered she could tell all her friends about the pony she'd ridden.

Hardy pulled up to the front of the house and helped us out.

Glancing at the garage, I saw Gage's car. He was almost never there on Sunday afternoons. My stomach did one of those funny flips that happens when you're on a roller-coaster ride, heading into the first big drop. "Gage is here," I said.

Hardy appeared unruffled. "Of course he is."

Taking Hardy's hand, Carrington walked her new friend to the door, talking a mile a minute. ". . . and this is our house, and I've got a bedroom upstairs with yellow striped paper on the walls, and that thing right there is a video camera so we can look at people before we decide to let 'em in—"

"None of it's ours, baby," I said uncomfortably. "It's the Travises' house."

Ignoring me, Carrington pushed the doorbell and mugged for the camera, making Hardy laugh.

The door opened, and there was Gage, dressed in jeans and a white polo shirt. My pulse rioted as his gaze went first to me, then to my companion.

"Gage!" Carrington shrieked as if she hadn't seen him in months. She flew to him and clamped her arms around his waist. "That's our old friend Hardy—he took us riding, and I was on a black pony named Prince, and I rode like a real cowgirl!"

Gage smiled down at her, his arm clasping her narrow shoulders securely.

Glancing at Hardy, I saw the glint of speculation in his eyes. It was something he hadn't expected, the attachment between my sister and Gage. He extended his hand with an easy smile. "Hardy Cates."

"Gage Travis."

They shook hands firmly, with a brief, nearly imperceptible contest that ended in a draw. Gage stood with Carrington still hanging around his waist, his face expressionless. I shoved my hands in my pockets. The tiny junctures between my fingers had gone damp. Both men seemed so relaxed, and yet the air was punctured with conflict.

It was startling to see them together. Hardy had loomed so large in my memory for so long that I was surprised to realize Gage was equally tall, albeit leaner. They were different in almost every way, education, background, experience . . . Gage, who played by the rules he'd usually had a hand in making, and Hardy, who tossed out the rules like a handful of Texas redbacks if they didn't suit him. Gage, always the smartest one in the room, and Hardy, who had told me with a deceptively lazy smile that all he had to do was be smarter than the guy he was doing a deal with.

"Congratulations on the drilling start-up," Gage said to Hardy. "You've had some impressive finds in a short time. High-quality pay reserves, I've heard."

Hardy smiled and lifted his shoulders in a slight shrug. "We've had some luck."

"It takes more than luck."

They talked about geochemistry and an analysis of well cuttings, and the difficulty of estimating productive intervals in the field, and then the conversation turned to Gage's alternative technology company.

"It's gotten out you're working on some new biodiesel," Hardy said.

Gage's pleasant expression didn't change. "Nothing worth talking about yet."

"Not what I heard. Rumor has it you managed to cut down on the NOX emissions . . . but the biofuel itself is still expensive as hell." Hardy grinned at him. "Oil's cheaper."

"For now."

I knew a little about Gage's private views on the subject. He and Churchill both agreed the days of cheap oil were almost at an end, and once we reached the supply-demand gap, biofuels would help stave off an economic crisis. Many oil people, friends of the Travises, said it wouldn't happen for decades and there was plenty of petroleum left. They joked with Gage and said they hoped he wasn't planning to come out with something to replace petroleum, or they'd hold him responsible for lost business. Gage had told me they were only half joking.

After minute or two of excruciatingly careful conversation, Hardy glanced at me and murmured, "I'll head out now." He nodded to Gage. "Nice to meet you."

Gage nodded, turning his attention to Carrington, who was trying to tell him more about the horses.

"I'll walk you to the door," I said to Hardy, profoundly relieved the encounter was over.

As we walked, Hardy put an arm around my shoulders. "I want to see you again," he said in a low voice.

"Maybe in a few days."

"I'll call tomorrow."

"Okay." We stopped at the threshold. Hardy kissed my forehead, and I looked up into his warm blue eyes. "Well," I said, "the two of you were very civilized."

Hardy laughed. "He'd like to rip my head off." He braced one hand on the doorframe, sobering quickly. "I don't see you with someone like him. He's a cold son of a bitch."

"Not when you get to know him."

Reaching out, Hardy took a lock of my hair and rubbed it gently between his fingers. "I think you could probably thaw out a glacier, honey." He smiled and let go, walking toward his SUV.

Feeling tired and bemused, I went in search of Carrington and Gage. I found them in the kitchen, raiding the refrigerator and pantry.

"Hungry?" Gage asked.

"Starving."

He set out a container of pasta salad, and another of strawberries. I found a loaf of French bread and cut a few slices while Carrington brought three plates.

"Just two," Gage told her. "I've already eaten."

"Okay. Can I have a cookie?"

"After lunch."

While Carrington got out the napkins, I looked at Gage with a frown. "You're not staying?"

He shook his head. "I found out what I needed to know."

Mindful of Carrington nearby, I held back my questions until the plates were fixed and set on the table. Gage poured Carrington a glass of milk and set two small cookies on the edge of her plate. "Eat the cookies last, darlin'," he murmured. She reached up to hug him, then started on her pasta salad.

Gage gave me an impersonal smile. "Bye, Liberty."

"Wait—" I followed him out, pausing only to tell Carrington I'd be right back. I hurried to keep pace with Gage. "You think you've got Hardy Cates all figured out after seeing him for five minutes?"

"Yes."

"What's your take on him?"

"There's no point in telling you. You'll say I'm biased."

"And you're not?"

"Hell, yes, I'm biased. I also happen to be right."

I stopped him at the front door with a touch on his arm. Gage looked down at the place my fingers had brushed, and slowly his gaze traveled to my face.

"Tell me," I said.

Gage replied in a matter-of-fact tone. "I think he's ambitious to the bone, works hard and plays harder. He's hungry for all the visible signs of success—the cars, the women, the house, the owner's box at Reliant. I think he'll throw away every principle he's got to climb up the ladder. He'll make and lose a couple of fortunes, and he'll go through three or four wives. And he wants you because you're his last hope of keeping it real. But even you wouldn't be enough."

Blinking at the harsh assessment, I wrapped my arms across my front. "You don't know him. That's not Hardy."

"We'll see." His smile didn't reach his eyes. "You'd better go back to the kitchen. Carrington's waiting."

"Gage . . . you're mad at me, aren't you? I'm so—"

"No, Liberty." His face softened a little. "I'm trying to figure it all out. Just like you."

I saw Hardy a few times over the next couple of weeks—a lunch, a dinner, a long walk. Beneath the conversations and silences and reconnecting intimacy, I tried to reconcile the adult Hardy had become with the boy I had known and longed for. It troubled me to realize they weren't the same . . . but of course I wasn't the same either.

It seemed important to figure out how much of the attraction I felt for Hardy came from *now,* as opposed to the past. If we had met now, for the first time, as strangers, would I have felt the same about him?

I couldn't have said for certain. But Lord, he was charming. He had a way about him, he always had. He made me feel so comfortable, we could talk about anything. Even Gage.

"Tell me what he's like," Hardy said, holding my hand, playing with my fingers. "How much of what they say is true?"

Knowing Gage's reputation, I shrugged and smiled. "Gage is . . . accomplished. But he can be intimidating. The problem with Gage is, he always seems to do everything perfectly. People think he's invulnerable. And he's very private. It's not easy to get close to a man like that."

"But you have, apparently."

I shrugged and smiled. "Sort of. We'd just started to get close . . . but then . . ."

Then Hardy had shown up.

"What do you know about his company?" he asked casually. "I can't figure out why a man from a Texas family with connections to big oil is fooling around with fuel cells and biodiesels."

I smiled. "That's Gage for you." And, with a little prodding, I told him what I knew about the technology Gage's company was working on. "There's a huge biofuel deal in the works. He wants to build a blending facility at this huge refinery in Dallas, and they're going to start mixing biodiesel with all their fuel, and distribute it everywhere in Texas. From what I can tell, the negotiations are pretty intense." I heard the note of pride in my own voice as I added, "Churchill says only Gage could pull it off."

"He must have gotten past some damn big hurdles," Hardy commented. "In some parts of Houston, just saying the word 'biodiesel' will get you shot. Which refinery is it?"

"Medina."

"That's a big one, all right. Well, for his sake, I hope everything works out." And, taking my hand, he deftly changed the subject.

Near the end of the second week, Hardy took me to a supermodern bar that reminded me of a spaceship, the sterile décor backlit with blue and green. The tables were the size of coasters balanced on soda straws. It was the latest place to be seen, and everyone in the bar looked extremely hip, if not exactly comfortable.

Nursing a Southern Comfort on ice, I glanced around the place and couldn't help noticing that Hardy was attracting attention from a few women. No surprise there, considering his looks and presence and charm. And as time passed, Hardy would be even more of a catch, more visible in his success.

I finished my drink and asked for another. I couldn't seem to relax tonight. As Hardy and I tried to talk over the blare of the live music, all I could think about was that I missed Gage. I hadn't seen him in a few days. Guiltily I reflected that I had asked a lot of Gage, maybe too much, in asking him to be patient while I tried to figure out my feelings for another man.

Hardy rubbed his thumb gently over the backs of my knuckles. His voice was soft beneath the biting staccato of the music. "Liberty." My gaze lifted to his. His eyes glowed an unearthly blue in the artificial light. "Let's go, honey. It's time to settle a few things."

"Go where?" I asked faintly.

"Back to my place. We need to talk."

I hesitated, swallowed hard, and managed a jerky nod. Hardy had shown me his apartment earlier in the evening—I had opted to meet him there rather than have him pick me up at River Oaks.

We didn't talk much as Hardy drove me downtown. But he kept my hand in his. My heart beat like a hummingbird's wings. I wasn't quite sure what was going to happen, or what I wanted to happen.

We arrived at the luxury high-rise and Hardy took me up to his apartment, a large space comfortably furnished with leather, hide, and stylish rough-woven fabrics. Wrought-iron lamps with textured parchment shades cast a muted glow through the main room.

"Want a drink?" he asked.

I shook my head, knitting my fingers together as I stood near the door. "No, thanks. I had enough at the bar."

Smiling quizzically, Hardy came to me and pressed his lips to my temple. "Are you nervous, honey? It's just me. Your old friend Hardy."

I let out a shaky sigh and leaned against him. "Yes. I remember you."

His arms came around me, and we stayed like that for a long time, standing together, breathing together.

"Liberty," he whispered. "I told you once that in my whole life, you'd always be what I wanted most. Remember?"

I nodded against his shoulder. "The night you left."

"I won't leave you again." His lips brushed the tender edge of my ear. "I still feel that way, Liberty. I know what I'm asking you to walk away from—but I swear, you would never regret it. I'll give you everything you ever wanted." He touched my jaw with his fingertips, angling my face upward, and his mouth came to mine.

My balance disintegrated, and I held on to him. His body was hard from years of brutal physical labor, his arms strong and secure. He kissed differently than Gage, more direct, aggressive, without Gage's erotic stealth and playfulness. He parted my lips and explored slowly, and I kissed him back with mingled guilt and pleasure. His warm hand moved to my breast, fingers lightly following the round contours, pausing at the sensitive tip. I tore my mouth from his with an agitated sound.

"Hardy, no," I managed to say, desire forming a hot weight in my stomach. "I can't."

His mouth searched the quivering skin of my throat. "Why not?"

"I promised Gage—he and I agreed—I wouldn't do this with you. Not until—"

"What?" Hardy drew his head back, eyes narrowing. "You don't owe him that. He doesn't own you."

"It's not that, it has nothing to do with ownership, it's just—"

"Like hell."

"I can't break a promise," I insisted. "Gage trusts me."

Hardy said nothing, only gave me a peculiar look. Something about his silence drew shivers up from beneath my skin. Dragging his hand through his hair, Hardy went to one of the picture windows and stared at the city spread below us. "You sure about that?" he asked finally.

"What do you mean?"

He turned to face me, leaning back and crossing his legs at the ankles. "The last couple of times I've seen you, I noticed a silver Crown Victoria tailing us. So I got the license plate number and had it checked out. It belongs to a guy who works for a surveillance company."

A chill rushed over me. "You think Gage is having me followed?"

"The car is parked at the end of the street right now." He gestured for me to come to the window. "See for yourself."

I didn't move. "He wouldn't do that."

"Liberty," he said quietly, "you haven't known the bastard long enough to be sure of what he would or wouldn't do."

I rubbed my prickling upper arms with my hands in a futile attempt to warm myself. I was too stunned to speak.

"I know you think of the Travises as friends," I heard Hardy continue in a level tone. "But they're not, Liberty. You think they've done you a favor, taking you and Carrington in? It was no fucking favor. They owe you a hell of a lot more than that."

"Why do you say that?"

He crossed the room to me, took me by the shoulders and stared into my bewildered eyes. "You really don't know, do you? I thought you might at least suspect something."

"What are you talking about?"

His mouth was grim. He pulled me to the sofa, and we sat while he gripped my nerveless hands in his. "Your mother had an affair with Churchill Travis. It lasted for years."

I tried to swallow. The saliva would hardly go down. "That's not true," I whispered.

"Marva told me. You can ask her yourself. Your mother told her all about it."

"Why didn't Marva say anything to me?"

"She was afraid for you to know. Afraid for you to get tangled up with the Travises. For all she knew, they might have decided to take Carrington away from you, and you couldn't have done a damn thing to stop them. Later, when she found out you were working for Churchill, she figured he was trying to make it up to you. She thought it best not to intefere."

"You're not making sense. Why would they have wanted to take Carrington away from me? What could Churchill have—" The blood drained from my face. I stopped and covered my mouth with trembling fingers as I understood.

I heard Hardy's voice as if from a great distance. "Liberty . . . who do you think Carrington's father is?"

CHAPTER 94

I drove away from Hardy's apartment building, intending to go straight to River Oaks
and confront Churchill. I was in more turmoil than I had been at any time since
Mama had died. I was strangely calm on the
outside, even though my mind and heart
were in anarchy. *It can't be true,* I thought
over and over. I didn't want it to be true.

If Churchill was Carrington's father . . .
I thought about the times we'd been hungry,
the hardships, the times she'd asked why she
didn't have a daddy when her friends did.
I'd showed her the picture of my father

and said, "This is our daddy," and I'd told her how much he loved her even though he was living in heaven. I thought of the birthdays and holidays, the times she'd been sick, all the things she'd had to do without . . .

If Churchill was Carrington's father, he didn't owe a damn thing to me. But he owed plenty to her.

Before I realized what I was doing, I found myself driving up to the gated entrance of the garage at 1800 Main. The security guard asked for my driver's license, and I hesitated, thinking I should tell him I'd made a mistake, I hadn't meant to come here. Instead I showed it to him and drove into the residents' parking section, and stopped the car. I wanted to see Gage. I didn't even know if he was home.

My finger was shaking as I pressed the button for the eighteenth floor, a little from fear but mostly from anger. Despite Mexican women's reputation for having hot tempers, I was pretty mild-mannered most of the time. I didn't like getting angry, I hated the bitter adrenaline rush that came with it. But at the moment I was ready to explode. I wanted to throw things.

I went to Gage's door with long, heel-digging strides, and hammered with a force that bruised my knuckles. When there was no response, I raised my fist to hammer again, and nearly pitched forward as the door was opened.

Gage stood there, looking calm and capable as always. "Liberty . . ." A question tipped the last syllable of my name. His light gaze swept over me, coming to rest on my flushed face. He reached out to draw me inside the apartment. I jerked away from him as I stepped over the threshold. "What's going on, sweetheart?"

I couldn't bear the warmth in his voice, or my own aching need, even now, to bury myself against him. "Don't you dare pretend you're concerned about me," I stormed, throwing my purse to the floor. "I can't believe what you've done, when I've been nothing but honest with you!"

Gage's expression cooled considerably. "It would help," he said in a pleasant tone, "if you'd tell me what we're talking about."

"You know exactly why I'm angry. You hired someone to follow me. You've been *spying* on me. I don't understand why. I've done nothing to deserve being treated like this—"

"Calm down."

Most men don't seem to get that telling a pissed-off woman to calm down is like throwing gunpowder on a fire.

"I don't want to calm down, I want to know why the hell you've done this!"

"If you kept your promise," Gage pointed out, "you have no reason to worry about someone keeping an eye on you."

"Then you admit you hired someone to follow me? Oh, God, you did, I can see it on your face. Damn you, I haven't slept with him. You should have trusted me."

"I've always believed in the old saying 'Trust but verify.'"

"That may work great for business," I said in a murderous voice, "but not in a relationship. I want it stopped now. I don't want to be followed anymore. Get rid of him!"

"All right. All right."

Surprised that he'd agreed so readily, I shot him a wary glance.

Gage was staring at me oddly now, and I realized I was trembling visibly. My rage had fled, leaving me with a sense of sick despair. I wasn't at all certain how I'd gotten to be in the middle of a tug-of-war between two ruthless men . . . not to mention Churchill. I was tired of it, tired of everything, especially the swarm of unanswered questions. I didn't know where to go or what to do with myself.

"Liberty," he said carefully, "I know you haven't slept with him. I do trust you. Damn it, I'm sorry. I couldn't stand back and wait when I wanted something—someone—this badly. I can't let go of you without a fight."

"Is this all about winning? Is it some kind of contest to you?"

"No, it's not a contest. I want you. I want things I'm not sure you're ready to hear about yet. Most of all I want to hold you until you stop shaking." His voice turned hoarse. "Let me hold you, Liberty."

I was still, wondering if I could trust him, wishing I could think straight. As I stared at him, I saw the frustration in his eyes, and the need. "Please," he said.

I went forward, and he caught me tightly against him. "There's my girl," came his low murmur. I buried my face against his shoulder, inhaling the familiar spice of his skin. Relief flowed over me, and I fought to get closer, needing more of him than my arms could encompass.

After a while Gage eased me to the sofa, kneading my back and hips. Our legs tangled together, and my head was on his shoulder, and I would have thought I was in heaven if the sofa hadn't been so hard.

"You need throw pillows," I said in a muffled voice.

"I hate clutter." He shifted to look down at me. "Something else is bothering you. Tell me what it is and I'll fix it."

"You can't."

"Try me."

I longed to confide in him about Churchill and Carrington, but I had to keep it private for now. I didn't want Gage to handle it for me, and I knew he would if I told him.

This was between Churchill and me.

So I shook my head, burrowing closer, and Gage stroked my hair. "Stay with me tonight," he said.

I felt fragile and raw. I savored the hard-muscled surface of his arm beneath my neck, the reassuring warmth of his body. "Okay," I whispered.

Gage looked down at me intently, his hand cradling the side of my face with infinite gentleness. He kissed the tip of my nose. "I have to leave before dawn. I've got a meeting in Dallas, and another at Research Triangle."

"Where is that?"

He smiled and traced my cheekbone with a lazy fingertip. "North Carolina. I won't be back for a couple of days." Continuing to stare at me, he started to ask something, then checked himself. He lifted from the sofa in a fluid movement, pulling me up with him. "Come on. You need to go to bed."

I went with him to the bedroom, which was dark except for the glow of a small lamp focused on the ocean painting. Feeling shy, I undressed and put on the white T-shirt Gage handed to me. Gratefully I crawled between the slick, luxurious sheets. The light was extinguished. I felt the weight of Gage's body depress the mattress. Rolling toward him, I snuggled close and hitched my leg over him.

Pressed together as we were, I couldn't help noticing the hard, almost scorching pressure of him against my thigh.

"Ignore it," Gage said.

That made me smile in spite of my fatigue. I brushed my lips furtively against his throat. The warm scent of him was all it took to start my pulse beating in a swift erotic tattoo. My toes delicately explored the hairy surface of his leg. "It seems like a shame to waste it."

"You're too tired."

"Not for a quickie."

"I don't do quickies."

"I don't care." I crawled over him with ardent determination, gasping at little at the flexing power of his body beneath mine.

A chuckle sifted through the darkness, and Gage moved suddenly, turning to pin me beneath him.

"Be still," he whispered, "and I'll take care of you."

I obeyed, shivering as he eased the hem of the T-shirt upward, peeling it back over my breasts. The tender heat of his mouth covered a taut nipple. I lifted up to him with a pleading sound.

His lips crossed my chest in a sojourn of half-open kisses, while he crouched over me like a cat. He nibbled on the wing of my collarbone,

finding the shallow depressions where my pulse stung, soothing it
with his tongue. Lower, where the banded muscles of my midriff
quivered at his touch, lower where every lazy exploring kiss turned
to fire and I twisted to escape the indecent pleasure, and he held
me there, still and tight, while sensation rushed and shattered all
through me.

I woke up alone, swathed in sheets that held the incense of sex and
skin. Huddling deeper beneath the covers, I watched the first rays of
morning creep through the window. The night with Gage had left me
feeling steadier, able to handle whatever lay ahead. I had slept against
him all night, not hiding, just taking shelter. I had always managed to
find strength in myself—but it had been a revelation to draw strength
from someone else.

Getting out of bed, I went through the empty condo to the kitchen,
and picked up the phone to dial the Travis mansion.

Carrington picked up on the second ring. "Hello?"

"Baby, it's me. I had a sleepover at Gage's last night. I'm sorry I
didn't call you—by the time I remembered, it was too late."

"Oh, that's okay," my sister said. "Aunt Gretchen made popcorn,
and she and Churchill and I watched the silliest old movie with lots of
singing and dancing. It was great."

"Are you getting ready for school?"

"Yes, the driver's going to take me in the Bentley."

I shook my head ruefully as I heard her casual tone. "You sound
just like a River Oaks kid."

"I have to finish my breakfast. My cereal's getting soggy."

"All right. Carrington, would you do something for me? Tell
Churchill I'll be there in about half an hour, and I need to talk to him
about something important."

"About what?"

"Grown-up stuff. I love you."

"Love you too. Bye!"

Churchill was waiting for me near the family room fireplace. So familiar and yet a stranger. Of all the men in my life, I had known Churchill the longest and depended on him the most. There was no getting around the fact that he was the closest thing to a father I had ever known.

I loved him.

And he was going to let loose with a few secrets now or I would kill him.

"Morning," he said, his gaze searching.

"Morning. How are you feeling?"

"Fair enough. And you?"

"I'm not sure," I said truthfully. "Nervous, I guess. A little angry. A lot confused."

With Churchill, you never had to lead gracefully into a touchy subject. You could blurt out just about anything and he would handle it with no problem. Knowing that made it easier for me to walk across the room, stop in front of him, and let it roll.

"You knew my mother," I said.

The fire in the hearth sounded like a flag whipping and flapping on a windy day.

Churchill answered with astonishing self-possession. "I loved your mother." He let me absorb that for a moment, and then gave a decisive nod. "Help me move to the sofa, Liberty. The chair seat's digging into the backs of my legs."

We both took temporary refuge in the logistics of transferring him from the wheelchair to the sofa, more a matter of balance than strength. I fetched an ottoman, propped it beneath the cast, gave Churchill a couple of small pillows to wedge against his side. When he was comfortably settled, I sat next to him and waited with my arms wrapped tight around my middle.

Churchill fished out a slim wallet from his shirt pocket, searched through its contents, handed me a tiny ancient black-and-white photo with tattered edges. It was my mother as a very young woman, beautiful as a movie goddess, and there were words written in her own hand. *"To my darling C. love, Diana."*

"Her father—your grandfather—worked for me," Churchill said, taking back the photo, holding it in the palm of his hand like a religious artifact. "I was already a widower when I met Diana at a company picnic. Gage was barely out of diapers. He needed a mother, and I needed a wife. It was obvious from the start Diana was wrong in just about every way. Too young, too pretty, too fiery. None of that mattered." He shook his head, remembering. Gruffly, "My God, I loved that woman."

I watched him without blinking. I couldn't believe Churchill was opening a window to my mother's life, the past she had never talked about.

"I went after her with everything I had," Churchill said. "Whatever I thought would tempt her. I told her right off I wanted to marry her. She got pressure from all sides, especially her family. The Truitts were middle-class, and they knew if Diana married me there was no limit to what I'd give 'em." Without shame he added, "I made sure Diana knew that too."

I tried to think of Churchill as a young man, pursuing a woman with every weapon at his disposal. "Jesus, what a circus it must have been."

"I bullied, bribed, and talked her into loving me. I got an engagement ring on her finger." He gave a sneaky laugh that I found sort of endearing. "Give me long enough and I grow on a person."

"Did Mama really love you, or was it an act?" I asked, not meaning to be hurtful, just needing to know.

Being Churchill, he didn't take it the wrong way. "There were moments I think she did. But in the end it wasn't enough."

"What happened? Was it Gage? She didn't want to be a mother so soon?"

"No, it had nothing to do with that. She seemed to like the boy well enough, and I promised her we'd hire nannies and housemaids, all the help she'd ever need."

"Then what? I can't imagine why . . . *Oh*."

My father had gotten in the way.

I felt instant sympathy for Churchill, and at the same time a jab of pride in the father I had never known, who had managed to steal my mother away from a rich and powerful older man.

"That's right," Churchill said, as if he could read my thoughts. "Your daddy was everything I wasn't. Young, handsome, and as my daughter Haven would say, disenfranchised."

"Also Mexican."

Churchill nodded. "That didn't go over big with your grandfather. In those days, marriage between brown and white was frowned upon."

"That's a nice way of putting it," I said dryly, aware that it had probably been an outright disgrace. "Knowing my mother, the Romeo and Juliet scenario probably made the whole thing even more attractive."

"She was a romantic," Churchill agreed, tucking the photo back in his wallet with extreme care. "And she had a passion for your daddy. Her father warned if she ran off with him, not to bother coming back. She knew the family would never forgive her."

"Because she fell in love with a poor guy?" I demanded in outrage.

"It wasn't right," Churchill admitted. "But times were hard."

"That's no excuse."

"Diana came to me the night she ran off to get married. Your father waited out in the car while she came in and said goodbye and gave back the ring. I wouldn't take it. I told her to trade it for a wedding present. And I begged her to come to me if she ever needed anything."

I understood what those words must have cost him, a man of such enormous pride.

"And by the time my father died," I said, "you'd already married Ava."

"That's right."

I was quiet then, sifting through memories. Poor Mama, struggling to make it on her own. No family to go to, no one to help. But those mysterious disappearances, when she would be gone for a day and then there would be food in the refrigerator and the bill collectors stopped calling . . .

"She came to you," I said. "Even though you were married. She visited you and you gave her money. You helped her for years."

Churchill didn't need to say anything. I saw the truth in his eyes.

I squared my shoulders and forced myself to ask the big question. "Is Carrington yours?"

Color mounted in his weathered face, and he gave me an offended glare. "You think I wouldn't take responsibility for my own child? Let her be raised in a damn trailer park? No, there's no chance she's mine. Diana and I never had that kind of relationship."

"Come off it, Churchill. I'm not an idiot."

"Your mother and I never slept together. You think I'd do that to Ava?"

"Sorry, but I don't buy it. Not if she was getting money from you."

"Honey, I don't give a fuck-all if you believe me or not," he said evenly. "Not saying I wasn't tempted. But I was physically faithful to Ava. I owed her at least that much. You want me to take a paternity test, I'll do it."

That convinced me. "Okay. I'm sorry. Sorry. I'm just . . . it's hard to accept that my mother went to you for money all those years. She always made such a big deal about never taking handouts from people and how I needed to be self-reliant when I grew up. That makes her a big fat hypocrite."

"It makes her a parent who wanted the best for her child. She did the best she could. I wanted to do a lot more for her, but she wouldn't let me." Churchill sighed, suddenly looking weary. "I didn't see her at all the year before she died."

"She was wrapped up with a guy she was dating," I said. "A real scumbag."

"Louis Sadlek."

"She told you about him?"

Churchill shook his head. "Read the accident report."

I stared at him, studied him, considering his fondness for grand gestures. "You watched the funeral from a black limo," I said. "I always wondered who it was. And the yellow roses . . . you've been sending them all these years, haven't you?"

He was quiet as I continued to put the pieces together. "I got a deal on her casket," I said slowly. "That was you. You paid for it. You got the funeral director to go along with it."

"It was the last thing I could do for Diana," he said. "That, and keep an eye on her daughters."

"Keep an eye on us how?" I asked suspiciously.

Churchill kept his mouth shut. But I knew him too well. Part of my job was helping to organize the rivers of information that flowed to Churchill. He kept tabs on businesses, political issues, people . . . he was always getting reports of one kind or another in deceptively innocuous tan envelopes. "You weren't spying on me, were you?" I asked, thinking, *Sweet Jesus, these Travis men are making me paranoid.*

He shrugged a little. "I wouldn't call it that. I just checked in on you now and then."

"I know you, Churchill. You don't just 'check in' on people. You're a meddler. You . . ." I sucked in a quick breath. "That scholarship I got from the beauty school . . . you did that too, didn't you?"

"I wanted to help you."

I shot up from the sofa. "I didn't want any help! I could have done it on my own. Damn you, Churchill! First you were Mama's sugar daddy and then you were mine, except I didn't even have a choice about it. Do you know how stupid that makes me feel?"

His eyes narrowed. "What I did for you doesn't take away a thing from what you accomplished. Not a single thing."

"You should have left me alone. I swear, Churchill, you're going to take back every cent you spent on me, or I'll never speak to you again."

"Fair enough. I'll take the scholarship money out of your salary. But not the money for the casket. I did that for her, not for you. Sit down, we're not done talking. I got more to say."

"Great." I sat. My mind was buzzing. "Does Gage know?"

Churchill nodded. "He followed me one day when I drove to meet Diana for lunch at the St. Regis."

"You met her at a hotel and you *never*—" I stopped at the scowl he gave me. "Okay, okay. I believe you."

"Gage saw us having lunch," Churchill continued, "and he confronted me later. He was mad as hell even after I swore I hadn't cheated on Ava. But he agreed to keep it secret. He didn't want Ava to be hurt."

My mind went back to the day I had moved to River Oaks.

"Gage recognized my mother from the picture in my room upstairs," I said.

"Yes. We had words about it."

"I'll bet you did." I gazed into the fire. "Why'd you start coming to the salon?"

"I wanted to know you. I was proud as hell of you for keeping Carrington and raising her on your own, and working your tail off. I already loved you and Carrington because you were all that was left of Diana. But after I met you, I loved you for yourselves."

I could barely see him through the glitter in my eyes. "I love you too, you high-handed interfering old jackass."

Churchill held out his arm, gesturing for me to come closer. And I did. I leaned against him, into the comforting fatherly smell of aftershave and leather and starched cotton.

"My mother could never let go of Daddy," I said absently. "And you could never let go of her." I sat back and looked at him. "I've always thought it was about finding the right person. But it's about choosing the right person, isn't it? . . . Making a real choice and giving your whole heart to it."

"Easier said than done."

Not for me. Not anymore. "I need to see Gage," I said. "Of all times for him to be gone, this has got to be the worst."

"Sugar." Churchill wore the beginnings of a frown. "Did Gage happen to mention why he was going on this last-minute trip?"

I didn't like the sound of that. "He told me he was going to Dallas and then to Research Triangle. But no, he didn't say why."

"He wouldn't want me to tell you," Churchill said. "But I think you need to know. There have been some last-minute problems on the Medina deal."

"Oh, no," I said in concern, knowing how important it was to Gage's company. "What happened?"

"Security leak in the negotiations process. No one was supposed to know the deal was going on—in fact, everyone at the table had signed a nondisclosure agreement. But somehow your friend Hardy Cates found out what was in the works. He took the information to Medina's biggest supplier, Victory Petroleum, who is now putting pressure on Medina to kill the whole deal."

All the air seemed to leave my lungs at once. I couldn't believe it. "My God, it was me," I said numbly. "I mentioned the negotiations to Hardy. I didn't know it was top secret. I had no idea he'd do something like this. I've got to call Gage and tell him what I did, that I didn't mean to—"

"He's already figured it out, sugar."

"Gage knows I'm the leak? But—" I broke off, turning cold with panic. Gage must have known last night. And yet he hadn't said anything. I felt nauseous. I buried my face in my hands, my voice filtering through the cage of my stiff fingers. "What can I do? How can I make this right?"

"Gage is taking care of damage control," Churchill said. "He's cooling things down at Medina this morning, and later today he'll pull his team at Research Triangle together to deal with the issues that were raised about the biofuel. Don't worry, sugar. It'll all work out."

"I need to do something. I . . . Churchill, will you help me?"

"Always," he said without hesitation. "You name it."

CHAPTER 25

The sensible thing would have been to wait for Gage to come back to Texas. But in light of the fact that he'd tolerated more than a few blows to his pride and an even bigger blow to an important business deal, all for my sake, I knew it was no time to be sensible. As Churchill says, sometimes grand gestures are called for.

I made one stop on the way to the airport, at Hardy's downtown office. It was located on Fannin in a towering aluminum and glass building with two halves that locked together like two giant puzzle pieces.

The receptionist was a predictably attractive blond woman with a smoky voice and great legs. She showed me in to Hardy's office as soon as I arrived.

He was dressed in a dark Brooks Brothers suit and a vivid blue tie the exact shade of his eyes. He looked confident, sharp, a man who was going places.

I told Hardy about my conversation with Churchill, and what I'd learned about his part in trying to ruin the Medina deal. "I don't understand how you could have done such a thing," I said. "I would never have expected it from you."

He looked unrepentant. "It's just business, honey. Sometimes you have to get a little dirt on your hands."

Some dirt doesn't wash off, I thought of saying. But I knew he would have to find that out for himself someday. "You used me to hurt him. You figured it would break us up, and on top of that, it would put Victory Petroleum in the position of owing you a favor. You'd do just about anything to succeed, wouldn't you?"

"I'll do what has to be done," he said, his face smooth. "I'll be damned if I'll apologize for wanting to get ahead."

My anger drained away, and I stared at him compassionately. "You don't have to apologize, Hardy. I understand. I remember all those things we needed and wanted and could never have. It's just . . . it's not going to work for you and me."

His voice was very soft. "You think I can't love you, Liberty?"

I bit my lip and shook my head. "I think you loved me once. But even then it wasn't enough. Do you want to know something? . . . Gage didn't tell me about what you'd done, even though he had the perfect opportunity. Because he wasn't going to let you drive a wedge between us. He forgave me without being asked, without even letting me know I'd betrayed him. That's love, Hardy."

"Ah, honey . . ." Hardy took my hand, lifted it, and kissed the inside of my wrist, at the tiny whisk of blue veins beneath the skin. "One lost deal doesn't mean shit to him. He's had it all since the day he was born. If he'd been in my shoes, he'd have done the same thing."

"No, he wouldn't have." I pulled away from him. "Gage wouldn't use me for any price."

"Everyone has a price."

Our gazes met. It seemed an entire conversation took place in that one glance. Each of us saw what we needed to know.

"I have to say goodbye now, Hardy."

He stared at me with bitter understanding. We both knew there was no room in this for friendship. Nothing left but childhood history.

"Hell." Hardy caught my face in his hands, kissing my forehead, my closed eyelids, stopping just short of my mouth. And then I was wrapped in one of those hard, secure hugs I remembered so well. Still holding me, Hardy whispered in my ear. "Be happy, honey. No one deserves it more. But don't forget . . . I'm keeping one little piece of your heart for myself. And if you ever want it back . . . you know where to find it."

Having never been airborne before, I white-knuckled it all the way to Raleigh Durham. I sat in first class next to a very nice guy in a business suit, who talked me through the takeoff and landing, and ordered me a whiskey sour during the flight. As we deboarded, he asked if he could have my number, and I shook my head. "Sorry, I'm taken."

I hoped I was right.

I'd planned to take a cab to my next stop, a small public airport about seven miles away, but a limo driver was waiting for me in baggage claim. He held up a sign with the handwritten letters JONES. I approached him tentatively. "Are you by chance looking for Liberty Jones?"

"Yes, ma'am."

"That would be me."

I guessed Churchill had arranged for the ride, either out of thoughtfulness, or the fear that I couldn't have managed to get a cab by myself. Travis men are nothing if not overprotective.

The driver helped me with my suitcase, a Hartmann tweed Gretchen had loaned me and helped pack. It was stuffed with light wool pants and a skirt, some white shirts, my silk scarf, and two cashmere sweaters she swore she had no use for. Optimistically I had also packed an evening dress and heels. There was a brand-new passport in my purse, along with Gage's, which his secretary had provided.

It was nearly dusk by the time I was dropped off at the small airport, which had two runways, a snack bar, and nothing remotely resembling a control tower. I noticed how different the air smelled in North Carolina, salty and soft and green.

There were seven aircraft on the ground, two small and five midsized, one of them the Travises' Gulfstream. Next to a yacht, the most blatant exhibition of extreme wealth is a private jet. The superrich have planes with showers, private bedrooms, and wood-paneled workstations, along with fancy stuff like gold-plated cup holders.

But the Travises, mindful of maintenance costs, had been conservative by Texan standards. That's sort of a joke if you've ever seen their Gulfstream, a luxury long-range aircraft fitted with fiddleback mahogany and soft wool carpeting. Also leather swivel seats, a plasma TV, and a curtained-off divan that folds out into a queen-sized bed.

I boarded the plane and met the pilot and copilot. While they sat in the cockpit, I had a soda and waited nervously for Gage. I practiced a speech, a hundred versions, searching for the right words to make Gage understand how I felt.

I heard someone boarding the plane, and my pulse went crazy and the speech flew right out of my head.

Gage didn't see me at first. He looked grim and tired, dropping a shiny black briefcase into the nearest seat, rubbing the back of his neck as if it were sore.

"Hey," I said softly.

His head turned, and his face went blank as he saw me. "Liberty. What are you doing here?"

I felt an overwhelming rush of love for him, more love than I could contain, rising off me like heat. God, he was beautiful. I groped for words. "I . . . I decided on Paris."

A long silence passed. "Paris."

"Yes, you know you asked me if I . . . well, I called the pilot yesterday. I told him I wanted to surprise you."

"You did."

"He's worked everything out so we can leave straight from here. Right now. If you want." I offered him a hopeful smile. "I've got your passport."

Gage removed his jacket, taking his time about it. I was reassured by the way he seemed to fumble a little as he laid the garment over a seat back. "So now you're ready to go somewhere with me."

My voice was thick with emotion. "I'm ready to go anywhere with you."

He looked at me with brilliant gray eyes, and I caught my breath as a slow smile curved his lips. Loosening his tie, he began to approach me.

"Wait," I choked out. "I have to tell you something."

Gage stopped. "Yes?"

"Churchill told me about the Medina deal. It was my fault—I'm the one who tipped Hardy off about it. I had no idea that he would . . . I'm sorry." My voice broke. "I'm so sorry."

Gage reached me in two strides. "It's all right. No, damn it, don't start crying."

"I would never do anything to hurt you—"

"I know you wouldn't. Hush. Hush." He hauled me close, wiping at my tears with his fingers.

"I was so stupid, I didn't realize—why didn't you say anything to me about it?"

"I didn't want you to worry. I knew it wasn't your fault. I should have made certain you understood it was confidential."

I was stunned by his belief in me. "How could you be so sure I didn't do it on purpose?"

He cradled my face in his hands and smiled into my streaming eyes. "Because I know you, Liberty Jones. Don't cry, sweetheart, you're killing me."

"I'll make it up to you, I swear—"

"Shut up," Gage said tenderly, and kissed me with a blistering heat that made my knees buckle. I wrapped my arms around his neck, forgetting the reason for tears, forgetting everything but him. He kissed me over and over, deeper, until we both staggered in the aisle, and he was forced to brace a hand on one of the seats to keep us from falling over. And the plane wasn't even moving. His breath rushed fast and hot against my cheek as he drew back enough to whisper, "What about the other guy?"

My eyes half closed as I felt the heel of his hand brush the side of my breast. "He's the past," I managed to say. "You're the future."

"Damn right I am." Another deeply uncivilized kiss, full of fire and tenderness, promising more than I could begin to take in. All I could think was that a lifetime with this man wouldn't be nearly enough. He pulled away with an unsteady laugh and said, "There's no getting away from me now, Liberty. This is it."

I know, I would have said, but before I could answer he was kissing me again, and he didn't stop for quite a while.

"I love you." I don't remember who said it first, only that we both ended up saying it quite a lot during the seven-hour-and-twenty-five-minute flight across the Atlantic. And it turned out Gage had some interesting ideas about how to pass the time at fifty thousand feet.

Let's just say flying is a lot more tolerable when you've got distractions.

I'm not sure if the ranch is an engagement present or an early wedding present. All I know is that today, Valentine's Day, Gage has given me a huge ring of keys tied with a red bow. He says we'll need a getaway place when the city feels too crowded, and Carrington will need a place to ride. It takes a few minutes of explaining on his part before I understand it's an outright gift.

I'm now the owner of a five-thousand-acre ranch.

The place, once known for its prime cutting horses, is about forty-five minutes away from Houston. Now reduced to a fraction of its former size, the ranch is small by Texas standards—a ranchette, Jack calls it mockingly, until a glance from Gage causes him to cringe in pretend-fear.

"You don't even have a ranch," Carrington accuses Jack cheerfully, scampering to the doorway before adding, "which makes you a *dude*."

"Who you callin' a dude?" Jack asks with feigned outrage, and chases after her, while her screams of delight echo through the hallways.

On the weekend we pack overnight bags and go to see the place, which Gage has renamed Rancho Armadillo. "You shouldn't have done this," I tell him for the dozenth time as he drives us north of Houston. "You've given me enough already."

Keeping his gaze on the road, Gage brings our entwined fingers to his lips and kisses my knuckles. "Why does it always make you so damn uncomfortable when I give you something?"

I realize there is an art to accepting gifts gracefully, and so far I haven't acquired it. "I'm not used to getting presents," I admit. "Especially when it's not a holiday or a birthday and there's no reason for them. And even before this . . . this—"

"Ranch."

"Yes, even before that, you'd already done more for me than I could ever repay—"

"Darlin'." His tone is patient, but at the same time I hear the uncompromising edge in it. "You're going to have to work on erasing that invisible balance sheet you carry around in your head. Relax. Let me have the pleasure of giving you something without having to talk it half to death afterward." He glances over his shoulder to make sure Carrington has her headphones on. "Next time I give you a present, all you need to do is say a simple 'thank you,' and have sex with me. That's all the repayment I need."

I bite back a smile. "Okay."

We drive through a pair of massive rock pillars supporting a twenty-foot iron arch and continue along a paved road that I come to realize is our driveway. We pass winter-wheat fields dappled with the wing-shadows of geese overhead. Dense growths of mesquite, cedar, and prickly pear crouch in the distance.

The drive leads to a big old rock-and-wood Victorian shaded by oak and pecan trees. My dumbfounded gaze takes in a stone barn . . . a paddock . . . an empty chicken yard, all of it surrounded by a field-stone fence. The house is big and sturdy and charming. I know without being told that children have been born here and couples have married here, and families have argued and loved and laughed beneath the gabled roof. It's a place to feel safe in. A home.

The car stops beside a three-car garage. "It's been completely renovated," Gage says. "Modern kitchen, big showers, cable and Internet—"

"Are there horses?" Carrington interrupts in excitement, tearing her headphones off.

"There are." Gage turns to smile at her as she bounces in the back seat. "Not to mention a swimming pool and hot tub."

"I dreamed of a house like this once," Carrington says.

"Did you?" Even to my own ears, I sound a little dazed. Unbuckling my seat belt and climbing from the car, I continue to stare at the house. In all my longing for a family and a home, I'd never quite been able to decide what they should have looked like. But this house looks and feels so right, so perfect, it seems impossible any other place would suit me half so well. There is a wide wraparound porch, and a porch swing, and it's painted pale blue under the ceiling like they did in the old days, to keep mud daubers from building nests. There are enough fallen pecans beside the house to fill buckets.

We go inside the air-conditioned house, the interior painted shades of white and cream, the polished mesquite floors gleaming with light from tall windows. It's decorated in a style the magazines call "new country," which means there aren't many ruffles, but the sofas and chairs are cushiony, and there are lots of throw pillows. Carrington squeals in excitement and disappears, running from room to room, occasionally hurrying back to report on some new discovery.

Gage and I tour the house more slowly. He watches my reactions, and he says I can change anything I like, I can have whatever I want. I am too overwhelmed to say much of anything. I have instantly connected with this house, the stubborn vegetation rooted so stubbornly in the dry red land, the scrubby woods harboring javelina and bobcats and coyotes, so much more than with the sterile modern condo poised high above the streets of Houston. And I wonder how Gage knew this is what my soul has craved.

He turns me to face him, his eyes searching. It occurs to me that no one in my life has ever concerned himself so thoroughly with my happiness. "What are you thinking?" he asks.

I know Gage hates it when I cry—he is completely undone by the sight of tears—so I blink hard against the sting. "I'm thinking how thankful I am for everything," I say, "even the bad stuff. Every sleepless night, every second of being lonely, every time the car broke down, every wad of gum on my shoe, every late bill and losing lottery ticket and bruise and broken dish and piece of burnt toast."

His voice is soft. "Why, darlin'?"

"Because it all led me here to you."

Gage makes a low sound and kisses me, trying to be gentle, but soon he is gripping me closer and murmuring love words, sex words, making his way down the curve of my neck until I remind him breathlessly that Carrington is somewhere nearby.

We fix dinner together, the three of us, and after eating we sit outside and talk. At times we pause to listen to the plaintive song of mourning doves, the occasional whicker of a horse in the barn, the breezes that rustle the oaks and send pecans rattling to the ground.

Eventually Carrington goes upstairs to take a bath in a refurbished clawfoot tub, and she goes to sleep in a room with pale blue walls. She asks drowsily if we can paint clouds on the ceiling, and I say yes, of course we can.

Gage and I sleep in the master bedroom downstairs. We make love in a king-sized poster bed, beneath hand-stitched quilts. Sensitive to my mood, Gage takes it easy and slow in the way that never fails to drive me crazy, drawing out every sensation until my heartbeat is hammering in my throat. He is strong and hard and deliberate, every gentle movement an assertion of something beyond words, something deeper and sweeter than mere passion. I go rigid in his arms, muffling a cry against his shoulder while he coaxes long, delicious shudders from my body. Then it's my turn to hold him. I put my arms and legs around him, wrapping him tightly in myself, and he gasps out my name as he surges and quickens.

We both wake up at daybreak as the wintering snow geese honk and flap across the fields on their way to breakfast. I lie snuggled against Gage's chest, listening to the mockingbirds serenading us from the oak tree by the window. They are relentless.

"Where's the gun?" I hear Gage mutter.

I hide my grin against his chest. "Easy, cowboy. It's my ranch. Those birds can sing all they want to."

Just for that, Gage replies, he's going to make me go with him on an early morning ride to check out my property.

That causes the smile to fade. There's something I've wanted to tell him, but I haven't been sure how or when to do it. I am quiet, playing nervously with the hair on his chest. "Gage . . . I don't think I'm up for riding today."

He lifts up on one elbow and looks down at me with a frown. "Why not? You feeling okay?"

"No—I mean yes—I feel fine." I take an uneven breath. "But I have to ask the doctor if it's all right before I do anything that strenuous."

"Doctor?" Gage rises over me, taking my shoulders in his hands. "What doctor? Why the hell would you . . ." His voice fades as it dawns on him. "My God. Liberty, sweetheart, are you . . ." He immediately moderates his grip, as if he's afraid of crushing me. "You're sure?" I nod, and he gives a delighted laugh. "I can't believe it." A flush of color has made his eyes startlingly light by contrast. "Actually, I can. It was New Year's Eve, wasn't it?"

"Your fault," I remind him, and his grin widens.

"Yes, I'll take full credit for that one. My sweet girl. Let me see you."

I am immediately subjected to an inspection, his hands sweeping over my body. Gage kisses my stomach a dozen times, then levers upward to pull me into his arms again. His mouth descends to mine repeatedly. "My God, I love you. How do you feel? Do you have morning sickness? Do you need crackers? Pickles? Dr Pepper?"

I shake my head and try to talk to him in between kisses. "I love you . . . Gage . . . love you . . ." The words catch sweetly between our lips, and I finally understand why so many Texans refer to kisses as "sugar-bites."

"I'm going to take such good care of you." Gage lays his head gently on my chest, his ear pressed to the rhythm of my heart. "You, Carrington, and the baby. My little family. A miracle."

"Sort of an ordinary miracle," I point out. "I mean, women have babies every day."

"Not my woman. Not my baby." His head lifts. The look in his eyes takes my breath away. "What can I do for you?" he whispers.

"Just say a simple 'thank you,'" I tell him, "and have sex with me."

And he does.

I know without a doubt this man loves me for exactly who I am. No conditions, no limits. That's a miracle too. In fact, every day is filled with ordinary miracles.

You don't have to look far to find them.

*Watch out for Lisa Kleypas' next contemporary novel,
also available from Piatkus:*

BLUE-EYED DEVIL

A turbulent but beautiful star-crossed love affair . . .

Hardy Cates is self-made, charming – and determined to carry out
his private revenge against the Travis family. So when he crashes a
Travis family wedding, the last thing he expects is to find himself
kissing his adversary Haven Travis in a dark corner. Hardy has
done many things in his life he's not proud of, but now he's trying
to rid himself of his roughneck past, which doesn't mean falling in
love with a rival – no matter how beautiful she is.

Haven, likewise, vows to stay far away from Hardy. Having had
her heart quite recently broken – and her body battered and
bruised by the man she thought she had loved – she's through
with men. That is, until she discovers that the temptation of a
tender-hearted, blue-eyed devil is hard to resist. And then,
when a menace from Haven's past appears, Hardy may be the
only one to save her . . .

978-0-7499-0904-8